JUNK DRAWER AT THE EDGE OF THE UNIVERSE

STEVEN REED JOHNSON

D1738886

CONTENTS

DEDICATION

Cathy Ambrose
Dennis and Cathy Brophy
Darcy Buck
Alex Childers
Nancy Cosper (Furman)
Elora Cosper
Jack Eyerly
David and Luann Furman
Lenny Furman
Jean and Ken Johnson
Kim and Perrin Stafford
Pam Wells (editor)

FOREWORD

In order to resolve conflict between his life and his art, Nabokov created a pastime. He choreographed changes in grammatical person, gender, and tense in order to transform his experiences into a third-person past, as remembered by a female friend. He or his friend Lidia might lead off the game on the terrace with, "The writer liked to go out on the terrace after supper," or "I shall always remember the remark V. V. made one warm night: 'It is,' he remarked, 'a warm night' "; or, still sillier: "He was in the habit of lighting his cigarette, before smoking it."[1]

Audre Lorde in her 1982 book, *Zami: A New Spelling of My Name*,[2] introduces the term "biomythography" to describe the woven nature of myth, cultural history, and the notion of telling one's story. "It is the expansive and inclusive process of self-construction and self-representation, a creative form in which I gain and enact my agency."

We all have an inner-narrator; even if not often aware of it. We seldom remember creating it. Having a narrator is like a having a butler for ideas.

For this novel I created a narrator, Reed Johnson, to tell the story. He has more freedom to improvise, fabricate, and speculate.

Reed is the same age as I am, but taller, more handsome, and fashionable.

As you will soon enough find out, Jack Ainsworth wrote most of the book. Reed wrote original drafts of chapters, the first chapter, The Holy Grail section, Postscript, and Footnotes.

Nothing in the book should be construed as real. After-all it is a novel.

---

1. "Playing Nabokov: Performances by Himself and Others," Susan Elizabeth Sweeney, *Studies in 20th and 21st Century Literature.* June 1998.
2. *Zami: A new Spelling of my Name*, Audre Lorde. W.W. Norton. New York, New York. 1982.

HOW I ENDED UP LIVING IN A RED
STORAGE SHED

If you drive I-205 on the eastern boundary of Portland, Oregon,
250 feet from where Woody Guthrie[1]wrote Roll on Columbia
Roll on, you might notice my neighborhood. It is a storage shed
facility. The buildings are bright red, and the entrance is marked by
large white pillars from the Gone *with the Wind* (Clyde says they are
real) plantation home. The sheds are gathered in a circle like covered
wagons. There is also a thirty-foot-high red Spork, badly in need of a
paint job. Thus, the name: Spork in the Road Storage facility.

On a clear day you might see me out in front of my 12' x 20' red tin
condo, under a fading red-white-blue outdoor umbrella, surrounded
by banker boxes. If you saw me—short, scruffy whiskers, long messed
graying hair, a ragged red Pendleton plait shirt, original cut Levies,
and dilapidated bedroom slippers—you would not think there's
someone who has figured out the meaning of life. I think that Ms.
Frank, my 5th grade teacher, a wrestling champion with a glass eye,
would be flummoxed that I turned out this way.

If you had read this novel, or knew Jack Ainsworth, it would come
as no surprise that I live here rent free. I also have a hot plate and
refrigerator. The owner of The Spork lets me use the office bathroom
and helped me install 2 skylights in the tin roof. The owner, Clyde

Horny—yes, his actual name, proudly displayed on his business card next to a photo of the Red Spork—owed Jack Ainsworth for finding a sexy mate for his jack terrier. The offspring were named Jack Jack, jack off, and Jack on.

I am not homeless. The Shire, the place I call home, and my family has for over a century, is just 3 miles by the way a crow would fly. The red storage shed is my Thoreau hut. My Walden pond is an 8-foot-wide green wading pool I sit in when it is hot. It might be the movie set for a Thoreau gone bad; a Superman bizarro alternative world where Thoreau had a meth lab.

I moved here, away from my home that is really like Walden, so I could finish my obligations spelled out in jack Ainsworth's Will and last Testament. At the Shire, loss and confusion surrounded me. It felt like entropy had the upper hand; the Entropy Evasion League had failed me. Everything was falling apart; the loves of my life were dying or had already passed. Do you remember that moment in Sartre's book *La Nausea* when the narrator sees roots of trees moving, tortured, clinging to life; a terrible and beautiful experience of fecundity. Anyone that knows the maritime climate of the west Coast of North America knows that life is like that almost all the time. Life is rotting, not shouting with joy. Closer to a Bergman movie than Rastafarian. The Shire, as Koslov,[2] a Biologist friend once told me, has the growth yield of the Amazon basin, at least for part of the year. Living in the fecund primeval forest and surrounded by the sights and sounds and knickknacks of my life was too profuse. I wanted laser beam attention.

Jack Ainsworth was a collector and extraordinary networker, a calling he and some others dreamed up in the 1950s, inspired by his father, Dr. John Ainsworth, and members of Random Lot. He also referred to himself as a social animator. He had files of information about 3000 people, mostly artists and other social animators, in the Pacific Northwest. The stuff chronicles an underground history of the region between the 1920s to the 1990s. Jack also had information about obscure collectors (post cards, oil rags, barf bags, navel lint) rednecks, street people, and bowling league champions.[3]

It would be easy to write a history of Portland, or more broadly Ecotopia[4] or the world, and Jack might only show up as a footnote and yet I am convinced without his presence here for 70 years, and his extended family, this part of the country would radically different.

He told me that the world was divided into two types of people (over a 30-year period he told me this at least 20 times and it was always different groupings) those who were afraid they might be in the backwaters or a footnote in someone else's more important narrative and those who didn't give a fig's ass. The latter were more concerned with clean dishes, clipping coupons, raising perfect kids, and buying a lot of shit to buy off entropy and avoid the black hole of their life. The way to measure all this according to Dr. John, Jack's father, was to figure out which ones were more afraid of dying and which ones were more afraid of living and how they were going to die.

Jack prided himself on being invisible. You had to dig deep to find him, and if you were digging around the edges, he usually found you first. That's what happened in our case. I had heard of the Gertrudea Stein Fellowship Club, a collectively run warehouse in Portland. I had seen the iconic Mr. Peanut appear in bold displays around town and on the roof of the dilapidated warehouse. It replaced a "Jesus will Save You," neon sign, with a twenty-foot-high Mr. Peanut[5] with an elegant calligraphic header: EAT. If you were a part of the primordial underground, you knew that stood for Experiments in Art and Technology.[6]

One of the difficult things about writing a book about Jack is that he changed history as he moved through life. Since he passed along Gus and I have unearthed over 30 personas he created with families, careers and effects spanning the globe, and documented through newspapers, magazines, academic-referred research.

It seems every day, as Gus and I tunnel our way through Jack's remaining archives, and continue the last Roundup theatrical performance, I ponder how many ways jack altered my cosmic projection. It is no longer clear to me what is my true story and the better one Jack created of my life. And even more disconcerting, that I feel I don't exist outside of the stories.

Jack helped thousands of people. Most of the time he did his work for free or people paid him with stuff. The stuff ranged from diamond necklaces to perpetual motion machines. At one time, it took up most of the 4th floor of the Gertrude Stein Fellowship warehouse.

Once you entered Jack's life you had a sneaking suspicion that he was orchestrating your life like the Wizard of Oz from behind a curtain. Because non-sequiturs were his normal way of conversing you also had to listen carefully. It was like having a hummingbird read a Henry James novel out loud.

Jack gave Uncle Gus and me both $100,000 in his will and all we had to do was finish his Last Roundup; complete the Chronicles of the Ainsworth Family that I had started soon after we met and find the missing box that contained Dr. John's epistemological re-imagination of the world; that in the vernacular of those days—I mean the 1960s—would *blow your mind*. Oh right, also I had to put together the stories of my life that were originally created over 30 years ago during the Arabian Nights' sessions that Jack fashioned to save me from oblivion. This clause in the Will also had a veiled death threat. "You will finish the stories or face certain termination." OK, maybe not so veiled, and Jack had connections. Or maybe I would die first and he would tell me at my deathbed, "I told you so." Over time, I realized he wanted me to discover his story of my story, and one other person's view of moonlight at the Taj Mahal—well at least that is what a cuckoo bird told Gus on a Last Round up trip, maybe more about that later.

When I met Jack, I wanted to be a writer. I imagined my life a series of astounding novels or countless short stories. When I met Jack, he told me my writing style was kind of William Burroughs-ether-acid-surrealistic-Unitarian-Buddhist. On another day he called it, "bullshit Jungian archetypal communications from your dead cat," in reference to poet Yates who did receive communications from his dead cat. My writing was a secret code in those days. If I had become

4

a famous author, scholars would have gained tenured track positions deciphering subtext and codes. I wrote in bursts fueled by alcohol, high-quality acid, on a Selectric typewriter. I could never know when to begin or end a story or how to choose which were important to tell. I also went through a stage of writing to get rich or be successful; writing kids' stories; travel pieces; even a stint as ghostwriter for a Playboy columnist. That paid well, and they invited me to the Playboy mansion in Chicago, which was withdrawn when I sent a photo of myself and my childhood friend Spermgate next to his mayo jar filled with cum from a year of masturbation.

My life changed the day I had an out-of-body experience when I opened a junk drawer. That was the day when a Seventh Day Adventist prayed for my salvation on my living room floor and I talked with Jack for the first time who called while we were praying. Now that I understand Dr. John's Random Knowledge calculator, I know that wasn't a coincidence but random order, a subtle but profound difference.

If only Dr. John had lived long enough to see the Internet. I don't know what status to give him in history; he may become a Nostradamus character or HG Wells. Only time will tell. What do you make of someone who in 1970 predicted that there would be a world brain he called the Mosaic and prophesied that a terrorist group would take down the world's most powerful empire with a Swiss army knife?

Dr John's missing box contained the concluding elements of his theory of Random knowledge. Jack was obsessed with finding the box. He had lost it—very uncharacteristic of Jack, who spent at least half of every day of his life reading and carefully filing stuff—and spent years looking for it. Jack had several boxes of his father's theories: notebooks, diagrams, correspondences from "experts" around the world, and from members of the Random Lot. In the bequest he asked us to make sense of it and find a publisher or otherwise distribute it for posterity.

Jack and Dr John were obsessed with lost and found. They believed we spend most of our life losing and finding things; at the micro-level a pencil or marble; at the macro level, our soul or purpose. Jack enlisted a graduate student in a study of the lost and found in our lives. For one year at the GS warehouse, just before I arrived, he randomly asked people, "Have you been looking for something in the last 24 hours?" and follow up, "did you find something in the last 24 hours. How many? I only found a one-page summary, with the statement, '82% of the subjects were trying to find things when asked; and 78% had just found something. 200 subjects; 1,200 inquiries.'

Uncle Gus and Jack were convinced that if I could put together Dr John's stuff in the right order, and importantly find the missing box, we would have a bona fide Junior Badger manual, like the one Huey, Dewey, and Louie carried around in Donald Duck comics that could answer any question. It could tell you how the universe started or what you were going to eat for breakfast the following Sunday.

Gus and I have continued Jack's last project, he called The Last Roundup as best we could. For several years jack had been re-distributing his archives to the receivers—the originators or the person who the document or thing really belonged to. We're talking hundreds of items, mostly paper format, some with clear recipient information but several hundred with only partial explanation or none. And returning items to their owners is not always as pleasant as it sounds. Gus had his life threatened, and I got punched in the face by a tiny woman much stronger than she looked.

The remainder of Jack's library and archive is but a shadow of its glory day. The stuff ranged from diamond necklaces to perpetual motion machines. At one time it took up most of the 4th floor in the Gertrude Stein Fellowship warehouse that took most of a small city block. Actually, there are over 1000 boxes in the shed. Uncle Gus and I left some of our stuff behind, as a "counter weight" (Gus's term) to Jack's biased history of the region. All the boxes are arranged on erector set like shelves; organized using Dr. John's Map of Knowledge scheme, an alternative to the Dewey Decimal cataloging system. One of the original Bay Area Revolting librarians[7] from the 1960s, said Dr. John's was like Dewey Decimal on mescaline. (#32) There are also many rare documents, including a Papal Decree from the 17th century, and Ralph's journal from his visits to Jupiter. There are files on at least 5,000 people whose lived between 1820 and the present; mostly residents of the Pacific Northwest. And there were my boxes, at least 30, although we found other stuff by or about me in boxes labeled things like 'records, 1972.'

I left a small space in the center of the shed open, defined by Jack's red round oriental rug, Kathleen's 1950s school desk, a reading lamp that reportedly belonged to Margaret Green Reed, mother of John Reed,[8] and a twelve foot long folding table where I organized the "stuff" Jack could not return during the last roundup.

I have started this story in so many ways—the end at the beginning or the beginning at the end, somewhere in the middle. I even once threw the pages in the air and threw darts until I hit a page to mark the beginning. Dr. John would have loved that approach. But I most often came back to the day when I first talked to Jack on the phone and I encountered a lasting metaphor for my life, a junk drawer that seemed to lead to anything and everything.

---

1. *"Guthrie documentary rolls on,"* Portland Tribune, April 6, 2011
2. Eugene Kozlov was biology professor at Lewis and Clark College from 1945 to 1966. In 1966 he moved to Friday Harbor, San Juan Island in Washington to serve as director of Friday Harbor Labs, otherwise known as Zoobot Program. He died at 96.
3. I am almost sure that John and Jack Ainsworth were related to the pioneering Portland businessman, John Ainsworth, but Jack said it was just a coincidence. My attempts to interview descendants of the other John Ainsworth, arranged through a descendent of the Couch family, failed to materialize. I could imagine our Jack doing what the historic Jack did. He was Grant Master of the Grand Lodge of Oregon; founded the Orient of Oregon and the Valley of Portland of the Ancient and Accepted Scottish Rite; and served as the first Sovereign Grand Inspector General of the Orient of Oregon.
4. Ernest Callenbach was an American author, film critic, editor, and simple living adherent. He became famous because of his internationally successful semi-utopian novel *Ecotopia* Published in 1975.
5. Mr. Peanut is the advertising logo and mascot of Planters, an American snack-food company. He is presented in his shell, and dressed in the formal clothing of an old-fashioned gentleman: top hat, monocle, white gloves, spats, and a cane.

Mr. Peanut was the mascot for the Canadian arts group, Experiments in Arts and Technology.

6. Experiments in Art and Technology (E.A.T.) was a non-profit and tax-exempt organization established to develop collaborations between artists and engineers. E.A.T. initiated and carried out projects that expanded the role of the artist in contemporary society and helped explore the separation of the individual from technological change.

7. *Bay area reference center. revolting librarians.* Celeste West described the city as "a trend-mecca–whether it be communal living, campus riots, gay liberation, independent film making... you name it and we've got it." But what San Francisco had, she argued, was not reflected in library collections unless somebody took the time to pull together "the elusive printed material." Thus, their newsletter *Synergy* examined the nature of library card catalogs, indexes, and selecting tools because staff believed such tools were mostly "rear-view mirrors" that provided little or no bibliographic access to the public's current information needs. By Sanford Berman—one of the original revolting librarians.

8. John Silas Reed, 1887–1920, as an American journalist, poet, and communist activist, best remembered for *Ten Days That Shook the World*, his firsthand account of the November 1917 Bolshevik Revolution, when Lenin and the Bolsheviks seized power in Russia. He was born on October 22, 1887, in his maternal grandparents' mansion in what is now the Goose Hollow neighborhood of Portland, Oregon.

RED SHED INTERLUDE, NO. 1: FINDING OUR WAY

THE VATICAN LIBRARY OR GRANDMA'S ATTIC?

U ncle Gus and I worked out a plan at the red shed and the warehouse. First, we made some practical decisions.

"Gus, There's an Office Supply not too far from here. I'm going to get a billion boxes."

"Well, that might too many," he said.

"Right. Meanwhile, you sort everything into three piles or areas."

"Wow, three," he said, "that is way cool. Jack would be proud of you. What three?"

"Well, paper is one, second one is all other stuff, and the third is junk."

"Shit, paper sounds good, but what exactly is the difference between the last two."

I was ready with an answer. "Junk is everything that Jack had to buy or purchase just to get by." I walked around quickly pointing at things. " Like this broken lamp, this rug, that old chair, that pile of coat hangers. Even his clothes. I don't think he would care what we did with his clothes or an old chair. He seldom used art. But he would care what we did with any paper and any gizmos. I walked around and pointed at some gizmos."

"Believe me," Gus said, "I know about gizmos. I invented the idea."

9

In fact, because we had paper strewn around, it looked like there was more than when we started. Both of us found ourselves immersed in boxes like quicksand. I found out things about Jack, myself, our community, and the planet, both disturbing and enlightening.

Here's what I figure. I was secretariat for 6 years. On average, there were 75 organizations with office space. 400 groups over the entire period. The group's average size was 3 staff. The largest was 15 (Crying of Lot 49). There were on average 20 public events a week. So that means over 8 years there were over 6,000 events. My best guess is that 10,000 people attended events there. The events ranged in size from 1 to 200 (in the Fishbowl room).

Lastly, the reports I compiled for a ten-year period, extended by Leland's ponderously detailed and well-organized reports while I was in my vagabond period, would make for extensive reading. 180 reports, 5,400 pages. That's not including the irregular reports Uncle Gus and others made over the 50 years before I arrived on the scene, another 5,000 pages. In total, there are 200 banker boxes related to the history of Gertrude Stein Fellowship club Just before I became Secretariat. Leland had institutionalized a protocol he called Armageddon Brian Storming (ABS). When I asked him about the name, he said Brian was the name of his favorite dog growing up. There was a sign-up sheet for scheduling use of the warehouse's 20 event spaces. If you put ABS after your event it meant you didn't mind if another group, regardless of the nature of the event, could be double booked. And then, who knows what might happen.

The Last Round Up

I put Gus in charge of locating Gertrude Stein members from the heyday period of the Gertrude Stein club. It was as though I had put him in charge of a high school reunion committee. He would come back with things like, remember Galactic Tom, who was voted most likely to succeed at nothing, well he now sells insurance for pandemics.

Gus and I continued Jack's last project, the Last Roundup. For several years he distributed his archives to the receivers—the originators or the person who the document or thing really belonged to. He left behind a map, (48" by 60") uncle Gus called the twenty degrees of Kevin Bacon[1] or pig for short. Jack passed along before he could distribute what he wanted to go back to the receivers. "October 15...Red shed broken into but nothing seems to be stolen but how would I know." (my journal entry)

One day Gus showed up at the red shed with 5 boxes, my junk drawer boxes, the original boxes I was pretty sure since there was a "Good Samaritan" sticker on one box—a group that Kathleen's father belonged to in the Bay Area. And another had my unmistakable handwriting, which just said "current stuff" not related to junk drawers, but clearly one of my banker boxes.

"Tinker bell had them," Gus said, apologetically. "My fault really, you know Jack also called her the good Samaritan," he said pointing to the faded label, "and no labels on the others, so I just figured they were all hers. You know she was a correspondence artist, so there was a lot of shit."

It hadn't occurred to me to look for my junk drawers. I think I had called them drawers for so long, instead of banker boxes, that I pictured them at the tiny house where I created them for Jack's first grand experiment with my head and life, not as things dislocated from their original and native state. When I found them—five boxes, they were no longer junk drawers but re-filed, re-packaged, color coded. In fact, my first response was they weren't mine. But then again, it was my stuff. The first thing I recognized was a tiny bowl with twisted seaweed, part of Japanese tradition wedding symbol, a half century old and not broken, even though my host father and his bride had long since died. Again, as with other things, Jack had usurped my life or meaning and once again I wasn't sure how I felt about it.

We tried to be all official like real estate representatives, as Gus said, and it didn't really work, like a dreadlocked surfer running a Swiss train. Gus took on the junk drawer stories.

He said, "Oh Right, I'll do my nephew's."

"Weird when you say it that way. How could Jack be anyone's nephew?"

"You don't believe me. I have his birth certificate."

"Ha. that's funny. Proof? Like Proof in this universe has any validity. Well, we have to divide it up some way. Of course, we have to start with you telling me everything you know about the junk drawer items and their stories and the connection between each item and everything else in the galaxy. You know Ouspensky [2]and all that shit. Right?"

"Here's what I remember. I hid the document in the most ironic and appropriate but weather proof place I could imagine. Sad to think how many days I pondered the place. I even moved the metal box to several places before finding the right one. Remember the HG Wells *Time Machine*. You put the machine in one place and might imagine historical changes; even that a building might be torn down and a new one in its place."

The final document I titled: *The Genesis of the Ainsworth Clan, 101 nefarious organizations, degrees of separation from the widening gyre, detectability variance, interlocking membership map, and persona fabrication since the Civil War.* well pretty sure that's what I titled it. It was about 200 pages, although there was also a pile (4-6 inches?) of documents, news clippings, photos, etc. It included my notes from the three official interviews we did. But Jack and Gus had insisted that I wouldn't need notes, that the tape recorder they had—the most advanced at the time that recorded body language, heart and breathing rates, and astral patterns—would be more than enough.

We have assumed Jack removed any record of the Ainsworth chronicle interviews on purpose. Much heated discussion. Soul and banker box searching. Gus swears he remembers exactly what he left behind. Audio tapes. Tapes could have gone bad. We found some snarly tape wrapped up around a toilet paper roll. We tried to get it to play and found some clues.

Gus told me Jack always acted like he knew what he was doing, even when he didn't have a clue. Something learned from Dr John, who said it over and over. Makes me wonder if Jack knew what he was doing when prescribing the junk drawer writing workshops, or if he was just making it up. Gus told me that Jack had cried when telling him about your junk drawers' experience.

But Gus also carefully transcribed the tapes. We had six sessions in additional to informal conversations, passing in the hall. I had many conversations with others at the Gertrude Stein but unfortunately didn't methodically record these.

---

1. Kevin Norwood Bacon is an American actor and musician. Six Degrees of Kevin Bacon or "Bacon's Law" is a parlor game based on the "six degrees of separation" concept, which posits that any two people on Earth are six or fewer acquaintance links apart. People challenge each other to find the shortest path between an arbitrary actor and Kevin Bacon.

2. Peter D. Ouspensky (1878–1947) was a Russian mathematician and esotericist known for his writing based on the Greek-Armenian teacher of esoteric doctrine, George Gurdjieff. In A New Model of the Universe, P. D. Ouspensky analyzes Eastern and Western thought and explains them in the light of recent discoveries and speculations in physics and philosophy. He explores relativity, the fourth dimension, Christian symbolism, the tarot, yoga, dreams, hypnotism, eternal recurrence, and various psychological theories. *New Model of the Universe*, Vintage books, 1971.

HOW I MET JACK

Preamble

I wrote versions of all three of pieces in this section. *Junk Drawer at the Edge of the Universe,* I wrote the day after I met Jack on the phone. The encounters with Hearing aid salesman, Jehovah's Witness, and my next-door neighbor, Jack, made of thin cloth. What I remember writing was more notes than a formal story. I remember wishing on that day I would be inspired by mysterious encounters, reminding me that while the universe is random, it can bring you beauty and wisdom. In jack's version of what happened, we agreed about our roles and roles and responsibilities, and impact on the known universe. But nothing in writing.

I left a version of *My First Days at the Gertrude Stein Fellowship Club* in the box I hid at the Funny Farm. But the version in this section seems more methodical and accurate. I wrote my version about the same time as I was beginning to mistrust Jack. I suspect he got some information from Gus, but Gus won't confirm or deny it.

How did you get here. The Technology Laboratorium fantasy came about because of one of Jack's homework assignments. During the writer's boot camps, I was to research and write up how we met. And importantly, how we almost met before we did.

I did mine the night assigned. Jack kept promising to provide his report, but he never did. We found it in the archives. It is more or less accurate, but it was not my writing style at the time.

THE JUNK DRAWER AT THE EDGE OF THE
UNIVERSE

I was coming home from a job interview when a woman in a Mercedes ran a stop sign and crumpled poor old Mr. Zoom's bumper, my $75 Nash Rambler. It was the middle of the day, and the woman, in a black suit, reeking of alcohol, gave me $200 (it was the 1970s; our rent was $75/month) if I would just forget it. I was excited to tell my wife, Kathleen. We were broke, and I was looking for a job or at least money to pay the overdue rent. I picked up a filet mignon and a bottle of Almaden wine, discerning wine for a college student or graduate, so we could celebrate our good fortune.

Kathleen and I had been re-negotiating the terms of our relationship since moving back to Portland, after we had dropped off the grid for two years. We had experimented with an open relation. When she got home, I absently asked her where she had been, assuming she had been out with one of her two friends, Peggy or Kay. She glared at me. Shit. Did I forget it was her birthday or our anniversary? Then I remembered she had been on a date either with the ontological firefighter or the suave Native American English professor and poet. "This won't work," she said, "if you don't care where I am," went into the bedroom and slammed the door.

I was torn. I wanted to go to her and apologize. Instead, I went to my study, a tiny room that was littered with books, newspaper clippings, piles of magazines, notes, drafts of chapter one of a dozen start-up novels, old diaries, memorabilia. I even had my parent's bank check stubs I had been examining to see if they contained evidence about the mysteries of my childhood. I took my job as a writer seriously. It was also my experimental mysticism laboratory where I attempted to move items with brain power as outlined in Ouspensky's *New Model of the universe*. My one success was tipping a pile of file folders by staring at it like a big dump was on the way. It turned out to be a 3.8 earthquake.

There was a very white, very blank, piece of paper in my typewriter. Exactly where I had left it. One line at the top, *The 100th greatest novel written by a white guy, Reed Johnson,* Our house was perpetually damp. The paper in the typewriter was limp like a Salvador Dali clock. I went back to the kitchen and made a gin and tonic the size of a glass of lemonade. I was in a different time zone than my neighbors. I went to work when they were coming home from work and often chased a Gin and Tonic with strong coffee or sometimes the other way around. The first sips brought a warm rush to my stomach and fired up my synapses. I wrote six sentences, then pushed junk off my mattress on the floor and collapsed melodramatically. Who was I kidding? I couldn't write. I wanted to fall asleep; the falling that came so completely when I was in a school class. Or pass out after a night of drinking. Sudden and complete oblivion would be nice. But when I laid down and closed my eyes nothing happened. I was wide awake. I couldn't remember if I had too little or too much sleep. My mind was racing like an engine on high idle. Pointless meanderings. Nothing I wanted to be thinking about. I had an alarming thought. What if I couldn't stop thinking? What if I could never sleep again? It wasn't as though I suffered insomnia. I had reasonably good sleeping habits. I could still stay up all night or I could fall asleep at the drop of a hat or mostly whenever I willed it. Whenever I had had difficulties sleeping I had my own equivalents of counting sheep such as trying to remember mile by mile family road trips or trying to remember the exact order of books in my father's gigantic library. I tried several routines but nothing happened. My mind continued to race. There was no off switch.

I went back to the kitchen. I thought I might turn off my brain by reading the Sunday newspaper comics but I begin to examine comic book conventions: different speech clouds, archetypal facial expressions. When Kathleen got up to pee, she found me at the kitchen table circling comic book conventions and taking notes. "You need help," she said shaking her head and went back to bed. I followed her to get a sweater. I looked at her lying on the bed. Her long blonde hair spread out on a maroon afghan; insect bitten lips slightly open. She was beautiful. When she had arrived on the college campus where we met, she had been dubbed Bridget Bardot by a fraternity. There was a bounty fund established for who bagged her first. It remained as one of the major victories of my life. Pay back for the many girls who had rejected me.

She opened her eyes slightly and faintly smiled. Ah, good I was at least partially forgiven. I turned back to the drawer to fetch my sweater and realized I had opened the wrong drawer. It was one of our junk drawers. There were hundreds of items. An image leaped to mind. Every item had string attached to it or most times multiple pieces of string, and these pieces of string eventually ran into other pieces of string from other people's junk drawers. I imagined the entire planet connected through everyone's junk drawers. There were patterns. Low and high density of tangled strong, long and short stretches. If I were God—or maybe that is what God saw when he looked in on us—I would be able to see the meaning of life.

I carefully slide the drawer out so I could carry it to my study. I glanced back to our bed. I didn't want Kathleen to see me removing it; more evidence that I was dancing the light fandango. I was alarmed by what I saw. I was lying next to her. I almost dropped the drawer. I had never had an out-of-body experience, and even though I was having one, I didn't believe they were possible. A mild sense of psychosis. I was beside myself. Ah, that's what that means!

My self in bed begin to wiggle and it turned into Morgan, our six-month-old puppy, who loved being under the covers. Morgan was our baby. He was a dachshund and Alaskan Samoyed who looked more like a medium-sized collie with cocker spaniel ears.

I found index cards in our kitchen junk drawer—avoiding the temptation to merge the two junk drawers, and realizing the floor was covered with stuff, I dumped this new stuff on the living room floor and with a ball of string, I created a maze of interconnected lines between items and story summaries I scribbled on index cards. If hypertext had been invented, I could have created links to links and text to subtext. Using my Rube Goldberg technology, stories emerged. A matchbook from Chico, California triggered a story about 500 pounds of almonds we had received from Kathleen's sister and brother-in-law's farm. There was a business card from the Good Samaritans Association. On the back of it Kathleen had scribbled, "how dad met mom." I had learned something new. If I were to pursue this enterprise there were many important questions, such as if everything was connected to everything then wouldn't the string just get tangled and wouldn't that mean I was no better off than before?

When I was ten years old, I saw a TV show where everyone in a town put one thing, they thought would inform the future about who they were into a time capsule. After watching the show I created my own. I piled stuff in the middle of my bedroom floor. My mother thought I was cleaning up my room, finally. It was difficult because I didn't want to give up things important to me in the now, and how the hell would I know what people would want in the future? Most of the time I thought the planet was going to die soon. That perspective was rooted early and has remained constant. So, what was important to save?

When I was finished with the time capsule, I buried it in our yard. I wish I knew where but I lost the map. The few indicators I did remember were altered. Trees fell. My father planted a garden. Moles and worms moved earth around. The only thing I remember that was in the metal box were baseball cards of the Brooklyn Dodgers. I might have been able to retire by selling the cards. But you don't always know what will be important. My dime store insight: Junk drawers are the best proof that Mark Twain was right—the world is a solipsistic boat load of shit—not an exact quote.

I might have gone on longer but ran out of string and index cards. The living room looked like a gigantic cat's cradle created by a schizophrenic patient. I had been awake for how many hours? I couldn't remember. My panic attack returned. What if I never slept again? I thought about how it might be a positive thing. If we typically sleep for 1/3 of our life, and I lived to 85 (based on my genetic actuary table. November 23 to be exact) then if I never slept would that mean I would live to be 113?

I couldn't just leave this maze covering the living room floor. When Morgan woke up, he would make a mess of it, the time-space continuum would be disturbed and Einstein might end up being only a postal worker. Ah, a reasonable solution. Using thumbtacks, I moved the maze from the floor to the ceiling and walls. Night turned into dawn by time I completed my task. This was working out fine. Kathleen and Morgan were both still asleep. I had to figure out what my life would be like if I never slept again, but I might talk Kathleen into taking photographs of my collage. She had a dark room in the dry part of the basement.

To understand what happened next, you need to know that one of my favorite books as a kid was *How to Get 1001 Things for Free*. My parents gave me a new edition every Christmas. They also gave me stamped post cards so I could send away for things. I was indiscriminate. I would send away for brochures about how to polish your silverware or photos of futuristic cars from Detroit. I just liked getting mail. I gave that up as a teenager when I was too busy being a juvenile delinquent but had taken it up again in the 1960s when I discovered the Whole Earth Catalog. It was like a grown-up hippie version of *1001 Free Things*. I sent away for catalogs, brochures, books, sample magazines. When I ran out of things to send for in the Whole Earth Catalog, I had expanded my search to include classified ads in magazines I picked up from the local Goodwill donation boxes.

I was just settling down in front of my junk drawer when there was a knock at the

Front door. A rare occurrence. It wasn't easy to get to our house. It was in the small gully of a polluted creek. The house was slowly sliding into the creek. In the winter a stream would form in the driveway and wind its way through our basement. Rather than remedy the flooding we created a Japanese garden: moss, tiny trees, a steam and ponds, a teahouse, and because we didn't have toy monks, we placed wooden toy soldiers. I based it on one of my favorite places, Kyo-Misu Temple in Kyoto It was part of my whole earth ethic: work with rather than overcome nature.

I could see in the rearview mirror we had nailed to a post—the only way we could see who was at the door—a ruddy-faced man who was removing a white cowboy hat and combing back his thin blonde hair. In an Edsel in the driveway there was a platinum blonde staring in her rearview mirror—Humm...I'm looking at a rearview mirror looking at Jayne Mansfield looking in a rearview mirror. An Escher moment. Then the cowboy leaned over the porch rail so we were face to face. He motioned to me to open the door, but I was distracted by someone else arriving on foot. Had he come out of the woods? The new person was dressed up in a black suit. Young and straight. The only people in this neighborhood who wore suits were Jehovah's Witnesses. Kathleen leaned out of bed and, somewhat alarmed, asked me what was going on. "Don't worry," I assured her, "it's just Avon calling."

Then the phone rang. I opened the door, and not thinking clearly about my next move, I invited my guests in while I answered the phone, "Is Reed there?" someone at the other end said. What the hell did I sound like? I almost hung up, but the voice sounded vaguely familiar. "Please hang on," I said, politely.

I put the phone receiver on a table, but it fell to the floor. The cowboy turned to me, "Ron Edsel with Miracle Ear. We sell hearing aids. Someone at this address sent away for a sample of our new compact model. Would that be you? Are you hard of hearing?" I avoided saying the obvious. And he added, pointing to the giant Edsel in the driveway, "God's sign you should buy from me."

The Jehovah's Witness held out a glossy brochure. "Well, can't help you with that" he said as he handed me the brochure, "but I'm a Rosicrucian, here to tell you about ancient secrets of the universe." I could picture the ad I had responded to, something about 500-year-old secrets revealed. How could one pass on that? Mr. Miracle Ear was pleased as punch. He grabbed the witnesses' hand, "Praise the lord. The president of our company is Jehovah's witness. That's why it's called miracle ear. I don't believe this. What a great coincidence. The design comes from one of John Smith's journals when he was in the desert."

Just to round out the party, I could see my neighbor Phil, who was always smiling and thought the gully was the best place to live anywhere on the planet, walking past the Edsel carrying a plant the size of a German Shepherd.

Morgan just then pushed his way into the living room, and for a flash exposed Kathleen, half naked. The guys were so engrossed with the vision of a naked young woman that the Rosicrucian didn't notice Morgan peeing on his shoe until the pee created a small stream that trickled across the floor and descended into a hole in the floor. The hole was clearly marked with a danger sign.

Phil was at the front door, "Oh sorry, didn't know you had company." (He knew. He knew everything we did). "But I have that snowberry bush I was telling you about." "Howdy," he said, turning to the hearing aid salesman and Rosicrucian. I thanked Phil and went to the kitchen to get towels to clean up Morgan's pee stream.

The Rosicrucian had a flash of brilliance. He got down on his hands and knees and invited us to join him so we could call forth guardians to protect this "humble home." I kept one eye open, just in case this was a scam. I pictured our homely scene from outer space. We were probably the only place on the planet with this confluence of capitalism, ancient secrets, and Mr. Roger's neighborhood. I could see Kathleen looking at us from the bedroom, now fully clothed. Maybe I wasn't a breadwinner, but I had engaged ancient guardians to pray for our home. I also wondered about future junk drawer items that might mark this day, like the Rosicrucian brochure. But if I started saving things on purpose, then I would enter the arena of the uncertainty principle. I was also surprised that no one seems to notice the entangled cat's cradle of truth on the walls and ceiling. Did I only see it?

I realized I had forgotten the phone call. They had probably hung up, but it was a good excuse to end the convocation. "This has been very nice," I said, "but there's an important caller on the phone whose been patiently waiting all this time." The three of them went out the front door. I didn't feel too bad since I knew Phil would invite them to his house. The blonde waved to me cheerily as they moved to his house.

I picked up the receiver and gave a halfhearted hello. It didn't sound like anyone was there but then, a smoker's raspy and deep voice, "I was moved by the invocation. Are the guardians enormous or invisible? I suppose...no worries about making me wait. A phone freak friend set me up with a special hold function. It's like having two lines." He giggled— A funny sound like he was pushing Jell-O through bad fitting dentures. "He can also give me a number to call for free long distance or an inside line to the Israeli secret police." I realized it was Jack Ainsworth.

I wanted to talk with him. I had many questions, but sleep deprivation was catching up with me. The best way I knew how to stay awake was to keep talking. I motor-mouthed my way through my out-of-body experience, my dream of a community laboratorium and my insight about junk drawers. Finally, like the Energizer bunny[1] with cheap batteries, I just stopped.

"You need to copy down this address." Jack said, "and if you have access to a WATS line, this phone number. It's in England. Dr. David Finney. He's studied junk drawers for 30 years. I have a paper he published I'll send you. It's a cross cultural analysis of junk drawers— not that it is always drawers, mind you. You know Eskimos use seal bodies. (Jell-O laugh) He analyzed 5000 junk drawers in America, Canada and England, and found that 78% of the contents had a significant story attached. That's excluding paper clips, rubber bands, etc. which he calls nihilities—although you'd be surprised how many nihilities have stories. He also found that—don't quote me here—but

I think it was like 60% of the contents could explain 58% of a person's life. There's a complicated formula I don't completely agree with, but it's still interesting." From this distant vantage point I wonder why I didn't doubt Jack's story. But at the time it seemed perfectly reasonable that he would know a junk drawer researcher in England.

I wanted to get off the phone. I felt inspired to write. But Jack kept talking—about the Crying of Lot 49, an underground communication system run by twins Thurn and Taxis; Quicksilver (whose real name may have been Michael Shamberg, who I knew as Mr. Gorilla Television) one of many traveling video porta pack troubadours he wanted me to meet. He told me about the Funny Farm[2], his family's 19th century homestead, now run by Uncle Gus., an anarchistic-techno refuge for vagabonds and rascals. He described the farm, but I was part of my brain was wondering why this, all of it, was happening. I think he described things like a drive-in movie theater on the farm, and part of Spanish sailing vessel on Mossy Brae, the 200-foot-high hill in the middle of the 300-acre farm—"think about it? It would mean the accepted history of this region is all wrong," he said in a dry academic voice.

He also told me about synergies in our lives. And added—the kind of insight I got used to with Jack—"I know you hate that word." One of his oldest friends (with hints she was more than that), Lilly, a gifted painter and dancer who worked with Ann Halpern and was life partner with the founder of Revolting Librarians in San Francisco. Lilly had been saved from an abusive alcoholic lover by friends of my parents. His aunt lived next door to one of my mother's childhood friends who was murdered by her son. I told him that the son had given me a comic book I buried in my time capsule, a DC Superman that might be worth a lot except I couldn't find it. And how that was related to my important insight I was calling the cat's cradle. Oh, you mean Kang Sok? Jack said, "the Bhutan name for it." He also knew about where I had grown up (Southeast Portland) what college I went to (Lewis and Clark College) , where Kathleen grew up, (Palo Alto) where Kathleen and I had homesteaded (Cascadia Oregon). A little weird, like talking to an FBI agent who doubled as a 10-foot-tall pineapple in malls.

He told me about his father, Dr. John Ainsworth, and his framework for finding truth and taking power away from the invisible council of elite rationalists through discovering random knowledge. It might change the world as we know it, he said earnestly. If I had been really listening that day, my life might have turned out differently. Throughout the conversation, I just took what he said for granted; not finding it strange that a stranger would know so much about me or trusting him as though he were my older brother or venerated teacher.

We hung up, But I didn't make it to my study before the phone rang again. It was Jack. With that delightful or irritating Jell-O laugh, he said, "about this junk drawer idea.... it's a little like counting cards in Vegas. But I think I can help you if you help me. Here's the thing.... We either make up our own rules or the universe makes them up for us, right?" He didn't wait for my answer, which was fine since I wasn't sure what the question was or the answer. "So, here is one thing we will do. I will produce the "Arabian Nights," just for you. You tell me good stories you live; you tell me shitty ones, you die." Girlish giggle. "I want you to take all the junk drawer stuff and put it into a banker's box, or however many it takes. It has to be banker's boxes. And another important rule, regardless of how many boxes. You have to stir them up. I mean, don't toss it like a salad or bouillabaisse, just gently stir it. Then once a month we'll get together and one of us will pull out an item and you will tell a story. Who knows, maybe I'll tell a story or two too. It has to be spontaneous and structured, you know, like Kang Sok is. So that's my proposal, what do you think?"

As though we were having a rational conversation, I replied, "So let me get this right. I am Scheherazade and you are the Vizier. Do I have to do the same balance of comedies, tragedies, poems, burlesques and erotica?" And do they all have to end with a cliffhanger?" I Paused to see if Jack was suitably impressed with my knowledge of Arabian Nights." He was not. Just stared right through me with Jack's black laser look. So, I continued, "I only want to tell stories about my childhood, I think."

"See," he interrupted, "you don't really know what you want or how to make a choice. But fine then just pick items until you get ones that prompt stories of your childhood. I'll take it to the Junk Drawer Council and request an amendment to the Random Junk Story Handbook" (the council and handbook, I found out later, neither never existed). And the biggie, I promise to get it all published."

"And what do I have to do for you?" I said, really just hoping to get off the phone.

He described the work of the Gertrude Stein Fellowship Club, which as far as I could tell was whatever he and Uncle Gus wanted to do. They organized events for the traveling minstrels and performing artists who yo-yoed up and down the west Coast from LA to Vancouver. They hosted the events at the Funny Farm, but it was too far out of town and there had been complaints from neighboring farmers. "But, now," he said, with a barker like zeal, "we can go big time. A female Fatale from the 1920s has donated a warehouse in the neighborhood called Old Town. She funded the Crying of Lot 49 Postal Service. I think because she's a stamp collector."

I agreed to help.

"No, that's not the way I see it" Jack said earnestly, "you are officially on the board of directors. I just created a new position on the board just for you. You will be secretariat, I'll tell you later what your responsibilities are."

By time we hung up, my ear hurt, and Mr. Sandman had disappeared again. I stared at the cat's cradle maze on the walls and ceiling, and examined the remaining items in the junk drawer, mostly nihilities. A broken pen. Spent camera flashbulb. A piece of gin fizz chewing gum from Japan (well that might be a story since I got it from the Japanese girl I fell in love with), bobby pins. A plastic clip-on earring. Where was the line between something and nothing? I pulled out a grocery list from six months ago. "granola." I didn't have it in my childhood. But cereal. Reading cereal boxes while my father read the newspaper came to mind. OK, my father. Not good. My father is an entire universe.

If I were going to map out how my story was connected to everyone else's story through their junk drawers, I was going to need a lot of string and a bigger space. Maybe *random* was just what we didn't have enough collective brainpower to figure out? Once we had a computer bigger than the moon and more powerful than a locomotive, then we could chart out every random event and would see the connections between everything. This was going to be a big enterprise. I would need something the size of a football field or a computer the size of our living room. I closed my eyes and picked items off the wall. I didn't put a white glove on my left hand as Jack had suggested, but I did note the time. The stove clock was blinking 10:00. Not that it was the real time. I then located the junk drawer items on the floor, and with my eyes closed randomly selected a handful of junk and carried it to my study.

Phone again. Guess who? "You know I assume?" He didn't pause long enough for me to respond. "In *A New Model of the Universe*, the experimental Mysticism chapter, he conducts an experiment on himself. He is never clear about what it amounts to? Meditation? Drug induced? He goes through stages of awareness and the "highest" one he says is mathematical. Past words, images, voices— oh right and down to even one voice, where he says most religions get stuck, you know God, Jesus, Mohammad, etc.-but he says beyond that then there is nothing but mathematical signs. He also observes that infinity is not continuation in one direction but infinite variation at one point. He stares at an ashtray for a long time. Ever do that? And realizes it is connected to everything in the universe. He finds a note to himself the following day, *a man can go mad from one ashtray*. Isn't that great."

I realized I hadn't told Jack I had already disrupted the scientific rules by creating the maze of strings and index cards. I explained what I had done and told him I would take it all apart and put it into banker boxes. There was no response. I realized there was no one at the other end. I said hello several times, louder each time.

Then suddenly, "Sorry," Jack said, "but Alfred, our 19-year-old cat, can't get into his cat box anymore so I had to help him. What were you saying?"

I decided it didn't matter. "Nothing important."

"Great. I'll see you Friday, right? Oh, one other thing. Would you mind if Uncle Gus is there too? He takes lightning-fast Native American shorthand he learned in World War II."

I went back to pondering my junk drawer. Was it a framework or a metaphor? Is it about all the junk? Just one drawer? What if I found a scrapbook or an old address book in the junk drawer? Those aren't random; it is organized junk. Photographs? Including photos in the inventory seemed like cheating. Cheating what? I was establishing rules for chaos. We had several boxes of photographs. I decided if I found loose photos in a junk drawer that was OK. Then the first photo I pulled out wasn't mine personally but from *Life* magazine; a famous one from the 1960s of a young woman sliding a flower into a rifle at the 1967 March on the Pentagon. I had the photograph because I was at the march in the front line, close to where the photo was taken.

I made another editorial decision. A rather big one that could skew the outcome. I included the boxes I carried around from house to house as we moved. Same principle, wasn't it? The boxes were filled with stuff I had considered important enough to save but not important for my day-to-day survival. Junk drawers? Junk boxes? I was making up rules in a scientific field that hadn't been born yet.

I walked to my late-night hangout, the Bomber[3] restaurant. I got to the top of our driveway; the vintage World War II bomber on top of the restaurant in clear sight. Turned back. Then turned around again. Cars and trucks hurtling along. If Morgan or I jumped into the traffic chasing a cute collie in heat, we would be dead. I couldn't decide, or was beside myself.

As I made my way back to the house, I realized I was finally feeling sleepy. In fact, it was overcoming me. I was weaving like a drunk. But I didn't want to sleep, not yet. I needed to inaugurate the junk drawer scheme. I could feel the stories of my childhood ready at the gate like greyhounds. I met Kathleen getting into Mr. Zoom. Where was she going? She was glaring again. But for which offense? Junk drawer schema covering our living room walls and ceiling? Inviting invisible guardians into the house? That we didn't have any money? That I had forgotten rules about our new open relation? That we were no longer in love?

"We need to talk," is all she said as she backed the car out.

I wanted to care. I did. But it all felt out of my control except for the junk drawer plot.

That's the last thing I remembered. Out like a light. When I woke up, it was dark and Kathleen was sitting on the floor next to me. I think she was trying to figure out if she still loved me. It hurt to have my eyes open.

She stood up, looked down at me, and matter-of-factly said, "Connie is coming over tomorrow and helping me move some of my stuff to Michael and Linda's. I think it's better if we separate for a while."

I was trying to figure out what day it was and the appropriate thing to say. I said, "Can I help?" She stepped over my piles and left. I tried to follow but fell back to the floor, fast asleep.

The solution to my writer's block had come about randomly. Right? I just opened the wrong drawer. Was it divine intervention? I had seen a replica of myself in another dimension. And then this random stranger had called, offering me a deal. Do somethings for him and he would turn me into a brilliant writer. The writer's block defined who I was or was not or who I wanted to be. I was desperate to get past it wherever it took me; jump off the cliff and land in a bog of crocodiles, or vat of jelly, or timeless bliss.

My First Days at the Gertrude Stein Fellowship Club

I went to sleep a married jobless hippie and woke up a bachelor with a new job, Secretariat of the Gertrude Stein Fellowship Club. Things were looking up. Well, not the bachelor part, but I even had a name for how to find meaning in the world through junk drawers. I woke during the night with a brief, satisfying smile, "I will call it string theory,"[4] not knowing the phrase was taken by scientists. I wasn't sure if the junk drawer thesis was real or just a metaphor. It was like the wisdom contraption developed by the Houyhnhnms in *Gulliver's Travels*, or Hermann Hesse's glass bead game. I was also excited about the Arabian Night's idea. Well, it was excitement blended with free-floating anxiety and dubiety. I had hopes I would learn what stories to tell and when to begin and end them. And maybe more importantly, why I felt compulsive about writing the stories. It seemed as much a burden as a blessing. Was compulsive storytelling a sickness or gift? When I had told Jack, I felt compelled to tell my stories. He had said, "You mean live life in the third person." Things with Jack could mean everything and nothing in succession like a strobe light.

I filled Mr. Zoom with my office and essentials of home—it all still fit in a car. Morgan put on his French beret and we were off to our new life. On the way we—well, I did anyway, although Morgan approved—sang *"Whistle While You Work."* Morgan didn't care for Disney anthropomorphism. The song became lodged in my brain for a month after that.

Now that the Gertrude Stein Warehouse was a part of my karma it looked different—looming, surreal and important. But maybe only so if you wore secret goggles. Jack had told me to park on SE 5th Avenue. I had only seen it from SE 6th Avenue where it appeared to be a normal, if somewhat run-down warehouse. There were a few people milling around. I'd say there were six hippies, five indistinct citizens of Portland, and the group that stood out the most, eight guys who looked like extras for what?....An IWW or stevedore union movie? Typical blue-collar guys—smoking, spitting, cursing, eye-cruising for chicks. But normal? Feeling like Sherlock, I noted something odd. They were all clean; their outfits looked they had rented them from a costume shop. It wasn't raining but dripping—off of gutters, five or six large sunflowers that had survived in a concrete desert.

Then one of the large doors opened on one of six loading docks.

A small man with a long white beard crawled out from under it, but he had to jump, nimbly, to avoid the door which came crashing down. "Fuckers, I told you that door needs to be fixed." I noted he directed his cursing at the hippies, not the blue-collar circle.

He rushed toward me. "Been expecting you. Uncle Gus to you. I've got lots to attend to and I'm late. He pulled out an oversized old-fashioned watch on a chain, "Get it?" he said. "Know the reference?"

"Yes," I said, "the White Rabbit."

He stopped quickly, "Jack wanted me to pass this on to you this... if I remember it right. He isn't sure about calling it—he didn't explain it to me said you would know— string theory. A friend of Dr. John's, another John, helped develop string theory and found black holes. He thought it was important you know about non-capitulating coincidence collusions? Your strings could just lead you to a black hole and your destruction."

He handed me a 3-ring binder. "Everything you need to know. Three hundred pages. The record reading time is three hours and the high score is 95." He eyed me. A piercing examination. "There is a hidden cache scavenger hunt coming up so I have little time, and this one has a big prize, four quotes from the sixteenth century, fifteen metaphors from the Tinker Creek fisher lady, and $100. You'll get yellow legal pad memo about all this if I can find the..." He turned to the eight identically dressed-in-blue workers, "Give me a name. Quick!"

Someone quickly shouted back, "Shawn."

"Right, so I will get you the Shawn manual soon." Turning to me, another drilling-deep examination, all through his thick eyebrows. "We just created the role of secretariat last night. Up all night doing it so hope you appreciate it." He opened the large door with ease. Stronger than he looks, I thought.

"That's right." he said, "so don't think just because you're taller you can take me down...

Answer to what? What I was thinking?

"So, the first thing you should do is the weekly roll call." He shuffled through the binder. "Here's a list of current tenants, and their rent payment schedule is here somewhere." We continued to walk as continued to describe the role of a secretariat, me thinking he's the size of Lewis Carroll's rabbit, yet I'm having a hard time keeping up.

"Remember, hardly anyone pays in cash so you need to know what everything is worth, and believe me, I have gotten everything under and including the moon...like? Oh, let's see...". He foraged through papers. Some paper flew away. He paid no attention. I could see that a lot of paper was blank. "Here's a list Leland made awhile back. He never dates things. Hope you do. Just kidding. He dates everything, and I mean everything! Like a chainsaw with pencils instead of teeth, meant for people with sharp wit.

"The warehouse is the urban outpost of the Funny Farm, but it is also an architectural version of the Badger manual. Get it?", Gus said, stopping abruptly.

I said, "No, I don't get it."

"You know it contains everything. An answer to everything. Amazing book, really. I mean Donald Duck's Woodchuck Manual. Eventually you will learn about the Badger Manual...The one I saw was about the size of a 1950s comic book and yet you could look up historical facts, how to make things, and even what happened yesterday to your Aunt Maple. You know?"

"And Jack wants a history of the place. You know the obscure thing I am referring to, right? Going back to the Random Lot in Seattle and controversy between Jack and his father that almost toppled world leaders—but don't worry about that." He stared into a spot in front of my feet, "You know it's not right? If it were, you'd be out of a job. You know," he said, doing a poor imitation of Donald Duck, "it's all in the Badger Manual. If you have a question about anything—and I mean anything—you consult the Badger manual." Then with a fake wistfulness, "this is all assuming we find the Badger Manual; that it is in the missing box. Don't get me wrong, the Gertrude Stein is a wonderful place to work live. A ripe place for a caterpillar to become a butterfly... but not like the heyday of the

Funny Farm." He made an audible sigh. He looked up at me. "I like to think of my laugh as a titter, not a chortle."

So, you may not be following this exchange, but neither was I. As I learned later, Gertrude Stein residents had their own slang, but also a way of talking that was in a gray zone between telepathic, non sequitur, and parallel monologues.

Gus went on. I was to maintain the Salon scrapbooks—all the tenants were required to deposit scrapbook materials at least weekly or face undesignated "sanctions." I also was to organize the People-to-People indexes, help make sure that the Crying of Lot 49 Postal Service ran smoothly, organize events, and finish a part of the earth catalog started by Rainbow Flute who fell in love with a Japanese Aboriginal woman and had gone feral in the outback of Australia.

"Which is another reason Jack thought you were in his karass,"[5] Gus said, while letting loose a slow whistling fart. "*The Mello Pages*, right... that's what you call your thing, right?" It didn't surprise me that he or Jack knew about it, even though I had only posted fifty flyers around town trying to find volunteers to help. It was part of the Technology Laboratorium fantasy, to publish an alternative telephone yellow pages.

"Oh, a biggie. We will give you $200 a month. That's besides free office space, access to the electronics lab, library, 15% discount at the Quality Pie restaurant. Jack will have to tell you what he wants you to do as far as people-to-people indexing. And He's been working on how the Arabian nights sessions will work."

Then in hushed voice, "and of course the missing box. And no, it's not like the park bench in *Waiting for Godot*. Real. Or if it is like *Waiting for Godot*, then you are the park bench."

It was hard enough to follow Gus, both physically and mentally. It became easier over time. I realized that was me adjusting to his pace and non sequitur nature of his brain—similar to Jack's, so I have to assume it was a family trait.

The Gertrude Stein Club was noisy. It seemed like Gus, sometimes without moving his mouth, like a ventriloquist. I heard him say, "Plenty of time for that later." His mouth didn't move, but one of the blue-collar workers who had been following us said fairly loudly, "You heard him right."

I shouted out, staring at several people, "Do people always follow you or are they following me?"

Gus, picking something alive from his beard, replied, "If they were going fast and had gone all the way around the planet then we're stalking them, right?" Chortle.

The offices I could see in were tiny. One or two desks. As though reading my mind, Gus said, "The average office size is about 1,200 square feet. Impossible, you say? Hang on to that thought. We're only on the first floor."

"So, what goes on here?" I asked. Again, Gus stopped, although this time I was prepared. I stopped before I asked the question. He looked at me as though I was in a Chevy Impala Plant and had asked *so what to you make here?*

"Dumb question, but I think on average—Leland might know better—there are between thirty and three hundred organizations as tenants or using the space for events."

"That's a kind of large range."

"You think maybe? There are about 2,000 events a year."

"So, five events a day?"

"No, more like fifty. But it's harder to get fix these days. About a year ago Jack and Leland institutionalized a new protocol they called Armageddon Brain Storming (ABS). There was a sign-up sheet for scheduling use of the warehouse's twenty event spaces. If you put ABS after your event it meant you didn't mind if another group, regardless of the nature of the event, could be double-booked. And then, who knows what might happen. Anyway, more about that later, we've got to move on...Oh, right, and there's been about 20,000 people here if you know what I mean since opening, whenever that was."

Another stop. Gus turned and whispered, "Sorry no one is friendly, but you know deadlines and Mercury in retrograde."

It seemed to me people had been friendly, although maybe not making good eye contact. But I didn't feel I knew Gus well enough to know when he was pulling my leg, especially since right then he pulled his leg, "Gout, runs in family. Another reason it's hard to give you an accurate account is things change. I suppose if you had a group like Mankind in Favor and Against Everything MFAE (pronounced Muff), you would not have to change your by-laws... your name can fit with any cause or mission. But take The Universal Center for Manitou Spiritual Advancement, which became the Esperanto Society for World Peace, which became the UnivesalOne Center. But the guru who ran the place, Shamu, sometimes known as Sadu, was changing his organizational name as he moved through life. "Duh, you know. That was the point, after all," He shouted out to a young blonde woman loaded down with file folders, "Wasn't it? When Shamu's harem started doing their collective masturbation in front of the governor's mansion, what were they calling themselves?"

"World Peace Through Ejaculation," I think she replied matter-of-factly and continued on her walk. She turned back. "I never did like that name."

Just then I noticed a man down the hall. I had only seen pictures of Jack, but it looked like him. He seemed to spot us and hide. But it was such a deliberate hiding. His beard and naked leg were sticking out in the hallway like the beginning of an exotic dance.

"Okay, on another subject, I'm not saying this place is like ritzy, but it is an entire block close to downtown, not falling apart, six stories." He paused and bent in closer to me, as though he were going to tell me a dark secret. "The average block in Portland is 68,000 sq. feet, while Chicago's is 217,000. So that means the Gertrude Stein has about 400,00 square feet, right? You know that expression, right, "We're not Chicago."

Gus started walking, talking with his back to me. "Yeah, I know where you're headed and you're as likely to find out how we afford it as you are to find the secret Coca-Cola ingredient, but let me put it this way: the patron's pockets are deep, there are places named after her everywhere, and we don't really have to worry about collecting rent... and she lives near Ursula Le Guin." Then Gus said very earnestly, "Do not try to find out who or talk about it with anyone. Very important."

I turned around. Gus was gone. A medieval vixen smiled and said, "Gus will be back in a minute. You have any questions?" I imagined the responses I might display, and decided on nonplussed, like nothing had happened. She was wearing a flowered peasant outfit, had red hair, and seemed like she always walked around in a bubble of sea breeze.

A voice from somewhere said, "That's Genevieve—seriously—she works with Leland. She doesn't know it yet, but she wants to be your assistant."

My stuff had already arrived. One box looked like it had been dropped in a mud puddle, but all the others were in tack. Morgan's bowl on the floor sent a cold shiver down my spine. I forgot where he was for a second and then realized Kathleen and I were ending our twelve-year relationship. "Ok, then I'm leaving you. Don't forget Leland will tell you about everything else."

There was a decent desk, although the top had carved initials, and a leg was missing, held up instead by bricks. There were five lawn chairs, a substantial floor lamp, and six large filing cabinets. "All yours to file," Gus said, pointing to the file cabinets. "Think of it this way. You could just go outside, collect newspapers or whatever you find, and file it. Or you turn information into knowledge, defeat entropy, add some time to your years and get early release." There were large windows and a partial view—another factory, and the tops of fir trees in the distance.

One other door. I figured a closet. I opened it and it was a closet, but the back wall was fake and slightly open. It was one of those doors that slide into the wall. I pushed it and almost fell back on the floor, thinking I had entered another space-time continuum. It was a large room with a noisy echo, sixteen-foot-high ceilings and in sight a small kitchen and bathroom with shower. I could live here. I realized that was a no-brainer. Probably many of the offices were also homes.

I fell asleep that night at my desk. Woke up around 3am with drool soaked into the ink blotter desk top. I found out that at night I was not alone. At that time the old building made sounds, distinct (pots and pans; radiator heating) and indistinct and mysterious—a sound of the ocean, pleasant moaning, a dog and cat fighting, someone yelling, "fuck off," and a mechanical sound, maybe a printing press.

The Technology Laboratorium Fantasy

Preamble

What we found in the archives after Jack's death about how we met, was a file folder, not a story or essay. There is a three degrees of separation chart showing the ways we almost met. Color coded and as Gus notes, using all 48 colors in a Crayola 48 pack.

- Photo of him and Anthony Judge [5] at a conference. I think it was the World Expo in Spokane, Washington. I created a people to people directory of all the futurists and networkers—including Judge—at the conference. Judge had written our bible at the moment a directory of all the networks of networks.
- An article talking about Captain Jack's unique dome where he is mentioned as the person who came up with the idea of using roll down car windows for windows in the dome.
- Meeting minutes on "ancient" mimeographed paper and purple ink with an attendance list that included himself, Steve Wozniak, and Bill Gates. (Not sure how this is related to our meeting).
- A thank you note from Larry Williams, director of the Oregon Environmental Council for his donation. We were always told that Larry had an affair with the pretty blonde who volunteered there. Same time as Kathleen dated a firefighter, most well known for being in a Fireman soft porn calendar.

When we moved back, we lived for a while at my uncle's house in the shire while he was off skiing with his war buddy, Smokes, and the likes of Mariel Hemingway (or at least that's what he told us). Then we found our home in the gully not too far from the shire. It felt like I was living in two worlds; now part still in the country, and part in the future. OK, so that is temporal and spatial. Is that OK to do? We continued to heat with wood, put up food for the winter while we both looked for jobs in our own ways. With money we made from selling our homestead, we bought equipment for the techno-laboratorium whose name kept changing. By the time I met Jack, I told people I was creating a community resource center—the more down-to-earth version of the Technology Laboratorium Fantasy. A center staffed by networkers who linked people with other like-minded people and resources. It was mostly a manual operation. I was laying the groundwork for an operation that would eventually be computerized, but at the time one could count how many computers there were in the city. There were the dozen Daddy Warbucks with mini computers and us. the hippies with revolution in our hearts and 64K in our computers.

Our purchases were in part practical and in part wacko. We had a Gestetner mimeograph machine, a thermal paper copier, an IBM Executive typewriter, darkroom equipment, video camera, and an alpha wave machine. It's the later that might give one pause. But the other equipment bought us friends. For example, how I found some people starting what they called the Home-Grown Library, and others starting the Poet's Warehouse, and our technology led me to Jack.

A part of me inhabited the same world as the geeks who became famous and rich. I wanted to connect people with other people and information and resources so they could change the world. It was a political cyber landscape; theirs was an electronic dorm or bar.

The fantasy—at least at first—was still embedded in our back to the land dream. People could live anywhere but still in effect be living on a college campus where our tribe members were just a virtual short walk away. And information, which was power, would no longer be owned or hoarded by a few.

So, imagine I am thinking about these things in 1969, but I was in the middle of nowhere. And I still believed the Shire, and this region was my home. While I was exhilarated by the chronicles and discoveries of the Homebrew Computer club[6] and the originators of "freenets" and obscure texts by people like Anthony Judge [7] about worldwide social networks, I was not in the epicenter. My life might have been quite different if we had moved to the Bay area then. I might have just gotten lost as a foot soldier with more well-connected people. But in Portland I was like a follower of Jesus in the wilderness. If there was anyone else thinking this way about the future of computing and social networks, and power through information, it wasn't hard to find them. Well, let me put that another way. Since there was no internet it was difficult to find anyone or anything (information or computing power) but there was also something inevitable about it. It was like I was talking a dialect. When I launched into my fantasy, people looked at me with indifference, skepticism or even concern that I might not have lights on in my caboose. But the special code words like networking would stand out and then someone would say—sometimes just to get rid of me—you should talk to so and so. And all paths seemed to lead back to Jack.

I went off to work every day, sometimes no further than from our kitchen to my study, sometimes to the public library or the Reed College library. I devoured underground newspapers and mimeographed fugitive literature. I toured the radical enclaves in the city and took notes from flyers on telephone poles. I made unsolicited calls to people I found who led me to other people. It was cosmic detective work, but there was no corpse or crime.

Kathleen was more selective and precise in her job searches, and it paid off. She became editor of an underground newspaper and volunteer staff at one of Oregon's first post-Earth Day environmental organizations. There was overlap between our worlds. I ended up writing the "access" section for the underground paper, since that fit in my cosmic mission. I was helping people find others who were trying to create the alternative universe. That's a pretty big task, as you can imagine. But Kathleen's and my path also took us in different directions. My path took me to the fringe. Every day I met or learned about people who were creating new organizations or projects or programs or whole movements, and spaceships and perpetual motion machines, artwork out of computer chips. Many of these pioneers were bright, others were dim. Many dreams were not destined to succeed.

In the techno-laboratorium period, I wasn't too interested in the political progressives. I watched the more radical progressives who rallied behind McGovern for president being replaced by the more establishment Kennedy people. The fringe people were once again pushed to the unfunded outskirts. In some ways, the passing of the torch wasn't all that different from any other generation. The progressives might smoke pot, and even take acid occasionally, but they would "settle down" and inherit the previous generation's progressive political work.

I didn't realize it at the time, but I was also attracted to beginnings. I was like fireweed in a clear-cut or burned forest; an early occupier plant. I helped organize an alternative lifestyles festival because it was where you met people who were starting new things. The names alone drew me to enterprises: the Apocopation Reconstruction Company, the Green Lace Wings Collective, Fat Chance, Jaybird Information Center, Observations from the Treadmill, Society of Strangers, the Living Systems Institute, Vocations for Social Change, Duck Soup Media, the Institute of Applied Energetics, Futures Conditional, Abundant Life Seeds, Float Town, Pot Walloper, Sumerian World Improvement Association, Universal-One Center.

I met people like Captain Jack. I spent several hours in Captain Jack's dome in the hills inside Portland. déjà vu. He never showed up. Similar to my first times at the other Jack's house, where he never showed up. Only a lovely woman, Millie, who at first seemed like she must be a watercolor artist or believer in fairies but turned out to be a raging Marxist who made me a delicious but hot as hell bowl of chili. All I knew about Captain Jack was that he was building a spacecraft and from a letter Jack shared:

"I was born on Saturn, but our family got kicked off the planet because my dad was fired from his job. We went off to Mars, but it was horrible there, so bushy and no social life. One night I was out with my check (did he mean chick?) and we ran out of gas. The gravitational pull brought me down to earth and ever since I've been trying to figure how to get back."

Instead of food, Capt. Jack drank Motor Cola. (his own concoction) One eight-ounce glass provided all the nutrition he needed for a month. On my first visit to the dome Leslie ignored me while I flipped through a pile of magazines and newsletters about habitat, in particular domes. I entertained myself opening and closing windows, which doesn't sound like fun, but the windows were from all types of cars and trucks. One of the windows even opened and closed electronically and played Beethoven's 5th. Finally, I asked Leslie what she knew about Captain Jack's spacecraft. She looked at me like I was in an Oregon forest looking for a Douglas fir.

"Duh, you are in it," Leslie said, "As always, the engine is a coat rack. In case you didn't know."

I went to dozens of meetings every week. I showed up like Forrest Gump, not always even understanding what people were trying to do, and never clear if I was on the cutting edge or in a swamp filled with loonies. I showed up at meetings that eventually led to stopping freeways that launched Portland's alternative transportation system; a crafts market that became the multi-million dollar Portland Saturday Market; made brownies as a member of the Men's resource Center to support the beginning of Portland's first Women's Health Clinic; signed a promissory note for $500,000 (while I was on unemployment) to buy a church that became a community cultural center; meetings that launched Portland's neighborhood democracy movement—at not just in one part of town, but I showed up at first meetings in neighborhoods in all districts of the city; launched a skills and service exchange and tool lending library.

I don't think my description of the technological-laboratorium-community-resource-center-world-brain was ever the same thing twice. But no matter how I described it or to whoever, people would tell me I had to meet Jack Ainsworth. Nobody could explain why I should meet jack. They might say "You know he does those salon things at the funny farm," or "He's the head council of the Entropy Evasion League," or "He brought Willie Wonka's cousin to town," or "he started the Crying of Lot 49 underground mail service," Or, vaguer like, "He's been doing this forever."

I knew what he looked like from an undated news clipping. In a photo he was standing with his Uncle Gus in front a carnival ride Gus had invented that was a giant lever with a hot dog at both ends. Jack appeared to be in his fifties; although he looked like one of those people who might have looked fifty as a teenager. He had dark, mischievous eyes. If he hadn't been smiling, he might look like Rasputin. Odd hairdo. He was partially bald, but instead of a bald top he had bald sides, like a Mohican.

I finally talked to him on the phone, and he invited me to his house. But he was never there. The door was always open, with a spectacular view of the city. There were refreshments, excellent wine, and state-of-the-art AV equipment. Most of the time there were other people there, all with appointments with Jack. People like a Bell Labs engineer who had dropped LSD and became a crystal artist or a swarthy Reed College student who had recreated Wilhelm Reich's[7] Organe box experiments. One day no one showed up, but the wine and refreshments were laid out. I ended up reading through what seemed to be a draft manuscript on how to start a community radio station, very similar to the popular *Sex and Broadcasting* by Lorenzo Miliam[8] which I had just picked up. I remember thinking it was kind of odd that the book was conspicuously open on a coffee table next to the chips and dip.

I met the traveling mistral group, "THEY-US," the collective that was trying to once and forever figure out exactly who "they" were who were always trying to get "us." We hosted a salon for them. A prize was given to the costumes that best personified "us" and "them."

I also met Phil. At least that is how he introduced himself. I found out later his name was Ralph and was living with Kathleen's friend, Jude. Phil told me Jack had saved him from a life of obscurity and uncertainty.

"Jack gave me the best advice I ever got," Phil said while trying to hide a bright purple spot on his head that reminded me of the one Morgan had on his butt after a major flea infestation. "He told me to keep an eye out for the man in a pink jumpsuit." He looked at me sincerely. "I can't tell you how many doors that have opened for me."

And how I met Uncle Gus, who acted as our host. He made sure we felt at home, helped ourselves to food and very good wine. When I first met Gus, I thought he looked like Jack, but then I realized he never looked the same. When I would try to imagine him or describe him to others, it was like I was describing Mr. Potato Head: different eyes, nose, face hair, even height and weight or age. What I remember from our first meeting was Uncle Gus's chronographer. It looked like a gigantic version of the White Rabbit's clock in *Alice in Wonderland*.

But not a clock, I had naively said. It looked like a speedometer and Lewis Carroll wouldn't have known about those, would he? And just exactly what did the door mouse say, Uncle Gus replied. You know that song by the Jefferson Airplane. Stuff like that drives me crazy, he said earnestly. Instead of miles, it was years. The arrow pointed to where his Gus was in his life. There was a red marker at 80 where he figured he was going to die. It was clear he was most of the way there. Every six months at a random time in the day, the chronographer would trigger a tape to go off with a random selection of music ranging from Armstrong's "What A Wonderful World" to 1950s rock-and-roll love songs. There were several features the owner could set. You could record how your days were going: stagnant, slow, flat line, speedy, exceptional, punctuated. Then at the end of each day it would reveal your life gap. I never learned what you were supposed to do with that information. After the third invitation, when Jack never showed up, I realized it was on purpose. Later he told me he called these events half-hazard, half-baked, and half-hearted salons.

43

1. The energizer bunny was created in 1973 as a mascot for Energizer batteries.

2. By now you are probably wondering what the relation is between the Funny Farm and the Arora Colony. They were within miles of each other and both founded at the same time. The strongest connection between the two is the Champoeg floor mill. I might have not known this if I hadn't found a finely carved wooden Buddha inside a Champoeg floor mill bag. The industrial side of the Ainsworth family ran the mill. Their largest customer was the Aurora Colony. They were ashamed of the Ainsworth clan and the Funny Farm, so they changed their name to Swan, descended from the Nedprunes of Coon Valley, Wisconsin. The Aurora colony was a Christian utopia founded by William Keil. There were about 600 people there. The equivalent today would be a commune near Portland with 20,000 people.

3. The Bomber was more than an advertising gimmick. "It's almost like a fairy tale story," maintains Milwaukie's Art Lacey, who owned and operated the 48-pump McLoughlin Boulevard gas station housed beneath the awesome WWII-vintage B-17G four-engine Bomber.

4. String theory grew out of work by John Archibald Wheeler, and further developed by Werner Heisenberg in the late 1930 and early 1940s. Black Holes. John Archibald Wheeler (July 9, 1911–2008) is best known for using the term "black hole" for objects with gravitational collapse already predicted during the early 20th century ,and for inventing the terms "quantum foam", "neutron moderator", "wormhole" and "it from bit"

5. From Kurt Vonnegut's *Cat's Cradle*, Dial Press. 1963. karass is a network or group of people who are affiliated or linked spiritually. A granfalloon is defined as a "false karass". It is a group of people whose mutual association is meaningless. Bokononism is a religion based on enjoying life through believing "foma", harmless lies.

6. The Homebrew Computer Club was an early computer hobbyist group in Menlo Park, California, which met from March 1975 to December 1986. The club played an influential role in the development of the microcomputer revolution. Several high-profile hackers and computer entrepreneurs emerged from its ranks, including Steve Jobs and Steve Wozniak.

7. Anthony Judge, January 1940, was director of the Union of International Associations. He published the *Encyclopedia of World Problems and Human Potential*, and the *Yearbook of International Organizations*.

8. Lorenzo Wilson Milam is an American writer and activist instrumental in starting many of the first listener-supported community radio stations in the United States, beginning with KRAB in Seattle in 1962.

GERTRUDE STEIN FELLOWSHIP CLUB

Preamble

As a last resort we conducted a straw poll, as outlined in the *Gertrude Stein Club Rules of Order* to determine if Henry Sycamore really existed. Two hundred votes were cast. I abstained, which made it 100 votes for *Sycamore alive*, 99 against. Jack had 2 votes and could have determined the outcome, but he was nowhere to be seen. So, Henry exists, and therefore the Annals is his, even though I showed them large sections in my handwriting.

We found the Sycamore's Annals in the same piles as my documentation of the Gertrude Stein period. That is, the documents are disguised to look like mine, down to the age of the paper and typestyle. Was this an attempt by Jack to show my professional and my personal sides of life? Why did he create my version of Gertrude Stein period and a persona (I assume), Henry Sycamore's?

But the Annals stood out. The other documents are public records—or that is made to appear that way, but these are stories about my personal life during the period. It was one of our earliest clues that Jack was doing more than just editing or recreating my work as secretariat of the Gertrude Stein fellowship Club. I told him about my 99-year-old aunt and being a caregiver for my grandmother when she was dying. I suspect he found more details in my personal journals; the ones purported to being destroyed in the Gertrude Stein warehouse fire.

The Gertrude Stein Fellowship Club Annals

by Henry Sycamore, 1985

> The Gertrude Stein Fellowship Club warehouse is an architectural manifestation of the Badger manual—the relatively small book that could answer any question. Amazing book, really. I examined comic books, and it was never bigger than a dictionary, and yet you could look up historical facts, how to make things, and even what happened yesterday to your Aunt Maple. You know?
>
> We are blessed to have Henry Sycamore's record of life at the Gertrude Stein Fellowship Club for several years. He kept roll calls he conducted monthly when rent was collected—rarely in the form of money but more often objects, such as muskrat pelts, ancient vases, etc. He also wrote up more impressionistic descriptions of the life and times of the Fellowship Club. That writing is the most important and easy to share material.
>
> — JACK AINSWORTH - SEPTEMBER 1985

I figure in the earliest roll call I may have documented one third of the warehouse residents and their projects or programs, at the most. In no particular order of importance, beauty or age. There was the Abundant Life Seed Foundation, which was either collecting seeds, assuming an apocalypse, or signing people up for the cryonic revolution. There was Ace Haynes, an alternative job counselor who in his spare time warned people about the coming end of the world. Naturally just down the hall was the Apocalyption Reconstruction Corporation ARC) who were trying to create a new economy based on protein coupons and who communicated with their communal farm up the Columbia Gorge using genetically modified carrier pigeons notable because of their purple feathers. And just in case Ace or the ARC failed, there was the Earth Reassembly Factory whose biggest project was constructing Noah's ark using a recovered coast guard vessel that was in the Warehouse annex on the east side of the river (rumored only; no one including Jack knew anything about it, or at least that is what he said. They had a competitor in their endeavor, Floattown, who had an abandoned barge on the river. The rumor never confirmed in their case was that they used underground tunnels in Portland's skid row used to kidnap derelicts into forced work on ocean faring vessels. The Institute of Entropic Energetics was a cosmic parody (their term) of the governor's Office of Applied Energetics. There were some "straight" operations, like the Dildo Press (lesbian literature press); the Living Systems Institute, design of solar and underground homes; a splinter group who didn't advocate underground homes after the leading national guru of underground homes was crushed in his own, called Here Comes the Sun; a chapter of Esperanto; Captain Compost and White Cloud Recycling, two small recycling companies, long before there was a market or interest in waste; the North Paranoid Climbing School, who led groups to climb rocks in eastern Oregon (although who also made furtive night time climbs on Portland office buildings). There were many arts groups in particular street performance groups, focusing on happenings and camp. But some of those groups traced back to Jack and Gus. It seemed everyone had one or both or their board or listed as primary staff members, including Experiments in Art and Technology, the Emma Goldman Collective, Great Western Radio Conspiracy, the Imagebank (brand was Mr. Peanuts), and Muddy Duck Acoustic Studio. There were also some subsidiaries of the Crying of Lot 49 postal service, including Dana Space Aachley (his name), Quicksilver messenger service, The Light Fantastic, and the Theobald Network. The Trekie who was obsessed with whether you could time travel and what you would change. You know, like if I move this lamp six inches when I am in 1923 and a boy misses it because it should be somewhere else and knocks it over and it burns down a barn that burns down a block where some guy running for president lives and it kills him etc. Kang Sok told me that one of his biggest regrets was that his son had buried in a time capsule out back of the warehouse, paved over for a parking lot, a first edition of DC Superman comics. However, Jack told me later Kang Sok wasn't a person but an ancient spell. Huh? Jack posted random signs about, some with clues about hidden wealth, others just random, like a haiku: Old pond / frogs jumped in / sound of water. Jack's version: Old Henry. Jack jumps in. Sound of chaos. Another sign announced a workshop that never occurred, as far as I know, from the Stone Mountain Trail Institute, about Metamorphism, an alternative to the Oregon Trail, blazed by 19th century hippies.

There were also many unaffiliated people who lived and worked there. They were allowed in by the once a month Deliverance Awards ceremony. They chose nine people whose commonality was a random color of the day. They interviewed candidates all day long and selected winners based on a questionnaire that no one ever wrote down. That is how Bertha ended up living in a room with a defunct furnace. Her entire mission in life was to link everything to LSD. When I arrived at the Clubhouse, she had 10,000 phrases and had conducted research on about 200. For example, the alphabet on LSD, Dog and cat fucking on LSD, Snail on LSD, snail getting rid of back of turtle on LSD, Jesus on LSD, eating a corn dog on LSD, free falling from 10,000 feet on LSD, a day at the Gertrude Stein warehouse hanging upside down on LSD. You get the idea, right?

The warehouse had the energy of a dysfunctional electoral campaign. At first I had no protective armor. I was vulnerable to every plot and excited to have so much going on in my life. My mood shifts reminded me of something I couldn't put my finger on. There were many people, many who I me, others who skirted by me without eye contact, others who seemed to always migrate together laughing about inside jokes. It dawned on me. It felt like I was back in high school except it was a high school on Jupiter and everyone took LSD with their pop tarts. Some days everything happening seemed not only normal, but it felt like I was part of an underground incubator where ideas for evolution of the planet were being revealed. At least I wanted to believe that. It seemed like a work release center. I met people, dozens. I developed routines like going out for coffee at the official Gertrude Stein club hangout, Quality Pie. I read through the Gertrude Stein manual.

When I asked Astrology Bill about Leland, he said in an irritating New-Age-pregnant-pause-and-beard-stroking-way, "as always the best thing to do in the warehouse when everything else has failed is to stand in one spot. It will come to you."

Sure enough, as soon as I stopped moving Leland showed up, in a creepy way, standing over my mattress on the floor which made his 6 foot 4 and 280 pound body seem even larger. Calmly, "I hear you have been looking for me."

Leland and I became good friends from the first moment, although as I learned later from many people, that's what everyone thought, but also no one, except for Jack, knew any more or got any closer than that first moment. He was a gentle giant who had been deeply harmed in the Vietnam war. Most of the time he just wanted to be useful. He collected information like it was firewood for the coming ice age. He made up projects based on vague directives from Jack. Jack told him he wanted to know about all innovative ideas as they emerged in Portland, "including the ideas that the originators don't know is original or before they even have the idea. You know, say it out loud or share it. And then cross-connect those ideas to understand the convergence." I can just imagine Leland saying, no problems, boss."

Leland tried several ways to carry out this task. The one he was working on when we met was a gigantic map of Portland, hand drawn by the mysterious Bob Benson who I had yet to meet. Leland then toured the city via bus and occasional taxi. He took photos of all flyers on telephone poles, and bulletin boards in coffee shops. He then analyzed these according to Dr. John's Map of Knowledge. I learned that from the Subversive task force in Portland. That's how they got some of their best information about the underground." he told me, explaining his innovation tracking system. He also clipped "relevant" newspaper and journal articles and organized them into scrapbooks. The scrapbook collection kept growing. And growing. Sometimes there was only one item like a news clipping for the *Coos Bay Herald*, "Coastal Alien Abductions," in the 1950s scrapbook. But when I point this out to Leland, he led me to one of many archival spaces in the basement.

"There you go," Leland said. "I would guess 200 linear feet. And of course, the stuff like sculptures and mummies things like that is somewhere else."

Leland lived in a tree house on the ground floor of the warehouse. He called it his watchtower. I had noticed it my first day at the warehouse but did not understand there was someone living in it. He had a phobia about not being able to see in all directions. He had also created a series of "hotlines," which were ropes connected to various offices and desks. The high ceilings in the warehouse made it possible to send his information along ropes and pulleys up and down hallways. "Limited," he told me earnestly as we looked at a color-coded series of ropes. With an elaborate pulley system, he relayed information attached to the ropes with clothes dryer pins. He would shout out, "Information coming your way." Sometimes the information was right on the mark: a flyer announcing events or copies of fugitive documents. He loved that phrase. "Fugitive document coming in at 4 o'clock."

Leland worshipped Jack, who had moved him out of a makeshift home he had under a nearby freeway ramp. Jack had given him a $100 bill and a tiny book, *Servant as Leader*, which Leland always had with him, rolled up in his back pocket. Jack moved Leland into the warehouse and gave him a job title, the Entropy Evasion League Secretariat. When I arrived, they changed his title to Entropy Evasion League Supervisor.

"Ironic," he said when he told me, "I mean everything is, isn't it?"

He made copies, ran errands, and was often the note keeper at meetings and public events. He had the most elegant writing style. He could make block letters in 4 point or 72-point size, and in styles ranging from English Gothic to Helvetica. He told Jack he had learned it from a guy who taught him about interstitial wildernesses in the city. He helped this guy map out the smallest "wildernesses" he could find in Portland, "He doesn't have a name? Nope, not pronounceable on this planet. I just knew him as the guy who created a Martian Passport.

With the help of our map making genius Bob Benson, he had created a spectacular map of the city. Together they had identified over 50 plant species that existed only in these tiny green spaces, some of which did not appear in the city's larger parks and green spaces."

A couple of months after my arrival, Leland and I went on our first roll call, a tradition that went on for years. I should add, it wasn't just me and Leland. Morgan and Leland fell in love. Their bond was so instant we made jokes about previous lives. I was jealous. Morgan would sit at the base of Leland's tree house. Not crying or begging, but with his head on the floor he would tilt his eyes up and he would watch every move. So Leland came to me and asked if it was all right if he sometimes carried Morgan up to the tree house. He was instantly the Gertrude Stein mascot. And of course, he wore his French beret. Morgan also loved our roll call days, and why not, everywhere he went he got treats and hugs. Leland was the perfect sidekick, an enforcer by sheer magnitude but gentle as a lamb. He frightened me mostly because he might just fall over and kill me, or if we turned corners quickly or went down narrow hallways, I was likely to get injured by accident, which happened many times. He had this laugh that made you want to hug him. But the laugh was tenuous, so much like the map he had hanging in his tree house that Jack had commissioned Bob Benson to draw. It looked like a kid's map of make-believe land, showing winds from the east called "laughing" and winds from the west called "crying," In the middle was a place called home. It was a bird nest, Leland's home with the wind blowing in all directions.

He also tried hard and often to tell jokes, but it seldom worked. That first day for our roll call, he ceremoniously brought out a gigantic photo album that looked like it was from the 19th century and showed me a list of the events and organizations that needed some spot checking. "There may be something suspicious," he said. That by itself was humorous to me. Suspicious in this context mean what exactly? "Let's see," he said, "we have to check up on the Barfarama event. You know purging in order to reach nirvana. And then the Vortex Lab is testing a new psychedelic drug, but we have a neighborhood incident in which a tenant told a homeless person to go fuck a duck and honk for it." He rattled on.

One thing about the roll call is that because of the names of groups most everything seemed humorous, either black humor or Groucho Marx kind of humor. "And Fat Change is having a fight over paper supplies with the Frog in the Well Collective and In a Nut Shell is siding with Guess Who—I mean the group not the question. And Pot Walloper showed up at the Reality Library event even though What I Mean told them not to. It was up to Rural Saturday but still... "

When reports like this made perfect sense to me, I knew I was becoming a part of the scene.

He turned to me to emphasize this— "it is not part of Uncle Gus's Armageddon Brain Storming process. So, they shouldn't have just showed up." This is when I think I won Leland over for good.

Without missing a beat, I replied, "You know, I think you should drop the Uncle Gus part of that title. I know you guys developed it together." That I knew about the process and spoke up for him made a lasting impression.

We didn't start the roll call and rent collection by going to tenant offices, but went to the catacombs so we could assess the state of tenant contributions. We had to give dollar amounts to what was there and assess if the value had gone up or down. The basement also had a creek flowing through it, Dodo Creek, named after one of Dr. John's sisters who died when she was three. It was a nice creek, only occasionally unruly, and someone had turned it into a putt-putt golf course. Over a tiny bridge and behind a giant door that used to be an ice cooler was the catacomb filled with, well, everything and anything but also all the item tenants had bartered for their rent. It looked like deep storage for a theater group—stage props, statues, costumes; and a staging area for a garage sale—lamps, chairs, kitchen appliances. Anyone could use the stuff, but Leland would provide entry and careful oversight. There was a strict lending policy.

"Isn't the creek a nice feature, don't you think," Leland said, motioning toward the basement creek, "Jack picked up the idea from some suburban yahoo." "That would be me" I said matter-of-factly.

The first time we wandered the hall doing roll call and collecting the rent, it felt like being an inner-city street grid person playing hide and seek in a suburban mall and cul-de-sac world. Hallways and offices looked the same, and more disturbing people and organizations and their goals and activities blurred into one another.

They held the board meetings at the local coffee and doughnut restaurant, Quality Pie. If people had escaped from the cuckoo's nest, they could be found here. The coffee was so bad it was good. The pies were colored-coated sugar. Anyone was invited to attend the Gertrude Stein board meetings. Which meant on some occasions we filled the restaurant. One time the owner—a retired the nationally known body builder—asked us to leave. Jack stood up and announced, OK, free coffee and pie at the Gertrude Stein warehouse. The restaurant emptied. We all stood in the rain until we were invited back in, and then Jack paid for coffee and pie for everyone.

It was also difficult to figure who had flown over the cuckoo's nest and who was a legitimate board member of tenant. My first board meeting I sat next to a guy who I ran into many times on the street who had obviously been told by some authority figure to not touch anyone. Problem is, he only had part of the instruction down. He touched and then drew back like he had been slapped and did it again and again. One day he showed me his prototype of a perpetual motion machine, a car battery attached to a small house fan. Just before the fan stopped, he would plug it into a wall socket. "Get it?" he told me, as long as I remember. Our killjoy overweight lawyer had to point out the obvious and sent him flying out of Quality Pie, knocking over a police officer on the way.

From minutes of one of the board meetings, a list of organizations who had paid rent—remembering a lot of the rent was in kind, like a pig, free massages, post life regression travel passes etc.

Show and Tell Nights

I researched the history of Show and Tell Nights at the Gertrude Stein Fellowship Club. I found documentation of show and tell events dating back to the 1930s, hosted by Random Lot in Seattle, Washington.

The first Show and Tell events Jack organized in the 1960s brought together as many people as he could find from his grade school who remembered their best show and tells. Things like a pet boa constrictor, which since it had been in third grade was now just the boa's skin, but the presenter's actual third grade teacher was there in a wheelchair. There was also dancing from Bavaria, Amazon river grub feasts, an Alchemist from Romania who showed how gypsies had created an atomic bomb in the 15th century. The North Paranoid Climbing School had a slide show of their mountain Climbing expeditions on peyote, Float town had room size replica of a future city they were going to float on the Columbia River. The Apocalyption Reconstruction Company discussed their protein-based economy. Short Bob and tall Bob were always there with their folding bikes, as was the Esperanto Free Planet group—with expensive translation dictionaries that seem mysteriously luxurious. Imagebank, always there with their Mascot, Mr. Peanut and complex collages. The Primal screaming collective and the Possum Living Collective had a feud no one could ever understand, although the shouting several times shut down the Show and Tell events. At one of those Short Bob was left over night in the Simulation Tank. the auditorium where Show and Tells where most often held had to close for several months because of a horrendous stench. Fortunately, Goddess Rachel with the Ocean in a Grain of Sand Collective found it was left behind by the Simple Living Collective when they did their Road Kill workshop. Fuck and Duck and Honk was most known for creative ways of sneaking unknown drugs into the events—mostly indigenous and organic ones from the Amazon rain forest. The only group that was never invited back was the group without a name who promote Barafaramas. The only group that brought the law down to the events was Dr. Abbott's irregular and uncertain health clinic because they had stolen the Wilhelm Reich Orgone machine from Reed College.

One of the salons that gained much public attention was when Jack Pratt showed up to cure all of Eugene's ailments by applying a 50-foot needle to the top of a prominent hill in the middle of the town. Jack Pratt was a drop out ad executive. He described himself as a social animator. He was an amateur photographer and filmmaker, and the first part of the scrapbook described his photographs and film screenings. The reviews were mixed. "Pratt is a component technician, but his subjects, and his way of organizing his art, reflects a lack of understanding of cultural tradition and reflects a condescending attitude toward his audience." There was a news clipping that described how he had been incarcerated in Salt Lake City because he had wired the courtyard in front of the Mormon Tabernacle to play rock-and-roll versions of sacred songs, and placed himself in the middle of the courtyard wearing nothing but a gigantic nylon with a sign reading, "Sinner."[1]

There were also rather official and well-organized events at the Warehouse like the Alternative Lifestyles Festival, held annually, and a Global Village high tech symposium, the Angel Eyes Psychedelic Fly-fishing workshop hosted by the arresting Angel Eyes from Mendocino, California. A science in the neighborhood workshop hosted by Neighborhood Technology Inc. of Washington, D.C. There are sparse descriptions of some events, no date, no number of people: Community Strengths conference, The Harvest and Barter Festival, a Leap Year conference presumably only held on leap year Februarys.Oh, and a kind of weird one. Melvin, my unpredictable childhood friend, showed up as a reasonably good magician. He had some standard things. But then he did this amazing thing by providing the name of every person who cleared their throats or farted—even the silent ones. He was only right about 2 out of 3 times but still damn, how did he do that. I came up to him after the show, but he denied ever knowing me. Weeks later, I found a card in my mail. Of course I remember you, but I had to pretend I didn't. You know show biz! May your life force still express itself as elephant flatulence.

Gertrude Stein Days, Jack's Version of Narrator's Life

Preamble

I wrote the following stories. I only kind of write them; edited by Jack. I read them several times. I was both pissed and honored, imagining Jack taking the time to rewrite my journal entries into "real" stories. Evidence? The ESP story, for example. I had never been to the funny Farm and the Chinese Fortune cookie factory is still there today. I have a photo of the invitation to ESP auditions on my bulletin Board. The community Novel compiled at the Home-Grown Library has my name as the first contributor. I have the original of the Vegetarian Map Maker's map of the Maritime Northwest.

Home Grown Library and the Mello Pages

Many new organizations and projects were birthed in church basements. The Home-Grown Library was at first in the basement of one of Portland's oldest churches. The Library collected fugitive literature and had a giant blank book that was a community-written novel. The book was 3' by 4' on very thick paper. They placed it on a tray on top of a paper Mache statue of an obscure Ainsworth from the civil war era. We called him Ezekiel. He was bent over with what remained of his head touching the ground, so in effect they nestled the book on top of his sizable butt I found a poster announcing the beginning of the Community written novel. Also, Carol, known in those days as Ruby Slippers, later a school district superintendent, and I met and she verified existence, promised to show it to me, but nothing happened.

Gus gave the loose collective that ran it a deal they couldn't refuse, free rent in the warehouse's basement with over 7,000 linear feet of erector set style shelving.

The group also put together one of the Gertrude Stein's most successful products, the Mello Pages, an alternative Yellow Pages. As with so many things during this time, there were other people around the country working on the same idea. Vocations for Social change in Boston assisted communities create yellow pages, and we visited a group in Seattle who were putting together a Part of the Earth Catalog for the Puget Sound. The group collected piles of information about Portland. They found out about every organization, old, new, imagined, futuristic. At one point they took the telephone yellow pages apart, and page by page tried to find alternatives. Members would walk the hallways shouting out categories from A-Z.

"Anyone got an alternative to zippers? How about ant farms?"

We were trying to create a parallel universe, and the Mello Pages was going to be the alternative yellow pages guide to the parallel universe.

Leland was the primary editor. It took over a year to complete, in part because it was like trying to fly a 747 with stoned airline pilots, and in part because his life was falling apart in so many ways. When asked why he did it by local TV interviewer, he said "normalcy therapy." Hunting, gathering, filing, creating schemes for organizing the world, seemed like a perfect way to escape the world. It was published. According to a reliable source, 1000 copies were distributed mostly at bowling alleys, gas stations, and alternative lifestyle shops. In the one existing copy there is a blurb by Ken Kesey, "Far Fucking Out." The TV interviewer asked Leland if he knew Ken Kesey. He replied, no but I wouldn't be surprised if Jack Ainsworth were Ken Kesey.

Earth Space Portland (ESP)

Then there was ESP—Earth Space Portland. Crazy Ralph first brought the group to our attention, but people tended to not pay attention to him. He told Leland, then who told me, that he was standing outside a phone booth when the phone rang so he answered it. He told me, "You know that place that used to be a Chinese fortune cookie factory? Well, now it's a movie recruitment office and a place where they are going to launch a rocket to outer space."

A couple of days after the event I went to the ESP "world headquarters" at the Chinese fortune cookie factory which had been there for as long as he could remember. But, now underneath the replica of a giant fortune cookie, there was a small handwritten sign:

Earth Space Portland
Temporary World Headquarters Forever
Film Recruitment this way

An astrology center across the street, and what might have been a disorganized junk store or a compulsive hippie scavenger's house, rounded out the small retail district.

As I approached the front door, I realized there wasn't one. Instead of a door there were strands of tire treads hanging from a bright orange bar that had snake eyes at one end and crudely drawn rattles at the other. As I got closer, I realized there was warm air pouring out of the building. A lot. It felt 10 degrees warmer by time I was twenty feet from the entry. There was a distinctive smell in the air, a combination of incense and gasoline. I had to duck down to get past the thicker part of the tire treads. As soon as I was inside I was greeted by several disembodied voices. The space seemed to go back —past piles and piles of boxes—for a long way. It was dimly lit throughout.

"Welcome." (female)

"Is that what we're saying now?" (male)

"If it were really happening, not just happening then what?" (female)

"I don't know what you're saying." (male)

"About time you got here." (female)

"Let the experiment begin." (same as first female)

"I've already moved on." (male)

I heard someone clearly say, "Have a seat," then the sound of a chair moving. As my eyes adjusted to the dim light I could see people, but indistinctly; fifteen people, more or less. One group was so still they looked like silhouetted stage props. There was also a woman with long hair who was wildly gesticulating to several others but she didn't seem to say anything. A mime?

I sat down in a chair that turned out to be a toilet seat without the toilet or plumbing (I assumed) and looked around the room. Not much to note, pretty barren. There was a map of the solar system with a speedometer below it that indicated the speed the Earth was moving away from the big bang. It showed the earth or the building was going 18,000 miles per hour. A poster for a book about the true meaning of apartment building gargoyles. A kid like-drawing entitled "Swordfish on LSD" that looked like a bouquet of sausages in a meadow. On the table—a large utility wire spool—there was an odd contraption. A space helmet is the first thing that came to mind—of the dime store variety. Just about when I had something else figured out about the space helmet, I was startled by a man coming up behind me.

"My name's John," he said as he sat on another toilet seat.

I rose, in order to indicate I would stand up and shake hands if appropriate, but it wasn't.

"I'm not hugging today," John said as he picked up the space helmet. "Phil's monitoring my brain waves on days with hugging and without." He turned the helmet around and screwed a large blue crystal into the round halo part of the contraption. It lit up. "I saw you admiring our outer space ESP transponder.

He let out a brief giggle, or maybe a noisy swallow, "I mean…there were other things that happened to me but I would have been mostly right there," he said, pointing to a bookshelf. "It doesn't really matter anyway," he said indifferently, "Don't take it personally if I don't remember you were here." He paused, stroked his beard, looked up suddenly, then down, "Let me put that another way. I am in the same space standing in the morning that is happening for sure and I don't remember you already, so not a chance I will tomorrow." Pause. "I hope that makes it clearer." He laughed, put his hands on his waist, striking a stance like a pirate or maybe a sorcerer. Then random voices.

"If you had come in you'd want me to pay attention to you, right?"

"But, he's not one of us."

"Stop! You j-shifted the attention zone."

"If the shoe fits, get an umbrella."

Now that I got a better look at the thing I could see that it was an upside down colander with small handles and three tiny legs. At the top of the legs there was a Frisbee with the center dug out so it was like a large orange doughnut.

"Ah, I know why," John said as he unscrewed the blue diamond crystal. "I didn't have the energy source in the right place, "this part comes undone and presto, the diamond drops into the middle of the force field." The blue diamond dropped from the Frisbee halo so it dangled and swung back and forth in the colander.

If there was one thing I had learned by living at the Gertrude Stein warehouse, it was how to act nonplussed. I said matter-of-factly, "I helped organize the event at the Gertrude Stein Fellowship."

John interrupted. "Let's clear up one thing right away. We are a totally separate subsidiary corporation of the Entropy Evasion League that made the presentation. We will use the data from the questionnaires ,but that's about it."

Even with my eyes adjusted there just wasn't enough light to catch John's expressions but I sensed he was inexpressive.

I continued, "Well, I just want to know about the film you are interviewing for."

"Well, can't help you there fellow," John said bending under the table to pick something up. "You came because you came, that's all I know. But, understand certain things before we can continue. You know what I mean?" He moved forward a little. Then he fell back in his chair and exclaimed, "Shit, I didn't mean transponder. I meant receiver. This is the receiver. Not the transponder. It's really not my area of expertise." He then brought his large pale hand out, palm up.

"Voila," he exclaimed as though he had done a magic trick, revealing a quarter with a hole in it. "This is for you. You know. I had been told someday it may save your life." I never refuse life saving devices so I held out my hand and the warm coin fell gently into it.

I realized it was silent; the only sound was a refrigerator. I looked around and all the people looked like silhouettes. There should have been some rustling or breathing. John rubbed the Frisbee part of the receiving unit.

"I'm calling Merlin, who I assume you are here to meet," he said and stood up. Then there was a loud noise and the bookcase in front of me moved forward.

"You may have to move," John said, matter-of-factly, "to make room for him."

Light poured out from behind the bookshelf and a tall lanky man appeared wearing a Pokka dotted top hat and sporting a mid-chest-length white beard. No clue how old he was. Without much of a pause he looked down at me in a friendly enough fashion, and said, "So I assume John has told you about our space travel plans? Let me show you our multi-processing on-board computer." He spoke with an accent I couldn't quite put his finger on. Maybe German or Austrian?

Merlin put his large hand on me, "Come on let me show you the computer." He turned to the silhouettes. "And anyone else that hasn't seen it all fired up."

"Lead the way," I said, the best I could come up with. I looked behind myself and could see at least three people following us. We ducked around the edge of the bookshelf into another room, at least as big as the outside one. Another man, wearing all green (hat, pants, shirt, socks, gloves) greeted us.

"Stop right there," he said rather irritated. "You will not get the full impact unless everyone stops right there."

I looked across the room. Although I wasn't sure what a multi-processing on-board computer would look like there didn't seem to be one. On the wall opposite us, where Merlin and the green guy looked there was nothing but one gallon gas cans with their tops crudely cut off. There must have been at least 200. Wall to wall. Inside many of the cans there were fan blades and the cans on the parameter were all lit by candles.

"Only the RAM's on now," Merlin said looking at me with wide-opened eyes. We're about to kick up the mainframe." I heard a loud click, like a circuit breaker and it was dark except for the cans with fans.

"Come on, who's ever coming," Merlin shouted. Several people moved quickly to sit on the floor near us. The dim lighting kept me from distinctly seeing the people. Although the woman closest to me whispered, "I'm just pretending to be a woman today." Then she said out loud, "Here we go." A flame shot up near the far end of the wall of cans followed by a series of noises. I couldn't identify them all. Mousetraps going off, car brakes, chainsaw, cords from a familiar rock-and-roll song (maybe the Stones?), the whir of a turbine like thing. Some of it real, some of it recorded. Hard to tell which was which. There were also screams (definitely recorded). "Slaves, you know," the woman next to me whispered. Then, one can after another, from one row to the next, the candles inside the cans lit up and the fan blades in most of the cans circulated; one after another until all 200 were flaming and fanning. This took 20-30 minutes. People made pleasing noises but no one spoke. I could smell the woman's perfume next to me as she swayed back and forth.

When the last one was ignited the audience, including myself, applauded.

"Now that's one heck of a computer, what do you say," Merlin said loudly.

"Incredible," I said.

We stared at it for some time then the bookshelf opened and a voice announced, "Drummer has produced a late dinner. You're all invited."

There were ten for dinner. We gathered around a pile of boxes that had a piece of plywood over the top that served as a table. I read labels on the boxes while waiting to be served. Tacoma, Walk of the Hands, 1976; Philadelphia, Arch of Disappointments, 1977. There was now sufficient light so I could see everyone, but nothing else had changed.

A very small woman, about my age, handled him a large bowl and spoke in a foreign language. I was confused; she said in English, "Esperanto." Oh, right well that explains everything.

The woman with the strong perfume to my left whispered, "She's trying to tell you the condiments are there on top of the computer chips.... Either that or she wants to marry you, kind of the same in Esperanto."

All I could see on the dining table they was what looked like electronic parts. Not wanting to eat computer chips, or fall victim to a joke about chips, I politely refused and begin to eat what was in my bowl, that was about ten different kinds of bean sprouts.

After we ate, Merlin took me aside, and said, "I want to be honest with you here...." He hesitated realizing he didn't know my name. "Sandalwood, that's what I'll call you. I have the feeling you're disappointed. I want to know why, Sandalwood."

It didn't seem that disappointment defined my feelings, but I asked him about what Ben had told me. "I heard you were recruiting people for a film."

Merlin stroked his beard and nodded, "Ah, you're too late. The caravan left yesterday." He folded his hands like he was going to pray. "I'm not sure you would have fit with that, anyway. You know it wasn't really a film. What they were going to do is get everyone there, have them create the world of the future and then just you know live in the future."

He looked furtively around the room, and then someone, maybe John, looked at him and shook his head, raising his eyebrows, and said, "no paper." He then handed him a felt tip pen. I said, "And what about Peter Fonda and Dennis Hopper?"[2] He answered me while shoving a large pink bean sprout into his mouth, "I don't know them. Do they work here?"

It's the Sand Crabs

My life could feel like I had entered a novel on page 42. Most of the time it was a Kafka novel or William Burroughs stream of consciousness. Befuddled by life creating art or art creating life. I seemed to attract crazy people.

The strained but continuing ties between my life and Kathleen's was well illustrated by our mutual acquaintance, crazy Ralph. He was clearly more in the warehouse world than the ivy league environmentalists. Jolly Tom the humor therapist, who lived on bean sprouts and dyed his hair a new color every week, one day whispered to me, "Don't think the guy's working with a full deck, or there's too many people home in his attic."

I met crazy Ralph through Judy, one of Kathleen's friends. It pleased Kathleen that Judy, who didn't have good luck with beaus, had a boyfriend. Judy was not someone you would suspect of knowing a person who had traveled to Jupiter.

When we walked into Judy's small and tidy apartment, Ralph was standing in the middle of the living room, stationed like he was an obedient dog staring at the front door; or, more specifically, the floor just in front of the door. He had flaming red hair that shot out from his head as though he had been electrocuted. A beaming smile and eyes wide open as though he were practicing the melodramatic stance for a play tryout.

"I was told about you the last time I was here," he said as he looked directly at me and ignored Kathleen.

"Really," I said, "and when was that?"

Judy greeted us from the kitchen.

"That's Judy in the kitchen," he said. "I mean when I got back from Jupiter." He then froze as though he were listening for another arrival at the door.

Kathleen did not deal well with non sequiturs or people who took trips to Jupiter. I avoided looking at her, although I could imagine her frightened look. She was probably fighting back a flight response, while I stood my ground with a matter-of-fact reply as though Ralph had just told me he had been to the shopping mall.

"So how are things on Jupiter?" By that one question, I endeared myself to him.

The dinner conversation felt upside down. Judy greeted Ralph's abnormal remarks with normal answers, but when Ralph said, "Dear, these pork chops are perfect. Just the way my mother did them," Judy looked worried. When Kathleen explained pending air pollution legislation, Ralph launched into a tangled theory about entropy and then insisted that Kathleen and he had known each other for years. He was glad to see she was again working on environmental issues and had gotten over the loss of Jenny, our dog. Weird. Part of that was true. Jenny was the name of Kathleen's favorite dog growing up. When Kathleen told Judy the environmental newsletter, she edited was at the printer, Ralph launched into another part of his entropy theory. He stared at Kathleen and earnestly pleaded with her, "Don't trap your soul in letters from the printer. I know you know that but you could be damned forever." He paused. Finally, a smile—a very fake one—emerged. "Well, maybe not forever. Just a long time."

About a week later, Ralph showed up at my office. He sat on the floor for hours. No sound or movement. It was remarkable self-control. I went off to a meeting and when I came back; he was in an animated conversation with Leslie who Gus was working, a Key Kesey community organizing project. Leslie was a beautiful red-head, very calm and kind disposition. They were having a reasonable conversation about how to get people to come to the Kesey event. It all seemed so—and too—normal.

Gus was helping organize town hall meetings in Portland that were a part of Kesey's Bend in the River (BITR) project.[3] Kesey had talked the Oregon Humanities Council into funding town hall meetings around the state to have a dialogue about what we wanted Oregon to be in the far-out year of 2010. This was 1974, which was the year the Sixties became the Seventies. It was when loose social movements coalesced into organizations and street leaders embarked on political careers or managerial jobs for NGOS. What this meant for BITR was that anytime you had a meeting, the room was filled with nascent leaders and too few followers.

When I went off to the bathroom, I expected Leslie to do the polite sidebar, "A little deranged but harmless." Instead, she put some flyers on my desk and said, "So I hope Ralph can come. I think we could use his help organizing." Huh? What did I miss?

It turned out that Ralph was a brilliant community organizer. There were about fifty people at this one meeting, all crowded into the Victorian home of a woman who would become Portland's mayor.[4] I was nearly to the end of my wits. It had taken over an hour just to establish an agenda and was probably going to take at least that long to assign a time for each agenda item. It was going to be another meeting that went to midnight, and it was making me feel we would be better off leaving the world to evil military-industrial maggots. There must have been ten people talking simultaneously when Ralph stood up. He held up his hand up like he was in a class. Strangely, everyone stopped talking.

"It's the sand crabs," Ralph said. "That's why we are in trouble."

A couple of people snickered; others looked around at each other, but it was still quiet as he continued.

"When I was on Jupiter last week, I was told by the Majestarians that the reason the earth is out of balance is because there are too many sand crabs. It is why they bounce."

There was silence in the room. To this day I can't remember what happened exactly, but I do know that within thirty minutes we had agreed about a plan of action and that everyone left the meeting in a good mood. Several people were singing, one group was dancing, and some people stayed behind to clean up dishes.

About a month after Ralph's skillful group facilitation effort, Judy called to tell me that Ralph was in the psychiatric ward of a local hospital. She needed our help. There was going to be a hearing to determine if Ralph could be released or should be sent to a long-term care facility. Apparently, Ralph had decided he wanted to go to Seattle (North) but had ended up in Gresham (East). The police had found him banging his head against a telephone pole. He wasn't severely hurt but bleeding profusely by the time the police arrived. Judy wanted us, along with two other friends, to testify on Ralph's behalf.

The hearing took place in a small room in the county courthouse. Ralph walked in accompanied by a police officer and psychiatrist. When he saw me, he said loudly, "So here we are again. They just don't give up do they?" I threw up my hands with a smile, looking at the Judge, as if to say, just an inside joke.

While the judge was the presiding officer, it was the psychiatrist who ran the show. I watched Ralph as he answered questions. There was something different about him. He looked like a grade school kid being asked to identify state capitals. He answered each question directly and succinctly.

"So why were you hitting your head on the telephone pole?"

"I was upset with myself for going to the wrong direction. I know Seattle is up."

"Have you felt different since being at the hospital?"

"Where?"

"Have you felt different in the last few days?"

Ralph said, loudly, "Yes, there is something different. I can hear a radio station through my teeth." The psychiatrist dutifully scribbled on his ledger pad.

"So, it says here you were a computer science major at Reed College. But you never got your degree. Why is that?"

With a straight expression, Ralph replied, "That stuff drove me nuts."

The judge shook his head. Someone laughed. That's when I realized they must have had Ralph on some kind of drug. He was flatlined. Drained of feeling. His answers were all in the same octave.

Then the judge turned to us. "This hearing," he said, "is to determine if your friend should be released or transferred to a facility where he can get help. The rules for determining this are quite simple. Is he capable of taking care of himself and is he either potentially capable of inflicting harm to himself or others?"

I was tempted to mention how I found him one day trying to

figure out how he could walk across a lawn without hurting insects that lived in the grass. He had figured out that with every step he killed thirty-five insects but said he drew the line at bacteria. But I thought that might not help his case. Not wanting to harm any life would not be a good defense.

In the end the judge released Ralph. "I can see," he said, "that Mr. Faraday has good friends who will support him. I hope that works. I recommend that he continue under the care of Dr. Willits, and that he stays on a regime of medicines that the doctor has prescribed."

Ralph looked pleased, as though his class project had received a blue-ribbon prize. As we gathered around him, the Judge came up to us, and in a paternalistic tone said, "Let me tell you something, I think anyone that hears a radio station with his teeth is nuts. But I can't pass judgment on that. I think you are all deluded. There are crazy people, you know. There is a difference between normal and abnormal. And it is important." He walked away before I could tell him about the article I had just read about how people with excessive fillings in their teeth complained about hearing radio stations in their head.

The last time I saw Ralph was the day I helped him move. He appeared with his pink suitcase and explained, "Judy told me the air was no longer fresh in the apartment and I have to move out." He fished around in his suitcase and pulled out a wad of cash. "See, I can pay for an apartment." He moved in very close to me and put a hand on my shoulder. "But don't get me wrong. I love you but it just wouldn't work for me to live with you."

We found an apartment within walking distance of Judy's apartment, an odd building that at one time was the international whorehouse for Portland's World Exposition in 1905.[5] It was difficult to move Ralph, not that he had much stuff. It was difficult to tell what was good stuff and what was junk. But, the most difficult thing was he kept disappearing. One time I found him moving his stuff from his new apartment to my place. His explanation: "Hard to keep track of change. It happens so fast."

I didn't see him for a month, and part of me was relieved, but I also missed him. So, I dropped by his apartment. He was gone. The landlord was cleaning up the last of his stuff, putting it into one box in the middle of the floor.

"Maybe you know how to get that stuff to him," he said.

I took the box. Another box to add to my collection. In the box there was one of Ralph's journals. It was written like he was trying to demonstrate he could not be held down by mere paper. The writing was contained inside squares and cartoon clouds and circles and pentagons and octagons, random questions and thoughts.

The title page: *What do You Think? Here's what I think you think—*

How long can you hold a thought?
why are there things you won't let me tell you?
Do I have to change myself or does the world have to change to accommodate me?
Is an idea a thing's fourth dimension?
When is an idea worn out?
What do I know that no one else knows?
Can I think about anything?
Can I love you if you don't understand me?
Is there only one way to say anything?
Am I just made up of what comes my way?
Have I lost the ability to be in the same place as my mind?
In the end will I have done more or thought more?
Does the world only make sense if we think about it?
Can I imagine the world without this sentence?
Would my life be very different if I could think of everything at the same time?
Should I try to talk to people like I talk to myself?
Is there someone thinking exactly what I am somewhere on the planet all the time?
If I could not remember what I just did a minute ago would I still want to live?

Can I drive myself outside of my mind? How much horsepower
would I need?
Should we make killing time a criminal act punishable by firing
squad?
Can you think of "it after too yet?"
What would happen if everything slowed down except for fish?
If I put just the right amount of time into a thought will it make
sense?
If I don't remember that I was born, will I not die?
Do I think more thoughts than the person next to me?
Do I create problems if I think of the right thing but in the wrong
place?
Do words make me think slower?

Months later, Judy told me she thought he might be living at the
coast. I think he went back to Jupiter.

The Elder Nudist Vegetarian Closet Gay Socialist Map Maker

A couple of weeks after the Mello Pages was in bookstores, a small
box appeared at the Club house front desk. It was a copy of the Mello
Pages taken apart page by page inside a used gray 3-ring binder. Every
page of our momentous directory was corrected and modified. I was
at first miffed. Who the hell was this? I imagined a petty bureaucrat
or ancient historian or John Deere cigar smoking journalist. But then
I recognized the penmanship style and realized it must be from Bob
Benson. Also, when I noted the way he wrote (and later how he
spoke) was like diction from the 19th century; formal British English.

We had one section we called "magic places." Something I took
great pride in. I had complied information about highest waterfalls,
places of little-known historic importance, and eclectic occurrences
such as when it rained salamanders in the suburbs east of Portland in
1918. My magic places section was dwarfed by this 19th century time
traveler. For each of my pages there were ten of his. For one county,
west of Portland, he noted, "partial representation from county

resource log with 3000 entries as of July 1972." I realized it was the author of *Oregon Non parks.*[6]

On our meeting day, he was waiting for me in the Mello Pages World headquarters. When I came in, he abruptly stood up as though I were a Master Sergeant and he was about to show me his bunk in the barracks. I noted that he did not make direct eye contact. He inscrutably combined a farmer and Ben Franklin intellectual. Overweight, with gray almost white hair, small bifocals, overalls, and a John Deer cap. He had already filled a table top with publications and maps. We shook hands. Another contradiction. His hands were strong but soft. I could also smell the faint odor of manure.

We spent several hours that day going through the Mello Pages and pursing obscure historical texts, and his inventory of special places on index cards. Absolute mastery of knowledge about the place we lived. I would throw out a fact, and he would nod, and then answer me perfect vest-pocket lectures, reflecting historical, botanical, geological, highway engineering, and literary knowledge. A renaissance farmer.

Bob was born in 1915 in Portland, where his family owned a rooming house. In the 1920s, wanting to leave urban life behind, with a dream of five acres and independence, his family bought land in Valley Vista, a tiny community along the extensive commuter rail system in Portland. They never really made a go of it. But, when I met Bob, he was still living on the family homestead, over 100 acres. The acreage was worth a small fortune but Bob never thought about selling it and instead he just squeaked by selling a few cows every year, cutting down trees to sell firewood, and his one business, map making.

It's hard to figure how Bob became who he was. Imagine growing up in the Portland of the 1920s and 1930s when it was still a rough and tumble place known as stump town. One thing to become an aberrant self in a metropolis, but quite another when you are a dirt-poor farmer in a remote outpost. Imagine being a nudist, vegetarian, socialist without a Castro District to find kindred souls.

Bob never got past high school, and yet he was one of the most knowledgeable people I ever met. There is a special collection of his writing, maps, and historical documents he collected; the Robert Benson Collection at the Washington County Historical Museum.

One time I asked him what Portland looked like before white settlement. Which led to an interesting discussion, and then two weeks later a hand-drawn map that showed off wetlands that had been filled, springs and creeks that had been buried in pipes, grasslands and forests where now there were housing developments. Maybe he picked up some of his intellectual curiosity from his family. His father was a carpenter who read Darwin and Kropotkin and who, as Bob said, like to speculate a lot about the future of humanity. But more than anything Bob was an ideal citizen of Carnegie's dream of public libraries for all. He haunted the public library year after year.

I didn't make much progress with this fantasy until Jack and I met and I became secretariat for the Gertrude Stein salons. It seemed like there was always room at the Warehouse for one more group or project. Leland told me there were 300 offices or rooms, not including large closets—which had been used for offices. I explained to Jack what I wanted to do. "Far out, far fucking out," he said. He got out a beautifully intricate map of the Warehouse I had not seen before. Leland used the map to keep track of organizations and individuals that came and went. Jack wanted to show me the available spaces, but I couldn't hear him. I called it a map and not a blueprint because that was the title: A map of middle earth, otherwise known as the Gertrude Stein Fellowship Clubhouse. The lettering was perfect. The map was really a series of maps. Each of the four floors were done in rich detail and from different angles: looking down, looking up, west, north, south, east.

"Oh, shit," Jack said and folded the map book, "I forgot Leland and Bob have a new one."

He pulled out a large sliding drawer from under a table. I told Jack I wanted to meet Bob Benson. But the meeting didn't take place for months. My other duties and putting together the Mello pages took up all my available time. And I had woken up one day and found my bed teetering on the edge of a cliff which I will explain later. I sometimes worked 18-hour days. It wasn't hard to enlist help. At one time I counted over 50 people who were helping: researching, writing, editing.

Bob drew a map that delineated our bioregion, before there were computerized mapping systems. Again, I had first asked an innocent question. What is our bioregion? I had been introduced to bioregional thinking through my friend Peter Berg.[7] I had been thinking as a bioregionalist but didn't have a word for it. A ha. I told Bob about bioregionalism and he, like me, seemed to intuitively know what I was talking about. I wondered what our bioregion would look like if you could see it from the North. Several weeks later, he showed me a draft map with that perspective. He never claimed to be a talented writer, and yet his legend that accompanied the map had the charm of a whimsical poet and the precision of a scientist:

"On a rare day of partial clearing, clouds separate to reveal the maritime northwest. On the east, the Cascade Range protects it from the thirsty plateau. On the west is the Pacific. Southward the Siskiyou and Trinity Alps palisade the Maritime Northwest against the bare brown hills and burning plains of California. Northward, though maritime climate persists, agriculture ceases, turned back by mountains that rise from the surf."

When you walked with Bob, it was like walking with a multitude of specialists or a hand held GIS multi-layered map. He might stop and point out a flower. "There's the corydalis, an extreme rarity, related to the bleeding heart but quite different in detail of the flower: to seed here, but when the whole thing is a spike of these odd-shaped flowers, it's quite impressive. That little fringe of vine with the lacy flower, that's the saxifrage. And there's the native waterleaf. There is also a weed waterleaf from Europe which is very coarse-looking. As you can see the native waterleaf is anything but coarse. I didn't know about that colony of tiger lilies... look at them. There will be quite a show when they get into bloom."

Bob and I wrote a column for a small rural newsletter, The Rural Tribune. We had missions. One day we tried to find cedar planks from a 19th century military road from Astoria to Portland. Another time we bushwhacked our way to a place in the Oregon coast range where three rivers had their origins all within a half mile.

One of our missions was to go to one of Bob's favorite places, a sacred site on Sauvie Island, just 45 minutes from downtown Portland. There were five of us that day. Myself; Bob; Zake, an Audubon activist; Frank, a Native American scholar; and Malcolm, a retired architect and our driver. Malcolm was an odd duck, close to 90, tall and bent over. He reminded me of a Sandhill crane. And not a competent driver. In fact, I suspect he was having mini heart attacks on our drive. On the highway where the speed limit was 55mph, he would suddenly slow down to 20 and turn around to tell us something in the back seat. Then he would jump lanes without looking about, speed up or slow down not in response to anything in particular. On one roller coaster stretch of the road, he told us how much he loved these roads as a kid. It was like a free roller coaster ride. Bob asked him to slow down because he felt like he was going to "spew his breakfast of oatmeal and blackberries." Malcolm just thought he was kidding and speeded up to get the full G impact. It was difficult to stick to our agenda with our lives on the line, while listening to normally polite and understated Bob squealing like a kid at the county fair. After our long and tortuous drive, we all got out of the car like we had been in the Santa Maria and finally found land after months on the open sea. I wanted to kiss the soil.

We stood at the end of a road with a boundary clearly marked as a hunting zone. It was off season so we were free to roam, but during hunting season if you didn't have a gun and license you could be fined $250. "Isn't that odd," Bob noted, "that if you trespassed on the land because it was sacred, there was no fine."

Bob explained as we crossed a meadow that much of the year was under water, "We are walking onto Oak island which is in the middle of Sturgeon Lake which is on Sauvie Island which is the largest island in a river in the USA where the fourth largest—depending on how you measure it, length, flow or area drained— and the 19th largest rivers come together. The natives called it Wapato Island. They named it after a plant essential to their diet while we named it after someone who exploited it."

Bob held forth as always telling us about historical events, and things like, "at the tip of the island on the north there is a magnetic anomaly. Perhaps related to the sacred nature." I knew this was a kind of Bob joke. Dry like bone. We walked quietly for quite a while. In part because we had to focus on where we were walking. There were areas that appeared solid but turned out to be like saturated tundra. Malcolm over a log and he went head first into the bog. Zake and I had to pull him out, which seemed to cause another seizure. Malcolm begin to repeat himself and nervously laughed. "boy who would have thought it," he repeated over and over. Sometimes his comment coincided with astounding facts Bob relayed or plants and birds he pointed to, sometimes the refrain was à propos to nothing.

Then we stopped. Bob pointed out how we were in the middle of a ring of ancient native oak trees. "Can't you see how it is a perfect ring. We don't know if Indians planted them this way, but there is anecdotal evidence."

We all looked around at the oaks. Magnificent trees and more or less in a ring. I felt something. A shiver. It was a magical place. And I've always had a low tolerance for woo-woo stuff. I would probably be the last to be brainwashed by a cult.

Bob continued. "We think Indians came here for coming of age rituals. There used to a rock here." He put his small pack on the ground and took out a drawing of a Native American standing on one leg on a rock. "I drew this last week. Just from my imagination."

Yet another skill I didn't know Bob had. The drawing was very interesting.

"The young man would stand here, maybe like this. In some difficult posture, we think that would strain you. You would stand for days until you were visited by your guardian who would then watch over you or you could rely on as you lived the remainder of your life."

"Boy, how about that?", Malcolm said, trying to hold up his wet leg, imitating the Indian in the drawing. I think we all wanted him to lower his leg, but too late. He was off balance and fell. Zake tried to keep him from falling and also fell. He broke Malcolm's fall, but now they were both wet and muddy.

"I think," Bob said, very concerned, "we should end our trip. We can always come back." Then he added, "We think someone stole the rock probably for their golf course lawn backyard in the suburbs for their koi pond, you know. I should say I have evidence from an unfortunate Indian I met who I think had too much lightning stew, if you know what I mean. But I have conducted additional research to authenticate his claim. I found a photograph taken in the 1940s. Slightly blurry, but you can see the large rock and the obvious footprint hole."

Malcolm said, "Boy, who would have thought that."

I shook my head in disbelief. I didn't know what to say. I was still trying to figure out if Chief Sitting Duck existed. I knew Uncle Gus pretended to be the chief on occasions, but he based it on a real chief, I think. I didn't want to wreck the story. I just added obliquely, "I know someone else who knows the chief."

Malcolm added, "Boy, who would have thought that."

A few weeks after Bob and I took the trip to Sauvie Island, I received a note from him. He was in the Veterans Hospital (another fact I didn't know about him. I couldn't imagine Bob in the armed services). He had colon cancer and would have to undergo many treatments. But, he wrote, "I don't think they have any remedies but I remain cheerful and can still read. Please don't visit me while I am in the hospital. I will soon be set free and will move to my sister-and brother-in-law's place. Much more convenient for your visit." While that may have been true, I also think he did not want me to see him reduced to a hospital gown.

In the letter was also a description of our visit to the Stonehenge monument at Maryhill Museum in the Columbia Gorge. There was a detailed analysis of the structure of the imitation Stonehenge, including a comparison of displays of shadow and light by the seasons for the English location and Columbia River location. It also contained a chart comparing the alternative explanations for the original Stonehenge.

When Bob moved to his sister's home, I visited him several times. He was fading. He lost weight, skin color, and his gray hair had turned to a luminous white. Most of the time he was in great pain. We never talked about his illness. I almost stopped coming. I learned from other dying people in my life that when yourself is reduced to willful surviving, then creating personalities to greet and interact with people, something we do all the time, can take away from the energy you need to survive in your primal state. To be the good son or mother is exhausting while being the good-natured golf buddy is not. When you are standing on the cliff looking into the abyss and simple movements are mechanical nightmares, then finding the personality software takes away from the energy or will power just to stay alive. Automated reptilian parts of the brain, like breathing, are no longer automatic. They take conscious effort and the dwindling life force has shunted from the immune system to creating conversation. For dying people, it was easier to be with health care workers. The self was more like a robot.

The second and third rung of family and friendships was the most difficult. To be father, mother, daughter, one had to gather the cellular troops who were preoccupied fending off invaders to create the personality. With a lover or closest of friends or family, you didn't have to do anything. They were inside you. When I told his sister about my concerns, she pleaded with me to keep visiting.

"He talks about each of your visits days before you come and after. I think he might just give up if he didn't have something to look forward to."

The last time I visited Bob, he seemed in worse pain. When he stood up to greet me, he fell back into his chair. The tiny room, with only one overhead light and an intense reading lamp at a desk, was littered with papers and maps. He had been there two months and filled the room. St Peter was going to have difficulty with his carry-on baggage.

It was October and grapes were just ripening. I had brought some from home because I fondly remembered how we used to sit in the picnic area outside his cabin—a discarded Forest Service log table, and lawn furniture—and pick grapes off the vines that were climbing up the cabin, while we ate lunches he made: peanut butter on saltine crackers, sardines, bananas, and Spam sandwiches, while we traded stories about our bioregion. I hid the grapes along with Ritz crackers and Tillamook cheese I had brought. It seemed ludicrous. He had given up eating, mostly. I made idle chitchat, rambling on about my activities and new maps I had found or articles in local historical journals. I was desperate to find a balance between idle chitchat and something that might interest him but not tax his physical state.

I then told him about an article I had read about Portland's gypsy population. Suddenly a change came over him, like an angel had swept through the room. He told me about the funeral of King George when thousands of gypsies had a parade with horse-drawn carriages on Broadway in downtown Portland in the 1960s. There was a settlement in the south end of downtown that had been demolished to make room for Portland's first urban renewal district in the 1960s. He told me about how he and his mother would walk through the neighborhood. She would clench his hand as they walked past colorfully dressed gypsy families. They lived on the sidewalk. "Odd," he said "isn't it we think that is abhorrent behavior. We create cyclone fence compounds and then think it strange when animals mark their territories with urine."

I realized as he told me about gypsies that the grimace of pain in his face disappeared. He sat erect in the depilated purple chair. His voice seemed more forceful. It was as though the Gideons had come through and told him that Jesus was waiting for him and he nothing to fear. It made me hopeful about my own demise. I had thought intellectual curiosity might give me something to do or sidetrack me from the inevitable collusion at the wall of death, but maybe there was hope. Bob's carnivorous intellectual curiosity was high-quality morphine. He espoused for a half hour on the gypsies which led to another espousal about Jews in Portland, which led to a recollection of houses and buildings that had been destroyed by urban renewal. Then he suddenly stopped and the grimace of pain returned to his face. "I need to rest," he said.

Knowing One Place like the Back of my Hand

Preamble

One of the homework assignments Jack assigned was for me to tell him about the place where I grew up. He added, "as though it was a secret or fairy tale land." I think he started calling it the Shire. In hindsight, I can see that these were serpentine research strategies. He was filling in gaps to create stories by and about me. I think this piece is like the genome code of everyone else around me, 99% the same.

The white beaver story had circulated on its own, but like the story passed around in a circle, it was greatly modified by the time it came back to me. The white beaver was now a competent magician and intervened in abusive domestic situations. Wait a minute, I've heard that before. Somehow my great grandfather's ghost stories had merged with the white beaver ones.

I know one place on earth like the back of my hand. It is a wilderness in the middle of the city with a creek running through it. At one end is Errol Heights, aka., Felony Flats, birthplace of Gary Gilmore,[8] a notorious serial murderer. At the other end is an upper-class neighborhood defined by the Reed College campus, substantial homes, and dense deciduous trees, more like an older Connecticut suburb than a Portland neighborhood. It is a unique geological space, defined by ridges on the north and south ends. The small creek, 24 miles long, eventually finds its way to the Columbia river. Tonya Harding,[9] the notorious skater, and Phil Knight,[10] founder of Nike lived in the watershed. The Northern branch of the Beat Poetry generation was conceived there. Not a mint condition stream. One writer called it the Chevy Impala of creeks; [11]David Duncan dedicated his novel, *The River Why*[12] to it.

My family's pioneer home is on the south ridge along a busy road. The road wasn't always so busy. When my older sisters were teenagers, their entertainment was waiting for a car to drive by hoping it might be teenage boys. The road became dangerous as the city grew. My neighbor's daughter was killed by a drunk driver when she was playing in the front yard. I used to tease her and just days before she was killed, she had gotten angry at me and dug her bright pink fingernails in the back of my hand. For months afterwards, I would stare at the impression of her nails in my hand, pondering death.

There is a long winding trail that leads through the forest to the meadows, wetlands, and floodplain of the creek. The traffic noise disappears and you enter another world. It is always dark in the forest. The floodplain of the creek is the only place lit by the sun. A biologist told us that our forest for several months of the year had the same vegetation yield as the Amazon rain forest. Before white settlers, including my family (1880), arrived it probably looked like dinosaur domain: ancient western red cedars and skunk cabbage. During my childhood years in the 1950s, the creek still supported a vigorous fish population. If we dropped a line in—usually a willow branch, fish line, lead weight and hook, an earthworm—we inevitably caught a native trout. In the fall we could catch returning salmon in our hands as they desperately tried to return to the upper watershed to spawn and die. We didn't know any better.

We had names for the landscape: the swimming hole, Pilgrim rock, the trestle, the butt (butte), the waterfall, the swamp, Buzzard Bait's shack. We built forts, rafts, dams, a dangerous but exhilarating rope swing, tree houses, contraptions to catch wild things, the cave dug by hand in the side of an unstable hillside. There was an interurban streetcar that ran through the canyon. We played chicken on the trestle. One friend lost. He fell from the trestle and was paralyzed from the waist down. I saw him twenty years after his fall in a wheelchair on the bus. He hadn't aged. On weekends and all summer, we spent entire days in the canyon. We returned to the comfort of our middle-class homes, filthy, with torn clothes, nursing nettle stings and bruises, and cuts from glass in the creek.

In the summer and fall there were wild berries, apples and pears from tamed and wild trees, and my father's bountiful vegetable garden. On warm summer evenings we might set up camp alongside the creek, pull together our food from the wild, including native fish and crawfish, set a bonfire, cook our meals and pretend we were the *Last of the Mohicans*. Of course, we might as likely wander down the streetcar tracks to a supermarket where a couple of dollars would yield sacks of hostess cupcakes, potato chips, penny candy, and soda pop in a can.

If I walk through the canyon now, as an old man, I can stop every ten feet and tell a different story.... That's where we found a dead octopus...The tree is gone, but that's where we found the skeleton of a man hanging by a rope....That's where Phil caught 25 carp in an afternoon (a sign the creek had become too warm to support native fish)....That's where Prudy, a teenage sweetheart who made all her own clothes, told me we were no longer going steady, and she was in love with a drummer from Paul Revere and the Raiders...Under that oak, the only one in the canyon, Huck gave me his white-handled knife in the shape of a sea lion head. See that Cedar stump?...My father told me that is where my great grandfather's guardian, the magical and inept, white beaver, lived...And that tallest of Douglas fir trees over there is the one Johnny Crawfish climbed and had to be rescued by Zeke, the obnoxious crow. I still have the trap my sister's boyfriend in high school used to catch muskrats, weasels, and river otters. He was killed in his day job at a local department store when he looked up an elevator shaft to see if the lift was coming. That stump is where I ran into my father when he was starting his work day around the place, and I was at the end of an all-night LSD trip. While he talked about tasks for me to do, interspersed with quotes from William James, I kept repeating, "This is my father...This is my father... What a concept."

There is a photo of me standing on the trail that led into the forest. I am fully weaponized—A BB gun, a plastic x-ray gun, a bullwhip over my shoulder, and bandolier. I took the photo with me when I was making my last appeal to the Draft Board to change my 1A status to conscious objector. I thought it was funny. But the fat Draft Board member who belligerently asked me what I would do if someone were raping my mother or my sister, would have thought it more evidence I was not against war, but just another kid, as he told me, who they could "turn into a fighting machine." I told him, "I know. That's why I have to refuse."

My father spent his life taking care of the place. While one of his closest friends, poet William Stafford,[13] created lasting monuments on paper, his legacy was our place. One of his pride and joys was a Japanese garden. A Japanese garden in the jungle? Like creating a Zen meditation gazebo at the super bowl. Talk about futility. One summer when I was bored, I created a 9-hole miniature golf course in a seasonal wetland.

There was a fallen tree where I went to talk to God. It was a Douglas fir that had toppled from the roots, leaving a gigantic hole in the side of the hill. Its roots towered above me. I built a flimsy lean-to out of boards and bows from the tree. The God who could topple this giant like it was a toothpick was maybe powerful enough to help me win over perfect, red-haired, Cathy, or at least help her remember my name when she passed me in the hallway at school.

Our family had many social gatherings on the place. My mother organized them. My father's role was to make sure the place looked perfect. He wanted people to envy him and admire how he had tamed the wilderness into a disciplined landscape. The most celebrated gathering was the annual 4th of July picnic. There might be over 100 people, mostly families from the small liberal arts college where my father taught. I was the oldest kid, and it was my place, so for one day of the year I was the center of the universe. When I said it was time to play croquet or Statue of Liberty or hide-and-go seek then that is what we did. Kit Stafford, Bill and Dorothy's oldest daughter, told me that what most impressed her was that I could eat a baloney sandwich with my feet.

The Golden Eagles, our gang, was a ragtag collection of white kids who lived in the neighborhoods surrounding the canyon. We experimented with altered states early on. We tried anything we could get our hands on. We drank bottles of Coca Cola with fistfuls of aspirin. We smoked crushed up licorice ferns in our school notebook paper. We stole liquor from my parent's liquor cabinet. To make sure we didn't get caught we only took tablespoons-full from different bottles, ending up with lethal and fowl tasting cocktails of vodka, bourbon, gin, crème de menthe. I smoked my first marijuana under the trestle with tough guys from Felony flats. I could increase my popularity in high school by having one of the best places to drink. We would get a wino to buy a case of beer and meet at the rope swing, swimming hole, or trestle, and then drink the beers fast so we could screw up courage to go to local drive-ins to pick up girls or get into fights. In college it was the safe and trippy place to experiment with LSD, Mescaline, psychedelic mushrooms. My intellectual college friends and I did this in my father's Walden hut, which I thought was fitting. We were retro-transcendentalists.

It was our sovereign state; our Lord of the Flies domain. Adults rarely ventured into the canyon. We made the rules. We governed with an iron fist and benevolence when we saw fit. While I was just a small white dude, I had monarchical rights because my family settled there first; we still owned a portion of the canyon; and the remainder, my family had donated to the City for a park.

The Golden Eagles could defend against most invaders into our territory. We enjoyed greeting the newcomers. Typically, one or two of us would walk casually up to the strangers and ask for ID. Then, depending on their compliance or defiance, one Golden Eagle after another would appear until the intruders were surrounded. There were about 15 of us and we had a substantial arsenal: BB guns, switchblades, bullwhips, slingshots, and brass knuckles we made in our foundry near the cave where in high school we made moonshine. Well, we called it moonshine, although it was really hard cider. A greaser from New Orleans who could have been a double for the Fonz, stole all the moonshine and busted up our still. We got back at him by stealing his hubcaps. He got back at us by pantsing Don, our white supremacist military historian Commie, and tying him to the jungle gym at the grade school.

There was a group from Felony Flats that scared the shit out of us, Gary and his dangerous friends. The only times we had encountered

Gary's gang had been disastrous. I came away once with a bloody bump on my head from a rock. They stripped Marvin and covered him with stinging nettles. If we saw them, we ran. We hurt people and sometimes stole from them because we were bored. Gary and his gang also did things because they were bored; but they were bored and angry. They had nothing to lose, and they had endured abuse and were impervious to pain.

After I went away to college, leaving my father and uncle and mother in their retirement years, things got worse. Without the moderating effect of the Golden Eagles, and encroaching urbanization, evil forces dominated. The canyon became like Mordor. The creek died. First there was nothing but warm water species, then nothing at all, as though there was an evil spell cast. Invasive species took over including English ivy and Himalayan blackberries. During the day, motorcycle gangs ran wild through the woods and along the abandoned streetcar tracks; at night drug and alcohol parties ran all night. The sounds of males running on speed and testosterone drowned out the sounds of wildlife. My uncle's house and my family's pioneer home were regularly burglarized. One gang of teenagers tortured and killed a 103-year-old man, probably the oldest man ever to be murdered in Oregon.[14] The gang broke into my house a week before they tortured the old man. There, but for the grace of God....

One time I was confronted by three butt ugly guys on Harleys. They were on one side of the creek and I was on the other. Sitting on their hogs, one said, "I think we should go over and fuck up that guy's lawn...oh right and him too. There was no one in shouting range. No cell phones. Inspired by who knows what insane guardian angel, I went totally berserk. I swore like I had Tourette Syndrome. Tore my shirt open. Jumped up and down. Ripped a small sapling from the ground and begin slapping the ground and my body. They stared at me, and back and forth between themselves, and then left.

When my father and uncle died, leaving my mother alone on the remaining acres, the canyon still in the dark ages and no magic ring found yet, I moved back to be my mother's caregiver and to see if I could reestablish my rule. When I first moved back, I was threatened, burglarized, surrounded by people living on the edge. There was a meth house on the east end. They had a horse that was starving. I would find him standing in front of my house eating from my garden. There was a toothless man who liked to prove he could get me anytime he wanted. He used glass cutters to cut a perfect circle in my picture window and removed just a pair of binoculars. He left a note, "gotcha," One night they barricaded my driveway so I couldn't leave in the morning. I was pinned down by a born-again Christian throwing rocks because I had refused to let his step son hug a tree in our yard to make amends to his mother who he had beat up. I found telltale signs of sad stories I couldn't make sense of; under a cottonwood tree a wet paper sack containing used rubbers; a women's slip and nylons; 2 beer cans, one filled with urine, a syringe, and the women's underwear section of a Sears catalog.

I had to hire a security guard for the times I was away. There was a turning point one night when I came home greeted by my security guard, a want-to-be Rambo type with high-tech gear. He was sitting on my deck where my uncle used to drink bourbon and watch the ducks on his pond. Rambo had camcorders set up at the boundaries of the property and a video display unit. It was new equipment, and he was pleased with how well the cameras worked in low light. He reported to me from his security logbook, "There were two suspect characters on the other side of the creek. I did nothing but just gave them the don't fuck with us look. They left." We watched the video displays. It had come to this? I used to be a leader of the Golden Eagles, now I was conversing with Rambo like we were in a war zone.

I despaired. I imagined finding an assisted living unit for my mom and moving to a low maintenance apartment in the city. Just give up. They won.

Imagining that gave me a cold and empty feeling. I imagined driving by our family home with someone else living there. I couldn't do it. I might die if I tried to save the place, but I had to try.

My 99-Year-Old Aunt Sits on a Whoopee Cushion

I was bored, waiting to go to my family's Thanksgiving at my sister's house. I had received a package from Jack's phone freak friend, along with a phone number for James Bond (well actually Sir William Samuel Stephenson,[15] who Bond was based on). I don't know why he sent me either. In the package was a small self-published booklet, "How to Get High Legally," and inside that a tiny satchel with a note: EAT ME. It was Hawaiian wood rose seeds, with a brief disclaimer, "a tranquil high, brief buzz, drowsiness. You should never—with or without the seeds—operate heavy equipment. You're a hippie."

OK, so it wasn't a good idea, but I figured I had hours to kill before the turkey dinner. I made a tea out of the small satchel. Bitter and warm, I drank it and laid down and almost immediately fell asleep. The next thing I knew, it was 3pm. It was at least a 45-minute drive and if I was late, I would be out of sync with my gene pool. When I arrived early for family gatherings things worked out better. It always felt like I was from another planet, but if I arrived late, it was like I didn't have a translator.

I quickly got dressed and climbed into my beater of a car and on auto-pilot drove to my sister's house in the suburbs. The wood rose seeds kicked in just as I entered the land of cul de sacs. I could have used some ether. What the hell did my sister's house look like? There was a part of me—the wood rose part I assume—that wanted to keep driving around until I ran out of gas. I found her house by spotting their jeep with giant tires and in the front yard her husband, mullet haircut and a menacing smile. He spotted me and gave me a signal, like he was pulling the air horn of an eighteen-wheeler. He moved in slow motion toward me. I had a brief sensation of seeing myself from his perspective. From that point of view, I looked like a hermit crab with telescopic eyes and a ponytail. I had the ponytail.

He gripped my shoulder like I was a side of beef and led me toward the house. "You got to see my new fucking workspace in the garage," he exclaimed. Each word seemed to stand out. Was it a fucking cool workspace? Or a workspace for fucking? You worked in a space, of course. If we didn't see it what exactly would happen?

Then I felt honored. The Chieftain of a village was going to show me his secret lair. I wanted to say something, but I couldn't decide if I should say it was awesome or amazing. I thought one was a compliment and one was an insult.

He pointed things out to me, a table saw that could buck up a wild boar, pegboards on the walls with carefully arranged tools, and posters of skimpily clad ladies holding screwdrivers and wrench sets. An image of Elmer Fudd in the Guggenheim came to mind.

I was distracted by a beautiful glowing necklace between a piece of blood-red wood and one of the largest pipe wrenches I had ever seen. Why would something so valuable be cast aside like this? I moved towards the necklace when suddenly the middle of it moved. Even more amazing, a necklace with a moving part! That's when I realized it was a spider and the necklace was a spider web glistening with water or oil. Now Mullet and I were both staring at it. I knew if I made eye contact with him; the jig was up. But then I got stuck on the concept of brother-in-law. He was my brother by law. I wanted to ask him what he thought of that. I remembered a third cousin once removed telling me when we met for the first time, "well you know you can't choose your relatives." But I was pretty sure he would think that was an insult. I also had the sinking feeling that if I laughed, I wouldn't know when or how to end it. Then I wasn't even sure he was my brother-in-law. They were married, weren't they? They got married in Los Vegas, didn't they? Or was that a television show?

Then there was a disconcerting image. Whenever I had a thought, I imagined it as a cannon. The cells in my brain were cannon balls. The synapses were the gunpowder. But every time the synapse fired, the cannon ball lifted off alright, but there was someone standing in the way with a big butterfly net. They wouldn't let the cannons hit their target. I decided not to share this insight with Mr. Mullet.

I looked at the brother-in-law and I thought he was on to me. I thought he said "the jig's up," but it was my sister telling us that dinner was served.

Everybody was talking fast. No one made sense. I counted. There were 18 of us, 19 if you included the after-image of my 99 year old Aunt Eva that seemed to follow my mother around. My ten-year-old cousin told me he was going to put a whoopee cushion on my aunt's seat. This seemed like an excellent idea. I wish I had thought of it. Maybe it was the beginning of a new tradition. Every holiday, whoever was the elder would sit on a whoopee cushion.

We filled our plates like they were wheelbarrows. I thought about reciting William Carlos Williams's poem about the red wheelbarrow. Wouldn't that be an appropriate substitute for grace? Forks were flying into mouths like dump trucks. No, not dump trucks. Fork lifts. Get it? Fork lifts. I momentarily thought I should share this joke. I might even be the hit of the party. Another insight: could it be that laughter wasn't good for my health? But how could that be? I had always assumed God was laughing most of the time. I needed to think about that later. But it might make a section for my official report on the uses and abuses of Hawaiian Wood rose seeds.

That's when I realized how many things I was: a citizen of the planet earth, an American, an Oregonian, uncle, brother, son, brother-in-law, cousin. I was not a daughter, banker, or dragonfly. That was good. But how could I be so many things? Did everything I say pass through my roles like a psychological filtration system? Again, maybe to think about later.

I answered questions, passing green Jell-O with carrots, laughing at teenage barf jokes. I could do this. My plate filled, but I kept adding to it. The colors were amazing. It was mostly white on brown, but then there were the red cranberries, the pink cinnamon apples, the olive-green canned peas.

While the conversation blurred on in the background, I felt my head getting heavier. It felt like my neck muscles were going limp or stretching.

The dinner in front of me got bigger and closer. Turkey, gravy, and those lovely mashed potatoes. Soft. If I let my head fall, then everything would be alright. It seemed like the right thing to do. Then out of the corner of my eye I saw my mother. It wasn't just my mother but all mothers in a linage that stretched as far as the wall of china back through time. And I thought everyone was staring at me. They were, and then they weren't. Like rolling a window up and down. Or like I was cupping my ears and hearing the ocean. And I knew it wasn't right. Even though I would enjoy letting my face fall in the dinner, it wouldn't be good for the people around me.

I said things. Auto-robot responding to questions, even making jokes and shuffling food in my mouth, passing food around. For a while everything seemed normal except for Mullet, who I thought was glaring at me now and then. At one point I thought he said, "I know what your fucking game is," either that or he said "pass the gravy."

My 99-year-old aunt came in from the kitchen to sit down. I glanced at my cousin and nephew and niece. They were on it. The whoopee cushion ready to launch. Barely able to hold in their laughter. She sat down and the whoopee cushion was outstanding. A long-protected bubbling fart. The younger generation burst into laughter, while the adults responded with mixed glee and uncertainty. I burst into laughter. But then I couldn't stop. While everyone else's laughter died down, mine became more intense. It felt like I was going to die of laughter. No, I mean really. The uncontrollable laughter was connected to the unconscious part of my brain that automatically regulated breathing. If I kept laughing, I would stop breathing. I couldn't do both at the same time. Although I had a choice. I could breathe or laugh.

I had just enough energy to get up from the table and go to the bathroom. I sat on the toilet. I was thinking it would best if I left. Crawling out the window I knew wasn't a good idea. I should tell them I wasn't feeling good and go home. A useful insight for future family get-togethers. In the future, as soon as I arrived at family gatherings, I would tell people I was feeling a little puny; that way I would have an easy out if I had to leave early.

I knew everyone was just outside the bathroom door waiting for me to flush the toilet so they could rush in and grab me. It didn't quite seem right. The hallway was small. Just exactly how were 18 people fit in the hallway? But it was quiet out there, like everyone was just waiting in the hallway to spring on me. I sat on the toilet for a long time. I must have nodded off. I woke up with a jerk that almost threw me to the floor. I grabbed for my pants and realized I had sat down on the toilet without lowering them. The wood rose state of mind seemed to have passed. When I went back into the dining room, people were taking dishes from the table, talking about the cranberry scare. Things were normal again. Maybe I would even stay for a while and have pumpkin pie.

Grandmother, Big Self

I had been in the alternative reality of the Warehouse for a couple of years when my grandmother died. She died in a hospital that was walking distance from the Warehouse. My grandmother, my mother's mother, never really liked me. She thought my mom could have done better than my father, and she transferred some of her disappointment and anger on to me. Come to think of it, I think she had a screwy relationship to all males. My grandfather reminded me of Heidi's grandfather.[16] My grandmother loved him, but also pushed him around. Her son, my uncle, was a racist with a quick temper. I feared him as a kid, and later when I was a long-haired draft dodging intellectual, I just avoided him. My grandmother also was a racist who called African American's coons up to her last dying days. She didn't understand why the restaurants Sambo's and the Coon Inn had to change their names.

My mom pleaded with me to visit her and I relented, even though I couldn't imagine what good could come of it. She'd take one look at me with my ponytail and beard and ask me, like she often did, why did I insist on hurting her and my mother? My mother explained, I suppose as a way of protecting me from outbursts or fits of indifference, that her liver was failing and what with the drugs, sometimes she didn't recognize anyone and well, she might just say anything. It meant nothing.

The first time I visited she was actually pleasant, so I decided to return, which was a mistake. As soon as I entered her room she said. "Why do you have to look like a girl? You are so much like your father. Why don't you love your country?" And she would point out what her son had brought her: Flowers, candy, and a coffee-table book about Liberace, who she loved—an incongruous fascination. One side of me wanted to punch out something like, "and you were called Minnie mouse when you were an exotic dancer in Astoria." (which was true) But I continued to return.

One day when I entered her room, I immediately knew something was different. She looked terrified. She tried to smile but cried. I was lost. I had only seen her cry once before, when my grandfather died. Otherwise she was stoic and tried to teach us likewise. "Be a little trooper," was one of her favorite lines. She was restless and clearly in great pain and talking nonsensically.

I wasn't sure what to do, so I just sat by the edge of the bed holding her hand. I looked around the room and thought how sterile it was. Some flowers and cards, but otherwise white walls and life support equipment. I wondered why, if they knew she was dying, she couldn't just die at home. (There wasn't much hospice care in those days). I called my mom to ask her why they couldn't send her home. My mother wasn't home, so I called my uncle. Big mistake. In his stern military voice, he told me it wasn't any of my business and hung up.

I watched her as she went in and out of sleep or unconsciousness. And then out of somewhere came this idea. What if I could describe her bedroom? Could I trick her into thinking she wasn't at the hospital but at home? I didn't remember her bedroom very well. I only saw it as I passed by on the way to the bathroom at Thanksgiving or Christmas. I remembered how many photographs there were. On dressers. On the walls. Everywhere.

"Grandma, I was trying to remember whose photographs you have on your dresser. funny I don't think I know all the people." She didn't respond. I added, "There's that really cool photo of grandpa in his explorer scout outfit that's on the wall." That was clearly the trigger.

She looked at me for a minute like she didn't know who I was and then started describing every photograph in the room. It was odd how I could ask her to describe something and she would just do it automatically. I think I could have asked her to tell me what was in her refrigerator and she would have. I'd say what plants can you see out the window or what else is on the dresser. No matter what the question, she would describe in great detail every photo, every knickknack, even clothes in her closet. While she was in this state of imagining, I could watch the pain wrinkles on her face disappear. People near death are supposed to remember details about the past, but not the present. What was this near-death ability? Photographic memory? More open to suggestion? Therefore, easy to hypnotic or brainwash for entering a cult?

From then on, every time I visited, I enticed her to imagine her bedroom. She would always seem calm during the inventory and afterwards, sometimes falling asleep remembering photographs on a dresser. I could repeat the exercise several times in one visit. I visited more often.

Then one day I met my grandmother's big self. When I walked into the white hospital room, she stared intently at me as I approached her bed and said, "You look beautiful standing there." What? Huh? That is not my grandmother. She didn't talk that way. She never thought of me as beautiful.

Without hesitation I bent over and best as I could, given all the life support tubes and wires, put my arms around her and nuzzled her face and said, "I love you." I remember thinking it was like she had taken a truth serum. She started telling me about the "coons" that had moved into her neighborhood.

I said, "Grandma, you know they aren't coons, don't you?"

She matter-of-factly replied, "Of course not. I know that."

Later her son came to visit. She seemed pleased to see him and held out her arms so he could hug her. He bent over, but I noticed he didn't really touch her. His embrace missed, and he closed his eyes. I realized he was afraid to touch her or repulsed by her.

After a while he left. I walked him down the hall as I had to go to the bathroom. When I came back to the room, my grandmother said, "He doesn't know how to love me, does he?"

"He's just frightened," I said. She died later that night.

---

1. The article was in the *Eugene Register Guard*, circa early 1970s. I was not about to locate it.
2. Dennis Lee Hopper was an American actor, filmmaker, photographer, and artist. He made his first television appearance in 1954, and soon after appeared alongside James Dean in *Rebel Without a Cause* and *Giant*. Peter Henry Fonda was an American actor, director, and screenwriter. He was the son of Henry Fonda and younger brother of Jane Fonda.
3. *Bend in the River.* One of the extraordinary events during this period was organized by author Ken Kesey. The Bend in the River (BITR) conference was funded through the Oregon Humanities Council. The intent of the gathering was to bring together Oregonians to envision what Oregon could or should be like in 2010. Leading up this statewide conference in Bend, Oregon, in 1975, Kesey, along with Kesey's followers, the Merry Pranksters, and young activists, held meetings in over 20 communities around the state to elect delegates and develop a slate of local concerns to take to the conference. one of the local organizers (Darling, 2001) summarized Kesey's intention as more art than politics. "Bend in the River," he said was like "the Twilight Bark in '101 Dalmatians." It's how you find out that everyone's still out there and what they're thinking tonight. And that you're not alone. It was where Senator Wayne Morse gave his last public speech, and where Kesey's band of followers, and admirers-- such as Rolling Stone photographer Annie Liebonitz, natural health advocate Andrew Wild, and alternative press guru, Paul Krasner, mingled with some of Oregon's future political leaders such as Oregon's current Secretary of State Bill Bradbury. Source: Johnson, Steven Reed, "Transformation of Civic Institutions and Practices in Portland, Oregon, 1960-1999. PhD dissertation 2002.
4. Vera Katz was an American Democratic politician in the state of Oregon. She was the first woman to serve as Speaker of the Oregon House of Representatives and was the 49th mayor of Portland, Oregon. She served as mayor from 1993 to 2005.
5. The Lewis and Clark Centennial Exposition was a worldwide exposition held in Portland, Oregon, United States in 1905 to celebrate the centennial of the Lewis and Clark Expedition.
6. *Oregon Non-Parks*, Robert Benson. Self-published, 1972. Available at Washington County Museum, Oregon, Robert L Benson special collection.
7. Peter Berg was an environmental writer, best known as an advocate of the concept of bioregionalism. In the early 1960s, he was a member of the San Francisco Mime Troupe and the Diggers. He is the founder of the Planet Drum Foundation.
8. *Shot in the heart,* Mikal Gilmore. Knopf Doubleday Publishing Group,2009.

9. Tonya Maxene Price (Harding), born in 1970, is an American former figure skater, retired boxer, and reality television personality. She is a native of Portland, Oregon.

10. Phil Knight, founder of Niki, was born in Portland, Oregon. He grew up in the Portland Oregon neighborhood of Eastmoreland and attended Cleveland High School.

11. *Pilgrim at Johnson Creek*, Bill Donahue. URL. March 1, 2000; http://billdonahue.net/pilgrim-at-johnson-creek/

12. Duncan, David (1988). *The River Why*. New York: Forbes Duncan.

13. A prolific poet, William Stafford often wrote about the American West while exploring universal themes. *West of Your City*, his first poetry collection, was published in 1960. In *Traveling Through the Dark* (1962). It received the National Book Award for Poetry in 1962. He lived most of his life in Lake Oswego, Oregon, and taught at Lewis and Clark College.

14. "Youths age 15 to 17 are arrested in Moorpark", Mack Reed, *Los Angeles Times*, November 13, 1993.

15. William Samuel Stephenson (1896-1989) was a close friend and colleague of the author Ian Fleming and was believed to be one of the models for the character James Bond. He was knighted in 1945 and honored as a Companion of the Order of Canada in 1980.
    https://www.bac-lac.gc.ca/eng/discover/military-heritage/first-world-war/100-stories/Pages/stephenson.aspx

16. Heidi is a work of children's fiction published in 1881 by Swiss author Johanna Spyri. It is a novel about the events in the life of a young girl in her paternal grandfather's care in the Swiss Alps.

ARABIAN NIGHTS SESSIONS

Preamble

The Arabian nights[1] sessions took place over about two years of my Gertrude Stein sojourn. There were four official sessions but there were also informal ones; like chance encounters in the Gertrude Stein warehouse hallways, sometimes lasting longer than the formal ones. There were also homework assignments, one of the longer ones resulting in "Knowing One Place like the Back of your hand," about my growing up in The Shire. Jack had this knack for asking me questions that, like the lick of a catchy rock-and-roll song, I couldn't get out of my head. Sometimes stupid questions like, "So let's say you want to persuade me—that is, if I were a girl—what story would you tell me?

Then there was what he called Writer's Boot Camp. Sometimes he mingled with Arabian Nights rules, although a few times there were specific "workshops." Jack would act like an authentic creative writing teacher; trying to pinpoint my strengths and weaknesses. At one point he found some of my oldest writing—although I don't know how he found those—and mocked me, but also pointed out how the 'primitive' writing revealed a 'writer's soul.' He was a good teacher. The only other good writing teacher I had was John Clellon Holmes.[2]

Arabian Nights Session #1—Welcome to the Inner Sanctum

Gus kept a key to the inner sanctum library where they held the sessions. I wanted to just act cool like it wasn't anything extraordinary when Gus pulled a book from the shelf and the entire shelf moved, exposing a room I hadn't seen before. Later I found out it was always a different book. There were probably 1,000 books, but no idea how many were fake.

As usual, Jack started talking as though we were in the middle of a conversation. "I reached 3,000 day before yesterday." No eye contact. Gus busied himself with video and audio recorders and other unknown machines, lots of wires. I wasn't sure what he was referring to but he more explicitly pointed to the tables with clean and tidy Banker's boxes.

"I reached 3,000 the other day. I mean people, not boxes. I'm not sure because people keep changing their names. You know, like Rainbow Flute called himself Mercury, as in wing-footed pony express the networking service, and people get married or die. You know the usual." He showed me my box. Every item was date stamped. It was impressive or alarming. "What are you, the CIA?"

"Funny you should mention that. Well, actually FBI." He pulled out a fat document. "You know this guy, don't you?" It was a friend from college, Jim Hansen. I hadn't heard from him since I helped smuggle him across the Canadian border to avoid the draft.

"You have to read it," Jack said as he thumbed through the document. "I suspect this is about you and your friends." He read, "A neighbor reported seeing strange bearded men come and go at all hours of the day and night." Isn't that a gas? Strange bearded men, you know, like Abe Lincoln or Jesus or Charlie Manson."

I had so many questions I didn't know where to begin.

The phone rang. Jack snorted as he listened, then covered the mouthpiece, " Merlin. Remember him?"

"I'm sure he didn't mean it," he said to Merlin, "don't worry, we'll come by and fix it." He hung up, turned to me, "you broke his tele transporter?"

Before I could answer he waved his hands dismissively, "We need to focus," and disconnected the phone, "but tell me—and I ask everyone this—does it remind you more of (a) The British Museum, (b) New York Public Library (c) Vatican library, or (d) none of the above?"

I did a double take. "Vatican. I was just thinking of it, and, well, because my uncle had this—"

"Enough, Jack said dismissively, "point taken."

Uncle Gus was surrounded by video monitors, a tangle of wires, and several machines that looked like they came from an H. G. Wells science fiction novel. Above him on the wall was a sign like one of those crocheted things you might see in grandma's house, that read, "We come into life, soft rip fruit, and leave like raisins that had the shit kicked out of us."

"Sorry," Gus said to Jack, he has to go out and come back in. We didn't get a good reading." Jack motioned to me rather curtly. I walked to the door feeling like I was in high school on my way to the principal's office. On my way out the door, a short man, shorter than Uncle Gus, shot past me and disappeared behind a row of banker boxes. On my way out, I looked at Uncle Gus. Every time I saw him, he looked different. This time he had a long, pointed, very white beard and was wearing a tattered brown suit and rainbow-colored tie. I couldn't remember if he had a beard the last time we saw each other, which was just the night before. I could have sworn the first time I met him he was taller than me.

"Go on," Jack said, "we'll call for you in a minute." I stood in the dark hallway, thinking about leaving. Absurd. Could I really trust the universe?

When I was summoned back, Uncle Gus was sitting at the table still tangled in wires, but it seemed fake; exaggerated; like he (or they) were hoping to measure my response.

The shorter guy was sitting next to him, also tangled. It was like a

Charlie Chaplin modernist black comedy. Was I supposed to respond? I refused. Behind them there was a clock like the Rabbit's in *Alice in Wonderland*, except the numbers were miles per hour.

Expecting I was going to ask him about the clock, Jack dryly noted, "it's the speed Earth is moving through the galaxy. Look," Jack said in a tone hard to decipher, "if we don't have rules then we no better than any other animals, right? We can always change them, likely will." He walked to a table with my stuff. More than I had seen at first. And it was all in brand new banker boxes. Jack motioned to the boxes like a game show host. "And we have reorganized your information," he said. "Your system seemed to make sense, kind of, and we needed it to be random for our purpose." He nodded. Up and down. He kept it up. Too long. And he had done it the first time we met. Maybe it would just go up and down forever. "Isn't that kind of amazing? That you can give meaning to these things, like breathing life into them. Nobody else can do that."

I interrupted, but he continued, "Yes, I know Kathleen or your mother might also, but think of it: after today, Gus and I and Ray (I guess the shorter guy) will all be able to tell stories about your things...and so it goes...."

When is a story no longer yours? As soon as you tell your partner? When written? Or written and distributed? What if you write it up, or just the notes about it and leave it on a park bench? How about a park bench in a foreign country where no English is spoken? OK, then what about you tell the story and like a chain letter or passing a word around in a circle it gets altered twice or one hundred times? Still yours at the end? Or what if it is the same basic stories but names changed or time frame changed? Yours took place in the 1940s, the other one took place a long time ago.

"You've met my Uncle Gus, right?" Jack said motioning to Gus. duh, I thought how many times have we been introduced but I didn't respond. Gus stood up solemnly, bowed at the same time as this guy who looked like a Martian ray gun.

Gus pulled out a snarly wishbone shaped branch and pointed to it like he was a game show babe pointing to what was behind curtain three.

Jack said, "Gus will record our conversation. I assume that is OK. He uses a Native American shorthand system." Gus held up a large blank book, bigger than his head. "And audiotape," Jack continued. Gus, still holding the wishbone, pointed to a large-reel-to-reel tape recorder. Jack motioned for me to sit opposite him at a long flimsy table, "Oh, right, and the wishbone. You're probably wondering about it." Gus held the two forks firmly and pointed the pointy end in a mock threatening way, and raised his thick eyebrows, smiled. "I do not understand how it works, but it's a lie detector. If you don't tell the truth, "Jack said, "it will shake. You know like a water Witcher."

I shook my head in a kind of "whatever" attitude.

"Seriously," Jack said. "It works. Let's get started." Jack motioned to me, and then to my boxes. "You kind of wrecked the moment but anyway, turn away, close your eyes, and put your hands to your ears."

I could hear a lot of movement, whispering. Maybe even another voice. It all seemed too solemn and wacky, but harmless. I kept saying to myself; you got a better way of dealing with chronic writer's block?

"Ah, Jack," Uncle Gus said, "if he holds his hands to his ears, he can't pull anything out of the box."

Jack waved him off. "I've changed the rules. I should have told you." Jack motioned to me. "Come, sit on my magic carpet." He sat down cross-legged on an oriental rug. I didn't know much about rugs, but this was not a dime store thing, and the luxury was amplified when I sat. It was thick and soft. The purples, reds, blues were brilliant and deep. It was a complex series of half circles leading to a center which seemed to be below ground level. Something about the design made it seemed three dimensional. "It seems rather magical," I said.

"It is," Jack said, with Gus nodding in agreement. "Don't worry," he said, "I will not pretend to be an Arabian prince. I will not behead you if I don't like the story... So, here are the rules so far. First thing is I can make up or change the rules as I see fit."

I nodded, knowing I was going to nod my approval to everything.

"Secondly, either I or Gus pull the items out. While we do that you close your eyes and cover your ears. I don't want the sound to distract you and the time you have to make an association between the item and a story to be the same. For now, you will pick out twelve items for each session. Then comes the speed story telling part. As quick as you can you tell us what comes to mind. No more than a hundred words. Gus's chronographer will count the words and give you this warning." He motioned to Gus, who honked a classic bicycle blub horn. Then we take the things along with your stories and get back to you once we discover the theme telling us what stories you should leave behind when you die."

"Not sure I like where this is headed," I said.

"I didn't just title these sessions Arabian Nights arbitrarily," Jack said, "We did our homework to understand the framework of those Arabian stories. The originals are of many types: tragedies, comedies, love stories, intrigue and adventure. One of the most intriguing elements is that Scheherazade's life hangs in the balance. If her stories succeed, she lives. If not, she dies."

"Keep in mind that what Scheherazade does is create a framework that guarantees she lives to see another day. Class, the answer is? *She leaves him hanging.* Exactly. You have a treasure at that point that no one else does. Think about that. It has to be a reliable teller, right? If we killed you and I completed the story, no matter how good my conclusion was, there would always be a sneaky suspicion that there was something better or more real or the truth. But also, curiously, there is no truth, right?"

"We thought of all kinds of things, but here's what we got. We call it the Cheshire Cat Punishment. You give us the only copies you have of your most precious documents, journals, personal letters, short stories, and all the writing and transcripts we create together. If you don't meet the obligations, we agree to torch the stuff, erasing your life behind you."

"Then there is the ultimate solution," Jack continued. "The Draconian Death Wish."

I think that was a professional wrestler's move.

Junk Drawer Items #1

Adlai Stephenson button
My family big democratic party supporters. It reminds me how a friend lived next door to Representative Edith Green, and I think I saw Adlai visit her there once before he was running for president. I also learned to associate Jews and democratic party. Since I was one of two people to vote for him in a dummy election, they always assigned me the same desk or lab partner with Gerald, the only Jew.

Wrestling magazine
The woman on cover was my 5th grade teacher. She had a glass eye which made it hard to figure who or what she was looking at. Very well-behaved class. I won her over because my mother was bookkeeper for a teacher's credit union and gave her loans with no paperwork.

Head of golden Santa Claus candle
It reminds me how I wanted an erector set one year and my parents gave me a world globe with a black ocean. I was furious, but I looked at them and realized I had power. I could dash them, even my father with his dispassionate fathering skills. I could just say like nice and move on or better, I could run out of the room crying. But I didn't. I spun it and had my finger land on Japan. Look dad, I landed on Japan. I learned how to lie that day.

Old picture of someone I don't know
The frame is 19th century. Studio shot. But my family has a

gazillion of these things, and no one knows who they are. Hey guys, you know I had an Uncle Gus in my family. He was a 19th century hippie, but I don't think it's him.

Photo hank Williams

Ah, my good buddy Dan. My first authentic gyppo logging red neck friend. I might be dead or be skinned alive, hanging from a western red cedar somewhere if not for him. He gave me that signed photo as way of apologizing for the night when two of his so-called friends invited Kathleen and I to their house and then threatened to have their way with Kathleen, but this skinny guy with a limp brought a 30-06 from the bathroom, shot it over their heads, shattering a cheesy chandelier. they took off. Never saw them again. Chuck was kind of the mayor of our town of 300 people.

Jail posting bail

A moment of pride. Like getting a letterman's jacket. I can still hear the metal door slamming behind me and Fred Jett and me faced the social world or a rural jail and watched as a kid who didn't look old enough to be in jail—rather the JD, was forced to masturbate in front of all of us while he was punched. We all had to punch him and share his fate. Why? Because he has struck his mother. And well, there's a line you know. They did it in our cell and we had to clean up the combination of jizz and blood.

Ad for Peyote

Remember, you could get it or use it if you belonged to a native American religion or church. A friend of mine did that long before the drug revolution. he was like his own merry prankster bus in our school. People just thought he was weird, never thought about peyote. He also saved all his masturbation discharges in a mayo jar. God, just remembered his mother showed it to me when folding the laundry. "Oh, boys will be boys," she said." And one day he took it I guess and comes up to our helpless science teacher with the unfortunate name of Mr. Swaim, which was mushed up into things like: Mr. Swarm, Mr. slime. So, He's talking to us about the periodic table and Andy just gets out of his seat walks straight up to within inches of Mr. Swarm, opening his eyes bug eyed like, "Hey, Mr. Slime you notice how my eyes are super dilated. You know what that means? And he lets go with this weird guttural sound of delight like a deep a huh and spit hits Slime's glasses. He has to remove them and says yes Andy, but please sit down. Andy turns around and whispers to me, though everyone can hear him, "peyote man. Imagine chugging a keg and then shooting up some raw sunlight and getting it on with Julie."

Selective service letter

One of many from them. I think this is the one, an appeal to the local selective service when this fat guy bent over me so I could smell stale cigar breath, and said, "Let me tell you something, young man. If there was someone raping your sister, I sure as hell hope if you had a gun you would shoot him. And besides which, if not now when we get you into the army, we'll turn you into a killing machine. My answer, yes, and that's why I won't join.

Vet bill

Oh shit, I said. I teared up. I had to put DC9, the name of a stray cat my father found, to sleep. He couldn't do it. So weird that he was a tough guy in so many ways, but he hated to see animals in pain. He more often cried about pets than people. DC9 was feral and wouldn't come near us for months. Then just a week before I had to have him put to sleep, I was asleep in the sun and was woken when his wet nose rubbed mine. I opened my eyes and froze. I didn't want him to run. But when I reached out to pet him, he twitched but allowed it. Then he trusted me. He got suddenly sick and couldn't even stand. Next thing he is laying on a cold silver table, I'm holding him as he gets injected with death drugs. I mean, so he finally trusts me, humans, and we use it to kill him. "right, like he's saying, buggers not going to trust them anymore." I was crying for him but also for my father and my uncle—who also cried more about pets than people." And I suppose crying because someday someone would put me to sleep too. The lie detector let out a wail like a German air raid warning. Yeah, I know the last thing was a lie...."

Arabian Nights Session #2—The Chronographer

The second Arabian night's session took place months later. Jack looked like he hadn't slept for days. I had never noticed how the bags under his eyes were heavy and brown. As though knowing what I was observing, he remarked casually, "They turn brown when I am worried. I think it is brain sediment. He turned to Gus, Isn't that right, Gus?"

Gus, distracted with his machinery, said, "I never see it your eyes always look blue to me. The wishbone is still in the shop. But...", he said as he pulled a sheet down from the wall and revealed the Alice in Wonderland rabbit's clock I had seen before, "I give you my chronographer," Uncle Gus proudly announced. "So, before it told us how fast we were moving as a planet. Okeydokey..."

He explained how the chronographer worked. Instead of miles, it was years. The arrow pointed to where Gus's great uncle was in his life. There was a red marker at 80 where he figured he was going to die. It was clear he was most of the way there. Every six months at a random time in the day, the chronographer would trigger a tape to go off with a random selection of music ranging from Louis Armstrong's "What A Wonderful World" to 1950s rock-and-roll love songs.

"Jack created a script for today's session," Uncle Gus said. Without a pause, he read from a stack of papers. OK, I wondered, but had gotten used to not asking, so why was Gus reading it, and why a script if he was right there?

"Remember," he said. "Jack wanted me to remind you that this is what you pay the big bucks for.... wisdom. And I quote... What is the difference between a junk drawer, scrapbook, time capsule and a pile of junk? Or what about a listing of your entire estate, including contents of all your junk drawers? What if I tell you to choose one thing for each day for the next month that you think is important. Then you say, *'Important? I never said what was in my junk drawer was important, did I?'* And so on and so forth." He came out from behind the table. "Just kidding. Here's what Jack wanted us to do. You're to pick three items and tell rapid stories.

I interrupted him, "What the hell? What about all the rules we set up in the first session? Why do we keep changing the rules?"

Gus stepped back behind the table, almost as though he thought I might hit him. "I don't know about that," he said matter-of-factly. I'll take shorthand and enter the data into my chronographer, which will of course later alert you to intersections. OK," Gus said, "Ray reminded me of a couple of things." He rummaged around in his papers. "Jack left some questions and minutes from our last discussion, but where the hell... Ah!" Gus shouted, "Isn't it good to find something."

Frankie added, "Sometimes I lose things just so I can find them."

"So here we go, Jack's session minutes:"

Was it random, really? How will we know?

Would it have been different if a stranger did it?

Will any item lead to all other items?

What would happen if your parents had kept boxes for you since birth? Each with a story attached they tell you on your 21st birthday.

Do photographs or stories steal your soul?

Gus lost a box of journals once and it was returned a year later. Is that amazing or not?

And now a quiz. OK, first one. Which of the following do you think is more accurate?

1. We come into life, soft ripe fruit, and leave like raisins that had the shit kicked out of them.
2. We come into life carrying several pieces of baggage: our genetic code, family plots, cultural binders, and most of all a set of instructions about what we can do while we are here. (I glanced at the wall and the crocheted Grape shit sign was gone)
3. or Is it a tale told by an idiot, full of sound and fury, Signifying nothing.

You could have also answered another question: Write the 10 most significant events in your life. But that seemed too obvious.

You know what, let's skip the quiz. I left a copy on your desk you can fill out later.

Junk Drawer Items #2

Orcas island menu

My older sister is dressed in tight leopard skinned peddle pusher pants. She was 15 and hated this vacation. The last one she went on with the family. She swore she would have a shitty time and did. She snarled for an entire week. I called her transistor sister, a derogative at the time for anyone that walked around carrying a portable radio shoved against their ear. Two years later she was pregnant and married.

Photo of my uncle's greenhouse

It was a photograph of my uncle's poor man's Greenhouse. A Greenhouse he created at the shire. To an undiscerning eye, it might just look like a large junk pile. He insulated walls with discarded sleeping bags inside plastic garbage bags.

He loved W. C. Fields movies better than anything. He didn't have friends or lovers, so he took me to movies. I saw him cry twice in the course of one week. Once at a Thanksgiving dinner when he bought 150 proof rum for the party punch and everyone got snookered. My mom turned the oven off by mistake, so the turkey was raw. We found her sitting outside in the rain nursing her rum punch. I found my uncle alone in my father's library, holding our cat Yasi on his lap, crying. Later that week he took me to a W. C. Fields Double Feature, and he laughed until he was crying.

Stack of old papers—maybe not mine

"OK," Jack said, "moving on." He pulled out a thick piece of paper. It looked like someone had tried to make it look like parchment. Burnt at the edges. Gothic looking script.

"Absolutely nothing comes to mind. Not mine," I said, puzzled.

"Oh, come on, the mind is never blank unless you are at level 19 in Scientology?"

"Shit, I don't know. Kathleen took a Chaucer class. Something I found on the street."

Gus and the stranger seemed almost angry, or at least extremely disappointed. Jack said, "OK, we'll just read it into the record."

Whoopee cushion

I remember a thanksgiving at my sister's. My nephew put it on my aunt Eva's seat. She was about to turn 100. When it went off, everyone laughed—except her. Which was fun, except I couldn't stop laughing. Like I was choking. Later I had to fight back the urge to just let my face fall in my plate of turkey mashed potatoes and lots of gravy. May have been the wild woodrose seeds I had taken earlier as a tea. Got the seeds for free from a company called Try Me.

Tattered Product Label
I think the crab king was the only person to threaten to kill me. I "stole" his Japanese girlfriend. She was living on the streets of Tokyo, an alcoholic when she was only 16. We petted in back seats of cars in college. When I think of her, I think of steamy car windows...well that and the fact I had my life threatened.

Carved ivory knife
A white-handled knife shaped like the head of a sea lion. I think I got that from my uncle. I mean, my mom's brother. He was stationed in Alaska during WW II. I don't know why I ended up with it. He hated me. Or what I stood for. Peacenik. But even that I let on that Santa didn't exist to my younger cousin. The knife not from my uncle but from this guy I met in eastern Oregon. A carnie hobo probably in his twenties when I met him, so to me, 14, he was old. He gave me the knife as a kind of contract that I wouldn't mess with this messed up kid he befriended in the shire where he showed up by coincidence years after I met him. This kid stole expensive equipment from Reed College and I caught him once trying to light our school on fire. weird cause it was mostly brick, and I laughed at him. And he shot a match at me with his match gun, almost got me in the eye.

Chocolate bar wrapper
I saved it on purpose thinking I might write a poem about it and add to my pension savings account because it belonged to congressional poet Laureate William Stafford. He was to dish out chocolate when our families went back packing.

Millie. Kiggins
News clipping of Millie Kiggins of Estacada Oregon having run in with Big Foot.[3] Millie was the first girl in Oregon to try out for guys high school football and get on the team.

Kathleen and I bought a house from her near Estacada and lived there for a year. In the woods that led down to the Clackamas river she and her father, Grover, had found big foot prints, now in the Smithsonian.

Note pad LSD trips

Jack gingerly handed me the next item, a wadded piece of paper on last leg. "Looks like it went through the wash. Don't think it's my handwriting. I struggled to read it, "We come into life, soft ripe fruit, and leave like raisins that had the shit kicked out of us." I glanced at Jack and Gus and the wall where I had seen this phrase in an elaborate frame. It was gone. I looked at the stranger, "I wrote it on an LSD trip when I figured out how to erase my ego and not get terrified.... next."

Rubber dart gun

Gus grabbed the stranger's suitcase, and they left. I went over to the box and covering my eyes pulled out another item. "Ah," I said out loud, "a rubber dart for a dart gun. What comes to mind is how wild Bill, our neighbor for a long time, who drank himself to death in his forties, had hair on the back of his hands. When I would help him spread bark dust, the dust would get caught in the hair. I was interested in any male body hair for a short while. Guys my age were sprouting hair everywhere, but not me...what the hell does all this have to do with dart gun....oh right well his daughter had a crush on me so he took us out together sometimes to get ice cream or would give us a couple of bucks to buy something so I bought a dart gun. But he grabbed it away from me with those hairy hands when I accidentally hit his little boy in the forehead."

Arabian Nights Session #4--Old Life Washed Away in a Tsunami

I don't remember how long it took us the schedule for the fourth Arabian Night's Session. A lot had happened, I know that. My old life seemed far away.

When I arrived in what I had thought of as my interrogation room, Jack seemed all business. Uncle Gus was in his usual position, surrounded by AV equipment. They had decorated the wishbone lie detector with tiny multi-colored Christmas lights. And there was a stranger sitting next to him. My first impression was that he looked like an Oxford academic. Not sure where that stereotype came from. A full gray beard and "natty."

"First off," Jack said, holding out a pile of paper. "If I didn't know better, I'd say parchment from medieval times." He handed me the pile, which seemed ancient. Through a beam of light, I could see pieces of the brown paper disintegrate in the air. A rusty paper clip held the papers together. I knew immediately what it was. I explained, but then declared somewhat in jest, "what is this are you changing the rules. You poked around in the box since our last meeting. What kind of science is that?"

"It was an accident. It fell out. That's still random, isn't it? So, what is it?"

I explained that it resulted from a conversation Kathleen and I had years ago, not too long after we met when I had opened a drawer in her kitchen in the house she lived in when we met, and thought it was funny the things that were in there. So, she later made me a list of everything in the drawer.

"Well, that's a fine kettle of fish," Jack said peevishly. "You told me you had this flash of insight the day we talked on the phone, but here you had this previous moment. Be honest with me or our methodology is compromised," and then winking at Uncle Gus, "that and/or sex life is damaged." He shook his head. "Kathleen may be the genius in this relationship. I should probably stalk her not you."

I looked over at Uncle Gus and the stranger. They were also shaking their heads. I felt like I had failed the parole board and was about to be sent back to my cell. Jack went over and secretly talked with the stranger. I couldn't hear them.

"OK," Jack said, "we can work with it. He handed me a red pen. Just randomly go through the material."

Jack turned to Gus with a quizzical look.

"Hey boss," Gus said, "ready whenever you are."

"Okeydokey," Jack said and dipped his hand into one of my boxes.

I held up my hand, "But what about the junk drawer list from my prior life?"

"Exactly," Jack said, "that's what it is, a previous life. We'll examine it when we do past life regression. Don't worry .that won't happen... So, what about the menu?"

"OK guys," Jack said, the jet plane won't wait what's it going to be."

The doctor was throwing things into a suitcase. File folders and underwear all mixed together along with what looked like a huge bargain pack of Alka Seltzer tablets.

"I would call it fog lights in the fog. That's the best I can think of."

I refused to ask them who the stranger was, although I had a suspicion it was the junk drawer theorist, old what's his name, but I also suspected it wasn't but just a friend or hired actor to pretend.

Junk Drawer Items #3

Broken 45 record—The Spiders in Japan

I am sixteen and I am in love with Kyoko. At the Kyoto train station, she seems to pay attention to everyone in our student group except for me. The blood flowing through me feels like ice water. Then, just as I am climbing on the train, she runs over to me. Oh, that smile! The ice water turns into warm bath water. She grabs my hand. I feel her soft skin. With the other, she hands me a 45 record by the Spiders. I will wait for you to come back.

Both Gus and Jack nodded in approval. Gus said, "125,000 to

one. That's the number of items in your box times your age."
Whatever. I pulled out more items.

Carved wood comb

I was going to say it was from Kyoko, but I think it was from
this other Japanese girl, a hotel maid, I was in love with. I
called her Ju Nana, which means 17 in Japanese. WE went on
a couple of dates. She spoke no English at all. We made out in
an abandoned baseball park. She wore a kimono for that date.
Ever try to get to 2nd base through that kind of clothing maze?

A string of 25 paperclips

In 7th grade I couldn't stop talking and the teacher forced me
to sit behind a filing cabinet for the rest of the year. Except
Parent's day, when we pretended nothing was wrong.

Perfume stick called Occur

That would not be Kathleen. She was the first girl or woman I
dated that never used makeup or perfume. Just Occur when
she was nervous.

Flyer in Japanese for West Side Story

I am with Bob and Randy in the Korean section of Kyoto.
We've decided to see how many bars we can go to in six hours,
but we only get to the 5th one where we almost died.

A flower pressed between pieces of wax paper.

A note. "first peony, 1943."—It's my mother's handwriting.
Before I was born. We sold flowers from our garden. We had a
stand along the road. A sign read, bouquets, please put ten
cents in the jar.

A matchbook from Eddie May's, a bar

The bar my parents met up with their couple swapping
African American couple. In the 1960s, my parents went to

Haight Ashbury just before the summer of love and crashed at a pad. In the 1970s they were briefly part of the swinging singles scene when they shared partners with a black couple. I walked in on my father with the woman.

SS President Cleveland menu
At the same time Gus and Jack shouted out, "we have a winner." Jack motioned for me to turn around. I could tell he was rummaging through one of the junk drawers, "Watch how now if I pull something out it will reveal the theme of your first assignment." I could hear them whispering, but not what they were saying. "Turn around." On the table was a menu from the ship we took on our trip to Japan in 1962, the S.S. President Cleveland. Memories of the ship flooded me. The sound of the engine in our steerage dormitory room that sounded like the heartbeat of the earth. Sailing out under the Golden Gate bridge, having never left the country except for Canada, and knowing my life was changing big time and forever. I told them about Liz, the 25-year-old woman from New York who took a fancy to me. Almost 10 years older than me. We met in one of the ship's bar every day. She thought what I had to say was interesting, and it seemed the more she thought that, the more interesting I became. Two weeks later, when we reached Yokohama, I was talking to anyone and everyone. Other people Liz's age, ship crew, exotic looking people with head turbans.

Tiny tan bowl with a nodded piece of seaweed
Jack pulled from the box a tiny tan bowl with a knotted piece of seaweed. "Easy," I said. Imagine I am sixteen. I have long hair. Less than the neat Beatle look. But all boys my age in Japan have shaved heads. I am with a Japanese man I only met the night before in Tokyo. We take a taxi to his house. Tiny and tidy house. The sliding front door opens and this ancient woman wearing kimono dives to the floor in front me.

Prostrate. Up and down like she is doing pushups. I want her to get up. Behind is Mr. Otha's 13-year-old daughter not quite on the ground but bowing." "too long, Jack said, matter-of-factly, "but we will accept it."

A worn, thin diary
"Nijo castle. 3 am some morning and I can't sleep so sneak out on to the streets of Kyoto. I recite the one Haiku I know in Japanese to Japanese workers gathered around a giant hole in the street."

High school grade report
"Late for my first class when I return to the USA, running up the stairs, and I run into this giant gawky student coming down. I am down 2 stairs from his level, and my head hits his crotch. "easy their brother If I want a blow job, I'll ask you." Wow, a giant with sense of humor. I later meet him around a campfire along the will. river and find out he is known as Mr. Light show of Portland. and his girlfriend is the daughter of friends of my parents, who have key swap parties."

Another broken record. The Dovell's Bristol Stomp
The Dovell's Bristol Stomp. A string of blind dates and disastrous drunken pickups at drive-in restaurants like Yaws in Portland. Rosemarie who is at least 4 inches taller than me and outweighs me by 20 pounds. She is plain and gawky looking, except when she dances the Bristol Stomp.[5]

Arabian Nights Session Extra Credit

Then there are the Arabian Nights' Sessions that Jack conducted alone. We found tiny boxes and manuscripts for 8. we dedicated three to Kathleen. The boxes had 200 items I have to assume he "borrowed" from our house before I moved to the Gertrude Stein Fellowship club. We found at least two stories based on found objects we never found, a five-dollar bill and the acknowledgment page to *None Dare Call It Treason*,[4] with a foreword by Dr. John. They also introduce him in the foreword as "second only to Charles Fort[5] in deep digging and crawling through libraries to find obscure facts and rats." I did separately tell Jack about the incident of being paid for just being a hippie and about the incident at the Shire with a police officer.

Hippie for a Price

It was the winter of 1968. David and I were walking back from the neighborhood tavern. Late. Maybe midnight. No one else on the rain-lit streets. Then a woman bolted out of a parked car, and then a man. They were agitated. We heard a "fuck you!" from the girl and then a "No, fuck you!" from the guy. We paused. One of those situations. Will we have to intervene? How big is the guy? But we were in our twenties. There were two of us. And David was tall and scrappy and I was still built like a wrestler. Shouting louder, the man put his arm on the women's shoulder but she broke free.

"Get your fucking hands off me!" She saw us and hurried toward us. We were officially involved. "I'm going with them," she said, and turned to us.

"That right?"

David immediately said, "Sure," and stood up taller.

I was dubious. The guy moved toward us a couple of steps, then paused. He flipped us the finger and got back into his car and left.

We went back to David's apartment. I'm sure we were both stupidly trying to get a better look at the girl and decide which one would sleep with her. I was wondering why she would trust us, two strangers in the dark.

In the apartment's light, I still wasn't sure if she was attractive. Her name was Cheryl, but that was her white name. She was Native American, and her tribal name was something like Meadow Lark. She explained how she had moved to Portland from the Warm Springs Reservation to go to community college. And at some point, she asked David if it would be all right if she stayed there the night.

When David went to the toilet, she spotted a *Life* magazine on the coffee table. It was *Life's* special edition about hippies. She picked it up and said, "See, that's how I knew I could trust you." I hadn't looked at the cover closely, but, oddly, the iconic hippie on the cover looked vaguely like me. David was still rather "straight" looking. With pony tail and scruffy short beard, I was unmistakably a hippie.

We talked for a while longer, and as dawn light entered the apartment, I got up to leave. When I was at the door, she hurried over to me, gave me a hug and a relatively long kiss, pressed something into my hand, and whispered, "That's just for being who you are." I figured it was her telephone number. I discreetly put it in my pocket. Outside, I took it out of my pocket. It was a $5 bill.

What I learned from Large Blue Thigh with a Gun

In my version of the sixties, everyone argued a lot. If I walked down the street, people made cat calls at my ponytail. I went to a party at my sister's house and when I walked into her front room one of her husband's friends in Marine garb threw me against the wall, denounced me as a Fairy-Commie-scumbag-hippie. Family gatherings turned into fisticuffs. I spent a lot of time preparing arguments or coming up with the best answer too late.

One day by chance, a police officer taught me how to argue in geological time. Leland garnered as much anger as I did, but because he was gigantic, most people only yelled at him from a distance or behind his back. But one day I invited him to come to the Shire. There was a back road into the property, and when I didn't want to have a family engagement but get out of the city, I came in that way. This day we encountered a police officer. (My family encouraged the neighborhood police to take their coffee breaks there. We had innumerable problems with vandals and burglars so we figured the police presence might defer some hell bent.)

We drove past the police car, and then it followed us to where we parked. The cop rolled down his window and motioned us over. Before I could tell him who I was, he asked for ID. As I started to explain how this was my home, he ignored me and repeated his request.

"Give me your ID first, then we'll talk."

"But he lives here," Leland said emphatically.

The cop took a hard look at him, "Well, when you show me your ID, then we'll know if that's the case, now won't we."

The car was blocked on his side by a wall of blackberries, so we had to saddle up to the passenger side. I handed him my driver's license and said, "Well, it won't tell you I live here. I grew up here but...."

"Let me examine the ID, then we can talk," he said more emphatically. He eyed Leland carefully. He was big, but Leland was bigger. He made sure we could see his gun. His blue thigh on the front seat was the size of a boa constrictor eating a lamb. Nice boots, and the gun which was not strapped in the holster. He could clearly have pulled it out in time to put several slugs in Leland's head. "So, what are you doing here?" he said while examining our ID.

Leland said, rather irritated, "Well, we're just walking around on his property. What are you doing here?"

Ah, shit, I thought. "OK, Leland, you didn't know this," I said, "but we invite the police here, so perfectly fine."

The cop seemed to ignore this exchange. "Well, your name is the same as the old man that lives here."

"Yes," I said, "my father's name is Ken and my uncle who lives right over there is Walt." It seemed a little strange that I was on the defense in my home. "Should I go over and get my uncle?"

Silence. "No, that won't be necessary," he said, softening. "No reason not to believe you. You know, can't be too careful. Just my job." He handed our ID back, and I figured it was over. But then he said, "So tell me, you seem like you're the right age to be in the armed services. Some reason you're not?"

Leland immediately answered, "Because neither one of us believes in the war in Viet Nam."

"Really!" the cop said.

And I knew we were in for something. Why didn't Leland tell him he had been to Vietnam and returned with physical and mental injuries that he would carry with him for the rest of his life?

"Let me tell you a thing or two about that."

And he did, and we responded. Back and forth. It was such familiar territory. Do you think freedom comes for free? (him) Do you really believe there is a communist threat? (us) Do you believe in free speech? (us) Yeah, and the right to bear arms too. (him) What would you do if someone were killing your mother? (him)

Leland loved it. He was bent over to get a full view of Mr. Blue while I looked around at the sky, watched a hawk overhead, then a squirrel checking us out, trying to remember what tree we used to have the giant rope swing on, occasionally adding my two cents.

The conversation took a peculiar twist when he asked us if we knew the book *None Dare Call It Treason*.[3.] He described the thesis which both of us were familiar with. He described a group that met in Portland to discuss conspiracy ideas.

"I am a patriot," he said.

This angered Leland, who declared his own patriotism and love for America.

I was trying to find some way to escape but leaned in past Leland and said, "I didn't know there was a group in Portland that followed this stuff. Where do they meet?" I'm not sure why I asked the question. Probably because I was always looking for unknown groups to list with the Mello Pages and other projects. I know I didn't have ideas about storming the meeting loaded down with automatic weapons.

Big Blue got a steely look on his face, put his hand on his gun and looked me dead in the eyes and said, "Look, punk, it should be obvious I know where you live. And if you know what's good for you, nothing we said ever happened. You got it?"

Leland seemed oblivious to this not-so-veiled threat and continued arguing about the conspiracy theory. I straightened up and looked up to the hawk flying over, and something clicked. Why on earth did I ever think I would win an argument with someone like Mr. Blue Thigh? It was a waste of time. Did I really think he might suddenly turn all nice and understanding?

"You know what, I never thought of it that way," I said. "Let's bring your people together with my people and smoke the peace pipe." We could sit here until the cows came home and nothing we said would ever sway Mr. Blue. And nothing he said would make us change our minds. I pulled at Leland and then bent down so I could look him square in the eye,

"No, of course not," Leland said, "We'd never rat on you or whatever, that's part of our code. I'm just glad we had the chance to talk."

I pulled Leland away, and then added, "We really appreciate that you came here. Sure, makes our life safer." Paradigm galaxies represented by us and Blue Thigh, with the only changes marked in geological time. Having an argument to build a bridge between us was like trying to stop the Big Bang with super glue.

Arabian Nights #344. Arabian Nights Japanese Anomaly

Preamble

You may have noticed a Japanese theme. I have had a lifetime fascination with Japan and many visits there, including when I was a teenager. But Jack was also fascinated not so much with Japan but with the Arabian Night's session when we pulled out an extraordinary number of items related to Japan. There were some rational reasons, like I had thrown a bunch of Japanese items into one drawer, but given what else was in the drawer, that made little sense. Japanese items didn't come from one trip, and other items in the same box were strewn over many years. I think it discombobulated Jack and Gus. Look, I knew the whole thing was staged—depending on sleight of hand, or way of distracting the audience (me in this case) so they wouldn't notice something otherwise pretty obvious. But, while it wasn't scientific, it was pretty random. They jiggled the Items, sorted, unsorted, thrown around, mixed up, to make it hard for things to cling to one another.

They both thought Dr. John had a name for this random selection, and a theory behind it but neither could remember where they heard about it. I was more expansive about that period of my life and emphasized how a trip to Japan took me to a different path I didn't even know was there: what I was like in high school, my personal transformation during Japan, and what happened when I returned to an American high school; it felt like I had time-traveled to school in another dimension.

Jack wrote it up. He conducted research about me and my friends. I didn't know that Esther, my high school girlfriend, had died until I found an article from Atlanta, Georgia, neatly taped to a corny red valentine card in the archives.

A tiny rush of small memories. So how does this one work in Dr John's random theory world? In that world there was a spectrum that went from random to fate or manifest destiny. There were pieces of string attaching us over time and place. If you could follow the pieces of string, you would understand why you took a footstep forward or why you had taken the last one. But what did it mean? If we had the big bang source code, would we discover the linkage?

One more item Jack had written up. I had once visited a friend who lived at Fort Ord in California. We had gone to Japan together. Jack wrote:

"I was on the Monterey State College campus attending a conference about using communities for university curriculum. The campus had been a military base, Fort Ord [1] and was in the middle of transformation into a college campus. They put me up in the residential area set aside for commissioned officers. I arrived at night and I did not understand where I was. When I went outside in the morning, it was creepy. The entire neighborhood was fit as a fiddle. Lawns and shrubs perfect, all the houses identical. I expected housewives of the fifties might at any moment prance out on cue for a musical about a creepy but also normal Pleasantville movie. The kicker, the mailbox for my house, listed the prior occupant as Lt.

Colonel John Ekleberger. Oh, how much Dr. John would have loved that."

She Had Eighteen Brothers and Sisters

In my junior year in high school, I was in love with Esther. She was a year older than me and everything was theater in her life. Stared in all the performances; had a hallway where all the theater wonks hung out. She was Catholic, which she used as a rationale for not going all the way. She had eighteen brothers and sisters. Only twelve of those lived in her house; the others were step-siblings who visited now and then.

The third floor in their Southeast Portland home was like a Dickensian orphanage. Her father was ancient and toothless. He chain-smoked. The younger kids loved to show me where he hung his boogers. From his chair in front of the television, he barked out orders. Often no one knew what he was saying because he couldn't find his dentures. His tone was obvious enough, so everyone yelled back what they were or weren't doing. When he managed to find his dentures in, he bellowed out specific names but often got them wrong.

"Dolly, shut the fuck up or you get the belt."

"I'm Nella June, not Dolly."

"Will all of you shut the fuck up!"

In the middle of this bliss, my parents told me the good news. We were moving to Japan for six months. How the hell could they do this to me? I had a girlfriend, a good source of beer, and my own plans, like Marrying Esther. All I knew about Japan was that everything cheap said "Made in Japan." That and one of my father's colleague's family were all killed at Hiroshima. And anyway, Esther's father had told me how he was second or third cousin in the Woolworth family and any day now they would roll in cash and he'd give Esther and me a house, car, you name it.

For a farewell party my friend, Dave, created a deadly mesh of alcohol made up of small dosages of at least six kinds of booze including Jack Daniels, brandy and Vodka, and he set me up with his girlfriend's sister, Barb, who was at least a head taller than me. I couldn't figure out if she was good looking or not. I thought she was when she danced the Bristol Stomp.[6] We played the Stomp a lot. I made it to second base before I passed out. Dave woke me at 3 am with a plan to go skinny dipping in the Columbia River. I was the designated driver, although I couldn't tell if I was still drunk or just half asleep. There weren't many cars on the road, but we ran into a carload of hoods from a rival high school. We were in my baby blue '53 Olds and they were in a souped-up Chevy. They challenged us at a red light. Rubber burning, we took off down a major thoroughfare. They would have won, except I floored it when we approached an intersection with a red light. I wanted to win, and I thought breaking might be even worse. Dave told me we were clocking 90 when we flew through the red light. When we got back to Barb's house, we were wide awake, so we drank more. I fell asleep wrapped up in Barb's body under a grandma quilt. I felt I was a child more than a lover. I left for Japan a few days later.

The letter from Esther was steeped in a perfume that provided me a Proust moment of gestalt memory. I think it is what she wore. I hardly wonder how Jack knew that, but really how? It is so old looking it looks like someone tried to make it look like an ancient treasure map: frayed edges, ripped out words, wrinkles like an ancient face. I had to put it up to the light and in places put specific words and letters under a magnifying glass. I kept the last letter, one she had written on the side of a fast food bag, and one on bright orange paper. There are some profound moments in her letters. In the orange ones, on a separate line, not related to what proceeds or follows: "Why is still a question to me. I mean, think about that for a minute...." She also compares herself to a snowplow, but all she was trying to do was be "different and perfect." Can you do both? I think I'm still trying to do that. She also told me that for the first time in her life she didn't have to be drunk to be with her boyfriend. That I let her be just who she was. She added that it was OK if I wanted to get drunk. She would understand. She must have been responding to a letter I had written when she asks, "why were you going 100mph?"

The bag letter is kind of charming. Apparently, she made her way across town by shrinking herself enough so she could fit into a fast food bag. She left herself in the bag at a bus stop and was picked up by a kid who carried her all the way here. He threw away the bag and miraculously it blew up to my front steps. Unfortunately, I wasn't there, so she left the bag with $5 that we had won in some kind of radio contest. She told me the bag was magic and that if I held the bag and thought about how much she loved me, it would transport me to her house.

When I came back from Japan, I was no longer high school kid. I didn't tell her I was back for over a week. Night after night I stood on the back deck looking out into the forest and listened to Sukiyaki and the falling rain, thinking about Kyoko, wishing I were back in Japan. When I finally got together with her, I knew it was over. She ran out the door when she saw me, embraced, and went for a long kiss. It felt like I was kissing my sister.

Then the classic. Heartbroken, she joined the air force. I never saw her again, although sometime in college I found her address in North Carolina and wrote her a letter. Her response reflected how so many things had changed. She had met Bill, also in the air force, just her type, I guess? "Bill's quite dominating and you could truthfully say I like it." She has had insights: "I know one thing for sure. I've grown up a little more and I don't think you would know me if you ever meet me again. Being out in the world makes you grow up. Life is so real." She also had forgiven me: "I hope you find love; you deserve to be loved." She closes with sage words of wisdom, "Well time flies and so do people. Be good but if you can't be good, then be careful and you can't be good and careful then don't get caught."

She died from a heart attack when she was in her fifties. I only knew this because I found a newspaper clipping in Jack's archives.

Metamorphosis

I was supposed to just stay with my parents while I was in Japan, but on the train from Tokyo to Kyoto my parents arranged for me to stay with Mr. Ota, a city government administrator from Osaka.

Mr. Ota took me to his office to wait while he went to fetch the mayor. I sat on the floor drinking green tea, contemplating how to greet the mayor—or some high up person—of Japan's second largest city. I wanted to be sitting if anyone came back. I don't know why. But finally, I got up and moved toward a sliding glass door. I opened it slowly. Smells and sounds entered the room. The wider I opened the door, more sounds entered until it was a roar. I walked across a small porch and stared out at a brown and gray city as far as I could see. It was impossible to take it all in. I tried to imagine telling the girlfriend I left behind or my best friends about this scene. They seemed so far away and explaining this seemed impossible. I was on another planet.

I was just coming back in from the porch when Mr. Ota came back with a half dozen formally dressed Japanese men.

"I want you to meet the mayor of Nishinomiya and the Vice Mayor of Osaka," he said. They spoke back and forth in Japanese as I held out my hand. Everyone bowed. I bowed. Then the most extraordinary thing happened.

I said, "It is a great honor to be in your beautiful country." And then added in Japanese, "Hajimamasta," meaning *pleased to meet you*.

Why was that so amazing? Well, where did it come from? I could tell you about the kind of drunks I had experienced or excoriating details about successes and failures trying to hit a home run with girls but how the hell did I know how to talk to Japanese government administrators? It was as though the curtain had opened in the Wizard of Oz, revealing a man pushing buttons. I didn't have just one self or ego, but many. While I saw myself only as the juvenile delinquent in an American high school, these people saw something else. I realized in a flash that I was not just that little self in the fishbowl of an American high school, but a multitude of possibilities.

Mr. Ota and I took a taxi to his house. When we arrived, we were greeted by his mother who fell prostrate at my feet. She repeated something over and over. OK, not covered in any handbook. What does a 16-year-old Juvenile delinquent when an ancient Asian woman falls to the ground? Mr. Ota just said she is welcoming you to our humble home.

The next morning, a loud noise like a gigantic vacuum woke me coming from my bathroom. I crawled across the floor and opened the door. There was a rubber hose the size of a boa constrictor coming through the window into the toilet hole in the floor. My first encounter with a honey truck.

Kawaii Baby

Not long before I left for Japan, I went on a blind date. When my blind date climbed into our car, she took one look at me and declared, "You got to be kidding. No way am I going anywhere with him.!" My friend Dave drove me home where I got fiercely drunk and wrote the first poem I had ever written. Something inane about seeing God's infinity in the starlit night. But even today, fifty years later, the poem can bring forth for me, if not for you, the feeling of rejection and smallness. In *Speak Memory*, Nabokov does a splendid job of delineating between a good and bad poem. He inserts a piece of doggerel so, so bad, but for him it brings forth a rush of memories and tears, but only for himself. A poem with an audience of one. An ad for a good shaving razor can do the same if it happens in front of a mirror like the one your father used. So what is the difference? The good poem and shaving add both evoke.

In Japan, it was like I had died and gone to heaven. If all the male students and I were in a pack, I was the one the Japanese girls and women flirted with. I fell in love daily with girls on the street, hotel maids, waitresses, host family daughters. Sometimes the girls were my age, but sometimes they were five or six years older. There was a popular song in Japan while I was there, "Kawaii Baby" ("Cute Little Baby"). That was one explanation for my success. Apparently, I looked like the American boy used on the record cover. Sometimes when I would be on the train or walking home around the end of a school day, small herds of Japanese girls would follow me singing that song.

We frequented a bar near our hotel in Kyoto and became known as regulars. It was a liberated bar. There were cross dressers and transvestites. There was also Emi, a woman five years older than me, and who, unlike some young Japanese women I met, sexually active and adventuresome. The first night I met her, she sat down at our table without an invitation.

She said, "I'm Emi, which means beautiful blessing, and I can help you learn about the other Japan." She sat down next to me. As the drunken conversation continued, she put her hand on the inside of my thigh, and when I noted it but looking at her, she just smiled confidently. I think it was the first time a girl or woman ever picked me up.

Over several weeks we met together or in our group. Then one night, only a week before our departure to America, she handed me a note. "I want to give you a surprise. Meet me tomorrow night at the main gate to Nijo Castle."

When I met her the next night, she was dressed in a Geisha kimono. She took my hand and put a finger to her mouth and then mine, indicating I should say nothing. We went to a small garden space along the Nijo Castle moat. It was too cold and hard to make love, but she undid her kimono and wrapped it around both of us and guided my hand from her breasts to stomach and below while her other hand found my family jewels. I doubt it took over three minutes when I exploded. While it didn't count as the time I lost my virginity, it would be years before I came close to the subsuming passion I felt that night.

I never saw her after that night, although she sent a gift to our hotel, her kimono sash that smelled like her for many months after our night together.

Arabian Nights Session #3--Mr. Death Shows Up

I braced myself for the Arabian Night's session like I was going to court. I had assembled facts and put together a narrative of Jack's life, his personas, and tangentially a biography of Uncle Gus, and histories of various institutions, EEL, etc. I was uncertain about much of anything but I knew the best way was to pretend I was. I also was going to take the upper hand by storming into the interrogation room, distribute handouts and pay no attention to their gaze or interruptions. It was a good plan except when I arrived at the integration room it was empty. Not just empty but void of any signs of inhabitation. Just one long table and several broken chairs. A beam of light from the one window (I could have sworn there was no window in that part of the room last time) aimed at the table revealed a layer of dust on the table and flotsam jetsam in the air. I sat on the table. I knew I was being duped but how or why? A spider emerged from under the table and scurried across pausing briefly on my pile of papers. I know he or she didn't but when it paused; I felt like it was staring at me. It said look at the walls. The walls were blank. No big deal? How about no outlets? But there would be a sign, right? New plaster filling in the old outlets? Just as I jumped off the table to investigate, I glanced at the door and realized there was a stranger. Standing inside. He may have been there all the time, behind the door when I came in. I stared. He stared back. I wanted to out maneuver him, then, everyone. But soon as I thought of a move— ironic twist, ambiguous wisdom, surrealistic improv moment, I could imagine how they would best me... It was chess and I was a checkers player compared to Jack and Gus. I imagined.... Who are you? Who am I? who do you think I am? Who do you want me to be? Don't you remember 4th grade? We sniffled glue together and locked the janitor in the bathroom? Or it was Gus or Gus had a son. Or it was my 4th grade teacher or Fred Jett after drug rehabilitation. The possibilities were endless.

The right move I realized would be to just go ahead with my agenda as planned. I adapted a persona; pretending to myself I was a

Ph.D. student presenting my colloquium. With prompt and ceremony. I placed out three piles of handouts, organized my overheads, even though there wasn't a projector, I planned to hold them up to the beam of light. Cleared my throat several times and decided I would face Jack, that is where he usually sat or stood or paced. When I stared in that direction, I realized the wall in back of where he stood was peculiar. When I moved back and forth so the light shined and then not on the wall it seemed like it reflected light. Ah....one-way mirror. I imagined Gus and Jack sitting behind the wall watching me, taking notes, snacking on pistachio nuts. I knew it wasn't true, and yet I could imagine it so well it was real. I really didn't know and more interesting I didn't want to know. It would make my presentation all the clearer. So, what the hell I imagined 50 people behind the wall watching me. I remembered a Twilight episode in which a man finds himself in a very comfy house but he doesn't know where and then an accident reveals he is in a cage and a mirror is revealed as a window with hundreds of people watching him. He is in a zoo on a foreign planet.

I organized my papers on the table, and put several piles of handouts, documents I was going to give to Jack and Gus. I was going to make use of the overhead projector, and Gus's lie detector in my presentation but I could wing it.

I tried to ignore Mr. Death as he slowly made his way toward me. Slowly as in exaggerated baby steps. While continuing to read Jack's biography out loud, part of me was trying to figure out how I was going to do the random lot thing. No box of stuff. Insight. Everything else is made up so why not? By the time I finished reading the stranger was 10 feet from me trying to make eye contact. When I was done, I carefully took papers out of the box that had my Jack notes and with a pen drew buttons on it: on/off, forward/rewind and crude picture of reel-to-reel tape. I then reached under the table, and like a very amateurish mime I placed "things" on the desk.

Junk drawer Items #4

Broken sun glasses

"Ah," I exclaimed as though I were unwrapping a birthday gift, "yes, a broken pair of sunglasses. How many have I broken? I had nightmare as a kid that heaven or hell would be like this gigantic tool shed or storage shed where everything you ever owned or broke was and you had to fix all of it and distribute the stuff to poor people."

Oly 4-star labels

There were one through four stars on the back side. If you had 4 stars you would score with chicks remember. Nolan the guy I hitchhiked with to Mexico had a box with probably 2000 4 stars but he never scored. Could be because he like a red-haired rooster. But he was also the guy that in the heyday of hippies was paid $5 to attend a fraternity party. Token hippie.

A smooth white rock

A smooth white rock with holes like Swiss cheese. My only French girlfriend found it on the beach and gave it to me. She was so far out of my class but I guess didn't know it yet or something. We had cool affair at the beach. Spend our days in an abandoned hotel pretending we owned it. But soon as we got back to reality, she had nothing to do with me.

Half bottle of Happy Feet, lotion for feet

Shit, don't know. Wait. Kathleen and got it in the mail when we dropped off the grid. I forgot how I sent away for things while we lived there. The Postmistress knew everyone, and everyone's mail. Whenever she handed me our mail, she took a hard look at me as though to either assess my evil potential or tell me if she wanted, she could have me run out of town in an express package. Kathleen and I though Pretty feet was weird because we bathed in the icy creek on our property. We left it down by the creek and watched it disintegrate as slugs and other animals had an orgy. Kathleen took photos of it.

The stranger handed me a note on an index card. It simply read, "not bad. Not good either."

Broken key chain
A broken key chain with half eaten or rotten chipmunk tail. Kathleen's mother thought it was funny. She gave it to Kathleen the first Christmas I spent with them in Palo Alto. In her stocking. The more drunk she got the more she could bring the conversation back to the key chain. How do you suppose they killed it? Was it road kill? She was neurotic but very bright. Had a high IQ, but she was like a muscle car from the 60s on car jack engine racing and nowhere to go. Her husband was sweet and smart. Kathleen called them the out of tune violin and bassoon.
I tried to imitate the sound of Uncle Gus's lie detector, that revealed tangential truth.

Page from Robinson Crusoe
A page from a hardbound copy of Robinson Crusoe. Not sure why I have a page. But forever the book is locked in my head as favorite time with my father when he would read to me in his Walden shed. The smells that's what I want back. I can describe them but can't smell them. I think if I walked into a space with all those smells: moldy sleeping back, his pipe, smoky pot belly stove, deodorant smell from one of those hanging air fresheners you usually put in a car. I would be flooded with memories. I'll even go out on a limb and say I would know answers to lives' persistent questions.

Photo from Pentagon
A famous photo. A girl sticking a flower into the rifle of a soldier at the 1967 March on the Pentagon. I was in the front row along with this iconic woman in the photo. What I remember about it was that some of us were in panic mode because the mob behind us of 50,000 people were shoving

forward and pushing us straight away into bayonets. Sheathed, but it wouldn't much matter. And you know what, it worked. There was more space for a while. Then they shot out tear gas and everyone panicked. I got several cuts and bruises but survived. I slept that night in Abe Lincoln's memorial, leaning on his gigantic foot. Huck, if you are alive and read this, imagine I slept on his foot!

---

1. *One Thousand and One Nights* is a collection of Middle Eastern folk tales compiled in Arabic during the Islamic Golden Age. It is often known in English as the *Arabian Nights*. The story concerns Shahryr, who is shocked to learn that his brother's wife is unfaithful; and then discovering that his wife has been unfaithful. He has her killed. Shahry marries a succession of virgins only to execute each one the next morning, before she dishonors him. Scheherazade, the vizier's daughter, offers herself as a bride. On the night of their marriage, she tells the king a tale, but does not end it. The king, curious about how the story ends, is thus forced to postpone her execution in order to hear the conclusion. The next night, as soon as she finishes the tale, she begins another one, and the king, eager to hear the conclusion of that tale, postpones her execution once again. This goes on for one thousand and one nights, hence the name.

2. John Clellon Holmes was an American author, poet and professor, best known for his 1952 novel *Go*. Considered: the first "Beat" novel, *Go* depicted events in his life with his friends Jack Kerouac, Neal Cassady and Allen Ginsberg.

   Johnson, as a writer, has great buried talent. He has a unique and special sense of words. His vision of life is his own. He's an outsider. As a person I found him guarded, intelligent, critical. He didn't say much in class; I could see the disgruntled word "hypocrisy" written in flames on his forehead, blinding him to certain things. I liked him; I tend to believe in people like Reed (they often write the standard toppling things 5 years after you've written them off as hopeless). But also, there's not much you can do for them. An avant-garde personality in the best sense. I would suspect that he's not yet mature enough, or bitter enough, to accept the ironic diminishment of himself which teaching requires. But under the psychedelia he is solid. (John Clellon Holmes, 1968).

3. Millie Kiggins. "What's so scary about Estacada?" Evan Jenson, *Portland Tribune*, October 28, 2009

4. *None Dare Call It Treason* by John A. Stormer, 1964.

5. Charles Fort was an American writer and researcher who specialized in anomalous phenomena. *The Complete Writings of Charles Fort, The Book of the Damned, New Lands, Lo! and Wild Talents*, 2011.

6. Bristol Stomp. **https://www.youtube.com/watch?v=CinviAVC5jY**

THE WRITER'S BOOT CAMP

Preamble

J ack just said he would help me with my writing. Like the ancient cartoon ad where man has sand kicked in his face as a weakling until he takes the Charles Atlas[1] and builds up his muscles. Jack would do that for my writing self. The Junk Drawer story format dominated the Arabian Nights sessions. For the Writer's Bootcamps, Jack attempted to use a formal structure. Kind of. He would pull out a piece of my writing from a box and critique it. Gus provided me transcripts of the sessions. I remember some writing, alleged to be mine; other examples, no remembrance.

Writer's Boot Camp No. 1

Jack was in his pseudo pontificator mode. If there was laughter it would be as fake as an earwig telling a knock-knock joke frozen in a carrot-raisin jello salad.

"Let's go back to the beginning when I decided you were sent to me for a reason," he said. "You remember this, right? It felt like I was here to help you create the epic story from all your junk. There were hundreds of items. An image leaped to mind. Every item had string attached to it or most times multiple pieces of string, and these pieces of string eventually ran into other pieces of string from other junk drawers. I imagined the entire planet connected through their junk drawers. In the present (now?) the strings reflected degrees of separation between people and places. Going back in time, the strings reflected a history of the planet." He stopped. Stared intently and then continued, "But I knew you were placed on earth to help me find Dr. John's missing box. Tit for tat. Blah blah. Probably hopeless, but let's dig in.

"First off, I don't know how to reconcile you, this rather boring fellow, with some of your writing. I can get the mechanical stuff how you want to write kids' stories or science fiction, and now documentarian, for example. But some of your current writing is William Burroughs[2] ether-acid-surrealistic-Unitarian-Buddhist. Or I found a diary you and Kathleen kept for over a month of everything that happened in a day. And I mean everything. The light reflected off your Irish charm cereal compared to the later from your Irish spring soap. The exact pathway you took while shopping and what hand you used to pick up the puppy chow. The story you didn't complete— which by the way seems to be a trend—about the Seed who saves the world thanks to an innovative and talkative crow who eats you and throws you up outside the forest that was a prison for all other animals in the world. Interesting maybe but not complete."

"I read the stories you submitted for MFA degree. In brief, here is my analysis. This alone should be enough to warrant your class registration fee.... Oh, right, you never paid me for anything."

Jack said all this staring at something on the wall just behind me as though he were practicing a speech in front of a mirror.

"You write in what the French call the historical present and very hard one to pull off in English. Flowering Judas has it. But it is almost too present, and I think makes the reader nervous, or at least me. Punctuation. No consistency. ponder it. Look at this one from Walter savage: I had avoided him; I had slighted him; he knew it: he did not love me; he could not." See, get the difference? Ok, so when grandma dies, flying not with the greatest of ease, what is it? She turns into Charlie Chaplin? Or did I miss something? Maybe all that's left for us to write is allegory if that is true you may be on the path but consistently stumble. You are dangerous when we move from romantic to the possibly fantastic, from reckless show sledding and hoarfrost skinny-dipping to that magical pond that freezes warts like a toad in a fairytale (didn't I note you have a wart on your hand) then it turns our beloved character Judd into a flat fairy tale character. Is that what you want? And finally, is Jamie a guardian angel Morgan Le fay or more Holden Caulfield?"

He then really looked at me, not the wall, and said almost plaintively, "All your early writing is like Nabokov's *Speak Memory*. Remember where he reads something he wrote as a child that works for him, but no one else. Not ready for prime time and public art. Your teacher grabbed you too soon, your art was still private, not public. Like the smell of turnip soup bright back delicious memories of Christmas past. Is that private or public? You could fill in the blank, the smell of 'blank.'

Jack's Critique of my early writing
"We should keep these early writings and my critique just in the far-out chance you become famous. Without the fame or notoriety (you could also kill someone) these are worthless purple blobs...loved that movie."

The Crabs
It had rained. The night was one for crabs to run wild. They were white with brown freckles and wounded like everything else on what was left of the earth. The salt water hurts their wounds and their heartfelt desire is to become a cocktail so their reincarnation can happen sooner rather than later. I must wait for Jaminan to come. He has told me he will come when the rainbow oil shadow in the pool of water disappears.

Jack: Your William Burroughs stream-of-consciousness stage

The Incredible Truskenanny

"Simon, finish my book. I am a rock island. Simon, be my lithologic traveler. The swan song is honking but no tears please. The jar on my head filled with water is arching sparks but the garden in my stomach is going to weeds and I am become dispersed atoms. Please keep in mind that all life is pain, not beauty. The world is breaking apart into metal shakes. Things just come to mind. It must mean the end is near. Ego has no control over what comes to mind. I know this now that time is relative and if there is any vision at all, then it is a dialectic which means no one suffers when they die except the living."

Jack: You know, like why not pretend you have a great novel and then work backwards to achieve it.

Fredrick Zederbog

Fredrick Zederbog, please tell me why the moon sails so swiftly through the clouds when you talk to me about meaning. Why do you look like the underside of a pillow and yet sound like a jackhammer? I depend just like you on contradictions breaking the spider webs. Like you, I am both delicate and vicious. I want to fall into one of your shell shot paradigms. Tomorrow I would like to wake with you and drink warm milk, read the headlines and laugh and then go put our heads in the freezer until we can stand it no more. Then we can laugh and eat tuna sandwiches.

Jack: I can tell it was written by a student in his own co-housing with students and away from parents for the first time

Hung Over

I laughed. I jumped. I sprang from wall to wall. I hugged the chair, the table, the stove, the iron, the refrigerator, the dishes, the noodles, soup cans, the pillow, the coat hanger. I threw the garbage in the air. I twisted. I bounced. I leaped. I kicked my feet. I kicked the walls. I rubbed the floor. I pulled my hair. I squeezed my nose. I shouted into the toilet bowl to free all alligators. I put the water stop in my mouth for a change. I ran and jumped into the shower and out. My neck was sore. My head ached. I could have drunk a desert. My legs were like snow in the living room. The moon was yellow. My bed smelled like burning marshmallows. I ran to the lake. Stripped my clothes. Filled my body with gooseberries. My feet sank into the sand. I felt the cold water while the sun turned orange. It was good to be alive.

Jack: Same. That rush of being sick as a dog and yet somehow "high" on life. A college student.

The Bouncing Alphabet
The bouncing alphabet exists in a vacuum veneered only by my consciousness. It is a race for race. The decomposition of innocence; from acquaintance to knowledge to objectification. Words there jump from one level to another. There are at times shattered anvils, beaten down by the slippery stirrups. Images there are drug through a constant temperature. Giant gray rocks are tied together by "to be" and "and" smooth slick lines of iron; iron twisted into phonetic shapes. The insulation between myself and who I am is separated by a fog of insulation. The vortex is made of shredded wheat.

Jack: When you followed analytic philosophers like Aj Ayer and figured out it could only lead to existential death or belief in God Got drunk with Dave. Got drunk with Fred Jett, Dave and Duncan. Picked up chicks. Got to 2nd base with Carolyn. Got drunk on elk Island with the sex machine. Got drunk with Shotput and Long Bow. Dave threw up what looked like white worms.

Jack: This is when you realized you were not like your friends in high school

From a journal: "Dave and I talked about the future and agreed we would be philosophical bums on southern California beaches."

Jack: And you wonder why you are the way you are? You are not living on a beach and you are not listed in the 100 top philosophers in the world list.

When I Look from my bedroom window, I can see some God's handiwork. The endless expansion of greenness. The sounds of life everlasting. The sound of the planet humming like insects in a meadow on a hot summer night.

Jack: Perfect example of Nabokov's distinction between public and private art. Brings a rush of everything for you and nothing for everyone else.

And then the beginning of something, "Alone and penniless, a dissolved man haunts the streets of Paris. He is known as the ghost of Dante street."

Jack: When you realized there was a fake world you could piece together from words you had read not experiences you had experienced.

The Dark Side of the Moon

Preamble

These stories derive from a combination of extrapolation from Arabian Nights junk drawer stories, and more debatably and deviously from "research" he conducted—i.e. material he stole from Kathleen's and my house during the time I was moving to the

Gertrude Stein warehouse. I am pretty sure I provided him with many of the details, but I never wrote them up. He and Gus tape-recorded the stories—of course lost in the Gertrude Stein warehouse fire. I don't think any of my stories lasted more than a few minutes.

Watching Jack's mind is amazing to me, more so than for you. At some points I can see exactly where mine ends and his begins (for example, the story of Mrs. Leach, in Demolition Derby section). I told him about Gary Gilmore encounters when I was growing up, but it was in an informal style. I probably said, "Then our neighbor, Bill showed up, a big guy, if out of shape..."

This is how Jack described it:

"Then a giant Grizzly bear appeared out of nowhere. It was Wild Bill. He let out a roar like a lion. While fat and out of shape, he appeared colossal. One look at hairy and gigantic Bill was all it took for Gary's buddies to hightail it. While their leader was still in a stranglehold, they weren't willing to stand still with someone twice the size of my father, knowing that their leader was being strangled by him."

Hindsight and blind sighted. Although who can blame me? It flattered me that Jack wanted to take my raw material and turn it into a coming of age story I wish I had, or maybe I did and didn't know it until I experienced it in third person. He read some of these stories at one of the Gertrude Stein Show and Tell events that I did not attend. Gus did. Most people thought he was talking about his own coming of age.

The Golden Eagles Rule

Our gang, the Golden Eagles, weren't exactly good boy scouts. We didn't carry guns. Most of the time we just did bad shit; and we protected our urban wilderness. One very hot and dry summer someone set the meadow in the park on fire. We sprang into action. We had the fire completely out by the time the Fire Department arrived. We heard through the grapevine who had set the fire. It was the same kid that I had caught trying to set fire to my grade school and then he had been caught stealing science lab equipment from Reed College. We figured it was our duty to catch him. One day we spotted him in the park. But he wasn't alone. There was some older guy with him. There were six of us, so we figured we could take on one other guy, even though he looked a little grizzled and scary. We strode right up to the kid and started pushing him around and accused him of setting the fire. Suddenly the other guy pulled out this gigantic knife and waved it at us.

"No one's doing anything to my friend, Little John," he said, poking the knife in my face. That's when I realized it was Huck. What the hell were the odds? How did he get from Eastern Oregon to my Shire, not exactly on the well-traveled paths of carnies and hobos. He forced us to shake hands with the arsonist-kid, although before we left he took me aside and told me he was going to straighten "Little John" out, but in his own way.

Huck insisted that we sit for a spell. He wanted us to share his meal: two cutthroat trout he had caught in the creek, crawfish, also from the creek, steamed with allspice, and sandwiches made up of beans and franks wrapped up in toasted balloon bread, and for dessert a chocolate bar and bowl of wild blackberries.

Huck entertained us for a while with on the road stories. He would slip wisdoms in that I found rather preachy. But it was kind of creepy that whenever I thought "bullshit," it was like he was reading my mind because he would glare at me. He might say, "Trust me, you do something bad, it will be returned on to you thrice." I was *thinking* thrice, what the hell is that? As though if you put it in biblical language it must be true? But right then he would glare at me. It made me involuntarily nod my head and smile knowingly. And sometimes, just to make sure I stayed with the program, he would throw his Jim Bowie knife into a nearby tree. Most every time it would land perfectly. And every time Little John would fetch it.

Then I noticed several intruders in the park. It was Gary and his gang from Felony flats. My mind was scrambled. I couldn't do the math or geometry. Huck wasn't a very big guy, but there were ten of us in total. Four of them. I could tell Huck had noticed them. I told him how this was a pretty nasty bunch; how they had stripped Malcolm and tied him to a tree and made a fourth grader eat a live snake.

All he said was, "Don't worry about it."

When Gary and his gang got within shouting range, Huck pulled out from his satchel one of the guns I remembered he showed me at my cousins Without hesitation he shot the thing several times, striking a branch above Gary, then even closer on the ground near Fuckface.

One of them shouted, "What the fuck you doing?" Confrontational but a little unnerved. "We're just minding our own business and I expect you to do the same."

They stood there, talked back and forth. Huck cocked the gun again, aimed it this time square at Gary.

"All right, all right, asshole, but we'll be back."

Huck was definitely our hero now. Although it was also likely if Gary had recognized us, we would pay for it.

We went with Huck to one of his friend's apartment near the amusement park, two doors down from where Gary Snyder[3] and others who ignited the Beat movement had lived. I smoked my first marijuana, pretended we were high, and listened to sexual exploit stories we had to also pretend we understood.

When we left, Huck took me aside and said, "Be good to Little John. OK? he's really a good kid. His father beats the shit out of him is all." With that, he gave me his knife. "This is for you, OK? I won it in a poker game from an American aboriginal in Alaska. It's made from genuine sea lion tusk."

One of the renowned battles in the annals of our gang, the Golden Eagles, for supremacy in the Shire was waged on a blazing hot summer day when we encountered Gary and his gang at the swimming hole.

We only knew Gary by name. The others we had re-named. There was Turdface, because he had a severe case of acne that made his complexion brown. There was Fuck Finger, who had this weird middle finger that was always halfway up and rigid. We heard he had his finger crushed in a car door at a drive-in movie, trying to yank some guy out who had stolen his girlfriend. And then there was Log head. While Gary was the leader, Log head was scariest to us. He was large, not muscular, just big. And he was always smiling, the kind of smile that made you uncomfortable.

While Gary and his gang were crazy and lethal, ours was just crazy. There was big Don, the military strategist who was known in school as a commie because he quoted Mein Kampf and Nietzsche. And red-haired Malcolm, the son of a minister. When backed into a corner which he was often because bullies loved to hate him, he would turn into a porcupine windmill. Spitting, yelling he would fly in all directions, swearing like he had Tourette syndrome. There was Tim, who had the biggest Mr. Johnson in our school, who showed it to anyone who was interested. My best friend Dave was tall and skinny. He may have been our best fighter. Wiry, and sometimes abused at home, he might have been able to claw his way to victory. Problem was, he was unproven. The only fight he got in, years later, revealed his weakness. A golden glove champion gave him one solid punch and broke his jaw. Gail, who we called Olive Oyl,[4] was the only girl member, and that was because she had endured an initiation by Big Don, a punch to the stomach. It had crumbled her, and she cried a little. We laughed thinking that was the end of it, but she stood up and said, go ahead, do it again. Don obliged her. She crumbled to the ground but stood up again. Go ahead, do it again. She could barely stand and struggled for breath. Don just shook her hand and welcomed her to the gang.

The swimming hole was a contested zone. It was the deepest hole with a place to dive, and it was on the eastern edge of the park. We wanted to claim it, but knew that Gary and his gang could take it from us at any time. It is also where Gary learned how to shoot a gun as described in his brother's amazing tale, "Shot in the Heart." So, on this infamous day burst out of the woods when we were swimming.

That was another thing about them. They didn't give you a preamble. They just launched into full battle.

The first rock struck Malcolm, which was a big mistake. I mean for us, not them. Malcolm collapsed on the ground, his forehead bleeding and then stood up quickly, holding out both middle fingers, he shouted, "Fuck you and God will fuck you too." And then for good measure, "And fuck your mother too." What the hell did he mean that God would fuck them too? Not that it mattered. We were screwed.

We had two advantages. We knew our territory every shortcut and trail. And my family's homestead was nearby. If we could just make it there, we would be safe, wouldn't we? I figured it was like a country. No border guards, but I thought there was an unwritten treaty. If we made it to our house, they wouldn't follow. We ran through jungle thick blackberries, following animal trails. But it wasn't as much advantage as I thought. Again, the imperviousness to pain factor. They tore through the blackberries. But we were able to maintain just enough distance that for a while we lost them. We could hear them swearing loudly and feeding off of each other's ludicrous metaphors and analogies. The only one I remember was, "We're going to turn you inside out so you can eat your asshole."

We crossed over the invisible border into our country and climbed the winding trail that leads to my house. They crossed over the border without hesitation. We still had a slight advantage. They hadn't found the trail but were slamming their way through underbrush.

At my house, a bad sign: my father's car was gone.

I wanted to go inside the house, lock the door, and call the police. But not Malcolm or Don. They wanted to take a stand using the arsenal we had created on the edge of the hill. We had a four-foot-high slingshot, not yet tested in warfare; several 150 lb. metal spools with cable that were positioned to be rolled down the hill; and an ancient Colt.45 pistol that, while not functioning, we hoped might appear so. We also had a BB gun (worthless unless we were 2 feet away with an eye in sight), brass knuckles (again mostly worthless) and a bullwhip.

I was also hoping that our neighbor Wild Bill might be home. Bill was a bear-like guy, out of shape and alcoholic. But he had a quick temper and could throw a bag of concrete around like it was feathers.

Don and I grabbed the four-foot slingshot, held in a place by a hole that should have been deeper. Malcolm had the bullwhip. He showed us, spinning in a circle, how they wouldn't be able to touch him.

Through an opening in deep woods they could see us. Gary was yelling loudest and started throwing rocks in our direction. Amazingly, several buzzed right past us. Good aim? Or random good luck? It was also disconcerting that they could see the house, and that didn't seem to deter them.

Just then my father drove in the driveway. Thank God. Well, at least I thought so, but then wondered what the hell it meant. Five twelve-year-olds and one tank-framed but short father, back from shopping. Just how tough were Gary and his friends?

My father got slowly out of the car with a sack of groceries. Malcolm ran at him, yelling, "There're these guys... we got to get um. They want to kill us. But we're ready for them." Malcolm, so pumped up, ran into my father and knocked his grocery sack to the ground and his pipe from his mouth.

"What the Sam Hill are you doing?' my father shouted." My father looked at his groceries on the ground and started to pick up his pipe when he heard Gary yelling. "Count the minutes you got left on the planet!"

My father had a way of roaring that could be every bit as scary as a twenty something's "fuck you." He didn't know where it was coming from but bellowed to the world, "Whoever the hell you are, you better get the hell out of here." He steamed over toward the side of the hill with Malcolm close by. The number or their ugly appearance didn't seem to deter him in the slightest.

Gary and his gang stood still, looking back and forth between themselves and up the hill at my father. A classic moment in warfare. The sides sizing each other up. Jerry stood still with a five-pound rock in his hand, ready for the slingshot. The spools were still poised to fly.

My father headed down the hill.

Gary stood for a moment looking at him, shot up his middle finger, holding it out in front like it was the mast of a ship, and yelled,

"Fuck you, old man," and starting ambling, not running, back down the hill, with his four comrades following. Their slow retreat seemed to further infuriate my father, who took giant steps, tripping several times as he lunged in their direction. Each time he tripped, he got angrier.

"Get the hell out of here. I ever see you around here again I'll bust your heads."

We all followed my father, although at a distance. We felt glee as the villains were on the run. They were retreating; we were advancing. I had the gun which I imagined I might pull on them at a distance, where they might not know if it was real or not. Jerry had several good size rocks and Malcolm had the bullwhip. I was leaning toward us as victors if it came to combat. But I wasn't sure. I had never seen my father in a fight. As we followed him down the hill, I wavered between wanting it to happen and not.

My father, with clothes torn and dirty, lunged through the underbrush. Gary and his friends seemed to laugh. Turdface rubbed his crotch and flipped us off as though he didn't have a care in the world, confident in their victory. They seemed to stop or slow down, and yet they were still retreating.

My father emerged first in the open meadow. Gary and his buddies were standing by our small muddy pond, facing us. They looked calm and determined. I examined them to see if they had weapons. It seemed like this would be the time to bring out brass knuckles, guns, or knives. Their hands were all accounted for, no visible weapons. It seemed like if I could see Gary's EKG it would be fast but even. He was amped up with adrenalin, but not stress or doubt.

I turned to my side to assess my comrades. No calm there. Malcolm looked like he might have a heart attack, and Jerry and Dan looked they were about to tell us their mother just called them home for dinner.

It was a Disney movie with my father as a grizzly parent defending its cub, charging ahead, overcoming fear, not considering odds. There was no turning back, no room for détente. From the moment he had dived over the hillside he was committed to head banging, no matter what the outcome. And we weren't in the equation. He was totally in his reptilian brain where his son and friends who had created the situation no longer existed. If Gary and his buddies toppled him like a ripe banana, he hadn't considered what they would do to us.

I'm not sure Gary and his gang grasped his determination. They must have seen this kind of blind determination many times, but maybe they couldn't believe that a pipe-smoking adult (he still had pipe in his mouth as he Leaped down the hill) wearing a beret would engage them.

But that's exactly what happened. Before any of them had a chance to put up a fist, grab a stick or figure out how to resist my father's charge, he had shoved Fuck Face against a tree. Still fifty feet away, I could hear his head hit the tree. Simultaneously, my father whacked Loghead with a stick. Blood gushed out of his nose. With the foot soldiers dispatched, he aimed at Gary. He wrapped his right arm around Gary's neck, and with his left hand grabbed his belt. Gary, taller than my father, was suddenly off the ground and spinning as my father turned in a quick half circle and tossed him against a large rock. Gary bellowed a "Fuck!" but got up, shaken and pissed. He couldn't stand up straight, but he hurdled himself toward my father.

We all stood to the side, my comrades and his foot soldiers, obeying some Western law about the two top dogs having the right to battle without interference. Watching the fury of my father was frightening. I wanted him to thrash Gary and his friends. I wanted him to send them to a deeper hell of pain; while the lawlessness and primitive nature of the energy swirling around us was frightening.

Gary then dove at my father and sent him to the ground. I felt a hopeless feeling of protectiveness. That was my father on the ground. Gary was on top of him. He slugged him several times in the face and shoulder. I grabbed a large branch nearby and realized the others were staring at me. Log head, with blood running down his face and shirt, glared at me. No interference. What a weird rule. We might be all fighting for our lives, but there were still rules?

Then my father got the upper hand by wrapping his arms around Gary's neck. Gary's arms flung wildly, and his face turned red. It didn't seem my father had an exit strategy other than to strangle him to death.

Fuckface, maybe thinking about breaking the rules, yelled, "Fuck, you're going to kill him."

Shit. Another permutation in the rule? That if your leader is being killed you can move or what?

Then a giant Grizzly bear appeared out of nowhere. It was Wild Bill. He let out a roar like a lion. While fat and out of shape, all appeared colossal. One look at hairy and gigantic Bill was all it took for Gary's buddies to hightail it. While their leader was still in a stranglehold, they weren't willing to stand still with someone twice the size of my father, knowing that their leader was being strangled by him.

My father let Gary loose, but just for good measure socked him in the face.

Bill swaggered over to my father. "Hey you're bleeding," Bill said to my father, and turned to us, "Everyone OK?"

We all absently nodded.

"Nothing," my father said calmly, then added, "Stupid fuckers."

My father explained to Bill what had happened as we walked up the trail. The four of us were quiet. Then my father stopped, looked back at me. He waited. Then, as I approached him, he put his arm around me. That's all. No words. I felt safe, like a cub in a cave, at least for the moment.

Demolition Derby

In the third grade, I refused to recite the Pledge of Allegiance. I knew the words, but I couldn't say them. My well-meaning teacher, Miss Smith, asked me several times to put my hand over my heart and give the pledge; each time I said no thank you, turning redder with each refusal. It was an election year and my parents didn't like Ike and wanted Adlai Stevenson for President. Maybe I thought the Pledge was like voting for Ike. It was the first time I knew that I was different. There was one other Adlai for president classmate, Gerry, the only Jew in the school. I was the only pantheist-transcendentalist-Quaker-socialist-Unitarian.

We called my fifth-grade teacher, Miss Anderson, the Dike, although I'm not sure we knew what that meant. She was built like a mastiff and wore drab clothes like a prison guard. She rarely smiled, and she had the best-behaving class in school. Before becoming a teacher, she had been a professional wrestler. We thought this was just one of those tall tales of the eighth graders until one of them showed us a wrestling magazine featuring Miss Anderson. On the cover she had an opponent in a headlock, with a horrified look on her face. She had quit her wrestling career when she had her eye poked out. She had a glass eye. The Eighth graders warned us, "Watch out, like she has eyes in the back of her head."

I didn't know what they meant until one day I passed a note to Karen who I had a crush on. It seemed to me the Dike was looking at the opposite side of the classroom when she suddenly bellowed out, "Bring that note here!" She read the note, crumbled it and threw it in the trash. Then all she did was stare at me. I could hear the crowd at a wrestling match. I saw my head superimposed on that wrestling magazine cover. "Don't pass notes in my class." I didn't.

In sixth grade you didn't want to get Mrs. Leach. Seriously, that was her actual name. Boys in Mrs. Leach's class had very short haircuts because if you did something bad, she grabbed you by the hair and pulled you out into the hallway, then wrapped you on the knuckles with a ruler and forced you to stand there. Sometimes there would be three or four boys lined up facing the wall like they were waiting for a firing squad. She was tall and skinny and wore floral dresses that looked like tablecloths.

We got back at her. It was rumored that Mrs. Leach didn't have muscles in her eyelids, and she had special glasses that kept her eyes open. I confirmed the rumor when I saw her in her car attaching her glasses to her forehead. So, we figured we would steal her glasses. I was still a bad kid in training, so the task fell to Ralph. For a couple of weeks, he did reconnaissance, hiding in the bushes outside her classroom. He waited and waited. Then one day he saw her take her glasses off and put her head down to rest. He ran inside, past Hermia, the large but slow janitor, rushed into her classroom and grabbed the glasses. She sat up, trying to find her glasses, and even brushed against Danny's arm.

"Who's there?" she yelled as she tried to open her eyes with her fingers, but too late. He was gone. And he had the glasses to prove it.

In seventh grade, I couldn't stop talking. If I wasn't talking, I was passing notes. One day after the teacher had told me to shut up for the third time, he asked me to come to the front of the room. I stood in front of him while he calmly took a book from his desk and hit me on my head, and then motioned for me to sit down. He said nothing. Rather, Zen like.

I went back to my desk and turned to Marcia, who had a crush on me, "Do you suppose I can sue him?"

He came toward me. I expected another bash on the head or worse and braced myself. He pushed me and my desk into a corner behind a filing cabinet facing the wall, and then just continued on with the class lesson. "Come on someone, what is the capital of the state of Washington?"

For the rest of the school year, I sat behind the cabinet facing the wall. If I turned around to look at my classmates, the teacher would motion me to face the wall. Eventually, I accepted my fate. I brought a mirror from home and put it on my desk so I could see what was happening. I emptied the bottom drawer of the filing cabinet and filled it with junk food and comic books. I took tests and did my homework, but no matter what I did, I always got an S for satisfactory. I answered an Algebra question by saying I had a crush on Sandra whose nickname was swivel hips; I got an S and a comment, "Student shows progress." I got one reprieve. On parent's day, the teacher moved my desk back. I never told my parents. Why ruin a good thing.

By eighth grade, I figured out that one of the primary goals of school was to be labeled special. If you were special you got unique books, and hall passes to go to another classroom with other special kids. If you were athletic you were let out of class to go to practice and treated like a rock star. Then there was leadership. We voted in fair elections, but it seemed like there were parents pulling strings. In my class, almost all the class leaders had dads who owned businesses. You even got privileges if you were failing. They called it Remedial. If we were having difficulties learning, maybe they should have called it something we understood, like stupid.

But I was average. Average at sports, average looking, and average in the classroom. Average didn't bestow special privileges. But I figured out there were two other ways to be special: to be funny or bad. I could be pretty funny, but I couldn't compete with jocks and class leaders who could get classmates to laugh, no matter how dumb their jokes were. So, I went for bad; and I got good at it. In my sophomore year in high school, the principal told me I had set a record for trips to his office.

I got caught at everything. Like the time I tried to lower a boy scout knapsack with office supplies, I thought we might sell, from the detention room to a friend waiting in the parking lot.

In the eighth grade, I wanted it to be the best Christmas ever. Not for myself, but for my family and friends. My mother gave me $20 to buy presents. But I had twenty people to buy gifts for. It just wasn't enough. I told Ralph, who had been bad longer than me, about my dilemma. He said, "Fuck, man, I just steal my Christmas presents." He offered to show me how. He took me downtown and showed me the ropes. The first couple of times I chickened out. There was a guilt and terror force field at the department store exit. When I finally made it through the force field, it exhilarated me. Since I had never won a race or had sex or taken good drugs it was my first encounter with the sublime.

Ralph told me I had great potential. I was small and had an innocent face which made me invisible.

After some practice runs with the master, I was ready to go solo. It was like a movie plot when the Kung Foo Master says, "I have taught you what I can. Just remember stealing comes from inside." I went every weekend. I had a watch for my dad, a fancy wallet for my mom, Chanel No. 5 perfume for my sisters. It never occurred to me that my family might wonder how I could buy $150 of Christmas gifts on a $20 budget. I had more than enough to make it the best Christmas ever, but I was addicted to the thrill.

One day I had grabbed a watch for my uncle from a gigantic bin and sauntered out of the store when a woman who looked like one of my mother's friends put her arm hand on my shoulder, and said, "Don't run, there's a plainclothes detective watching you." Firmly holding my arm, she escorted me back into the store. I knew I was going to hell, but it felt cool to go in an elevator past the shopping floors to the administration's inner sanctum.

My mom came and picked me up. She asked me on the way home why I had done it. I told her I wanted to make it the best Christmas ever. She cried but quickly wiped away her tears. At home, my father smacked me twice, once on each shoulder. I ached like I had just gotten tetanus shots. All he said was, "What the hell's the matter with you?" which was his response to everything I did bad. Swearing off all crime, I took everything I had stolen, put it into a big box, and floated it down the creek.

In the early 1960s, school administrators tried to hold back the rock-and-roll cultural revolution by dictating fashion. There were rules about skirt length, hair length, and odd ones about shoes. White bucks made popular by Elvis were forbidden because the powder that kept them white was everywhere like patches of snow. Shiny black shoes were also outlawed because guys were using the reflection to stare up girl's dresses. In the course of two years I was suspended from school first for having my hair too short (shaved) and then too long (Beatle length).

You also couldn't have your shirttail out. In my social studies class, one of my friends came to class late with his hanging out. The teacher, who always seemed to be angry and smelled like horse manure, pointed to the door and yelled, "Out. To the principal's office." As he turned to leave, I stood up.

"Then you have to take me too," I said as I pulled out my shirt tail.

I suppose I expected it might be the beginning of the revolution, not Che Guevara's, but the one launched by "Rock Around the Clock" and "*Rebel Without a Cause.*" Nobody followed.

Then there was poor Mr. Swaim, our physics teacher in high school. He loved science but didn't stand a chance in the brutal climate of an American high school. He had bright curly red hair, thick glasses, and wore his pants high, which meant his Mr. Johnson bulged. We endlessly debated whether or not he had an erection. One of my friends, Peter, said he had heard about a disease where a guy had a perpetual erection. We got very creative at asking questions that not so subtly masked double entendre about hardness.

"So, Mr. Swaim, is this a hard science?"

"Exactly what is between a rock and a hard place?"

Peter was ahead of his time. He had a black light in his basement and his parents bought him alcohol, as long as it was just beer and we stayed at his house. One day in Mr. Swaim's class, Peter told me he was high on Peyote. In the early 1960s you could legally send away for Peyote buttons from the North American Native Religion association. I didn't have a clue. The only high I knew about was drinking beer. He was above the law and scrutiny of the man because it was like that moment in Cool Aid Acid trip (it was the same year Ken Kesey took acid for the first time.) When the explorers on the flagship Further were pulled over by the police, and the police just figured they were college kids who had too much to drink. One of things Peter loved to do was respond to Mr. Swaim's scientific assertions with great enthusiasm. It was hard to call him on it since he was just embracing a learning moment. He would jump out of his seat and bellow out, "Aha! I get it! Simply Amazing!" All Mr. Swam could do was embrace his enthusiasm, "That's good Peter." And without a touch of irony, "Isn't science amazing!" Before sitting down, Peter turned to the class and grabbed his Mr. Washington, "I know it excites me."

On the day he was high on peyote and he got up from his seat and walked right up to Mr. Swaim while he was lecturing, pushed his face up close and said, "Hey Mr. Swam, look at my eyeballs. The pupils, I mean. Look at them. Aren't they huge?" Mr. Swaim didn't even last the year.

I have a tiny journal I kept for one summer. Lyrical and repetitive. Got drunk. Got very drunk. Got drunk and cruised for chicks. Went to Rooster Rock and got drunk. I was sixth to do it with the sex machine on Elk Island. Stole shit and got drunk with Dave...

I was in jail or Juvenile detention five times. Odd to me how abnormal and edgy my life was. I will not compare my growing up to an urban teenager in inner city Detroit, or even white trailer trash in the broken down inner suburbs. We had a girl we called the Sex Machine who would do ten guys a night on an island in the river; a friend came to school high on mescaline; "fairies," as we called them, jerked off popular kinds in Boy Scout tents; several friends were killed in playground fights; another committed suicide after losing big time in a poker game within fifty feet of one of our state senators; I belonged to a gang, the Golden Eagles, who had to fend off a famous serial murderer; and my mother's best friend growing up was murdered by her son.

I went to one high school reunion and when I tried to tell some seamy stories, classmates acted like I was from another planet or at least another high school. I wondered if I made it up. But I know I didn't.

While school administrators thought the main purpose of sporting events was the game itself, the more important event was the post-game rumble. We poured out of the gym or stadium and the battle began. One night one our "class leaders," just started it by throwing a garbage can through the Tastee Freeze hangout across the from the rival high school, which is now curiously known as the "Tabor Commons." There was this one group that included a state wrestling champion and another who ended up playing defensive tackle for the Dallas Cowboys. Depending on the sports season, they would drive up just as the game ended, like an episode of "The Untouchables." They had a beautifully restored black Al Capone Cadillac, and they were dressed in vintage gangster outfits. As people poured out of the gym or stadium, they would either stand perfectly still and just stare at any boys from the opposing high school. If some guy dared even look in their direction, *what the fuck you looking at?* Or, *if you ever want to have kids in your life, start running.* They rarely got into fights. Nobody challenged them.

There were other nifty diversions, like the one Fred Jett dreamed up where you just drove around the school after a game, randomly picked some guy, usually with a girl, jumped from a slow-moving car, and coldcocked the guy, shouting whatever nonsensical thing that come to mind, "That'll teach you to talk dirt about my girlfriend," or "You even think about fucking my sister, you're dead, you get it?"

Halloween was always a blast. Somehow, we all knew where to meet. Word would get past around in the hallways and classrooms. The mob would swell to 25 or more teenage boys, ready to raise hell. We walked the streets of *Leave it to Beaver*[9] neighborhoods, stealing candy from kids or pants them; throwing pumpkins at cars; tearing out flower beds. All the while handing around concoctions of hard liquor stolen from parent's liquor cabinets. There were some kids we knew and for some reason just hated. We must have pantsed Malcolm a dozen times. Once, when he had the nerve to wear his boy scout uniform, including sash with merit badges, we stripped him clean and tied him to a telephone pole at a busy intersection. We didn't avoid getting caught. In fact, if the police didn't come after us then we had failed to raise hell.

There were also underlying sexual perversions, bestiality, undeclared but accepted homosexual behavior that seemed out of proportion to journalistic or academic assessments of that period. I woke up one night in the tent shared by six other guys at boy scout camp and watched the lonely nerdy unpopular kid giving a blow job to Rob, one of the most popular kids in the school.

While we tried to kill ourselves in a variety of ways and were very creative in how cruel we could be, our self-destruction tool of choice was quarts of beer and driving while drunk. And just think we did all this with mostly just access to alcohol and few weapons. Just imagine what we could have done if we had meth and AK-47s.

Etched into the towel dispenser third floor unisex bathroom: "

Just how bad were you? Evil is in the beholder's eye. Prove it jerk wad!" That was it. Challenge to me? Why third floor? In over a year in this reality, only the second time I had used it. How long had it been there? But I felt challenged to show just how bad I was. No, I hadn't killed anyone, although only God or angels kept that from happening. Like the night on a double date and guys from a rival high school, the year when no one dare challenge our high school because we had a class of jocks that could pick up any high school by the foundation and shot putt it across the city. But me? I was just a small guy in between classes, but I did my part. On double date, when they challenged me, I didn't think much about taking off at the green light in my baby blue Oldsmobile with glass pack mufflers and floor it. Incapable of stopping half a mile down the road at a red light. No time to consider who might come the other way, a family man coming home late with his empty lunchbox looking forward to peeking in on his tiny son or daughter. Others in the car said I was hitting 90 when I went through the red light.

So I wanted to show Jack, Gus, anyone, just how fucking bad I was.

The Sunny Side of the Moon

Preamble

"So, from your utter darkness, shallowness, depravity and nihilism," Jack asked me one day, "could you see the light at the end of tunnel, or could anyone else see your puny beam of light, with your soul running on AAA batteries?"

I replied, "I was kick ass evil—maybe not like Gary Gilmore, but rotten to the core as far as I could tell, and yet all these people seemed to think I had a heart of gold. Like Eric Hoffer[5] who stayed with us a couple of times, said to my father, 'Ah, this one, he has a velvet heart.' Are you kidding me? We—20 or more of us on Halloween—would storm through neighborhoods, tearing up old ladies' gardens, running stoplights while my blood was mostly alcohol."

I told Jack the story about procuring a flashlight at an army surplus store for my earliest backpacking experience with poet William Stafford and his family. Here Jack served as a good editor, not changing any facts but just editing it to create my desired effect. The same goes for the piece about the Grundtvig Free School. He conducted research to figure out who else had arrived in Estacada from the Black Mountain School in North Carolina. That just seems genuinely gracious and respectful.

Headlights in the Fog

My family, and our family friends, often went car camping. But backpacking into wilderness was rarer. My first wilderness experience was a trip instigated by William Stafford, to the Mt. Jefferson Wilderness. It was going to be a father and son experience, three fathers and their four sons, that is until Kit Stafford, a natural born feminist at age 8, insisted that she go too.

To prepare for the trip, we went to the REI of that period, Andy and Bax army surplus store. While the dads picked out what we really needed, I wandered the store trying to figure out what I could buy with my two dollars. I was obsessed with flashlights, a fetish I inherited from my uncle who always had the biggest and brightest ones. And there it was. A gigantic green flashlight powered by a six-volt battery. I just had to have it. But it was $4.95. Now keep in mind there were no bar codes. The price was drawn on the lens with an easily erasable pen. I realized that if I removed a part of the 4, it became a 1.

Heart beating, I carried it to the cashier. Bill was cashing out at the same time. "What you got there?" he said, pulling it from my hand and shinning it to the ceiling. "What a beam!" he exclaimed. "And under $2. Isn't that good luck." The cashier rang it up, and I was out the door.

It was a fairly arduous trek into the wilderness. Backpacking equipment was primitive. I used a Boy Scout pack whose straps scored my shoulders with red marks and boots that produced open sores. But there were also magic moments along the way. The water from cold springs in tin cups. And the chocolate! To this day, I always take a giant chocolate bar with me when backpacking. Bill was the chocolate custodian. At each stop for water, he would dole out two squares for each of us. He could never be talked into three.

We set up camp in the wilderness park. The boys had a campsite a few hundred feet from the men and Kit. I could hardly wait for dark so I could use my magic flashlight. I thought I could shine it all the way to top of giant fir trees. After dark, Bill came over to our camp. "So" he said, "let me see that flashlight." I proudly handed it to him. He shined it to the top of a tree. "Well, I'll bet...", he said, in a secretive and unmistakably coded fashion, "you could almost shine it all the way to the top of the mountain," and with a complex smile, added, "imagine all that for just $1.95."

Grundtvig Free School

Estacada is a small logging town along the Clackamas River, 30 miles southeast of Portland. I have always been inexplicably drawn to the town and the river. When you reach the eastern end of town the paved highway continues but eventually splits into two gravel roads. They have paved all the other highways that pass through the Cascade mountains. So, it feels like you are not passing through the mountains but going into them. The town itself has little to offer. Its most notable "attraction" for years was the Safari Club, a restaurant and bar displaying the owner's wanton slaying of animals from all over the world. I remember in particular a giant Polar bear with a pissed off expression that leaned over a table. It felt like he might grab your burger or just fall on the table.

My first recollection of Estacada is standing in a meadow, between the town of Sandy and Estacada, with William Stafford, his son Kim, and my father. We were there scouting land that we might buy together. I was 10 years old. We were going to create a commune. It was the 1950s, so commune had more of a 1930s or transcendental connotation than a hippie one. My father had told me about Brook

Farm, and he had built a small shed in the woods in back of our house modeled on Thoreau's Walden hut. My great grandparents supplied flour to the Aurora Colony,[6] a 19th century commune, south of Portland. And my father and Stafford both spoke with high regard and skepticism about Glen Caulfield, who had moved to Estacada to live off the grid and start the Grundtvig (Danish Folk education) Free School. (Sadly, we never bought the land. A road not taken.)[7]

At about the same time that Glen was trying to live off the grid in Estacada, a splinter group of teachers and students moved to Estacada from the Black Mountain School in North Carolina. The splinter group was led by John Wallen, who was critical of what he saw as too great an emphasis on the arts and felt that the arts as they exited were too esoteric. He presented a community service plan in the late 1940s, through which, instead of teaching, he would have been a liaison between the college and the surrounding area for projects related to class and local arts and crafts activities. The plan was rejected, so Wallen and a group of students pooled their resources to form a commune that would have an integral relationship with the surrounding community. He left in February 1948 to find a location, and the following summers several students joined him near Estacada, Oregon. For several years they lived together as a farm cooperative and had a woodworking shop. To create for the small logging community a sense of history and traditions, they started a timber jamboree with dances, logging skills, and a crafts exhibition. When the group dissolved, many of the members moved to Portland (where several taught at the Catlin Gabel School) and remained a close community of friends.

For a short period, Kathleen and I lived in Estacada. We bought a small house and two acres on Horse Heaven Ridge, high above the Clackamas river, four miles south of Estacada. We bought the land from Millie Kiggins and her father, Grover Kiggins. In the 1930s Millie tried out for the Estacada High School football team, probably the first woman in the state to do so. She also had an encounter with Bigfoot and created a beautiful garden surrounding the house that Kathleen and I bought and lived in for several years—a house that

Millie told us she lost in a poker game to that damn "aboriginal woman." Millie also by pure chance found and purchased the flour milling equipment that used to be my Great Grandfather Swans at Champoeg, one of the first floor mills in the Oregon Territory.

The Carny who Loved Abraham Lincoln

My Aunt and Uncle and cousin Danny lived in a tiny town in the dusty wheat fields of Eastern Oregon near The Dalles. In the summer of my 7th grade I visited them and that is when I met Huck, the rambling carny worker who loved Abraham Lincoln.

On the drive there we stopped at Celilo Falls. It was still a colossal waterfall, and a sacred Native American fishing site, but it would soon be buried under the lake behind The Dalles dam. I felt like I had time traveled back to the wild west. There were "real Indians" standing on rocks casting nets and what to me looked like spears. My cousin's town still had boardwalks, and the only hotel in town was like a set from the TV show *Gunsmoke*.

My uncle, my father's older brother, had been student body president at the University of Oregon, and his wife was homecoming queen. By the premature end to their lives, my aunt was an alcoholic and my uncle killed himself through alcohol and too many high cholesterol breakfasts. Danny, who was adopted, also died from alcohol abuse in his forties.

Every morning my cousin would take a bloody Mary to his mother's bedroom. I could see him fluffing her pillow in dim brown light, which reminded me of a movie I wasn't supposed to watch like *A Streetcar Named Desire*. I slept in the basement surrounded by guns, crossbows, cowboy memorabilia, knifes, and civil war swords. My Uncle could have stood off the commies if they ever had any reason to come to Eastern Oregon.

Everyone knew everyone in town, and my cousin, six feet tall in the 8th grade, was a local sports hero, good at basketball, track, and baseball. He could walk behind the fountain in the drugstore and make himself a shake or dish up a scoop of ice cream. We could also go into the two taverns in town. We couldn't buy anything, but my cousin could sip beers or hard drinks from men playing poker. There were real cowboys everywhere; some with holstered six shooters. Their hands were like dry branches. I didn't want to shake hands. They would know by my soft hands that I was a city slicker.

My aunt swerved around the house, swearing and breaking things. She disappeared every day by the middle of the afternoon. Around dinner time my uncle asked Danny to fetch her from one of the taverns. Sometimes she'd be asleep in someone's living room or backyard. Everyone seemed to know where she was.

On the walk back for dinner, she'd be sloppy and sentimental. She would stop, grab one of us and then the other, stare at us through her bloodshot eyes, and tell us what good boys we were and how much she loved us. I would smile back, but it made Danny either sad or angry. One time when he started crying, my aunt yelled at him, "buck up sissy. Life's a bitch!"

I had met other people like Huck at the amusement park near my home. They fascinated me. They kept their cigarettes rolled up in their tee-shirt sleeves, swore non-stop and seemed to live free and glorious lives filled with booze, and drugs, and lots of women. Or at least that's what they told us. Huck was different. He was quiet, rarely swore, and when he talked about women, it was respectfully. He was working on a railway project. He had a room in the town's hotel. My uncle didn't approve of him so we had to sneak over to the hotel which wasn't easy in a town of 300 people. He bought us beers a couple of times, but only two at a time. Once he trusted us, he showed us his prize possessions. One was a Colt 45 that looked like it was out of a Roy Rogers movie, and the other was a collection of books about his hero, Abraham Lincoln.

One day we went to the hotel, and he was gone. He left a note for us at the front desk, along with an ornate but cheap replica of the Gettysburg Address. *Remember these words*, the note read, *until our paths cross again*. I figured I never would see him again.

A Rainbow on the Dark Side of the Moon

Preamble

Jack had the chapters "Falling in Love while being reconstructed" and "Wormhole Between the Shire and New World Order." attached to each other. That makes a kind of Jack-sense. I was recovering from my own reconstructive psychotropic surgery (LSD, etc.) When I met Kathleen. Peculiar that she isn't mentioned in "Falling in love..." Much of that piece could have been constructed by research using underground press of the period.

Reconstructive Psychotropic Surgery

In the 1960s, Portland was an outpost. If you said you were going to the city, you meant San Francisco. Seminal events, cultural innovations, elements of the alternative universe and the zeitgeist were transmitted via underground press and by traveling vagabonds who yo-yoed the coast from LA to Vancouver BC. We called them networkers. They were manual versions of Facebook. If you wanted to know what was happening and find your tribe in Portland, you went to The Switchboard—a hotline and typical office of cinder boxes and milk crates; a few cafes like Mountain Moving café (if you were lesbian) or the Charix, Ninth street Exit, Arbuckle Flats, or Lair Hill Park known as the hippie park.[8]

I fancied myself more an artist worrier than a political one. The nomenclature of change agent appealed to me. I took LSD for the first time in the spring of 1965, which I mark as the beginning of my psychotropic reconstructive surgery period. I administered an illegal and non-surgical lobotomy on the JD part of my personality, Draconian trying to get past the hormonal and societal border guards. Kids, don't do this at home; just because it kind of worked for me doesn't mean it would for you.

While Portland was just an outpost, it didn't mean you couldn't get your hands-on high-quality psychotropics. The first LSD I took was one degree of separation from Owsley,[9] the heaven's chemist.

During one period I had a large artist's sketchbook that was in part a journal for my experiences, while several pages were doused with blotter acid. My connector gave me the journal with five pages neatly marked off to indicate mellow, semi-functional, and supreme trips. There was also a tiny packet on the last page called draconian.

My first exposure to mind-altering drugs—aside from binge drinking—was with invaders of the Shire from Felony Flats, when I was 12 years old. Some days us card carrying Golden Eagles wandered around the Shire like Ginsberg's poets of the night looking for a fix to boredom. Boredom was our cancer. It followed us around like a DDT filled cloud bank.

One day we were just wandering around the shire, desperately trying to find something to kill boredom. We jumped down a slope to duck under a bridge over the creek and encountered three dudes who looked like Hell's Angel wannabees. I realized one was our nemesis, Gary. My heart was pounding, expecting the worst. But something was different. It was like we were in a parallel universe, like Superman's Bizarro world. They were smiling and laughed at us.

"Jesus man, you scared the shit out of us," Gary said.

I said, without thinking, "yeah right, like we could ever scare you. This is probably just a dream, you know?"

That really made them laugh. One guy laughed so hard he tripped and fell into the creek, which made them laugh harder. I thought it was a trick. Like if we laughed too, they would say, "what the fuck you laughing at." Then one of them handed me what I thought was a cigarette while he helped his friend.

"Go ahead he said, take a toke just don't Bogart it." I did not understand what he was talking about. Toke? Bogart it? As he grabbed his friends' hand, he added, " Panama red, so don't waste it." I didn't know what that meant either, but I realized it must be marijuana. Dave grabbed it from my hand and took a long suck and immediately coughed like he was dying, which made the one guy let go of his friend who fell back into the creek. David handed me the cigarette. Again, they were all laughing, but then the one guy grabbed Dave, and said, "so you think this is fucking funny, do you?" and pushed him into the creek. I knew I had to do it. I turned slightly away and drew smoke into my mouth without inhaling. When I let it out, I said, "good stuff." I learned quickly. It seemed what you did was laugh and be clumsy. I tripped on purpose and fell into the creek laughing.

And I had an inspiration. I knew a thing or two about crawfish and knew there was a lot in this part of the creek. With no one noticing I grabbed a big one with only a left pincher and threw it at Dave who batted it away. It struck the biggest guy who had said little. When the crawfish hit him on the head, he grabbed it and crushed it in his hands. I guess that was the funniest thing any of them had ever seen. Dave and I told the story many times. And the story grew in later versions: we smoked all afternoon and had a crawfish fight and then as all good stories in those days one ended with naked girls. In one story, mean Gary pinned down a girl we named Penny, and had a crayfish pinch her nipple, which got her excited and they made out right there in front of us.

The book that led me to LSD in 1965 was Aldous Huxley's *Heaven and Hell*.[10] Even the title was enough to draw me to the enterprise. It felt like my life could go from heaven to hell in an instant. Most of my old friends were still drinking and cruising. My new found intellectual friends were drinking, smoking some pot, and cruising for existential answers. All-night parties with my intellectual friends drove me close to the edge. Their questions made sense; their answers just drove me closer to the brink. The answers rarely seemed real. They were satisfied with blueprints or answers that just led to more questions. And they could face all the most challenging basic questions of life, love, meaning and death and still want the same things my high school friends wanted: a beautiful woman at their side. That was the ultimate spoil from the war, even if you didn't really know how to make the thing work (i.e. have an orgasm). But there was also some coolness in being an existential eagle scout. You got that by books like merit badges. And having witty answers like the right knot to tie for different circumstances.

I really wanted answers. If someone had said they could give me real answers but I would have to kill myself, I would have struck the bargain.

My favorite book at the time was *The Little Prince.* At breakfast one day, about 6 months before she died, out of the blue, he handed me a first edition and said, "remember how much you loved this book as a kid?" I didn't know why she gave it to me and ignored it for several weeks, but then when I read it, it was like I had a decoder ring. It wasn't the same book. It wasn't a fantasy kids' story. When the fox tells him how to tame him so they can become friends and how then they will have expectations and rituals it was about the love I wanted. But when he allows the snake to bite him and tells the narrator to not worry, that although it will look like he is in pain not to worry for it is the only way for him to get back to his planet. It all made sense. To fully experience the beauty of life, one had to experience pain.

There was another coincidence that led me to my LSD therapy. A bleak New Year's Eve I spent alone. I had nowhere to go and my parents were away for the weekend. There was a fierce windstorm, and I watched my favorite old growth Douglas fir outside my bedroom window strain in the wind. I was mesmerized by the wind's desire to take it down and the tree's ancient and magnificent power to resist but the outcome wasn't clear. I thought I could see the trees' gigantic roots the size of weightlifter legs stretching underground being pulled from the ground. I prayed. I don't know to who. I didn't have a God in mind. I was so much a part of this drama that it took me a while to realize I had a pain emanating from my stomach or back. At first it just felt like diarrhea cramps. Great, not only was I going to be alone for New Year's but experience it with the flu. But the pain kept growing, reminding me of times I had gotten stung by a bee and first thinking it was like the sting of stinging nettle but one that kept radiating out. So, with this pain. It grew. Maybe god was telling me the tree is falling. When the tree fell my pain would go away. Or I would die. I had never had such excruciating pain. It radiated throughout my body. I must be dying, I figured. Just like that. Out of the blue, I was having a heart attack. I couldn't stand up so I crawled across the living room floor, through the kitchen to my father's library where the phone was. it seemed to take forever. I called a hospital (there was no 911 in those days). In the middle of the raging pain, I had enough sense to crawl back to the living room and unlock the front door and laid there. The wind was still howling. I could watch my guardian tree still struggling to survive. you and me both. Then the strangest thing happened. The pain seemed unrelenting, but then for a moment it would go away. During these lucid seconds I had no pain, and it seemed like it didn't matter. I might be dying, but it was alright. I had memories of wonderful moments in my life like sitting in a boat on the mirror like stillness of Diamond lake fishing with my father and the first time I kissed Marcia at a 7th grade Halloween party and looking at our Christmas tree one night after everyone had gone to bed. Then the pain would return. And go away. It almost felt like I could control it. Either that or I couldn't tell the difference. I had what felt like an original thought, my own, not one I had read or tossed about in my college all night existential dialogues. That pain and pleasure were the same or there was just a thin line between them and that it was the same border land as there was between crying and laughing.

The ambulance arrived, and with a brief description of what I felt, one of the attendees immediately diagnosed my condition.

"You have a kidney stone. Don't worry, you won't die."

He gave me a shot of Demerol and by the time we arrived at the hospital the pain was gone and I was in a state of euphoria. Not just pain free, but I was in an inviolable bubble where my life, at least for now, was perfect. There was a purpose and I would not be alone forever. Also, I perceived that I had multiple selves, but one was more than the sum of its parts. The goal was to find one's authentic self. Lying in the hospital bed, I perceived how thin the border was between pain and pleasure. I remember I said to one nurse, "Is it that white comprises the absence of black or the other way around." I also thought about how the questions about life and death and meaning were not just intellectual bantering. There were consequences to your answers that started with the right questions but didn't end just with clever retorts or quotations. We were the equivalents of 17th century explorers. Space, the final frontier. No, not really. The final frontier was between our ears. I had a responsibility to find out what was unique about me. I was the intersection of forces that were me and only me. Once I tapped that, everything I said would be true. I didn't need to understand the textbooks or get good grades or get the chick under my arm that everyone would envy; any or all of that might follow if I answered the more basic question about who I was. When the doctor came in to show me an x-ray of my kidney stone I was crying.

"Thank you," I said. "Amazing, isn't it, that I wouldn't have had this happen if I didn't have a kidney stone? But I get it, to find truth and beauty you have to experience pain." What I didn't tell him was that I decided to embark on the most dangerous journey of my life, a journey with Mr. Tambourine Man.

The prime source on campus for quality LSD was this guy my intellectual posse nicknamed Donovan, after the folk singer who they thought of as a phony imitation of Bob Dylan. He was always in full hippie garb, as though he had made purchases from an alternative LL Bean Catalog. And yes, everything was "far out" to him. He traveled the I-5 corridor at least once a month. He would return with new albums: Grateful Dead, 13th Story Elevator, Jefferson Airplane, and with a cornucopia of drugs. Everyone in that sub culture knew exactly when he returned. The orders went in and the mood of the campus changed, at least if you were wide awake you noticed. But it was 1965, and most people didn't have a clue. It was like that Kesey bus excursion (Kool Aid acid trip) when young people acting weird, even police figured were, just kids acting up, maybe theater majors or at worse they had drunk too much. There were conversions every week. I remember one in particular, a star long-distance runner, straight as an arrow but then he came into class on a Monday, and his relatively short hair was tied into a tiny ponytail and instead of his usual dress shirt he had a Hawaiian shirt on and a smile that wouldn't end.

So, this star athlete just suddenly says, "How do I know that when you say something is green, the same thing I mean when I say it?"

The class was a poetry workshop, so I suppose it was a vaguely relevant question, more than it might have been in say a chemistry class. But we knew what had happened. Donovan was back in town with a stash of LSD, and there was another student who had fallen through the crack in the cosmic egg. He told me later he just couldn't imagine why he would want to run. So competitive. What's that all about, really? I mean I'm now a Ferdinand the Bull kind of guy.

Donovan volunteered to be the guide for my first trip. He had me fill out a kind of questionnaire. I don't have a copy, but I remember some questions, which included: Name three places where you feel safe. What are your biggest fears, first in life, then about the trip in particular? And some odd questions like: if someone trapped you in a collapsed mine, would you rather be alone or with a person who bugged the hell out of you? Would you be more likely to cry if a dog died or a person you didn't really know?

Although the Shire was first on my list of safe places, he ruled it out. We went instead for a triplex of a friend of his. There was an experienced tripping couple who lived next door who I liked and trust, but nobody in the other apartment, it belonged to his girlfriend who was out of town. For music to begin with, we had Bob Dylan. For when I felt it coming on, Pachelbel's Canon.

He also brought over a large suitcase of psychedelic toys: several types of kaleidoscopes, a strobe light, black light, candles, a collection of concave and convex mirrors, a book of optical illusions and Escher drawings. He also left me with a suite of albums from Moody Blues to Beethoven. He blessed the drug before I took it, although he seemed halfhearted about this part of the ritual. The best advice he gave me was, remember nothing bad is going to happen. Just a day like any other. He took me next door and Barbara and Greg assured me they were cramming for exams and going to be there all day and night and I could come over there anytime I wanted to. He then gave me his phone number and left.

When the drug started coming on, I played music, tried out the different toys, indulged in the enhanced sensory world. All cool, but by the second hour I wasn't doing anything, other than going from sitting, to squatting, laying, standing, stretching. It felt like I was preparing for an Olympic marathon event. I spent ten hours in that house, but I can hardly remember any details of my surroundings. I was not in the outside world, but inside. I realized that day that to me the trips my friends had told me about meant very little to me. The outside world was beautiful, or that is more beautiful. Everything was lucid and amplified. But to me it was therapy. I knew that this was the way I could get back to that moment in Japan when I realized I was someone other than the JD I had been pretending to be.

It seemed each time I took LSD there was a different focus of attention. That first time it was about pain and pleasure.

There was a wooden banister on the stairs in the house I grew up in. At least up to a point of age and weight, I could coast part of the way down the stairs on the bannister. It was a morning ritual. I would slide down the bannister and enter the kitchen smelling of bacon and Swedish pancakes. My father would be in the dining room hoarding the paper. He would leave out a couple of shriveled pieces of bacon and batter for me to cook up my own paper-thin pancakes. One day I was too big and pulled the bannister out of the wall. Fortunately, my father was already out in the yard working that day and I could rescue the bannister, and as long as I or anyone didn't use it as a slide, I never had to confess. If I had my father would have angrily said the usual, "What the hell were you thinking?" parental Zen kaon question.

In my mind I had jumped from bed to bannister, naked, and when I jumped onto the bannister it turned into a razor blade. It sliced me neatly in half and then when I jumped off at the bottom my body, just as cleanly and neatly, came back together. In the seconds or moments as the razor slit into my body there was unmitigated pain. But it wasn't normal pain, emanating from a place in my body, like when I fell from a rope swing, 20 feet onto a gnarly branch or the time my sister slammed a door on my smallest finger and almost decapitated it. There was no single source of pain. It was that the whole world was filled with pain. As far as one could see. Everything about living was painful. Breathing, walking, being in love and losing it, and most of all a sense that every moment moving forward through time was painful. Unless you could stop time, there was no avoiding pain. That is all there was. Living was pain or pain was living.

Now I felt like I was truly in higher education. A joke I could hardly tell anyone, surely not my family or my childhood friends. I didn't even feel right telling my fellow trippers. They wanted to know about the sounds and smells or talk about their multiple orgasms'. Had Timothy Leary had 2000 orgasms, or something like that, as reported in *Playboy*? I wanted to tell them about how I was moving from one kind of self-destructive behavior to another. I was destroying oneself in order to create a new self or find my true self. It wasn't a cruise ship but a voyage like Ponce De Leon. I didn't expect to become a perfect person, as cool and boring as that might be but Huxley's metaphor of *Heaven and Hell* rang true—I read that, *The Little Prince*, and certain chapters from Ouspensky's *A New Model of the Universe*, often during my therapy with Dr. Tambourine man, my favorite Dylan song.

In another trip, the primary metaphor was that life was like this hallway that went on forever with doors every 20 feet. When I walked down the hall, I could open any door I wanted. If I didn't truly examine myself, then more and more of the doors became forbidding. Out of fear I might even lock them, afraid that demons or bad memories or narrow minded, thoughtless, inattentive versions of me would pop out and scare the shit out of me. Once I was free, then I could walk the hallway and open up any door I pleased. There would be scary shit behind some doors but it would be like water off a duck's back. Doors where everyone's subtext was visible and I could see what people were really thinking of me while they hid behind clichés and platitudes. Behind another door was a windstorm that would pin me against a wall, giving me a sense of exactly how brief and meaningless my life was; behind another was a blazing fire from hell reminding me of just how horrific my death might be; behind another a fear that there would be no torture and pain in my death, just loneliness. I would be in a shed in the middle of nowhere, burn the last piece of compostable material and then freeze to death utterly alone, and then like Scrooge I would see life after I had left and people would be joyous or more likely indifferent. It would make no difference. The mountains would still stand there in their beautiful and indifferent granite.

I discovered why I could do what I was doing: I had a good ship. Underlying all the self-destructive behavior, self-doubt and self-loathing and depressing thoughts about my intellectual smallness and my lack of pheromones, I had a robust ego. As though I had watched artisans build my ship from the best of wood and nails and glue and knew that whatever the elements could throw at me, I would still wake up in the morning on calm seas and the day would seem miraculous.

I recognized the relative strength of my ego as a floating log raft on a sea that went on forever, in all directions, and as deep as the highest mountains on Jupiter. My ego or self was relatively stable and reliable. When I took LSD with Dave, I realized his ego was a mutable tangle of plastic and roots, limbs, and discarded Barbie doll parts. His ego had been torn apart while serving in the Vietnam war. We were both on LSD. I would go to William Burroughs, a stream of consciousness rifting on him. It was fun to me; terrifying to him. In a normal state he could suppress, repress, transform what I told him into harmless gum drops. If I told him I was watching my ego disappear in the sunset, he saw it. He experienced it and it was terrifying, like it was to my grandmother when she was dying and would float off into empty space where she didn't exist. One day in front of the refrigerator I explained how to use the disappearing railroad line in the distant horizon as a way of watching his self disappear into nothing. I realized he was furiously chewing the inside of his mouth. His eyes reflected pure horror as though a leopard were leaping from a tree toward his jugular. He couldn't stop the performative meaning of words. When I said watch our egos disappear, he did, and he was left with nothing.

When Donovan left town, he offered me a sweet deal, and a delightful gift, a leather-bound journal that inside had three separate sheets of blotter acid. It wasn't like I had a plan to take LSD every day for six months to beat the Guinness book of records, it just happened. If I had been a reasonable person, I might still have some of that left. Instead, I took some almost every day for six months.

Things just fell into place. A friend had to go back to his home on Long Island to take care of his favorite aunt, who was dying and didn't want to lose his house that was within walking distance of the college. I talked my parents into the move and told no one about my course of action. At first, I was fairly nonfunctional. I would forget to eat, lose track of days, stay up for days and nights in a row and missed most of my classes. After a while life on LSD seemed like the norm, without seeming like an abnormality. First, I went just to my late afternoon and evening classes when I might come down. Even then nothing and everything made sense. It was like everything was in all capital letters. I WAS IN A CLASS. Every word was a universe on to itself. Everything teachers, students, clerks, winos, squirrels, made perfect sense. Even vacant sorority girl's blather made sense. There were so many things that would make me cry: Hallmark card, *Anna Karina*, homeless person, *Madame Bovary*, watching room freshener and Hamburger Helper ads. I could feel those women's satisfaction smelling their house enveloped in lemon aura. It was important because it was the human condition. We all were in that, no escaping it. It was sad to me that people smelled. I wanted to tell people I loved them, anyway.

By chance I watched Disney's movie *Old Yeller*,[11] and thought I would never recover. If I had had a video recorder or TiVo, I would have watched Old Yeller being put down over and over. The pain and sorrow were all enveloping like a dense fog on the Thames. There was nowhere to go. Once again it was that proximity of pain and pleasure, sorrow and joy. I made a list, that sadly I can't find, of opposites that were not. I called them borderland guard words.

Here's a scary thought: I did everything normally, including driving. I discovered this auto-pilot (kids do not do this at home). It was like I was in a foreign country; while I was thinking in English, I was speaking French or Spanish; or the reverse. Even though everything was interesting and fruitful and important from sow bugs to warning signs and signals and stop signs, some part of me knew which things to pay attention to in order to survive.

Just as with driving, I found a kind of autopilot life. I could read without every word being a separate universe. From the academic standards' perspective, it was a mixed bag. One professor told me I was the only one he could imagine helping the other students understand William Burroughs. Great way to direct me into chaos. Published stream of consciousness.

One professor, a family friend, a member of a small pack of professors who as part of their commitment to the 60s counter culture broke down the barrier between students and faculty, refused to grade one of my papers. His comment:

"I can't grade this. Really, it falls outside the range of A-F. And I'm not saying therefore A+ of F-. I don't know what it is. All the sentences make sense. The structure and flow make sense, but I don't know what it means. And I don't mean, like I often do, that I don't know what you mean. Or you aren't clear. You are, but I just plain don't know what it means." It was a paper about *Paradise Lost*, that incorporated Tom Wolfe's *The Electric Kool-Aid Acid Trip*, Chaucer, Aldous Huxley, Scottish botany, astrology, and an obscure Ukrainian poet who never existed, and included a summary of some insights while on acid that seemed to me to be quite reasonable.

When I cried out to the universe to tell me the meaning of life when I was drunk during my teenage life, all I got in return was a blurring, spinning world like I was on the spin cycle; on LSD I got answers in code. Ouspensky says that the universe first answers you in your voice, all ego; then it returns answers in multiple voices; and finally, in the most crystal-clear state, the answer is returned through mathematical relationships. I couldn't get past the code or multiple voices. Little did I know then how eventually God, tired of my insistent whining like a mosquito, would answer my questions.

It also felt like every day my small self had less control over me. The sheets of blotter acid were disappearing. The notes I took from trips were shorter and shorter and more obscure. Although one day I took notes about everything that happened to me. And I mean everything. The entry for the one day was over 100 typewritten pages. There were more obscure notes from the trips than remaining paper dipped in acid.

Then Donovan left in the middle of the night with a gay guy who looked like the Disney character Goofy headed for Stephen Gaskin's[12] Farm in Tennessee. He left me a small gift of Orange Sunshine acid that he said came straight from the Grateful Dead through their road manager.

I'd been keeping a journal called "Signposts." By now the pages in my journal soaked in LSD were gone. I filled the Signpost Acid journal with strange notes and drawings that I always expected to lead me back to the epiphanies, although they rarely did. My friend Dawn had drawn me the best illustration of the process. A small Hansel like character in a deep wood staring with wide-eyed amazement at a roughhewn sign that said "signposts." In most ways, the journal scribblings didn't really matter. Words didn't hold the back the floods or encapsulate the typhoons. Sometimes it felt like a house restoration project, but more often the self I was creating was from the ground up. Unlike many of my friends, I wasn't building on a foundation started in high school. I had to destroy oneself in order to make room for the new one.

I created a theme for each of my remaining hits of acid, as though I was cramming for my Western Civilization final exam. I suppose it was my own version of Kesey's Acid Tests. Of course, it was a stupid idea, as anyone knows you have little control over what happens. Like trying to create an agenda for a meeting of anarchists. I had a big sheet of blank paper for each theme: death, life, love, etc. Having taken it so often, I controlled it better than some might, but everything was (duh) interrelated so no matter where I started, there I was (double duh).

And there was one word that just never let go: love. No matter where I started, I always came back to love. I was nothing without it even if I didn't know what it was.

· · ·

Resettling America One Redneck Village at a Time
  Preamble

During the Arabian Night Sessions there are at least three items that evoke stories about Cascadia: the head of colored Santa Claus candle; photo of Hank Williams, and a letter from the Selective Service. There is also a heavy set of allusions to iconic figures of the 1960s: Ken Kesey, Neal Cassady and Paul Krassner. [13] That makes sense. Informally we talked about them, and others like William Burroughs. I may have told him about the blue house in Cascadia where day trippers gathered to take LSD, but the stoned-out hippie fire is his imagination. Gus says I told him about our desperate measures to fit in, and the ways we measured success, like getting high-quality firewood as a measure of our acceptance, but that's about it.

First You See it, then You Don't

We bought land up a river that flowed from the Cascade mountains to the Willamette River. Each river flowing down from the east and the west had new settlers in the 1960s and 1970s. We moved to a small town, Cascadia. In the late 1960s and early 1970s young immigrants from California overran Cascadia. When Haight-Ashbury hit bottom, hippies colonized Oregon. Thousands. In one summer alone 10,000 moved to the Illinois valley just south of Cascadia. It was the third largest migration into Oregon after the original white settlers and ship builders during World War II. Many of the new hippie pioneers didn't make it. The ones that moved to the Willamette River floor or on low foothills bordering the river more likely made it. They tended to be more serious farmers. The ones that moved, like far out, into the mountains, tended to not make it and move back into the grid. Or they dived so far into an alternative universe through psychotropic drugs that they never came back. In the Cascade mountains the career options were limited: logging, working the green chain, or logging and working the green chain. There was always the growing marijuana option.

Rivers like the McKenzie which flows through Eugene, and past Kesey's college, University of Oregon, had well-educated tribes and bus caravans; ours, the Santiam was more sparsely re-populated. I don't think it really mattered to Kathleen. She just wanted to live in the forest and be amongst her animal spirit friends.

Our town had a population of 300. Most people speed through Cascadia without realizing it's a town. Unknowing tourists are regularly run off the highway by logging trucks trying to make 3 runs a day from the dwindling supply of Douglas Firs east of the town. If you turn off the highway and cross over a white covered bridge, there is a post office, and state park that in the 1920s was a health spa that touted the healing qualities of the fowl tasting mineral springs.

Our life off the grid was exactly what we fantasized. Every day was like a peasant's workday in the middle ages. We measured time by light and shadows; eating, drinking and evacuating moments. When we made love, I felt swarthy. Standing in our field in the middle of summer I could hear the earth's hum or song. And just like in the middle ages we had ticks and lice and we were constantly dirty. While we didn't have a lord on a white horse riding through the fields to intimate or beat us, there was a park ranger who came periodically to remind us of where the border was between us and public land.

Our property adjoined Cascadia State Park along the Santiam River in Oregon. Cascadia itself was dropped out, and our place, a mile up a gravel road, and then another ½ mile up a dirt road was even further dropped out. The town of Cascadia was a post office, tiny store, gas station and Grange building.

That I arrived in this tiny gyppo logger town alone, and with a ponytail, did not bode well. I figured when Kathleen arrived my status would go up some. A young, beautiful woman with long blond hair and insect bitten lips would go a long way. Meanwhile, the best I had to offer was Morgan. And he was a good commodity. Morgan loved to ride shotgun in Mr. Zoom. If you said, "Morgan, shotgun!" he run to you and lifted his front paws up and down like a cat kneading bread. You could tease him for a while but he would eventually get it. He would make a noise that sounded like, "ah fudge," and once more swear to himself he would not be duped. He also insisted on wearing my French beret. If I was wearing it when we got in the car, he glared at me. If I started the car before I gave him the cap he would howl. Once I placed it on his head, he sat perfectly still right next to me as though we were on a date. If our road trip was too long, he would lift a paw and drape it over my arm on the steering wheel. I would lift it off. Back on. And off. Finally, I would tell him, "Morgan fuck off we're not going home yet." He would move across the seat and lean against the window. Then he would look like he was coming home from a binge on the left bank. One time the beret fell off. The passenger window was open, so he hung his paw out the window. He reminded me of my high school friend Shot-put who would roll up his sleeve and hang his arm out the window when we were cruising for chicks.

The first time I stopped at the local grocery store-gas station-bar in Cascadia Morgan waited in our white crummie (which also gave me some currency since it looked like everyone else's truck) wearing the beret sitting upright in the passenger seat. I saw several guys in cork boots and red plaid jackets walk by and break up laughing and one came in and said, "did you see that fucking dog, thinks he's cool or something."

Morgan had other traits that helped us gain friends. If you put coffee or alcohol in front of him, he would snort and shake his head like he was a temperance tee tootler. He laid down to eat resting his jaw on his bowl which made him look drunk or hung over. Once he made friends with someone if he saw them even at a sizable distance, he would cock his head back and howl. It became a matter of distinction to be friends. Also, if you walked with him, he would run ahead, hide and then leap out like a vulture and push his lips back and his teeth out. The local teenage girls who visited me—mostly as a place they could smoke and tell me about their raunchy boyfriends —loved to take him for a walk.

My first encounters with the locals were unsettling. When I bought food at the tiny store, famous for two yolk chicken eggs, people in the store would stop shopping or talking and just stare at me, and then follow my exit until I drove away. Deliverance came to mind.

Then I met the informal mayor of the town, our neighbor Dan; Dan, his wife and two teenage boys, both the size of small pickup trucks. He was a pleasantly alcoholic logger with an easy laugh who loved nothing better than to drink whiskey and tell stories. Everyone loved him in town and he became our entry into the community and our guardian. Dan visited the day after I arrived. He came early in the morning with Wild Turkey whiskey, his drink of choice. I knew I couldn't say no, and I knew it was the end of my day. He stayed for a couple of hours and as soon as he left; I went into the tent and passed out.

I knew part of the problem was that I was not only a hippie, but I was a loner. When Kathleen arrived, she might make a big difference, but that was still a month away and I might be dead by then. I knew the soul of life in small Oregon towns was the tavern, so after shopping one day I strode across the street to the Mill In Tavern. It was still daylight. I figured if I came early enough the locals wouldn't be drunk and I could get back to my place in daylight.

I forgot it was always nighttime in taverns. It seemed very familiar: pool tables, a long wooden bar with pickled eggs on the counter, and about a dozen logger types and two women. Conversation didn't exactly stop but they duly noted my presence. I ordered a draft. I could hear some conversation directed at me, "lives up Beverly rock road." "He's From Portland..." Nothing too disparaging. Then a cork boot wearing angel came in with a flood of light behind him (I kid you not). It was Dan. Everyone warmly greeted him. I raised my hand the pope had blessed tentatively and miraculously he headed right for me, "Hey, it's the professor. How the fuck are you?" He put his hand on my shoulder, and grasped my bicep (Thank God, I had been doing hard labor helping my father at the Shire). "A beer for me and the professor here." It was like the Pope had blessed me. I didn't know where he had come up with my nickname, but the more I thought about it later, drunk in my tent with my head spinning, it was perfect. It was respectful and disparaging at the same time. It gave me some berth of behavior. I could be weird without being threatening. I was a part of them but different.

By the end of the evening I had played darts with someone, pool with someone else, learned a Hank Williams tune, learned to lie about how I felt about the war in Viet Nam, learned at least six new words for an erection, and knew who had the best firewood in town.

We built a cabin in 6 months enough so the first heavy rains we laid in bed and listened to the rain hit the roof. That first night we both laid in bed staring up at the ceiling just listening. We were dry; what a miracle. We were English literature majors and had built a house that protected us from the elements. It was a live of routines: wake up in the cold (in winter) start a fire, have breakfast cooked on the wood stove, and some mornings sitting in front of the kitchen stove, and then girding up the strength to make a run to the outhouse. It may have been the most peaceful part of my life, before or after; but I also knew it couldn't last forever. Kathleen and Morgan knew they could live there forever, but for me the routines shrank time. With nothing new or unexpected, except an occasional deer leaping past our house, time was shrinking.

The locals didn't know what to make of the new pioneers. The gyppo loggers and others treated them like unwanted invaders. But, they were curious. The local teenagers new from Life Magazine coverage that these newcomers had newfangled ways to get high, and the women didn't wear bras and were easy. And there were mysteries like the family (kind of...one guy, three women who looked like they had last been at the Playboy Mansion, and 2 small kids that never wore clothes) who built a large tutor style home on 15 acres of stream front land. Each of their neighbors lived in mobile homes. The guy's name was Spinoza, and he drove a customized 4-wheel drive vehicle worth two local family's income for a year. Just where the hell did they get so much money? Nobody yet thought about how the new immigrants were making small fortunes growing pot. Everyone knew about pot but it was something that came from Mexico or Columbia.

There was a row of cheap houses right along the highway that many of the new immigrants settled in. One in particular, just known locally as the blue house. It was hard to tell how many people lived there. No one in town knew, and likely people living there also didn't know. We lived way off the highway up our own quiet road, a mile further down the highway so to get to the "city", Sweet Home, a town with 4000, we had to drive past the blue house. We had met some people so whenever we drive by, we waved or honked, even though most of the time we didn't know who we were waving at. Many of the hippies looked alike. And they like to gather in the overgrown front lawn where there was a tipi and several tents and rotating school buses. They had this enormous back yard that went off into the wilderness so we always wondered why so many of them choose to sit by the freeway where log trucks with tons of old growth logs roared past. They just sat there sometimes staring at the road.

At first the local teenagers didn't take to the new immigrants. One group threw a sack of shit with firecrackers at Spinoza's fancy truck. Big mistake. Spinoza was a big guy. He worked out by throwing 100-pound rocks into the river. He had this kind of deadly serious way of talking. About the incident he just said in a calm voice, "they really shouldn't have done that." He figured out who it was. He bought their homestead and tore down their house. One of the other teenagers was found tied to a telephone pole with a big note, "don't fuck with me. OK?"

After that the teenagers made friends with the new immigrants. Which worked out some ways fine but in other ways the culture clash was a little unnerving. They introduced the local teenagers to marijuana and LSD and they begin to act kind of screwy. Like one day Kathleen and I were talking to the postmaster along the back road when this beat up station wagon came barreling down the road with two giant naked assess hanging out the rear end. The postmaster watched the wagon go by, without turning to me just noted, as though he were noticing a hawk fly over, "That was Chuck's kid Big John driving. I didn't think he had his license yet."

One of the celebrated moments in the new immigrant history was the night the local teenagers figured a swell trick to play on the day trippers. They knew that every Thursday night the trippers and the more established hippies gathered at the blue house to share food and the latest imported drugs. It was a party that lasted all day and night. The rest of the story is all second hand so I'm not sure exactly how it was carried out. I know the local teens had a hangout at the foot of Mossy Brae, the town's landmark rock that rose several hundred feet in back of the town center. There were several caves, and the teens had fixed one up as a den of inequity. Everyone knew about it including parents and the police, but they seemed to let it be as long as there wasn't anything terrible. So, I imagine some of them sat around and conceived the plot there and gathered their supplies for the mission.

There were a lot of day tripping hippies that particular night. A converted school bus had arrived the week before. The story goes they were gathered around the woodstove while one of the new refugees, known as Blonde Bill led the group in a yoga practice, when suddenly without warning the house burst into flame. Just like that. As one guy told me later, "It was a regular conflagration. You know, like a firestorm." Several people shot up and sprang into action, diving for their stuff, saving drug stashes and babies, while others continued their yoga practice. Some people were panicking and screaming while others stayed calm or didn't know what the excitement was all about. By time the first alert hippie got to the door, the fire was out. It was quiet until one person summarized the situation, "wow was that brimstone?"

The Teens had doused the house—of cedar shake construction—with lighter fluid and ignited it. Between the sponge like nature of cedar shakes and the thick most air of an Oregon Forest, the lighter fluid caught fire and then evaporated. The town endlessly debated this incident. Did the teens really know what was going to happen? Was it funny or hilarious? It turned out to be a bonding experience.

Rednecks to the Rescue

How much I was accepted into the community only became clear about a month after Kathleen arrived. There was one other neighbor between our place and Dan's. It was an abandoned homestead. All that remained was a dilapidated cabin, small barn, and a few apple trees which the bears loved. It was rumored to belong to a Doctor from Albany but we had seen no one there. One night about midnight there was suddenly the sound of cars and trucks, light beans this way and that way, and then loud male voices. I snuck down through the woods to get a better look. When I was close enough to hear, but also close enough to run back to our place I shouted out, "Hey, who's there?" The voices quieted down and then a belligerent voice shouted back, "Who the fuck wants to know." And another voice, "why don't you come down and find out." That was enough for me to hightail it back to our tent. I instructed Kathleen to drive down the hill and find Dan. It seemed like a reasonable strategy. While she was gone, I snuck down the hill to get a better look at the extras from Deliverance. I got closer than I had before and figured out that it was the Doctor from Albany. Emboldened, I came out of the forest and announced myself. "your neighbor. Not that you knew you had one. I know you right you are the doctor from the White Knight Health Clinic in Albany?"

We had a pleasant conversation and then I remembered the mission I had sent Kathleen on. I excused myself and went to find Kathleen. I was walking down our long driveway when all hell broke loose. Coming up the driveway with spotlights blaring into the woods, gun shots, screaming and whooping a caravan of rednecks fully armed. I stood in the roadway signaling them and heard one of them shout, "There's one of them now." I heard Kathleen exclaim, "No, that's my husband!" The cars came to a crashing halt. With the drunken force of gyppo loggers staring at me with hands on instruments of destruction, Kathleen explained to me how Dan wasn't at home so she went to the tavern and he wasn't there but his friends rallied to help. The battalion continued to drink beers and one guy fired off random shots into the woods, and said in disgust, "Shit let's go get the fuckers, anyway!"

"Just joking," the guy said, who looked like the left side of his face had been hit by a log on the green chain, a fairly frequent occurrence in these parts. After we thanked our army, we joined our neighbors and once more I found myself hung over in the morning trying to build a cabin with only hand tools. But it also felt like they had accepted us into the community.

After two years of living in the forest primeval and drinking moonshine with local rednecks, I was restless. I felt disconnected from the world. I would sit in our white GMC crummie, listen to the radio, and eagerly look forward to the mail. Using the car radio, I could only pick up local stations. I bought a portable radio that had short wave frequencies. More contact with the world. Then I wondered if I could pick up more stations if I put an antenna up in a tree. I thought if I was going to climb 50 feet up a Douglas fir to install an antenna, why not build a platform where I could sit and listen to the world? Kathleen put up food for the winter while I hauled lumber up the tree. Two weeks later, I could sit on the platform. The platform swayed in the wind; dipping me over the hillside, glimpsing the Santiam River, then back to our field and house. I was connected. I could listen to Brother Epley talk about his magic prayer pillows in St Louis, or George Armstrong and his money producing Church in Texas, or Wolfman Jack from Los Angeles.

Then one day I got a copy of the *Last Whole Earth Catalog Supplement*. The only other mail we were getting was letters from family and returns from my responses to classified ads in magazines I picked up at the garbage bins in town. Getting an information-rich and current journal was a memorable event. I couldn't figure out why I received it. I wasn't a subscriber. Then I realized why. The editors for this last edition were Ken Kesey and Paul Krassner, editor of the Realist. I subscribed to the Realist, Krasner's surrealistic anarchistic journal, in 1967, and now four years later I was apparently still on his mailing list.

I walked back to our house from the post office a mile away. The walk to and from the post office was one of Morgan's favorite pastimes. He almost always ran out of pee by the time we got back home. It was a very large territory to mark. I decided the only place to understand this thing dropped into my life was under the Elf tree, an ancient Douglas Fir whose massive limbs created a mossy carpet around it. It wasn't hard to imagine elves dancing around it. I sat under the tree and read the catalog from cover to cover. I had an epiphany. Someday soon we would all have access to computers, the storehouse of all knowledge, and direct access through telecommunications to anyone on the planet. I wanted to be a part of constructing the world brain. I wanted to move back to the city. I knew Kathleen would not agree and be devastated by the idea. I developed a strategy as I walked back. This vision could not wait. I would tell Kathleen that someday we could move back here, or anywhere, and be in the center of things. There would be no backwater. We would be connected to vast networks of people around the world and the grassroots would uproot the established powers. And there was a new role to play. I would be a networker. To sell it, I also came up with a name that would blend high tech and organic earthy life. We would call the enterprise The Technology laboratorium.

In the coming weeks, I eventually wore Kathleen down. We would move back, but live at Cascadia part of the year, and when the Laboratorium was up and running, we would move back. I knew with great certainty we wouldn't. Not because I would resist or go back on my promise. I imagined that in four or five years something would happen to us. We were at a fork in the road and our paths, while parallel, were slowly but inevitably drifting in different directions.

For the next month I wrote game plans and created diagrams and proposals, matrixes, and calls to action. I put the stories I had been writing about growing up in a box. We found a couple with two goats and five dogs to rent our place and moved back to Portland. I finally felt like I had a mission or quest in life. I was the Don Quixote of the information age.

Thanking Ken Kesey and Paul Krassner

I was able to thank Ken Kesey and Paul Krassner for their role in changing my life when Kathleen and I moved back to Portland to create the technology laboratorium. In 1974 when Kesey organized Bend in the River, a state wide Chautauqua or visioning process about the future of Oregon. The process that went on for months leading up to Bend was a chaotic Merry Pranksters event with many of the original Pranksters involved. It was documented by Rolling Stone, and photographed by a then unknown photographer, Annie Leibovitz.[14]

Paul Krassner and I were at the same table at the Bend convocation, listening to Senator Wayne Morse[15] gave a rousing and strangely stilted speech. He seemed ethereal. It was almost like we were watching a black and white film. He had terminal pancreatic cancer. His cadence was from another era, hardly fitting this crowd, who were admiring. Here was the only senator who voted against the Tonkin Gulf resolution that launched the Viet Nam war. While I watched him, I had the incongruous memory of seeing him get out of his car at another congressperson's house, Edith Green's, from my friend's club house. I was twelve then. The clubhouse was the attic of a garage. In the clubhouse we played poker and smoked cigarettes, and poured through a collection of Playboy magazines. We separated the playboy section of the clubhouse from the "casino" by a blanket so we could discreetly make love with the centerfolds. There was a small window overlooking Edith's yard. I knew who Wayne Morris was because my parents were democratic precinct leaders. It didn't at all seem odd to me when Michelle, my favorite playmate, did her two-dimensional magic on me. It was probably about the time Lyndon Johnson persuaded the Senator to join the Democratic caucus. At the time, the rendezvous with Michelle was more important to me.

It was the Senator's last public speech. He died a couple of months later. Thanking Paul Krasner for his part in a big change in my life was anticlimactic. He laughed and said, "far fuckin out," and then walked away. I wanted to tell him that is the same thing Ken

Kesey said about a book I had published. What is it with you guys and far fucking out?

---

1. Charles Atlas was an Italian-American bodybuilder best remembered as the developer of a bodybuilding method and associated exercise program which spawned a landmark advertising campaign featuring his name and likeness.

2. William Burroughs was an American writer. He was a primary figure of the Beat Generation and a major postmodernist author whose influence is considered to have affected a range of popular culture and literature. Burroughs wrote eighteen novels and novellas, six collections of short stories and four collections of essays.

3. "Gary Snyder talks writing influences, Reed College and Portland," Jeff Baker, *Oregonian*, June 16, 2011.

4. Olive Oyl was Popeye's girlfriend. Popeye the Sailor is a fictional muscular American cartoon character created by Elzie Crisler Segar. The character first appeared in the daily King Features comic strip Thimble Theatre on January 17, 1929, and Popeye became the strip's title in later years. Oly was skinny and wiry.

5. Eric Hoffer wrote ten books and was awarded the Presidential Medal of Freedom in 1983. His first book, *The True Believer*, was widely recognized as a classic, receiving critical acclaim from both scholars and laypeople.

6. One of the more successful American utopian communal societies in the nineteenth century was founded on the Pudding River in Marion County, Oregon, in 1856. Named for a daughter of the leader of the Christian communal group, the Aurora Colony (or Aurora Mills, as it was also known) grew to a population of over 600 individuals who followed the basic Christian beliefs of Wilhelm Keil (1812-1877). The Aurora Colony became known for its orchards, food, music, textiles, furniture, and other crafts and its communal lifestyle and German traditions https://oregonencyclopedia.org/articles/aurora/#.XzHPpS2ZNoI.

7. *Those were the days my friend we thought they would never end*, Steven Reed Johnson, Prepared for William Stafford Workshop Lewis and Clark College, 1994. http://docshare02.docshare.tips/files/23932/239320370.pdf

8. Johnson, Steven Reed, Transformation of Civic Institutions and Practices in Portland, Oregon, 1960-1999. PhD dissertation 2002.

9. Augustus Owsley Stanley III, 1935–2011. Stanley was the first known private individual to manufacture mass quantities of LSD. By his own account, between 1965 and 1967, Stanley produced no less than 500 grams of LSD, amounting to over five million doses. He was also soundman for the Grateful Dead. One of Jack's friends was their road manager.

10. *Heaven and Hell* is a philosophical essay by Aldous Huxley published in 1956. Huxley derived the title from William Blake's book *The Marriage of Heaven and Hell*. The essay is an account of Huxley's experiences with mescaline. Publisher: Harper, 1956.

11. Old Yeller is a 1957 American drama film produced by Walt Disney. It stars Tommy Kirk, Dorothy McGuire, Fess Parker, and Beverly Washburn. It is about a boy and a stray dog in post-Civil War Texas. Considered one of the all-time tear-jerker scenes when the boy has to shoot his dog.

12. Stephen Gaskin was an American Hippie icon best known for co-founding "The Farm", a spiritual intentional community in Summertown, Tennessee.

13. Paul Krassner was an American author, journalist, comedian, and the founder, editor, and a frequent contributor to the magazine *The Realist*, first published in 1958. Krassner became a key figure in the counterculture of the 1960s as a member of Ken Kesey's Merry Pranksters and a founding member of the Yippies. He died on July 21, 2019, in Desert Hot Springs, California.

14. Annie Leibovitz is an American portrait photographer. She photographed John Lennon on the day he was murdered, and her work has been used on many albums, covers, and magazines.

15. Wayne Morse was a United States Senator from Oregon, known for his proclivity for opposing his party's leadership, and specifically for his opposition to the Vietnam War.

THE AINSWORTH CHRONICLES

Preamble

This is Jack's version of a transcription of the series of interviews I conducted with him. I recorded them and took notes but never wrote up a transcription. As I recall there were five interviews, each one lasting five hours. On average, the transcription of one hour of an interview is 40 typed pages or 10,000 words. So that means Jack whittled down about 1000 pages to two.

Johann Storedal Olson and Sigred Olson were living at the family homestead, Storedal, in Norway, when in 1897, they gave birth to Dag Storedal Johansson (that is, the son of Johann Olson). Through relocations; the whim of Immigration Office staff; a scandal in Coon Valley, Wisconsin; and his constant urge to wander and learn, he eventually became known as Dr. John.

They migrated to America when Dag was four. At Ellis Island, the immigration officers changed the family name. They thought it was confusing that the parents were Olsons, and the kids were all Johanssons. They gave them a new family name, Johnson. Johann was furious; almost punched one of the officers. In retribution they renamed Dag, Dr John. They said he looks like a doctor. He had saggy eyes that made it like he was wearing spectacles and a birthmark near his mouth shaped like a smoking pipe. They also refused to print a last name on his immigration paper.

They moved to Coon Valley, Wisconsin. This is where Dr. John got in the habit of running away. The first time Dr John ran away from home, he was four years old. His parents panicked, as did the entire town of Coon Valley. Bears, falling off a cliff into the river, or kidnapping all came up as possibilities. Three days after he ran away, he reappeared; sitting at the kitchen table eating rolled oats and milk as though nothing had happened. When he was asked, he finally told his parents, "an Indian took me to a secret place." He told the same story to anyone that asked. At first everyone figured it was just his fantasy until one day Olava saw a large Indian carrying John on his shoulders across a field. They disappeared into the forest and John reappeared days later, alone.

His parents weren't negligent parents, just distracted. They were hard core socialists and involved in protests and strikes and writing polemics. Several times when he went wandering, they hadn't noticed for a couple of days.

It wasn't unusual for John to be absent. He didn't enjoy playing with the other children in the family, preferring mental activity to physical. For a while his parents put a collar and rope on Dr. John to keep him nearby. But he always freed himself; or the mysterious Indian freed him.

Then he discovered the town library. A tiny library set up in the town's first fire station when a new one was built. Town folk donated most of the books and magazines. The most popular donations were Reader's Digest books, romance novels, National Geographic, out-of-date almanacs and encyclopedias. But to John it was heaven. The library was a five-mile walk. If he started at 6am he would arrive at ten just when the librarian arrived. He started doing this when he was eight and by the time he was ten he had read everything in the library.

It did not surprise anyone when John disappeared one day and he wasn't heard from for months, until his parents received a postcard with a half-naked mermaid on one side, and his note on the other, "Found library bigger than I can digest in a lifetime." He had walked to Chicago. In Chicago he fell in love with Elizabeth Maggie who was a follower of Henry George. Jack insists you can't understand his father if you haven't read George's work. Elizabeth is also credited with creating the board game Monopoly.[1] Dr. John worked on it first with a decidedly leftist twist. If you ended up with too many properties, an anarchist was likely to kidnap you. Henry George was also in love with Elizabeth. He even challenged Dr. John to a duel.

Also, My father loved gyroscopes. He met Elmer Ambrose Sperry[2] in Chicago in 1930. He was by chance invited to an early meeting of promote business leaders and scientists who were planning the Chicago's world fair to be opened in 1933. Of course Dr. John was always trying to understand chance encounters real meanings. When Sperry described his gyrocompass at a luncheon and applications in navigation, Dr. John was focused on the social milieu more that the invention.

I should warn you that when you find his journals you will find references to Gyroscope but not always the device he named people that. People he thought were screwy but maybe also geniuses. And another thing he invented he called that. Gus renamed it. The only one I think is here at the warehouse. Gus renamed it the Chronographer. He can show it to you.

Dr. John went back to Wisconsin. There he found out his parents had responded to an ad in a radical publication in Oregon. The ad was from a Major Ainsworth about his daughter Olava (Oldegard) Ainsworth. An offer for the appropriate gentleman to marry his daughter and in the bargain acquire 360 acres near Portland, Oregon. A catch. the suiter would have to take their name, Ainsworth.

Dr. John was a writer for the *Firebrand*[3] and a member of the Academy of Socialism and the Friends of Henry George,[4] who had a sizable following in Portland. You know in those days if you were radical; you knew everyone else that was; like John Reed[5] and the irritating love of his life Louise Bryant there weren't many places to gather. Also, nobody made much money. They spend days in the nearby mountains picking wild blackberries to can for winter survival.

They called themselves the Random Lot. Members were anarchists, socialists, single-taxers. One notable person in their circle was affectionately known as Dr. Urine,[6] an early advocate of the initiative and referendum process. The Firebrand family, those publishing the journal and others loosely affiliated with the group, tried to make ends meet while attempting to live off the land in the countryside near Portland.

Another Random Lot member was Rodney Cameron[7] who opened a bookstore in the heart of the civic elites' territory in 1938. While not rich, he had lucked out when a cousin left to find gold in California, leaving him a partially completed building that was going to be a dry goods store. When the cousin was killed in a mining accident, Rodney inherited the property, completed the building, and opened Cameron's A Novel Idea bookstore, which became another place for the progressive members of the Random Lot members and followers of Henry George. Cameron had a fair selection of books, at least for a remote, rugged town like Portland was in those days, but the size of the collection was supplemented by special collections such as the large collection of matchbook covers anywhere on the west Coast, and the largest ball of string, maybe anywhere in America. No way to contradict it, so he claimed it.

He never seemed to take care of himself, one of the few bachelors Jack knew. His hair was usually tangled and dirty. He only wore one costume: blue jeans and a gray sweatshirt, with black tennis shoes that were falling apart.

Rodney turned his bookstore into a place for meetings. Meetings for groups like the Webfoot Postcard Collectors Society,[8] the Madame Blavatsky Study Group,[9] the DiceLife Foundation[10] —a group of people who rolled dice to plan their lives "a kind of astrology, I think," Mr. Green said—and the Stone Mountain Trail Institute, a group of unorthodox historians who were writing the history of the Stone Mountain Trail, an alternative to the Oregon trail, where pioneers had, as Jack would say, "discovered the counter-history."

In 1911 the Random Lot members in Portland created the People's Library in defiance of the white founding father's leadership. To Random Lot members, the founding of the library was an iconic battle for freedom of information, one they ultimately lost. The first library was the Mercantile Library, which was funded through subscriptions by the business elite.

The People's Library had originally been the public library until Frank O'Conner became the librarian. Frank's idea of a library didn't sit well with the community. Frank and other Random Lot members didn't see a library as a place just for books. It was about ideas and knowledge and bringing people together for exchanging ideas. Instead of using the public funds for more books, he hosted events, and he focused the collection on scrapbooks filled with photographs, quotes, pamphlets, and books. There was a notebook called "Death" and another called "Anxieties." They also created their own books, pasting together local texts and famous authors. Interesting that in one correspondence a member refers to as the Home Grown Library, a turn of phrase that was used again in the 1970s by radical librarians. Eventually someone donated a building for their library, symbolically on the east side of the river—home of the people, not the civic elite. John was a leader of the cause and at least for a year lived in the library basement.

Delving into the Heart of Randomness

Preamble

We stand on the shoulders of geniuses as Isaac Newton noted. Dr John read widely. He was familiar with the western civilization cannon but was proud of how he knew many of the central tomes of every country, in fact of most all tribes in the world. If you don't believe me check out the Badger manual. Not like Ainsworth was the first to think of the "world brain". Ainsworth often quoted Vannevar Bush,[11] whose 1945 Atlantic article is sometimes considered the forerunner to the google world. Dr John often sympathized with thinkers and inventors out of synch with their time. Two centuries ago Leibnitz[12] invented a calculating machine which embodied most of the essential features of recent keyboard devices, but it could not then come into use. *I am like Leibnitz struggling with a system that has no device.* Ainsworth says at one point. Babbage[13] could not produce his great arithmetical machine. His idea was sound enough, but construction and maintenance costs were then too heavy.

What follows is Jack's version of a transcription of the series of interviews I conducted with him. I recorded them and took notes but never wrote up a transcription. As I recall there were five interviews, each one lasting five hours. On average the transcription of one hour of an interview is 40 typed pages or 10,000 words. So that means Jack whittled down about 1000 pages to two.

JA: In the mid-1970s my father, Dr John, wrote a book titled *Delving into the Heart of Randomness.* It was 800 pages. He went to a couple of printers locally; I think one was Binford and Mort Publishing.[14] Old man Binford wasn't interested. It would break their budget, but they became friends. He went to San Francisco and New York. He carried it with him. When he started the box was brand new. Crisp white for grapefruits, I think. By time he got back to Portland the box was brown, taped together, and the manuscript was thicker. It had soaked up water along the way. That's when he realized that publishing was absurd. It was at the heart of what he was trying to undermine, and here he was expecting them to publish it. He printed 100 copies and distributed it through the Crying of Lot 49.

RJ: Why was publishing absurd?

JA: The preponderance of the material is my father's attempt to find a matrix for mining information randomly that would create usable knowledge. He carried out hundreds of experiments. For example, convinced that people, inadvertently, held crucial information for other people, he worked out complicated formulas that involved moving in each of the four directions from your home, writing the 6th, 9th, 27th, and 110th words that you saw or heard after you walk exactly 13 minutes. Then you waited for the next person to use each of the words and asked them, "Do you have something to tell me." He had figured out that over 60% of the time he discovered a critical value for his life. I really do not understand how many of these theories and experiments he carried out, but I suspect it is at least hundreds if not thousands. After many years, he discovered what he thought was the best tool. And, you guessed it, that's what was in the missing box.

RJ: I had a feeling.

JA: Another key document is *Random Theory of Knowledge: Overthrowing the Power Elite.* In *that*—remember, this is the mid 1970s—he wrote, "In the future the Mosaic will create complete mathematical versions of ourselves.Through this self-emulation, the intelligence of the swarm will be revealed. We will no longer seek knowledge through rational deductive thinking, but through plucking relevant knowledge through random encounters. It will be known as fractal knowledge, and the machines that serve us as Mosaics."

RJ: This sounds somewhat prescient.

JA: You think? "The masters of the world control the world through rational thought behavior and deductive scientific thinking. They do this by creating a Master Story that everyone believes. The Master Story is overcome through flying below their radar by random knowledge seeking and swarm networking. The intelligence of one worker bee is nil, the swarm is all powerful. My father imagined a Mosaic, or "world brain", with all knowledge that all people can use and where they all have access to each other. He did not imagine personal computers, laptops, or I-Pods. At the period he developed the theory the assumed computing model was the minicomputer. He was concerned that computers could also consolidate power, so he envisioned a decentralized network of small (large for his day) computers, available to the public through telephone booths, libraries, laundromats, schools, and ham radio networks.

I am proud that my family has been on all three Portland Police Subversive's task force. In my father's case for trying to create a world brain.[15]

RJ: Go back a minute, Tell me more about the Laundromat

JA: My father's breakthrough about random knowledge came about—of course—randomly when he was at a coin-op laundry. He had picked up a flyer advertising a Rosicrucian speaker in town. He put it down on the book he was reading *Spangler's History of the World*, then put coins in the dryer. When he came back to his book, he realized a sentence from the flyer and from the book lined up just so and created an answer to a question he had been pondering: How do you know if you really dance to a different drummer? The answer was: He listened to the wrong counselor...

Jack: You ever think how we might be related? I mean Johnson's (maybe Olsons) from Norway. Probably are, I would venture. That's a little weird, what say?

RJ: I have never researched my family. They are from Norway. I think along the western coast line. OK? Can we get back to your life?

Jack: I think it all really started in Norway 250 years ago. Although my father swears it goes back to the Middle Ages. I have a photo of the house in Norway where Johann Olson set up a special room for doctoring historic documents. They created forgeries of Norse history in the Oslo Public Library; added deadly snakes to postcards; hid secrets in paintings that hung in notable Inns. That kind of thing. It's also where the fairy fetish started. Someone showed me a photograph of a Norwegian hunting scene where 2 fairies are hidden in the leaves and moss under a dead Moose.

Dr John Sightings during the Gertrude Stein Fellowship Days

My first meeting with Dr. John was about six months after I moved to the Gertrude Stein warehouse. I noticed a strange looking man (and that is in the context of the Gertrude Stein Fellowship club) sitting in Leland's nest office. I figured he was a stranger; all the regulars knew better than to mess around with Leland's nest. He was sitting, but I could tell he was tall, taller if not bigger than Leland. He looked most like someone from the Old Testament painted by El Greco. When I looked at him, he stared back in a penetrating way that made me feel like I was the stranger. He had a strange birthmark near his mouth. He mumbled, "don't know who the stranger is in town, right?" That is from a song by Bob Seeger, not the forbidden son of Peter Seeger but the one famous for saying 'the multifarious masses of grapes turned to raisons through life considered as God's horseplay." His voice trailed off and he went back to staring at a book the size of the desk. I wanted to find Leland. In case he didn't know that someone was in nest.

Then I found this entry in one of my journals:

"The only time I met Dr John. Standing side by side, Jack and Dr. John looked unrelated, like a stork and Penguin or Mutt and Jeff. The analogy was all the more striking since Dr. John, tall Mutt like, was wearing a stove pipe hat, a vest with watch chain hanging from a pocket. A time traveler from the 1890s. It was also disappointing; that

Jack had a father. Dr. John didn't say much until he launched into one or another of his favorite topics. He had a cadence reminiscent of Native Americans. Spaces between conversation bits. You would say something and he would stare at you as though the words or meanings hadn't reached him yet. Then he was like the stereotypical old timer sitting in front of the dry goods store "some say that..." "I suppose that's true, but...."

Then at another point, with conspiracy thinking sneaking into my brain, Crazy Ralph stopped me one day and said, "you know there's something weird I need to tell you. And Jack did not put me up to this. But the Dr. John I knew had a fuck ugly mole just below tee-shirt level. I hadn't thought about it but walked in on him getting a massage and you know how you notice something more when you don't want to notice it. I did not want to look at the mole. It looked like a shaved guy's Mr. Johnson, the way it dangled with a sack. Well anyway, it wasn't there and there was no scar. I moved closer to look at it and I think he Impulsively covered himself."

Dr. John looked different whenever I saw him. When I asked others, they said things like, "well not really. Maybe a little. Wears what he finds in the goodwill bins. Doesn't seem to age much.... "

One day I was walking past the Gertrude Stein board room, that is the Quality Pie restaurant, when I noticed Crazy Ralph. I'm not sure how it became one of my responsibilities, but I felt I had to protect Ralph from the community. He was talking to a man who looked like he had picked up 1980s business man gear from the Goodwill. I was late for a meeting with Dr. Joseph Miller[16] who was helping develop an archive of about Portland's water system, and I wanted to hurry along. But then realized it was Dr. John. No one had told me he was in town. I hid behind a telephone pole so I could get a better look. Some people were in the way and I couldn't get a clear look by time I did Ralph was there by himself, but still talking. Not unusual for him to be talking to no one or phantoms. Then someone put his hand on my shoulder, cleared his throat—in the same way Jack did—maybe a family thing? "Well, stranger getting a good peak at the genius from Jupiter? It was Dr. John. quoting Crazy Ralph's version of entropy "Entropy will always increase unless we all shoot up diamond dust. The purity of the diamond molecular structure will create new balance in the universe." He held out his hand containing small white pebbles.

Dr John was also a regular fixture on the streets of Portland. He knew the notion people were after him was absurd; that was conspiratorial thinking, the paranoid that made sense out of disorder. Of course, they weren't after him. They were just doing what they thought they had a calling for, and he was in the way. Or was it that way? But Things didn't just happen. Of all the things that might happen, only certain things did. Take for example what Ass Hole—his preferred name, the preacher from We Are One Church, who lived on a stone bench in front of the Portland library—said to him one day, "So what's it going to be? Are you going to be on the stage or in the audience?" Ass Hole giggled and then started talking about how the Veteran's Administration wouldn't give him money for a new arm. What Ass Hole had said fit perfectly with his interior monologue of the moment. He was wondering about his role in life. Did he want to be a part of history, however small, or just be in the balcony looking at the stage?

Dr John died during my sojourn at the Gertrude Stein Fellowship club. Leland told me but then added, I guess you don't know this part but he dies all the time and then magically reappears, although one time it turned out to be an actor Jack hired. He videotaped people's responses to determine if they were amazed or perplexed.

Jack didn't know for certain when or where his father died. I think the last time they saw each was when Jack went to San Francisco to fetch him from a homeless shelter and bring him back to Portland. While Jack was packing up his belongings at the shelter his father went outside to grab a smoke and never came back. A year after that, a Random Lot member told Jack he had moved to an abandoned resort town along the Salton Sea. He had died, so the rumor had it, when he was creating an art installation that showed the relationships between everybody on the planet. It was based on research he conducted at the Mormon Church and his theories of random knowledge. The Random Lot member had sent jack a photograph of what was left of the installation. He estimated the piece was ten miles long. The largest pieces were giant rocks labeled "nuclei," the smallest were tiny preserved insect bodies, and he had labeled, " illume." Along with the photo was a brief description, "Over time spiders will randomly connect the nuclei and the ileum, and the age of Aquarius will be born. All people will be connected to all other people through the world brain." Ring a bell? It reminded me of my junk drawer epiphany, and made my playful insight seem like it was part of the lunatic fringe. I wondered why Jack never mentioned this to me.

---

1. Elizabeth (Lizzie) J. Maggie was born in 1866. Lizzie was a firm believer in Henry George's writing, specifically the book *Progress and Poverty.* In a 1936 interview with Lizzie appeared in a Washington, D. C. newspaper, criticizing Parker Brothers. Maggie spoke to reporters about the similarities between Monopoly and her own Landlord's Game.

2. Elmer Ambrose Sperry, Sr. (1860—1930) was an American inventor and entrepreneur, most famous as co-inventor, with Hermann Anschutz-Kaempfe, of the gyrocompass and as founder of the Sperry Gyroscope Company.

3. Anarchism on the Willamette: The *Firebrand* Newspaper and the Origins of a Culturally American Anarchist Movement, 1895-1898, Alecia Jay Glombolini, Portland State University, Master of Arts History Thesis, 2018.

4. Henry George was an American political economist and journalist. He promoted the "single tax" on land. His writing was popular in the 19th century America and sparked several reform movements of the Progressive Era.

5. John Reed. https://oregonhistoryproject.org/articles/biographies/john-reed-biography/#.XzHYAC2ZNoI.

6. William Simon U'Ren, known as early as 1898 as "Referendum U'Ren" for his single-minded devotion to the cause. He earned a law degree in Denver, and then moved to Iowa, Hawaii, and California before settling in Milwaukee, Oregon, in 1889.

7. Cameron's Books and Magazines, or simply Cameron's, is Portland, Oregon's oldest used bookstore and one of the largest vintage magazine dealers in the United States.

8. The first known reference to a "Webfooter" in Portland was at the Lewis & Clark Expo in 1905. The Webfooter was a mascot for the fair. He was actually a frog. Post card collecting was a popular pastime in Oregon's early days. One of the earliest known post card clubs was known as The Oregon Postal Card exchange.

9. The Theosophical Society is an organization formed in the United States in 1875 by Helena Blavatsky to advance Theosophy. Theosophy is the belief that knowledge of God can be achieved through spiritual ecstasy.
10. The Dice Man, a 1971 novel by English professor George Cockcroft (writing under the pen name, "Luke Rhinehart") tells the story of a psychiatrist who makes daily decisions based on the casting of a die.
11. Vannevar Bush was an American engineer, inventor and science administrator, who during World War II headed the U.S. Office of Scientific Research and Development (OSRD), through which almost all wartime military R&D was carried out, including important developments in radar and the initiation and early administration of the Manhattan Project.
12. Gottfried Wilhelm Leibniz was one of the most important logicians, mathematicians and natural philosophers of the Enlightenment. He became one of the most prolific inventors in the field of mechanical calculators. He also refined the binary number system, which is the foundation of all digital computers.
13. Charles Babbage was an English a mathematician, philosopher, inventor and mechanical engineer. He originated the concept of a digital programmable computer.
14. Binford & Mort Publishing is a book publishing company in Hillsboro, Oregon, United States. It was Founded in 1930. At one time they were the largest book publisher in the Pacific Northwest. The privately owned company focuses on books from the Pacific Northwest and has printed many important titles covering Oregon's history.
15. The City of Portland created a red squad, during and after World War I, to "watch" the subversive threats of socialists and union activists. After World War II, the City established a red squad to monitor organizations that might plot revolution. Then the City of Portland established a subversives watch program within the Portland Police, during the 1960s and 1970s to watch over subversive blacks, Native Americans, Youth, or anyone stapled a flyer on a telephone pole. They had the best collection of these flyers. The files kept, and sometimes still preserved, are remarkable historical records of organizations that might not otherwise even make it to newspaper content. Jack was proud that his family has been all three times on Portland's subversive watch list. *"In Case You were wondering... intelligence gathering was more than a one-person operation,"* Portland Tribune, September 27, 2002.
16. Joseph L. Miller Papers, 1909-1995, Oregon Historical Society. Papers include in-depth material on Joseph L. Miller's crusade to collect and organize information on the Bull Run Reserve and watershed and to expand public awareness of threats to famed pristine water through formation of the Bull Run Interest Group (BRIG) and lawsuits he initiated against the U.S. Forest Service. Bull Run is the principal source of water for Portland, Or., and other smaller communities in the area.

RED SHED INTERLUDE NO. 2

Progress Report

The reality of life at the red shed is a mess. We spend a lot of time organizing and reorganizing. Keep in mind that Jack was picky about organization; he rarely let entropy get the upper hand. He wanted us to discover some things in a certain order, which I don't want to reveal in the chance it would dispel some mysteries. Sometimes he started something and never finished it. For example, even though you read about the Gertrude Stein Fellowship Club early on, we didn't piece together all the narrative until much later. The material about Arabian Nights and Writer's boot camp went through multiple drafts. A multitude of voices or eyes of perception complicated it. There was Jack's, and Gus's, and mine; several diaries from *outside* observers; audio and video tapes; and written transcriptions or summaries of those tapes. Also, Gus and I had disagreements about what really happened that went on for days. We almost came to blows, and several times didn't talk to each other for weeks at a time.

The Red Shed itself is moldering. A phrase we came up with as we observed how many creatures we lived with from lichens, to mice and moles and an occasional raccoon. I got bit by the racoon and went to the ER. But the invasion was subtle and insidious too. The paper was the home for critters, mildew. A letter from Kathleen was rolled up from the bottom, the home for a fairly enormous spider that Gus noted danced (maybe a Polka) away when we found him. There is also the outside world. Certain cars drive by or even into the parking area to examine us (or we are just paranoid). Including a guy who looked a little like my father, who took a photo. But that turned out alright since he dropped his camera and dashed away. We crushed the camera along with the spider from Kathleen's paper—by accident.

Is Gus for Real? Mistrust Creeps in

Gus wanted me to trust him. He seemed to want the same things I wanted most of the time. But. Sometimes I imagined that the puppet master, Jack, had written Gus detailed notes about how to proceed. The details were more Hieronymus Bosch (Dutch painter) than Singer portraits. I pictured Jack's instructions to Gus as a massive tree, with branches branching out forever. I wanted to review everything that we had already reviewed. The uncertainty principle crept in. I had trusted Gus when he provided me with Arabian night session transcripts, and many other documents and stories. But the uncertainty was like how a photograph displaces your genuine memory. I remember a photograph of my older sister. We were sitting on a blanket in our meadow in mid-summer sunlight. She was smiling big time. In front of her was a small whicker picnic basket and belongings, small plates, cups, napkins, utensils. She had won it at the Oaks amusement park.[1]

My sister had rotten luck with most everything in her life from a bad part of a gene pool to loser husbands. But she always won things. Nobody else in the family. But the photograph is what I remember of her. Gus's account of the Arabian nights had erased my own memory of it.

· · ·

Remember the Hippie Home and the Red Necks?

I remember twice I stood outside the red shed with most of Jack's stuff. I had a 5-gallon gasoline container, ready to torch the red shed. I wanted to wipe it from the face of the earth. But then I started laughing. *matter is not created or destroyed.* Shit. So, I stopped myself. Another time—or so Gus told me—he found me standing in the parking lot with a selection of boxes. I told him it was just the stuff that made me hate jack. He read from the first sheet he picked up—of course having to point out that nothing was random. He read "I hated and loved him in such a wide range that the hate tail met the love tail and were tangled in a knot like a giant box of extension cords and garden hoses." we both laughed and it became a running punchline..."I hated and loved him like a tangled love like the orgies of grape vines and blackberries in the summer."

Once I threw hundreds of pages in the air and threw darts until I hit a page to mark the beginning. Dr. John would have loved that approach. But then I remember the day when I first talked to Jack on the phone and when I encountered a lasting metaphor for my life, a junk drawer that seemed to lead to anything and everything.

Here is something I am Glad I didn't include in the Manuscript

One other thing you need to know is the trail of sorrow I have been on for years. The loves of my life died in succession. Kathleen moved on, dying in the Oregon Desert with the leader of a motorcycle gang who helped her die in peace following Native American ways. You may not sense my grief as I begin this story, but that should tell you something. I have been able to use the quest for the missing box as my surrogate quest and a way to soak up my sorrow. But then again, isn't that what we all do all the time. I used to think life was all beauty interspersed with pain; but I realize that the underlying sound of the universe disintegrating into a black hole is the state of things, and we have to grab moments of beauty as they slide past us. I often feel like I am the sole survivor of a holocaust wondering around a desolate planet hoping there still may be love like I have experienced, but that may never happen; the best I can do is hold moments of beauty as long as possible. My life expands and contracts. It expands into the infinite universe and then contracts into a junk pile of details with no meaning; soundless and not even any fury.

Some days I feel like I was just born yesterday, other times I feel like I am on the last leg of a multiyear relay race. The finishing line is in sight and still not clear if I will drop off the edge of an infinitely tall cliff with the bottom either marshmallows and pillows of goose feathers or a bath of hot chocolate or blood. I have spent so much time in the last decade caring for, or at least waking every day thinking of someone else's relay race, that I don't know if I am tired beyond tired, or so stressed I am tired. When I am that tired, I get bored; I think.

Organizing the Archives: good idea and bad ideas

We used Dr John's alternative to the Dewey decimal system for organizing the achieves. But when that couldn't hold back the tide, we turned to traditional systems like Dewey Decimal and Library of Congress.

The problems of creating an information system were many. We were just organizing information or data so traditional systems worked. But we were also tracking over 100 publishing plots involving piracy of my writing and life; Jack's personas; word-of-mouth clues about the meta story. As Gus pointed out in one stellar chart, the 100 documented plots easily created 1000 networked plots that spanned the planet much as Ouspensky's ashtray did during his mystical experiments. A deep principle behind Jack's work was the Ashtray. In simple terms that one can start with anything—like an ashtray in an English Gentleman's library and from there connect to everything. As though Kevin Bacon had been making movies since the beginning of humanity. So, if everything leads to everything else, what's the point?

Sometimes the red shed was like a parody of Dr. Frankenstein's lab. We ran over to each other with eureka moments. Uncle Gus darted in, under the radar as he liked to call it—I hadn't seen or heard him until it was too late and he shocked the cow out of me—and his eyes were bulging like a Darwinian bug gone bug eyed and hyperdriving, "I got it." he said as he unfurled a 15 foot long sheet of paper. "It's a matrix," he announced, as though that explained everything from Adam's apple to the invention of post electrical magnetic curing and brain wave interpretation.

"A way to figure out what Jack was up to over all these years. Matrix you know what it means, right? It was like your random junk thing, right? Or maybe they are related? It's an organizational structure in which two or more lines of commonality or communication may run through the same individual."

"Well, that doesn't sound very related to what we are doing."

"No," he said as though he were explaining quantum physics to Nascar race attendee, "I'm thinking more about a decoder, you converting multiple video or audio or written channels into a discernible universal code. Or that we create a device for routing single or multiple inputs into a multiplex of outcomes. Well or we could just fall back on creating a chart or graph that shows relationships between information we shared openly or Jack stole from me.

"Right, I suppose we could do that."

Slowly, patiently, I reminded Gus about the guy who showed up at a show and tell then became a permeant fixture under the steps on the 6th street entrance. He advertised he could tell you the answer to any question in 5 minutes or less. He would disappear into this cheaply made portable closet, painted gold with one giant red rose, then come back out. We never found any secret ways in or out or wires or anything. And he wasn't stumped. Like he could tell you about the weather on the day King Henry VII was married or what you had for breakfast. He would conclude each session with, "that's all I have to say on the subject."

Why do we keep finding things?

We reached breaking points often. We didn't want to find anything more. But still we did. Boxes inside boxes. I found 75 of Kathleen's letters that almost went out to a Rebecca during a Last Roundup outing. The letters were mingled in with Rebeca's recipes based on the replacement of sugar with honey. And this befuddled me. I vaguely remember that I asked Jack to safeguard some of Kathleen's letters. But when or why?

Tinker Bell had my original junk drawer boxes. I forgot there was such a thing. When we first set the ground rules for Arabian Night sessions, Jack requested that I fill some boxes with stuff from junk drawers so I could draw random items for the sessions. He had some rules about that process we found later. A few index cards with rules like—if you fill a banker box half full with items from an actual junk drawer then you may fill the rest of the box with stuff from the floor of the room you work most often in. Maybe these rules were meant for me; Gus says that Jack followed the rules. So, I have no way of knowing how much of my junk drawers were filled with stuff from the floor.

Stuck in one continuous 78 record grove

Mike Spreck called me. (no, you don't know him and he will just appear this one time) The phone rang at the red shed. I forgot we even had one and couldn't find it. But of course, it was in the box labeled "technological inventions Dr John and others." Guy on other end, "you're hard to track down. Say do your parents still have that Fischer speakers?" Huh? But I decided just go along with it; never asked his name. "No, you're just a month or so too late. sold it or them whatever way you say that." Then I figured out who it was. Only one critical question, "Do you still have your mayo bottle of jizz."

"Sure do, "he said. As though I had asked if he still had that Gibson guitar, "but no babies yet. And I've mixed it with all kinds of jizz, like cats and raccoons. You wouldn't know who you sold the speakers to, do you?"

When I told Jack this he told me about Harry Smith, one of his mentors, an extraordinary collector, who lived in the same building as Jack for a while in the 1940s.

Manuscript in Parallel Universe

I knew Henry Sycamore didn't exist. But then Gus came back from an extended Last roundup trip and announced he knew where Henry lived. His informant had told him, "well he goes by the name of Leland. He showed me the two-hour long film he had produced." OK, lots of mysterious to unpack with that one. First, was it just a coincidence his name was Leland? And then there is the film. Just when or how did a film get turned into the document we had? Just to cut to the chase of this one. We never found Henry, although we found someone claiming to be Leland. And we never found a film, even though we chased down several clues to no avail.

What Goes around Comes Around

Gus's 55th Last Round-up trip was over 500 miles. Gus told me about one of the round up recipients had been in Denmark and visited a Grundtvig Free school. There he found a tiny book of poetry by Glen Caulfield, I think that was the name. It stood out to him because on the cover it said, *Free Times Press*, Estacada, Oregon. You just don't see Estacada that far away, from well, from Estacada.

The Great Gertrude Stein Fellowship Club Fire

Whenever I couldn't find something it would come back to the great Clubhouse fire of 1979. When I look back on it, it seems so obvious. The fire had consumed whatever Jack had wanted it to consume. Even though luminaries like Space Cadet Bill the astrologer had pointed out, "Funny don't you think, the fire mostly burned your stuff and while Mercury passed underneath Jupiter." He explained the unique alignment of the planets, so long and in so much science bending detail that I forgot the more important fact. I just figured the fire was like a temptress who could change appearances to suit the fancy of an observer. The fire also burned everything belonging to Leland. Ok, but that wasn't realistic since Jack created him as a character in a novel.

Just a few months back I ran across a couple of files and documents supposedly lost in the fire, but guess what I found the stuff in Jack's archives. If fact, I wondered if there had been a fire. I was off taking photos—a wild goose chase—of a downpour of salamanders in Estacada, and when I go back the big stuff, furniture, etc., had been recycled and all my papers were in several boxes. The boxes were labeled either "mushed," or "pristine but of little value," and "pristine of some value."

Then a mystery, of course. Some of my things (documents, journals, articles) I found seemed to be forgeries or reproductions. So maybe there was a fire and jack wanted me to think there hadn't been one? And one more portentous thing. I found a copy of a contract between me and Jack; a contract I had assumed was only verbal. The first line I read was,

"If narrator is found to fabricate, outright lie, exaggerate or take part in paradiddle activity, we will burn a proportionate volume of his precious papers."

From my journal around the time of the fire

There was a suspicious fire at the warehouse a few days after my 3rd Arabian Night's session. That would have made it July, 12. Why suspicious? Well, the fire apparently started in 4 places almost simultaneously. Three of the locations were in my domain. The fire destroyed two of my Gertrude Stein scrapbooks, tape recordings of the first two Arabian nights sessions, and. The fourth location was in Leland's area. But all he lost were piles of magazines he and others saved for clipping graphics. The Fire department investigated and agreed it was arson, but gave up on the investigation after a couple of months. The primary fire inspector would have liked to shut the whole place down as a firetrap, or as he was heard saying to a police officer (who later was discovered to be the leader of an illegal subversives group in the police bureau... more on that later), that "the whole fucking commune fairy shit hole should be burned to the ground." But he couldn't do anything about it. The building after all belonged to one of Portland's most powerful families. The Fire department enforced some codes that forced substantial changes at the warehouse. In fact, some dwellers mark it as the beginning of the end. The freewheeling days were over.

To me it meant I had to reconstruct some history of the Gertrude Stein events, and my own chronicle. I was also suspicious of both Jack and Uncle Gus. While they acted innocent and had legitimate alibies —they were both out of town—and I couldn't figure why they would do it, I suspected them. Another game? If so, one that seemed more dangerous than others. The fire inspector pointed out how close the fire burned to a storage area that had cleaners and solvent. The whole warehouse could have been engulfed.

With the Fire department unwilling to further investigate, we did our own. Mr. Astrology was the lead suspect. Unlikely, he did it alone. Also, he had an alibi. He was in the hospital after having the shit kicked out of him but some Sierra Club backpackers who did not take kindly to his elaborate campground on Mt hood, that look most like an Arabian nights carnival camp, used to ensnare gay cute guys in "those perfect short pants with round boob-like knees."

---

1. Oaks Park is a small amusement park located 3.5 miles (5.6 km) south of downtown Portland, Oregon, United States. The park opened in May 1905 and is one of the oldest continually operating amusement parks in the country. The 44-acre park includes midway games, about two dozen rides that operate seasonally, a skating rink that is open all-year, and picnic grounds. It is also home to the Herschell–Spillman Noah's Ark Carousel, a historic wooden carousel constructed in 1912.

THE MANY FACES OF JACK AINSWORTH

Preamble

I fell in love with jack several times. One of the first was during an early interview when he told me how he was inspired to live the life of an invisible improvisational artist. It didn't come to him out of thin air. He was descended from generations of other like-minded artists; His father, Dr John in particular, and the members of the Random Lot. As someone said, with a deep laugh, when I told him I was writing a biography of Dr John, and in effect Jack and history of the Ainsworth family. "Right he said, so you are writing an authentic chronicle of Jack who changed history as he went along. Good luck."

I knew Jack had personas, but I did not understand how many and how extensive the subterfuge. There were at least 30 personalities I gleamed by going through his boxes. There were no instructions about what to do with the alter egos. Should we write obituaries for each one? Continue their stories? Write up an expose? Store away the ego remains in the last resting place and leave it to whoever is around 20 years from now?

By prying through Jack's journals, I figured out how he came up with the idea. He was about 10 years old. His father often took him to the main Portland Library. His father loved the public library although he also thought the library, all libraries, represented one element of the hypnotic trance the ruling class thrust on the masses. Information and stories were free, uncaged, ethereal, and it all belonged to everyone. Once it was in books and then in libraries, they could use it to further the power of the elite.

The People's library is a Crack in the cosmic Egg

One day Jack was in the natural history section of the county library trying to make sense of butterfly patterns, when he noticed an old geezer with a remarkable set of pens and tiny brushes. He was slightly hidden behind a column and had a ridiculously large piles of books on the table. He was doing something illicit. He observed everyone, especially the staff. If someone came nearby, he would make a comically melodramatic gesture like "Eureka!" and scribble in his notebook. Jack could see he was doing something to a large book. He was writing or drawing on it. He was marking up public property. Jack tried to get a closer look, but the old geezer caught his eye dead on and wouldn't let go. He felt like a fish caught by a hook. The geezer motioned to him. One of his father's golden rules of parenting was to talk to strangers, not avoid them. One of his bedtime lectures was about wandering strangers who invisibly altered history.

Jack cautiously walked over until he was behind him. The book on the desk was a beautifully illustrated guide to English gardens and conservatories. It was open to a fine illustration of magnificent lilies in the Kew Royal Botanic Gardens. The old man smiled mischievously. He smelled of alcohol and pipe tobacco, very similar to his father's. He said, "You know that game, see if you can find what is wrong with this picture?" Jack nodded. "So, see if you can."

Jack looked carefully, not sure what to look for. There was so much detail and texture. Then finally he spotted something under a giant leaf. " An elf or something, isn't it? What's it doing there?"

The man laughed loudly, drawing the attention of a librarian. The geezer's smile and laughter turned quickly to panic. He quickly gathered his pens and brushes, and put the book back on a shelf. Jack felt like he was part of a James Bond plot. As the librarian headed toward him, he whispered, "And that's how you change history. Think about it," and then scurried out the door.

Jack did think about it. Often. He went back to the library and examined the illustration. The man had replicated the illustrator's style. It might be years before it was discovered, if at all. It was surely illegal and maybe immoral. Yes, definitely immoral. But, then again, his father had often talked about how the powerful controlled history which was the ultimate power, more than money or sex or owning things. And here was this scruffy nobody in the middle of nowhere in a library among many of the thousands in the world, thinking he could change history by vandalizing a book. But what if there were others like him; and just how could this small act change history? He imagined a rich woman who loved gardening, discovering it and then telling someone who told someone else. He figured out that this book was first published at the time when fairy art was in vogue in England, so the public wanted to believe in fairies.

About the same time Jack told me about the library incident he also told me about meeting by chance a seminal collector and mentor, Harry Smith.[1] They lived in the same apartment building in Northwest Portland, in the 1950s. Curiously I found a reference to one thing Harry collected, according to his friend Allen Ginsberg; that was several years' deposits of his semen in the back of his freezer for alchemical purposes.

Salvador Dali Dead lifting rocks in the Kitchen

There is a humongous truck stop a few miles east of here. Jack and Gus were always fond of it; me not so much. Last week Gus stopped there to get gas on one of his Last Roundup Trips to drop off 25 haikus to Cindy Rukus that she wrote in high school—now 40 years ago. She had sent them to Jack over a two-year period along with wonderful, sophisticated innocent drawings.

It was a game they played by mail. She would send several poems and several drawings, and the trick was to match them. Salvador Dali was Cindy's favorite artist, which may give you some idea about the difficulty of matching writing to picture, and who she was; 15 and found Dali in a rural redneck high school—which coincidently is where my father taught for several years. While Gus was waiting in line to pay for his gas, the guy in front of him starts talking about a guy who lifted rocks as part of a talent show in Talent Oregon. He thought the funny thing was a talent in talent Oregon. Then several truckers got into a conversation about how difficult it was to lift boulders more than barbells. I knew where this was leading, more or less, since one character Jack had created in Sweet Home—near to Talent—was Don, a Ferdinand the bull kind of guy who drove around Sweet home in his broken down tan station wagon with three Japanese-Aki and huskie dogs each weighing 140 pounds plus. In a diary entry jack runs into Don and noticing he his locking his car, says, "yeah you can't be too careful." Don bug eyed, and earnestly says, yeah, I know. They might take my stereo. Shit, Jack thought. like someone would try to break into a broken-down station wagon with almost 500 pounds of flesh tearing dogs owned by guy known in town as the one who lifted boulders for his lunch break.

Passing the Word Around in a Circle

I knew jack performed this kind of improv because he told me he did. But imagine what like to research an act where the basic nature of the act is to change the meaning of a word or phrase or story as it is passed on. Gus figured out that if you passed a 6-word phrase around a circle of 25 people, you might have 150 pathways. And that is assuming they are sitting near each other in a circle. Jack's improv was maybe among 10 to hundreds of people all around the globe. Talk about random.

Gus told me about one game. "For several years I got a postcard from jack, maybe every other month. With an assignment. I loved it. Cloak and dagger stuff. I was never sure how it was supposed to add up. I still have the cards somewhere. But one might read, "With at least six people able to hear you, in 3 places, like a post office, or a restaurant—do at least one of these 25 miles from your home. Say to your friend—if you can, choose a friend who looks like a hippie..."They pushed her in her hospital bed over the side of the cliff." So, I did that one. Here's a weird thing about that (as though the whole thing wasn't). I was in one of the last Coon's Inn restaurant when I hear a guy nearby say, "the lighter fluid caught quickly on fire and just as quickly went out. Think it was because of the cedar shakes." Weird in one of the other games I played I was supposed to pass on, Wow, that was weird did anyone else see the house go up in flames as he passed the dubbie on to the next person in a circle. when I looked at the next person, in astonishment, the guy looked back. I realized he thought I was flirting. So I left. He looked like a guy that might have a knife gash scare across his chest.

I don't have quantitative evidence...well, I do have some of the original postcards. but I mean from others.

Well, not quite true. It come up in Last Roundup interactions a few times, but I was focused on other things. Oh, and he did it at the Quality Pie...you know that right. You were there a couple of times. like the one where one guy said, "Remember who used to hang out here who created a perpetual motion machine?" The other said, or what I thought he said was, "How much did Jackie pay you to say that." the first responded, "Five bucks, how about you?" When a third person madly interjected, "are you fucking serious! He only paid me a dollar," and then threw his pie on the floor and stormed out, leaving a server wondering what had just happened. Gus came out of nowhere and helped the server clean up the pie, and said, "Don't worry about it, that was Jacobin. He always does that."

But you know what the most disconcerting ones were? The stories he published that you claimed were yours, like Levitating the Pentagon, were proceeded by word-of-mouth reports. I can think of at least 4-5 times where I overhead parts of that story. One time on a bus and when the person saw me starting at them, when they said, well he told me it was part of the underground railway system, I didn't say I knew it was." And then they both flew off the bus and disappeared.

Love letter and memorabilia forgeries

World renown calligrapher Lloyd Reynolds trained Jack[2] at Reed College, the same guy that taught the genius who created the code for good typefaces for the first Apple computers.[3] Jack was interested in the artistry and then the history of typefaces, one of those under-appreciated elements of the history of the planet. Jack was skilled at calligraphy, but also able to create forgeries of almost anything. Hancock and the Declaration of Independence no problem; or someone in a nearby restaurant booth writing checks. He also extended the writing forgeries into memorabilia. I heard about but never saw an entire box he created of love letters and memorabilia celebrating a young couple's love. He followed them and when they moved; he switched out one box for another. As I understand he always did this with a kind heart—not things like hidden affairs but more like supposedly lost diaries revealing painful or beautiful sides to a person.

He did this to one of my high school girlfriends, Prudence. It was a nice sweet romance, and we had parted friends, but it was also a kind of mysterious breakup more for her than me. I couldn't explain why I wanted to break it off. I knew it was something weird, like class differences. I was off to a quality college; she had a clerking job at Nordstrom's. Apparently, it took her over a year to respond to a package Jack sent her with heartfelt reflections on my love for her and how we were star-crossed lovers. She asked me (Jack) about getting together. But I (Jack) never responded, and I didn't know about this exchange for over 20 years.

1001 Things for Free in the Mail

Gus told me that Jack's fascination with classified ads was inspired by my fascination with sending away for free things in classified ads.

"You know how you were fascinated with classified ads, the period when you sent away for anything free in magazines? Humm, how Do I know that? I guess from Arabian night sessions." He paused as though he were running through memories, although I knew he was just buying time. "nope it was from you first phone talk. "How do you know about that. I never told you, did I." Nope. well yes, off and on. but Jack had a transcript. He rummaged through a nearby box "somewhere in here." "Ah, the old paper rummage thing," I said, with ironic smile. "I know that one. I learned it from jack. I could sit here all day as you rummaged and we would then move on, but..." Gus pulled out an old reel to reel tape.

"I'm not sure Jack loved this stuff like you did. But he did after he met you, even if he wouldn't admit it. He got it from you. In those days when you were entering the Gertrude Stein days, there were a lot of classified ads everywhere. Remember, whole tabloids of nothing but classified ads, like Nicol ads. I found some stuff in the archives. Jack had kept ads he ran and their answers but I doubt it was everything. So, I conducted research. I examined the classified ads in the Oregonian, a Portland underground newspaper, several suburban weeklies. 1 paper per month for 12 months. Then just to add a random element to the mix I examined daily newspapers in Denver, Santa Fe, San Francisco, three of Jack's favorite cities. This took me several months. I found 20 suspect classified ads.

Alone Alone on a wide wide sea

Gus figures jack put messages in at least 2000 bottles into all the oceans and most of the seas of the world. But it wasn't just bottles in the ocean. He also routinely did graffiti in public bathrooms, wrote on sidewalks. We found photo documentation on one installation at the Oregon coast. A public bathroom. The original line was " you think just a coincidence that dog is god spelled backwards?" There were 25 photos taken over a 3-year period with other people's contributions like "Drunk at Dave's with sad lab Timmy," "cat spelled backward is TAC."

Jack also liked to leave to-do lists, love letters, half poems, opening lines to novels. In coffee shops, rest stops, cereal rows in grocery stores. Keep in mind that Jack often elicited others to help him, from the Gertrude Stein, surviving Random lot members, and often random people on the street. He did "rounds" this way. He handed out one liners like "Did you hear Mary had a baby but is still a virgin." Jack rarely knew where or how far these rounds went. With the Mary one he had documented after one year it had become, "Did you hear the one about the Donkey who gave birth to a cedar tree?"

Gus told me pontificating with his horseshoe pipe, that we all do it. It can be fortuitous, fluky, unintentional, intentional or inessential or essential. Yeah right, whatever that all means. Look it up in the Badger manual. how stories get passed around, like the one about lovers at lover's lane driving away with a bloody hook stuck to their car door.

Jack's Personas
Preamble

We know creating personas is a long Ainsworth family tradition. Below, I summarize some characters Jack and Dr John created. I doubt we found all of them. There is at least one instance where Dr. John created a fictional character who created a fictional character.

Mr. and Mrs. Blassner

Jack created Mr. and Mrs. Blassner as leaders in occult fiction and fact. They were publishers of The *Occult Today,* a quarterly publication that published the work of many of the best-known writers on the occult. They were also known for the costumes they wore to conferences and gatherings, most often as Siamese twins. Jack also created Al Zimmerman, a fanatic contributor to The Occult Today and other publications. He was also an employee at CERN in Switzerland, rumored to have worked on a world brain. For that work, he was shortlisted for a major scientific journal.

.   .   .

The Nome sisters, Bertha and Bella

Jack loved post cards. He created the Nome sisters who were founders of the Web-footed Post Card Collector's museum in Portland. We found one photograph of the supposed Nome sisters standing inside their museum in which all the walls, and the ceilings, and the floor were covered with postcards.

Beatrice Mumfield

Beatrice Mumfield was probably Jack's first persona since he based her on his experience in the public library when he superimposed fairies in notable botanical books. She was the distant relative of English royalty. In a confessionary tome, she admitted to altering the history of fairies in text and graphics in at least 50 libraries around the world. Jack had several folders about Beatrice, with news clippings, academic articles, biographical information, photographs, even a passport.

Larry Cliff

I told jack the story of Larry during our Arabian Night's session. Over many years he planted counterfeit news about him as he grew up and gained a reputation as a sanitary engineer—a phrase he supposedly coined.

Dr. David Finney

A British scholar who studied junk drawers for over 30 years. I found the article Jack referenced in our very first conversation, *A Cross Cultural Analysis of Junk Drawers and the role in Order*. It was just a copy of the article itself. It was reproduced with early copier technology, so it was faded. By "coincidence" on all 40 pages, the upper left corner was smeared with oil, so the journal's name was not visible.

Liverpool, England

Here's a funny one. Liverpool England conference, Civic life in an era of digital communication. Way far ahead of the times. Dr. Finney, known for analysis of junk drawers, appears on stage with Mr. Blassner to debate the question, Will the Occult Gain Footing in Digital Era? Mr. Blassner said,

> *In the future, the Mosaic will create complete mathematical versions of ourselves. Through this self-emulation, the intelligence of the swarm will be revealed. We will no longer seek knowledge through rational deductive thinking, but through plucking relevant knowledge through random encounters. It will be known as fractal knowledge, and the machines that serve us as Mosaics.*

Pretty sure Dr. Finney is Dr. John, the summary of his first presentation is verbatim from Dr. John's primary publication.

Then with Mr. Blassner he details how the occult is a way of making sense out of disorder and therefore a way of undermining the masters of capitalism.

He enlisted the owner of a Harley-Davidson Motorcycle shop, a failed thespian, to play the part of Mr. Blassner and a professor from the University of Liverpool to be Dr. Finney. The professor did it in exchange for Jack helping with an AI experiment in which a life like robot answered any question by being fed answers from computer lab at the university.

---

1. Harry Smith was born May 29, 1923, in Portland, Oregon, and his early childhood was spent in the Pacific Northwest. Harry's parents were Theosophists, who exposed him to a variety of pantheistic ideas, which persisted in his fascination with unorthodox spirituality and comparative religion and philosophy. Smith's broad range of interests resulted in several

collections. He donated the largest known paper airplane collection in the world to the Smithsonian Institution's National Air and Space Museum. He was a collector of Seminole textiles and Ukrainian Easter Eggs. He also considered himself the world's leading authority on string figures, having mastered hundreds of forms from around the world. From Harry Smith Archives.

2. Lloyd J. Reynolds was an American calligrapher and professor at Reed College who taught classes on creative writing, art, and calligraphy.

3. Charles A. Bigelow is an American type historian, professor, and designer. He received a MacArthur Fellowship in 1982. Along with Kris Holmes, he is the co-creator of Lucida and Wingdings font families. Bigelow received a BA in anthropology in Reed College and was a professor of digital typography at Stanford University from 1982 to 1995.

JACK THE IMPROV ARTIST

Preamble

Junk Drawer item stories inspired most of the stories in this section, but not the story about my great grandfather's ghost. I told Jack about the ghost, and Gary Gilmore, and my great grandfather, in the writer's bootcamps. In hindsight, I can see a pattern. Over time, Jack asked me many questions about these events. But he knew how to ask the questions, and spread them over time, so I didn't notice a pattern.

The junk drawer items. The Olympia 4 star label is the root of Ringo Starr in Ensenada, Mexico. Pushing Minnie and a Burning Bed into the Columbia River comes from the jail bail posting documents. Levitating the Pentagon photo of a girl with a flower in National Guardsman's rifle.

Here is what Gus had to say about the origins. "The stories he published that you claimed were yours, like Levitating the Pentagon, were proceeded by word of mouth reports. I can think of at least 5 times where I overhead parts of that story. One time on a bus and when the person saw me staring at them, they said, "Well he told me

it was part of the underground railway system, I didn't' say it was."
And then they both flew off the bus and disappeared."

"And of course," Gus continued, "he took off from the random
item in session #1, the receipt of your bail posting when you and Fred
were arrested in Clatsop County....to quote you from the transcript, "A
moment of pride. Like getting a letterman's jacket. I can still hear the
metal door slamming behind me and Fred Jett and I faced the social
world of a rural jail."

The Bonneville Salt Flats Time Portal

By Catalo Pazino
Shimmer, Quarterly Journal of Fine Arts[1]
Fall 1990

When I went out to get the newspaper in the morning Dave was
sitting in a lawn chair wrapped up in his sleeping bag. He looked like
a caterpillar with a beard. "You want to go to Mexico?" he said. In
those days I usually ended up with a "why not?" more than "why?" It
was simple in those days to leave. I filled up my boy scout backpack,
grabbed a sleeping bag and left a note for Kathleen, "Dave and I are
off on hitchhiking trip. Will call. Love you."

Our first ride was with a muscular guy in a Chevy with a corvette
engine who loved tailgating unsuspecting motorists and then passing
them like they were standing still. He was a born again Christian and
Jesus was looking out for him; or so he told us when we got out and
he pointed out his bald tires. Our most frightful ride, well at least
until our ride later in Utah, came at dusk outside Boise. A black
Lincoln Continental pulled over. "Brand new," the overweight guy in a
Hawaiian shirt told us." The car reeked of alcohol. The car sailed like
a catamaran. I glanced over at the speedometer. We were going
100mph. I thought of excuses to get out. Then the guy's head hit the
steering wheel. "Shit," I yelled to Dave who had fallen asleep, "the
fucker is dead." It was a four-lane straight road. I was able to push the

fatso back into the seat and steer it but his foot was heavy on the accelerator. Dave climbed out of the back seat and got down on the floor. It looked like we were having a kinky ménage à trois

With considerable effort, several swerves onto the gravel shoulder, we could push him down on the seat, leaving me just enough room to steer the boat and bring it to a stop. We left him in a gas station parking lot.

We had heard hitching a ride in Utah was difficult, so we were delighted when on the outskirts of Salt Lake City, we were picked up by a red 1950s Studebaker in mint condition. The driver was American Gothic. He didn't say much. Dave jumped for the back seat again, leaving me the responsibility of keeping up a conversation. We drove for a long time through boring suburban strip malls, following the coastline of the Great Salt Lake, with brown and white mountains further to the west. Mr. Studebaker didn't respond to my dialogue starters. His longest sentence was, "Nope, not any colder than any other year." My internal warning lights went on and off—headlines of disembowel hippies followed by rationalizations: Mr. Studebaker was John Wayne like.

We finally broke free of the city. He said, "have to pull over to take a leak." Odd place, I thought. No trees. Nothing to hide behind. In Fact, nothing. He pointed west. That's the Bonneville Salt Flats. Pointing to what looked to me like sand or ocean or lake or a flat rock. Stand on your head and it might not look any different. Definitely Escher country. I was thinking it was nice he was sharing the landscape.

Dave came to and clumsily got out of the car. "What the fuck? Where are we?" Bonneville Salt Flats, I said matter-of-factly. Mr. Studebaker pushed past Dave, grabbed our gear and threw it on the road. He opened the passenger door, and from the glove compartment pulled out a gigantic pistol. "Both of you back away from the car." Dave and I looked at each other. For real? As though he knew what we were thinking, he blasted the gun twice, once in the air and once into Dave's backpack. "What the fuck you doing?" Dave said. He said, " I Don't think you better care what you're thinking?" our

Mormon driver said. Huh? He kept the gun directed at Dave and started to get into the car, but added, "You fucking hippies, this is one place you better never come back to....oh, right and guess what it's getting up to 110 today. Only 85 now. He laughed. With that, he sped off. We both stood there watching the car until it disappeared. It took a long time for the car to disappear, which is when I realized we weren't on, or anywhere near the freeway. I couldn't remember turning off. And there was nothing. Really nothing. No buildings, no electric poles.

We constructed a make-shift tent out of our bedrolls, clothes and pieces of a road sign that had the letters E and R. It was just large enough that we could hide our bodies from the blazing sun with our feet dangling out. It was impossible to figure out the line between the earth and sky; mirage and reality. I saw houses, cars, rocks the size of skyscrapers, highways, people walking. Dave said even the unicorn he saw nearby couldn't help us.

Then I saw something moving toward us. I thought about warning Dave. Were we sitting in the middle of the freeway? It kept getting bigger; from jack rabbit, to car and then semi-truck or RV. I shook Dave to wake him. He sat up. "Shit." he said, "a VW bus." A VW bus was as good as an AAA tow truck or Good humor ice crème truck. I agreed, though if that were true then it was likely we were dead. No other reasonable explanation. Dave calmly started taking our tent down as though we had just been waiting for a greyhound bus. I knew it was just a hallucination. But it sure the hell was very real. Even the sound of the engine. The hallucination stopped right in front of us. It was an amazing mirage: A VW bus with an intricate mural: a mountain, lake and meadow and a Native American in feathered headgear. Then the engine turned off, and it was silent. The van door opened and someone came around the side toward us. Then Dave agreed it must be a hallucination. "What the fuck?" he said. Standing in front of us with the glaring sun creating an aura around her was a goddess. Long blonde hair floating in the air like a Clairol Shampoo ad. "I suppose you want a ride," she said, then bent over, pulled up her skirt. "Excuse me, but I've been holding it for miles. My name is Bonnie."

She asked us where we were going. I told her San Francisco, although that made little sense. I thought we were headed for New York, or was it Mexico? How the hell did we get here?

She opened the van door. Our mirage became even more real and fanciful. It was a living room. A small couch, a polar bear rug, refrigerator. "OK," Bonnie said, "one of you has to ride here with me. I snorted some coke awhile back but I will need a rest and besides I don't want it to feel like I'm your chauffer." Dave was already in the living room. He looked like he had just climbed out of a World War I trench. She bent over the front seat, exposing perfectly shaped tan legs and pink underwear. This really was the best hallucination I'd ever had. She opened an ornate metal box. "Most any kind of drug known to humanity." Simultaneously, both Dave and I said, "This can't be happening." She replied, "jinx, you owe me some coke." I was thinking this must be real. But why couldn't we get her to understand our state of amazement? "We might have died out there, you know. Can't thank you enough." She smiled at me, started the engine, turned to Dave, "cassettes are in the Quaker Oats box."

The first hitchhiker we picked up seemed normal and innocuous. He had a beat-up guitar case littered with souvenir labels of American cities. Although, I didn't care for his hairstyle, Chicago box top. It might be either military or prison. He was very polite, so I figured it was military. He said, kind of formally, "Thank you for picking me up. You'll find me to be good company. Really, thank you." But then it started. "what do you call a cow jumping over a barbwire fence? ... Udder destruction." Then he rolled off several 3rd grade level jokes. Bonnie and I continued to talk. He ignored us. Then I realized he was telling the first joke again, and the others followed in exactly the same sequence. And again. And again. New one on me, a pathological joke teller.

By time we got to the Nevada border, we had picked up two more hitchhikers. The first one, Frank, was a tall skinny guy with tattoos; a house painter who had left his sweetheart because she had cheated on him. The other was Bernie, a Black teenager from New York City. He told us he was on the lam, which struck the obsessive joke teller as hilarious. He kept repeating, "on the lam." Frank showed us a carving he was whittling. He said it was one of the reasons he left New York.

"You left New York because of a lamb?" Bernie asked.

Angrily, Frank said, "It's not a fucking lamb it's my 6th grade teacher." Frank looked to be about 16.

"How the fuck did you have an affair with your 6th grade teacher?" Bernie asked.

Frank held the knife close to Bernie's face, "Not when I was in 6th grade, you fuck face."

Bonnie suddenly pulled off the highway, slammed on the brakes. "OK, I want everyone to calm down. And I mean now or you'll swivel up on the salt flats like your penis after a cold shower." Everyone was quiet for a minute, then jokester started laughing hard. "Now that's funny. Really, that is really funny!"

Everyone nodded complainingly. Bonnie pulled back on the highway and I told the story about Mrs. Leach, my sixth-grade teacher.

"The thing about Emily, "Bernie told us, "that was so sexy, I kid you not... was that one of her ears was bigger than the other. That used to drive me nuts... she was white too."

"Fuck, you got to be kidding me," Dave said, "that's fucked. I mean weird ears is one thing but white? You mean like balloon bread?" Again, that struck Mr. Joke as hilarious. He laughed until he was crying.

Bonnie insisted that I sit in the front. Then for a while I drove. Everyone was good at talking, less so at listening. The bus was noisy, and the music was loud. The repertory of bad jokes continued.

At one point Frank abruptly turned off the cassette player and looked at Mr. Joke "what the fuck is it with you?" He turned to the rest of us, "I mean right, he just tells the same jokes over and over. Is he all here? The lights on, but no one home? I think you should worry about him not me."

"Huh? Did we say we were worried about him or you" Dave said.

I don't have to tell jokes," Mr. Joke said, "Did you hear about those people who ate themselves when their plane crashed in the Amazon?"

"Yeah, that's more comforting," Dave said. Frank and Bernie helped themselves to something in the drug cache.

Bonnie put her hand on my thigh, "But not you honey, OK? That's all I ask. Some pot, that's ok but nothing else." I agreed, wondering what hitchhiker handbook rules she was following.

The sun was low in western horizon and the sky was turning orange when we arrived on the outskirts of Lake Tahoe. We found a campground and collected money for dinner. Bonnie and I went to town to find a supermarket. While we stood at the meat counter trying to figure out how much hamburger we could afford, I asked her, "So I just got to know. Why did you pick us up? I mean single woman—and beautiful one at that—and you pick up 4 strangers. And all of us strange in our own ways. You know some kind of dark magic or karate?"

She put her hand on my shoulder. "Here's what I figure. I left Madison to get away from a control freak boyfriend (she had already told me this). The first night I was scared. I left my engine running all night in a rest stop between two RVs with old people in them. But then I had a flash. I'm doing this trip not to just get away from something, but to start something new. But I didn't know what. You know I wanted a sign. And you guys were it. When I pulled off to pee. You think I looked unreal; well, you did to me too. When I saw you, I thought I was hallucinating. When I saw you, I could see your aura. It was a soft purple, my color. Or that's what my I Ching reading that morning told me. *Look for your answer in something purple...* or something like that." She picked up a package of hamburger patties. "These are a little more expensive but seems like a good deal. What do you think?" I nodded vacantly. "The rest is history," she concluded.

Shit, was my thought. She was right. I could never make a move on her. And while I might not be able to fend off would be rapists, I would probably try.

At the cash register she added, "one thing I ask is that you sleep in the car with me and just you. Then with a sweet but boundary setting comment, "you in the front seat and me in the back."

That evening we had a picture-perfect campground: part leave it to Beaver, part Blade Runner. We even had s'mores. I think each person was high on a different drug. The cosmic bubble of the period of American history was shining brightly. A cast of unrelated characters who in real life would have passed by each other, but in our virtual world of hitchhiking we created a congenial world. If we hadn't all looked so wildly different someone would have thought we were a family reunion. Although our only encounter with another camper revealed our true colors. A man from a gigantic RV came by offering leftovers, and I could see in his face, as the light from the fire allowed him to look around, that our social network confused him. A homecoming queen with two derelicts, a black teenager whittling a weird provocative woman on a stick, and a mental institution escapee, me a stereotypical hippie, and Dave who looked homeless, with wide-opened eyes reflecting the fire.

We told stories of the road and laughed a lot. Bernie had figured out a way to have Mr. Joke tell just the right joke on cue. Dave told yet another version of how he had gone crazy in Vietnam. Bernie confessed that he was on the lame from a botched convenience store robbery in New York.

As the evening wore on Frank told more sexploitation stories regarding hard dicks, sluts with gigantic bazookas. Frank even made a halfhearted grab at Bonnie but fell short and almost landed in the fire pit. Bonnie seemed unconcerned.

Then people faded one by one. Frank got up to pee and never came back. Mr. Joke dozed off in place. Then Bonnie, looking at me said, "well time to hit the hay." She got up and reached out her hand and pulled me up. I stretched as though we had done this many times; yes, time for me and my lady to hit the sack. Wow, how many times could I say I was heading off with the woman that everyone else wanted to be with?

Dave, who had not been in on the earlier pledge, looked at me with surprise. This had never happened to us before. He always got a prize, and it usually left me feeding off the bottom. I threw water on the fire and followed Bonnie back to the VW. She slide open the van door and climbed in the back.

"Remember, you're in the front seat. Thank god not bucket seats," she said.

I dutifully climbed in the front. She threw me a sleeping bag and then quickly undressed. The dim dome light revealed her perfectly tan and shapely body. She undressed as though we had known each other for years. But then I realized she undressed as though we were brother and sister and ten years old. Absolutely nothing sexual. She had made the right call. I was probably the only one that was not a threat. She turned off the dome light and then asked me to tell her a story. I made up a story about Herman the worm and one of my father's magic white beaver stories.

The next day we drove across California, most of the time singing songs like *Kookaburra sits in the old gum tree* and "the ants go marching two by two," as though we were returning from summer camp. Frank and Dave left us. I visited a friend in Palo Alto, so Bonnie dropped me and Bernie outside Berkeley.

It rained. Bernie and I found refuge in an abandoned car. There had been a fire. The seats and dashboard were melted. Bernie told me more about his life in New York, living with an abusive uncle and his partner who played tricks to get food on the table. We pretended we were in a stolen car on the lam. He gave me a whittling stick I hadn't noticed he was working on. It was of a small bear in a gumdrop tree. The last thing I remember Bernie doing was yanking the steering wheel off and handing it to me, "I'm fucking tired, here you drive."

Levitating the Pentagon

Leland Johnson
Mountain Men Journal for Real Men[2]
June 1992

There were 25 buses from Ann Arbor that made the journey to the 1967 March on the Pentagon against the war in Vietnam. Our bus broke down in Beaver Falls, Pennsylvania. We were told we could wait for a replacement bus or hitch a ride. I had a ponytail, scruffy face hair, and was wearing my long gray wool coat from Goodwill. I figured the attractive girls would be the first to be picked up and I would be the last, if at all. But I was one of the first. A yellow Jaguar convertible stopped clearly in front of me.

"You look like a fur trapper or Indian fighter," said the very straight-looking man about my age. He pushed open the door. "Name's Phillip. Hope you like the Kingston trio," he shouted above the roar of the jaguar.

Great, I thought, I'm off to levitate the pentagon, stuck in the fifties.

"I'll bet you're going to the march, right?" he said as he shifted into a higher gear. I could see the speedometer teetering around 100.

"Right," I shouted, "bus broke down." That's all we said for a while.

Hang down your head, Tom Dooley....

At one point I caught him smiling at me, and thought, ah shit he's a fairy.

As one eight track tape ended, he said, "I teach at the University of Pittsburgh. I'm on my way to University of Maryland to continue my research on LSD." An undercover cop who likes the Kingston Trio? Or just a gay psychotropic drug researcher and a fur trapper from Oregon racing toward a peace demonstration in a yellow Jaguar

"Really," I said, passively, "that must be interesting work."

"I've never taken it myself, you realize. We're giving it to mental patients." I remembered reading about the research in Ramparts magazine. "You ever taken it?" he said, giving me closer scrutiny. The undercover cop scenario seemed likely now.

"No," I said, "I've thought about it but never found any."

He laughed, and pointed to a small silver suitcase in the backseat. "Well, you landed in a car with probably some of the best LSD in the world, "Right there. Ten thousand hits."

We missed Washington, D.C. and ended up on a blue highway in Virginia. Frank stopped to pee. He reappeared with an ancient looking black dude and approached the car.

"This here is Jim Jacobsen. He knows how to get to the Pentagon."

It was boiling hot, and they were both panting and sweating. He looked like a time traveler from the 19th century. All we had to do was give him a ride and he would show us a secret way into the Pentagon. Frank re-arranged things in the car, carefully moving the LSD suitcase to the trunk, and we headed off.

Along the way he kept us entertained us with stories. "A cousin of mine moved to Portland. He ended up moving next door to a serial murderer. Well, he wasn't that when my cousin moved there. I just figured it out after reading the newspaper."

We reached a tiny town and Jim had us pull into a parking lot behind an auto wrecking yard, then down a dirt road that ended at what looked like an abandoned rock quarry. Phillip parked and Jim explained how there was an abandoned rail line here. Rumor was that during the civil war period it was part of the underground used to smuggle blacks to the North. I had grave doubts on many levels. Jim himself seemed trustworthy, but an underground tunnel? Where would I end up? I imagined skeletons, rats, bats. Pitch black. Death by slime or asphyxiation by ancient poisons. Like most people I thought of it as a literally a tunnel, not a series of safe houses, maps with safe routes.

Jim led us around the base of the rock. He kept saying, "trust me. Here. Trust me. It's here." Phillip was getting antsy, and said, "Look, I'm late as it is. I better leave." He held out his hand to shake mine. "I'm leaving you in good hands, right?" Not really, but it didn't seem like there were many choices. Go with Phillip and hitchhike from somewhere else or follow this weird lead. Today I would have gone the safer way, but then I was listening for secret instructions from my karass. Before I knew it, the red Jaguar was gone, and it was just me and Jim.

I was humming to myself, "lions, tigers and bears oh my" from Wizard of Oz. Stuck in my head, but with my own words, "rats and bats and slime oh my..."

"Lordy. Lord, there it is," Jim shouted. Relief. It wasn't even a tunnel or cave as I imagined, more a gully. "If I remember right," Jim said, "it goes like this for a while, then there's a tunnel that you crawl through for a while and then a grate that will take you right where you want to go.

Then he walked away. And there I was. How the hell did I get to this point in my life? On my way to a peace march and I end up on the underground railroad. Led here by pacifists in my life: Hideo, whose family was killed in Hiroshima; Cleo who told me that every time I walked on the grass I killed insects, which haunted me as a kid; and William Stafford, Oregon's poet Laureate, who wrote of his experiences in a Conscientious Objector camp during World War II, in *Down in my Heart*.[3]

I walked for about an hour in the small gully, climbing over fallen trees and small slides. Then sure enough just as Jim had said the gully became a tunnel. It was dark but not as dark as I anticipated because there were small air vents.

Then I heard voices and the distant sound of cars. Then there was a grate above me; and something I didn't expect. I was staring right up into the crotch of a soldier. If I jumped up, I could have touched his shoe. I leaned against the wall of the storm drain wall in the shadows, trying to figure out what to do. Was I really inside the Pentagon grounds? Clearly, I couldn't go up through this grate.

I moved forward in the shadows. The tunnel got smaller but there was lighter. A light at the end of the tunnel. Finally, a literal use of that metaphor. The tunnel ended at a rotted wood frame. I pushed at it; the wood crumbled. I peeled it back and I was able to poke my head out. I was inside a hedge. I could see an open meadow, soldiers everywhere, although at quite a distance from where I was. And, a mammoth building. It was the Pentagon.

I cautiously stepped outside the hedge, staying low to the ground. Then all hell broke loose. Someone spotted me and shouted which launched dozens of soldiers in my direction.

I tried to remember my nonviolent Quaker training. Don't sit. Don't run. Hands out, palms up. Or was that with an angry dog? While some soldiers moved quickly toward me, there was also a commotion halfway across the field. There were 20-30 people with placards running and shouting. I thought they were demonstrators but something odd about the group. I couldn't quite put my finger on it and then I realized the group had no color. It was inconceivable that 20 peaceniks would all be dressed in gray and black tones. I couldn't read the signs but could see what looked like a Nazi Swastika. The soldiers headed toward me quickly changed direction and headed for the Swastika.

There was another burst of people near to where the gray flannel suit battalion had emerged. This one was more colorful. Ah, good peaceniks. They were running at full speed toward the Swastika people. Soldiers were converging from all directions. I realized that the second group was all women. Well, kind of. Maybe. As they got closer to the Nazis,[4] I could see everyone's relative size. It was like an army of Amazon women had come out of the Jungle. These were not diminutive homemakers or young college women but more like stereotypical Russian track and field athletes. I could walk out into the open and nobody seemed to notice me. I was invisible.

The Amazons grabbed the Nazi signs and the Nazis and begin battering them with the signs. The Nazis tried to fight back but were outnumbered or outweighed. So much for white male supremacy.

While I wanted to see the conclusion to this alien performance art piece, I realized it was my opportunity to make a break for it. I hurried but calmly toward the edge of the meadow. The soldiers had left gaping holes in their perimeter. I came to a small wall. A four-foot jump and I was on the street grid of DC. But without a clue about where to head; but it didn't take long to figure it out. Helicopters overhead and the heartwarming sound of *"One, two, three, four! We don't want your fucking war!"*

"Hey, hey LBJ, how many kids have you killed today?"

I turned a corner and found myself on the front line of the demonstration. We continued on to the front steps of the pentagon, close to where I had originally emerged. Someone told me the Fugs were levitating the Pentagon. It didn't seem to move, but hey anything was possible.

You know that famous photo of protestors, in particular a young woman, pushing flowers into the soldier's rifles? It was an iconic moment in our history. It was also scary as shit. I was in the front row and put a few flowers in rifles. But, do you know what's it like to be in front of a surging mass of 30,000 people. Maybe the bayonets were sheathed but it wouldn't make much difference when a mass of people were shoving you forward against a force of soldiers who had been ordered to not move. Some of us futilely tried to pass the message back to not push forward. Right, try to tell 30,000 people anything. Being short I bent down and crawled away from the front line. Although that didn't work too well because it seemed every direction, I went I ran into soldiers dispensing tear gas.

I wondered around the rest of the day and into the night trying to find my friends or anyone from Ann Arbor to no avail. I knew where the buses were to meet the following day but had nowhere to stay for the night. I walked the length of the National Mall and ended up at the Lincoln Memorial. Once again, I was invisible. I climbed over a small chain link and laid down, leaning against one of Abe's gargantuan feet. I wished I could have told Huck, my Carnie friend who loved Abraham Lincoln, how I slept on Abe's foot.

Pushing Minnie and a burning Bed into the Columbia River

Jonathan Aims
Surfing USA newsletter, Santa Barbara, California

Preamble

Gus met Charlie on one of his Last Roundup Trips. He gave him a copy of *Pushing Minnie and a Burning Bed into the Columbia River* and told him it was published in a low budget surfer newsletter out of Santa Barbara.

"And of course," Gus continued, "he took off from the random item in session #1, the receipt of your bail posting when you and Fred were arrested in Clatsop County....to quote you from the transcript, " A moment of pride. Like getting a letterman's jacket. I can still hear the metal door slamming behind me and Fred Jett and we faced the social world or a rural jail and watched as a kid who didn't look old enough to be in jail—rather the JD, was forced to masturbate in front of all of us while he was punched. We all had to punch him and share his fate. Why? Because he has struck his mother. And well there's a line you know. They did it in our cell and we had to clean up the combination of jizz and blood."

It was the early 1960s and Beach Riots were held every September in Seaside, Oregon's honky-tonk sea resort. We were able to score five fifths of Johnny Walker Red through a retired alcoholic rodeo clown who was helping my dad clean up the Shire after a disastrous wind storm. I had a 53 Oldsmobile. When you down shifted, it sounded like Robert Mitchum's car in the moonshine movie, Thunder Road. We started out with four of us, Fred, Dave, Jimmy, and myself. We went to Astoria, just north of Seaside, where we were going to stay overnight in an abandoned nursing home that belonged to Fred's grandmother, that was on a bluff overlooking the Columbia River.

We rolled into Astoria, rolled down our windows, rolled up our sleeves, and hung our arms out the window to show off our biceps, and sang thunder road. Nobody seemed to pay much attention to us. The nursing home was at the end of dead-end road. Fred couldn't remember where it was, so it was dark by the time we got there. We stayed up late drinking Johnny Walker. Fred entertained us with stories about ghosts who haunted the nursing home. The most notable one was about Minnie, his grandmother, who ran the nursing home. She had been jilted by a lover, so she kidnapped him and tied him to a bed ("right here in this very room"). She was going to light the bed on fire and shove him out onto a balcony and over the cliff, but someone had alerted the police who surrounded the nursing home. Minnie lit the bed on fire but as she went to shove her lover and the bed over the cliff her leg got tangled in sheets and she got dragged with him.

Someone must have heard us and reported us to the police. We cleared out and ended up sleeping the rest of the night on a beach just north of Seaside. It was probably 4am by the time we got there. I tried to sleep, but it was difficult. All we had were moldy blankets from the nursing home. When I finally gave up sleeping Fred was already or still drinking. When we spotted a helicopter overhead, Fred lifted a bottle of the Johnny Walker and saluted them with a, "Fuckin A!" I couldn't resist. I started in on the Johnny Walker. By time we packed it in and get to the beach riot, we were three sheets to the wind. In the parking lot, two cop cars were waiting for us. Fred was good at talking his way into and out of things. Probably for the same reason he had a nearly 100 percent batting average for getting chicks to give him their phone number—another reason I liked to hang out with him. The police let us go when Fred made up a story about us visiting his aunt who lived in Seaside and needed her medicine.

We tried to make it into Seaside on small back roads just in case they were lurking around. We were almost there when a cop car parked on a side street spotted us, turned on his flasher and siren, and began pursuit. I kept driving, waiting for Fred to come up with a plan. "Fuck if I know" is all he could say. I kept moving. "Yeah," Fred said, "fuckin A, give them a run for their money." The world was a blur, adrenalin cursing through my body, I floored it. Life on the edge, eluding police in a VW bug. The next thing I remember is we were behind bars and some guy scary looking guy was staring me close up and said, you fucking almost hit the mayor's wife.

First time for me in jail, third or fourth for Fred. Immediately, a short guy wearing a white apron greeted us, "Name's Buzz and if there's anything you need you know who to come to."

"Fuckin lying brown nosing fuckface is who you are," a mean-looking guy with deep acne scars, said. Turning to us, he said, "what he means to say is he has special privileges because he spends more time here then at home. Just a lousy drunk and wife beater." Buzz headed toward a buzzer by the door. "What... you want me to hit it?" he said defiantly. "Do whatever the fuck you want. Someday both you and I are going to be out there at the same time." It was a pretty awful night. Guys puking. Some teenage kid with thick glasses in for hitting his mother or grandmother, which didn't go well with the inmate morals.

Two weeks later, my uncle drove me back to the Clatsop County Courthouse to hear my sentencing. My uncle hardly said anything to me about my arrest. It was like we were going on a vacation. He had a black Mercedes Benz. He had removed the back seat and torn out the wall to the trunk so he could use it as pick-up truck. There was also a horrible stench coming from the trunk. I peeked. It was a black salmon, rotting, covered with maggots.

I thought it was really nice that for the trip to the coast he had installed a lawn chair to replace the back seat. There was a rubber cord lying on the lawn chair. A poor man's seatbelt, my uncle explained. I slept off and on. At one point I woke up and couldn't see his head. He was bent over rummaging through a pile of maps and we were hurdling toward a car coming the other direction. "Walt," I yelled, "this is a two-lane road!" He swerved just in time back into his lane.

Ringo Starr Turns up in Ensenada, Mexico

Jack Ainsworth
Indigo and Chartreuse
San Diego State College student literary journal
January 1989

At the end of my junior year in college, I came down with mono. The mono was like a stalled storm front in a valley. Every day I woke up feeling the same. Then my friend Rolodex—called that because he had many friends but couldn't remember anyone's name—invited me to Hollywood. He smoked a prodigious amount of weed. He lived with his father. He stashed his weed in his father's freezer inside fake frozen dinner trays. We had talked about taking a road trip to New York City so he could show me his hipster friends, a term he noted was older than beatnik or hippie.

I didn't see how I could muster strength to drive a car which at the time was an ugly but totally reliable 1958 pink Chevy Belair I called the pink turd. I woke up the next morning and felt exactly as I had the morning before, and decided, in that way you can only do when you are young, that a road trip was exactly what would cure me. By the time I got to Eugene, the plan seemed to be working. I felt achy, but not sleepy. Jazzed to be on the road. I drove on.

There is a plateau when you enter California, near the town of Weed, the heart of the Klamath Swirl.[5] It is the epitome of nowhere. I have a fondness for the place. When I was in college, on one of many spontaneous road trips to San Francisco; it was after-all the city and the center of the known universe; I took one of the best pees in my life. I leaned against a snarly dead madrone. The pee was long and satisfying, but I realized no one knew where I was. That is, my parents didn't know. I was on my own. I knew also that I had my entire life ahead of me. When I climbed back into the car, I told my car mates about my insight and called upon us to swear allegiance to a higher cause. Even if we don't know what the fuck, we are doing we should pretend we do." Well, I don't know about that someone said, but there are some foxy Haight Ashbury chicks and good drugs." Someone else added, "If the Knights of the roundtable were around today, they'd be getting magic potions from Owsley, not Merlin."

Rolodex's bungalow was a classic crash pad. I was never sure who lived there and who was visiting or who knew who. The bathroom was special. It was entirely wallpapered with aluminum foil. Which was cool, but also it looked out on a Universal Studios parking lot. One of the unwritten rules was that you should sit there long enough until you saw someone famous. I didn't have to wait long. The first time I sat, I saw Dick Clark arrive. Sitting on the throne I shouted out, "I'd give it a 90 for dancing to." He glanced around. I doubt you could see into the bathroom, although you might see reflected light from the aluminum foil through the palm leaves.

A couple of days after I arrived, we went on an expedition to Venice beach; a week long party at one of Rolodex's cousin's house. I ended up being the designated driver because everyone in the house had taken LSD for breakfast.

My Hunter Thompson moment on a freeway. From the back-seat Rolodex yelled, exit. Next exit. I looked ahead to 3 possibilities. Fuck which one. I shouted, but all I heard was the guy with Spock Ears say, "What I'm saying is I am sure he robbed the bank. He is wanted, but what I meant is I don't know if they know who he is. If they did, then they would want him. See what I mean. They don't know him they're looking for." They were talking about Jessie, who slept in my room with a gun under his pillow. I heard Rolodex say louder, just take an exit, it doesn't matter which one. Shit, since when does it not matter what exit. But LA, maybe it doesn't. Then I realized the guy with a premature gray beard they called the original space cadet was whispering to me, "Is it coming on yet?" "What the fuck you talking about I shouted. Rolodex answered me. "What he means is, is the acid you took in the Jell-O coming on yet?" I screamed, what the fuck you talking about," as I exited. The ramp swept out over the city. I could see the ocean and multiple levels of freeways filled with cars in all directions. "Wow," the space cadet said, "I never get tired of this view. It takes my breath way." It didn't feel like I was driving, more like we were on a carnival ride. It even seemed that everyone was leaning into the curve—and we had to or the car would tip over—as we descended the exit to the grid of Venice Beach. "What the fuck you talking about," I shouted, glimpsing Rolodex in the rear-view mirror. "The Jell-O," He repeated, "I can see the ocean," someone said. "remember that game as a kid. First one to see the ocean gets a free snow cone, or gets laid or something."

Didn't anyone care that they were being driven by someone on LSD? I was trying to focus on the road while checking my ego and doors of perception. I had never had LSD, so I wasn't sure what to expect. I turned to the space cadet in the passenger seat, which freaked me out since it was Rolodex. "How the fuck did you get there?" I said, amazed by my graceful stop at a traffic signal. "The challenger has landed," Rolodex said. He put his hand on my forehead, "Not to worry, we were just kidding you. Learn to trust your internal robot."

A couple of days later, Rolodex and I hopped into the pink turd to go to Mexico; in theory, a test run for our larger trip to New York. Tijuana seemed too fanatic, so we drove on to Ensenada. The plan was to get a reasonable hotel room with a view of the ocean but we first stopped at a bar which was followed by another and then another. By time we got to our fourth bar we ran into people we knew. During this period in my life, I could drink a lot. We interspersed margaritas with potato chips and pork rinds. At this bar a guy came up to us with three Mexican women who looked like they might be anywhere from 13 to 30 years old. "I told you I would find women for you," he said. I didn't remember his pledge, and it was hard to hit the recall button because one of the dark-skinned Lolita had her hand down my pants. Hey, the guy shouted, drinks are on Santa Claus (Rolodex) and Ringo Starr (me).

I think when we came into this last bar; I had $200. Rolodex probably had another $100. I think somewhere along the way I learned how to speak Spanish, either that or I was speaking Japanese. Either way, the girls seemed to understand me.

I vaguely remember going to the bathroom to vomit and then being carried to a booth. The next thing I knew, it was morning. One of the girls was in the booth with me. Close up she looked like Sharon, a girl I had a crush on in 4th grade. Maybe it was because I had to pee badly. I had lost all possibility of making it with Sharon in 4th grade when I had shot out of my seat when I saw a puddle appear around my shoes, and yelled, "someone peed on my shoe." It was Sharon's. Then Rolodex was shaking me and dragged me to my feet. We gotta get the hell out of here. We may owe someone for sleeping with the girls. Well, I don't know about you, but I don't think I did anything with Chiquita here." She hadn't stirred, and I had a flash that maybe she was dead. We first got into the wrong car. What's the odds of there being two pink 58 Chevy? We drove in silence to the border. I was hung over but, in a crystal, clear way. Life was good. I wondered out loud, So Rollo, you know sometimes I wonder if I like this part of drinking the best. You know when there is no headache and it just feels like the world is floating along harmlessly. It just feels like nothing can harm me. Well, he said, "I hope you're right since we're at the border and I can't remember if I left the sinsemilla bud and vial of cocaine at home or not." I made a promise to God. If he would just let us pass through the border, I would try to do something with my life.

My Great Grandfather's Ghost and Another Serial Murderer

A Story based on my story told to Jack during an Arabian Nights' Session and a local newspaper article written long after the event.

I only figured out the role Jack had in this story by chance—yes of course maybe there is no such thing. I had been trying to figure out more about my family tree, prompted by the many questions Jack and Gus had asked me about my tree that I could not answer. I agreed with them when they told me family histories were often just believed with little evidence. Stories got passed along generation after generation. I went to the pioneer cemetery where some of my family is buried. I knew how to find the spot because there was a gigantic sequoia and a small angel stature, dedicated to I suppose my great great aunt who died when she was four. When I approached our plot, I noted there were three people there taking pictures of my family's plot. At first, I figured it was photographers. It was a pleasant site in the Macabre way of cemeteries but then I heard one of them say, "OK, so it says Tideman Johnson on the tombstone that means nothing." He was holding a photo. I know this is the guy I saw. I mean the ghost."

A natty young lawyer looking kind of guy, in pin-striped shirt—like seeing a dreadlock hippie showing up at Daughters of the American Revolution picnic in Topeka—entered my office holding a pack of papers and without an introduction, read to me the following. No introduction. Just launched.

"Don't you think it is rather eerie to read about your life in a book by someone who grew up to write for *Rolling Stone* magazine, author of *Shot in the Heart*, Mikal Gilmore. He describes the far east boundary of the shire we fought over, Across the street lay the train tracks that carried the aging trolley between downtown Portland and Clackamas County's Oregon City. Just past the tracks ran Johnson Creek—in those days, a decent place for swimming and catching crawfish—and beyond that there was a large densely wooded area. It was rumored that teenagers gathered at nights in those woods and drank and had sex in hard-to find groves. It was also rumored that a gruesome murder had taken place there years before, and that some of the body parts from the crime had never been recovered and still lay buried somewhere among the trees. And he hits the nail on the head describing the contested zone, "Up the hill behind our house was a neighborhood known locally as Shack town, where laborer's families dwelled. Drive a few blocks past that and you would hit the old moneyed district of Eastmoreland, where you could find the state's most prestigious school, Reed College. If you were to draw two concentric circles on a map—the outer ring, a loop of wealth; thinner one, a wheel of privation—then our home on Johnson Creek Boulevard would lie at the core point of those circles. A null heart, in the inner ring of the city's worst back country."

Maybe that is more painfully true than weird, but then Uncle Gus even though he denied it, slide a newspaper article under the Red Storage shed door one day, just when I was putting the finishing touches on this manuscript and preparing to close up the Red shed, that described how my great grandfather was haunting the woods, Mikal describes. The woods have a name, my great grandfather's, Tideman Johnson Natural Park. He died in 1913.

So anyway, this guy, Jacobsen, reported seeing Tideman's ghost in the woods and neighborhood. According to Jacobsen, my great grandfather broke into people's garage and made loud noises, especially when there was a family fight. He was a spook counselor. Then there're the bones. In the neighborhood adjoining Tideman Johnson Natural, Jacobsen's mother was picking out big "glacial stones" in her garden and every time she hit one, she hallucinated the rock was a bearded man's head. This freaked her out and ruined her gardening experience. The bearded man was the same man Jacobsen encountered.

They reported Tideman to be a kind of spaced out, like a new age hippie that didn't quite get enough of his past life regression workshop materials read before he died.

"You, know," Jacobsen said, "I got this feeling from him, you know, like he was just cruising, just sort of there, taking it all in."

The other thing is that he started showing up in the neighborhood wherever there were family disputes. He scares the shit out of the aggressor who runs back into the house for make-up sex. Apparently, he also likes kids. Jacobsen's six-year-old daughter ran into him and just called him the funny old man. They decided if they could bury him, his bones, the right way—following a makeshift ritual obtained through the Tibetan Book of the Dead—then Tideman would might wander off.

Now imagine the story of Gary Gilmore and this, Jacobsen moved here from Virginia with his mother and younger brother, on the run from their serial-killer dad. Talk about bad karma. His family ends up moving to this urban wilderness in Portland, the breeding ground for Gary Gilmore. What's the odds of that? So, Jacobsen and his friends perform the ritual and bury the bones deep.

And here's the part that gets to me a little, if it's true. It worked. They didn't see him after that.

All this leaves me a little unsettled. Like why didn't Tideman visit me? I'm still around in the shire. And these dudes re-buried him. What does that do to his karma wheel?

---

1. I found a *Shimmer* Magazine that published between 2005 and 2018. It was referred to as a journal of speculative fiction.
2. There is a *Mountain Men Journal*, but not "for real men." The current editors were adamant they had not, would not, ever and forever, publish anything like the Pentagon story.
3. *Down in my Heart*. From 1942 to 1945, William Stafford was interned in camps for conscientious objectors for his refusal to be inducted into the U.S. Army. The book is a memoir of those years. Google Books. Originally published: 1947.
4. On Oct. 21, 1967, demonstrators began filling the Mall midmorning. Speakers included writer Norman Mailer, poet Robert Lowell, pediatrician Benjamin Spock, and Clive Jenkins of the British Labour Party, whose remarks were interrupted when a member of the American Nazi Party tried to punch him at the podium. *Washington Post*, Oct. 19, 2017.
5. David Rains Wallace is an American writer who has published over twenty books on conservation and natural history, including The Monkey's Bridge (a 1997 New York Times Notable Book) and The Klamath Knot (1984 Burroughs Medal).

DOING THE RIGHT THING

Preamble

After I read "Rage, Rage Against the Ordinary," for the fourth time I fully understood the expression, "he laughed until he cried; he cried until he laughed." Add some anger and disbelieve. I could have written the stories, right? I knew what it must be like for a celebrity with a ghostwriter. It was my story. It was my life. All jack had done was complete some sentences, put it in a proper order. I knew that wasn't true too. I tried it. I sat down with the journals and tried to write another version. After an entire afternoon and evening I realized I was lacking perspective, style, order.

Rage, Rage against the Ordinary

Even though Kathleen and I had separated, we talked almost every night on the phone. We went on dates, showed up at people's parties. Most people probably figured we were still living together. The pain in Kathleen's shoulder didn't go away. Over several months she had an array of tests. Her primary physician, founding member of the local Physicians for Social Responsibility, either fell in love with

Kathleen or adopted her as a daughter which sometimes helped and sometimes hindered the quality of care. He recommended exploratory surgery with the assumption that it might be a pinched nerve. We all figured her pain, swelling, and decreased ability to use her arm had come from her fall on the ice after our argument.

I took Kathleen to the hospital the day of her operation. The surgery took longer than we expected. The doctor came out and with his surgical mask dangling around his neck told me that the pain in her shoulder was from a malignant growth in a lymph gland. A very aggressive form of cancer. It was a movie but with no music sound track. I distinctly remember the sound of coins in a vending machine and then the sound of a Milky Way candy bar descending from the Shute. And while the Doctor continued his pronouncement of most likely death, I wondered if the person had put in exact change. How much were Milky way bars these days?

In the movie script, I would have asked him how long she had to live. But, I stared at a mole that moved up and down with his Adam's apple (and had time to wonder again if that meant women had an eve's apple). As he tried to move gracefully away, I was imagining asking Leland about boxes so I could move to Michael and Linda's. It was the right thing to do. I wondered if we should sleep in the same bed and noticed that the doctor was now down the hall, and like in a movie, he was signing something on a clipboard. It was hard to tell if I didn't believe him or just blindly accepted the verdict. I wanted to tell him how she had stopped breathing as a small child and almost died. She had wondered often if she was never meant to be here. But then he was in front of me again and he was shorter. He told me to not believe in that new age babble about unorthodox cures. But that was only imagined. *He* was a nurse, and *he* was telling me that Kathleen was still out of it and she had not been told about it. "It?" What was it? Her impending death? But imagined or not, why would he feel the compulsion to tell me that?

I moved out of the mutant home and into Michael and Linda's. We had two rooms but slept together at night. For Kathleen's cancer the only procedures were warlike radiation therapy, a localized agent orange or radical surgery. Remove her arm and entire shoulder.

Week after week I went with her to radiation therapy. I would sit in a waiting room trying to mask out the painful stories around me. Wives and husbands, sons and daughters, all with similar stories. Patients would come into the waiting room grimacing in pain and leave grimacing with another kind of pain. People I saw week after week would just stop coming; as though a mysterious Alien were whisking them away.

The radiation therapy seemed much worse than the cancer. Her right arm filled with fluid. Enlarged and tight, her arm reminded me of crawfish I would catch as a kid with one gigantic pincher. We struggled with a battery of pain medicine, trying to find a compromise between sedation and stupidity and wakefulness and pain.

I knew the right thing to do was stay with her no matter what. Even though the wonder and romance of our relation had ebbed, it didn't really matter. She needed me.

She also had unfaltering support from Mike and Linda and their two small girls. The home was so normal. We had dinners together, often with guests. We had birthdays and homey traditions like canning fruit, baking cookies. The girls, Annie and Jessica, 4 and 6 years old, had all the time in the world. To them a tragedy was having ice crème fall from a cone to the ground. But they always got a new scoop. Neither Kathleen nor I had imagined ourselves as parents, but Annie and Jessica treated us as though we were an aunt and uncle.

Some nights Kathleen's pain was so great she would go to the partially finished attic space where she could writhe in pain until the pain medicine would kick in. I might find her there on the edge of sleep but on a razor blade of pain, holding on to Annie's security blanket she had given her when she was told why she cried a lot. She mastered a groan that vibrated her entire body. She transferred the pain to me if we embraced.

We had our most poignant talks just as the pain meds would kick in. I came up one night and she was softly crying, "I don't know if I can go on," she told me calmly, "what's the point?" I asked myself the same question every day, not for myself but for her, and every day I had different answers or none or more questions. "Well, the point is," I said, as I petted the security blanket, "to either do battle and win or to know why you are here or why this happened to you." She looked confused and somewhat angry. "What difference does it matter why it happened to me? the chosen one? Random? that I sinned? If I am dead will it matter?"

My answers were too intellectual for her. She was brighter than me. A straight-A student forever, and not just a good student that knew how to play the game. She was creative and original, although too shy to shine in the classroom. She could memorize a poem and tell you in a nutshell what else the poet was trying to tell us. But I had more patience to wind through mazes of intellectual chicken wire. I liked the chase. I wanted the foreplay to last forever; Kathleen would rather get to the point. The immediacy of her illness, pain, and ultimate demise had magnified her impatience with tangled arguments. I felt some of that myself. Words didn't cut it. Thinking about it just created more mazes.

"Well," I said, "if it were me, I would rage against the dying of the light."

"That's you" she said, I don't want to rage. I just want a normal life."

A part of me understood that. I could accept it as a legitimate strategy. The ordinary was a reminder that as George Harrison said, life goes on within us or without us. In that context canning preserves, or washing the dishes, was a sacred act.

"I guess from my rage I would find the courage to either do battle or to live my remaining days with force." I paused. She was now in fully medicated state and near to sleep. I continued, "I suppose it might look like I was living an ordinary life but it would be like I had been given permission to ask for the truth and expect people to not waste my time...which is probably what we should ask of people, anyway." I turned to her. "Doesn't it seem like you should be able to demand that every moment is a peak experience?"

Saying it out loud, confused me for a minute. Isn't that why I had taken LSD for months? But I wasn't in pain when that happened. Just past the sunny alpine meadow there was a dark forest, death, that you knew gave life to the meadow. The bad trip, unless it was some unscrupulous dealer giving you junk drugs, was getting lost in the forest. I suppose I thought dying should be one gigantic acid trip.

I wanted to take it back. She was in pain and dying, and I was telling her she had to live up to the gift God had given her. Some gift. Shit. I wanted badly to change the subject, to tell her whatever she chooses to do I would love and support her. I felt like a disappointed parent when their child brought home a C on their report card. Fortunately, she was falling asleep, so I spooned up next to her, avoiding her bloated arm, and hugged her tightly. I was crying but was able to say, "Whatever you do will be right." Even though I wasn't sure I meant it.

It became harder and harder for me to escape this other side of reality. The normalcy, while enjoyable and comforting, was festering inside me. I had reoccurring flights of fancy in which I would throw fresh baked zucchini bread through a window or tell the kids on their birthday they were going to die too. I felt like I was the only crazy one in a house of perfectly reasonable people. Another movie set. I was a zombie in an episode of "Leave it to Beaver." [9]

We didn't sit idly by. When the Tumor Board (a legion of doctors who reviewed cancer cases like a parole board reviewing Charlie Manson cases) reviewed the lack of progress through radiation therapy and recommended the radical surgery option. We rejected it. We tried alternatives. There was mega-vitamin therapy, which we heard about indirectly through the basketball player, Bill Walton. This regime meant Kathleen would take fistfuls of pills several times a day. We stealthily imported laetrile from Tijuana. Kathleen received acupuncture treatment, still "outlawed" by the medical establishment. When her primary doctor found out about it, he attempted to have that doctor excommunicated through the Medical Examiner's board.

We had another attic session. This time Kathleen confronted me with a declaration. I needed to accept the path she had chosen or leave. She wanted me to stay. She needed me. I was the only deep love she had experienced in her life. But I was undermining her choices. She told me that my rage and my insistence that she do something wasn't helping. She wanted the normal life and maybe it was hiding from the ugly truth, but the other way, my way of looking at the world and her disease was scary. She needed me to accept the inevitable. She was dying, and she chose to live with good friends and watch the girls grow up and plant a garden and can fruit and read books.

What brought her joy was Toby, the corgi, a stray dog who had just wondered into the kitchen one day sniffled Kathleen's leg and fell asleep on her foot. And now he never left her side. That to Kathleen was divine intervention. It was the kitchen, more than any other room that represented life to Kathleen. A time lapse of a day would reveal food being cooked, dirty dishes appearing and then being cleared. The smell of breakfast food displaced by lunch and dinner food. Neighbors who stopped by with flowers, giant zucchinis, and the most recent cancer cures.

We looked at each other for a long time. I knew my answer had to be sincere. If I stayed could I get fully behind her choices? It wouldn't work if I just politely accepted the judgement. I could obviously say yes or no. But instead of yes or no, I asked her what kind of God she believed in.

"Isn't it pantheism or something like that?"

She looked at me hurt and dismayed, but reluctantly replied, "I suppose Native American. Which is a kind of pantheism." She turned away from me, and with some anger said, "But what good does it do to figure this out. You're so intellectual. I just want to know that you are there for me no matter what choices I make. The choice I make is to live here together as a family. Can't you just say yes or no?"

She was skipping my thought about Pantheism and I didn't even know where I was headed with it. I dropped it. And choking back tears, I said, "I will do the best I can". More tears, "I just don't know if I can do it." I imagined my life in the coming months. I would drink or get stoned more. I would make up excuses to go away now and then.

Over the weeks following, I fell back on my word repeatedly. I drank more, although everyone else did too. I smoked pot and scored cocaine occasionally so I could feel like Superman. We continued our meltdowns in the attic. To the rest of the world, she was a trooper. Occasionally she would wipe back tears at dinner when the pain was great and run to our room and come back with bloodshot eyes. But our verbal contract stated that when we were alone, she could scream in pain and talk about the unfairness, angst and dread, blackness and terror. And my part was not to solve the problem, but just hug and comfort her. For the most part I accepted this; it was a reasonable contract. But it took its toil; like knowing someone had a secret lover or an undercover identity. Occasionally during her melt downs, I could sneak in spiritual thinking. I brought home Native American books like Castaneda's tales of Don Juan, which we read together. I was building up to courage to tell her I should move out when something extraordinary happened.

I was building up to courage to tell Kathleen I should move out, when something extraordinary happened. Kathleen had held on to a volunteer job during her illness, editing an environmental magazine. The group held an annual retreat in various wild places in Oregon. That year they went to a small Inn near the Malheur wildlife refuge. From Kathleen's perspective, not much happened on the trip. It was beautiful, and she was pleased that she had found a balance with her pain medicine that allowed her to be in the wild.

A week after she got back, a stranger called her. As she later reported it, he tried to reassure her over and over that he wasn't stalking her. This man, Roger, had seen her at the wildlife refuge as she came out of an outdoor bathroom. She remembered him, vaguely. They had smiled and said hello. She remembered seeing him climb on a Harley with several other bikers. A small, harmless looking motorcycle gang. She remembered thinking, now there's a world foreign to me. She almost hung up. But it was the silence that kept her on the phone. He said nothing. She could hear the sounds of nothing in his background. He could probably hear the twins in her background. But she was curious too. After all, he had gone to the trouble of finding her which he explained hadn't been easy and only possible because his ex-wife, a nurse, and member of Kathleen's environmental organization knew about the group's retreat, and showed Roger a copy of the group's newsletter with a photo of Kathleen. And through some more detective work, he had gotten our phone number. check repeat some?

She finally broke the silence. "How did you find me?"

He explained it was because one of the women in her group was his ex-wife's sister. She had shown him a picture of Kathleen in the environmental journal. He had then called the environmental organization and pretended he knew something about a secret logging contract for Opal Creek wilderness area. Clever choice since that was one of Kathleen's most passionate concerns.

She agreed to meet with him only if he would come to our house. The day he came over, I remember, was very clear and Mt. Hood in the distance was very white. It was spring and there had been little melt down. When Marry and I both exclaimed about how pretty the mountain was, Maya I think for the first time could see the mountain. Until then she had not understood that it was huge but far away; instead of small (like one of many houses) and nearby. While Kathleen's life was disappearing, hers was expanding.

We were all home that day, both curious and guarded. More the later when he arrived on his Harley, looking very much like a gang member. It seemed strange to see a dusty Harley in the driveway next to our two Volvos.

They sat on the enclosed glass porch looking at the Mountain. He struck her as an odd combination; part Harley, part hippie, but kinder than she had imagined. She was nervous but not freaked.

After a few pleasantries he said, "Do you know who Don Juan is?"

She stared at him and as she told me later, something opened up inside her. Because we had both been reading a book, the Crack in the Cosmic Egg, she used that as a metaphor. They talked for several hours that day. She provided a cursory summary to the family and then later in bed she tried to express a deeper sense of the encounter.

I was mystified and disturbed. I was in wonder at the coincidence, but dumbfounded. How could the messenger come in beat up dusty leathers on a Harley? Just how far did God expect us to stretch to find salvation clues? Was it a scam? Was he just stalking her? Even though she was disabled, she was still radiant. How did the universe work? A gazillion actions and reactions, decision or lack of decisions, and your life goes one way and not another. Nature just culls two people in the middle of nowhere, so they meet? And he just happens to be following Native American spiritual practices?

Although I didn't fell certainty, I expressed it. "In our safe attic space," she asked me, "Do I follow these weird marching orders? Is this a karass or a granfalloon?" There was a long pause and I could feel her staring at me. I knew whatever I said she would run with it as though I were a parent giving her permission to go to summer camp.

I said, "You have to follow it."

On the side, I did some sleuthing. I enlisted the best private detective I knew, Jack Ainsworth. When I told him the story, I expected he might ask me troubling questions reflecting my own doubts, but he replied he would see what he could find out.

We found out where Roger lived, a barge on Summer Lake in Southern Oregon, that he had no police record, had not finished high school although teachers had good things to say about him. His art teacher said he had talent working with metal and wood. He liked to find things along highways and turn them in art. She laughed remembering one he called the Duckbill Platypus which was a duck with a bill that looked like a plate and there was a white cat, made from animal skins, sipping milk. He had dropped out to take care of his mother and a sister when their father had committed suicide. He was a reasonably skilled carpenter. And yes, there was a small motorcycle gang. But hardly a dangerous crew. They were known in the Summer Lake area, but not for anything horrendous. The gang was really three friends and Roger's brother. And yes, they were interested in Native American religion. They hosted sweat lodges and an informal group that read the books of Don Juan. It was a little hard to imagine, but the group met at the Paisley Public library. A librarian informant told Jack he thought they were no-goods but as

Jack added she was a member of the local Lions Club auxiliary and had a love or leave it bumper sticker and thought Native Americans were communists.

They continued to get together, most often at our home. Then one day he proposed they drive to Summer Lake. It seemed strange that day to see Kathleen with her long blonde hair pouring out of motorcycle helmet. I felt like a parent watching their only child leave with a cult leader, or with the leader of the pack. They spent a week on the barge in Summer Lake, and when she returned, she had decided to move there.

The Importance of the Ordinary

This isn't technically my story. But, since I originally read it 20 years ago, I haven't re-read it. I may have changed it. It is from Antoine de Saint Exupery's *Wind, Sand, and Stars*. He wrote *The Little Prince*, the best children's story of all time. My mother read *it to me* when I was a kid. When I read it again in my twenties to Kathleen, I understood it in another way.

I tell the story from *Wind Sand and Stars* when I am trying to remind myself or others why the ordinary is important. It is near the other life equation I often wrestle with: is life mostly pain with occasional stabs of beauty, or is it mostly beauty with occasional stabs of pain.

The book is an account of Saint Exupery's adventures flying mail routes across the Sahara and Andes. On one harrowing flight off the coast of Spain, he becomes lost in thick clouds. He has no sense of direction. For all he knows, he may be going away from the continent out over the vast Atlantic Ocean. At one point he is so disoriented that he has the sensation he is flying away from the earth, into outer space. With only the drone of the engine surrounded by clouds, he loses a sense of time and experiences a complete sense of calm. It doesn't matter. He will fly until he runs out of fuel and descends into oblivion.

Then miraculously he sees lights and the coastline. Still with a sense of sublime indifference, he realizes it is the town he was headed for. His radio, which had stopped working, comes on and he is able to get instructions for landing. He lands the plane and then walks a short distance to the café he often frequented. He wonders briefly why he is not more thankful or even exuberant about landing safely. He orders coffee. He takes a sip of the very hot and bitter coffee and burns his tongue. With the taste of bitter coffee and the burning sensation on his tongue, he suddenly weeps, thankful to be alive.

Creating the Sequel

I replayed the movie of Kathleen and Roger taking off on his Harley many times; and I edited the versions so often it was hard to remember which was the truth. There goes my wife (still odd to me to say I had a wife even while I lost her), on the back of a Harley, with someone (Roger) who had a vague similarity to Charlie Manson, but who was a serious follower of Castaneda's Don Juan.

One time Roger came with two of his friends, part of his motorcycle gang. When they took off from our quiet Portland neighborhood, it sounded like the beginning or end of a "Born to Be Wild" movie. That was Kathleen, the woman who had grown up in Palo Alto with Joan Baez,[1] a straight-A student dubbed Bridget Bardot in college. She was on her way to a secret enclave near Ft Rock, not that far from where she was born, the way a crow would fly. But her karma yarn might have only gone as far as Stanford, where she had been accepted and had an affair with a professor while she was still in high school. I thought about sending a photo of her on the Harley to the high school alumni association: *Kathleen Kellogg on her way to Native American spiritual encampment run by motorcycle gang, in her second year of lymphoma cancer.*

The old Kathleen listened to Bob Dylan and Joan Baez; the new Kathleen, Hotel California and Margaretville. What would you find in her junk drawer to reconstruct her life? Well, not a drawer, but could you deduct her story by what she left behind?

The tattered copy of *A Separate Reality*

A poem written by the Stanford university professor who
Kathleen had rendezvous with when she was still in a high
school near the site of the National Accelerator Laboratory.

A pipe made from a deer antler, Roger's first gift to her she
had left behind by mistake after an all-night drinking binge.

Then I see our ordinary family waving to the new Kathleen,
blond hair fluttering underneath the helmet etched with a Golden
Eagle., as she left for her new life. I remember thinking, wow, she
belongs to a Golden Eagle gang, like I did when I was a kid. Just a
coincidence? Later that evening, the kids watched a special about
Abraham Lincoln. I remembered the carnie I met in eastern Oregon
who loved Abraham Lincoln. Kathleen would have been roaring past
the town where I met him.

We didn't know what to say to each other. But thank god for kids.
They knew what to say. "You promised us we were going to go to the
zoo." Ah, the ordinary. Michael weeded while Linda packed lunches. I
could not get myself to go back inside the house. I figured everyone
expected I would keep living there. Kathleen would be back often.
She was continuing with treatments at the hospital. If I went back
inside it would be like eating a hamburger when I left Japan as a
teenager; it would be accepting that life just goes on.

But I wanted answers. I thought maybe now that the angel of
death was somewhere in the high desert hundreds of miles away, I
could put that search on the back burner. But, nope. In fact, the
potency of my longing was stronger. I wished someone could
brainwash me. I wanted to be a true believer. I envied my aunt (the
one who sat on the whoopee cushion; lifelong Christian Scientist.
She told me when she closed her eyes, imagining her death, she
could see Jesus with outstretched hands. I wanted to walk down
ancient cobblestone street to a church like the Florence Duomo in

Florence and feel the presence of God. Hell, even running into L Ron Hubbert would have been nice.

That day I had stood in the yard for a long time, watching the sun rise and light up the city below, and then walked to the Gertrude Stein Warehouse. I didn't expect Jack to be there, but he was. He listened to me rant and rave about fairness, truth, beauty, death, life. He was in his sponge mode, a trait I sometime forgot about him. As much as he pontificated or had you run gantlets of non sequiturs he could also just listen. As I wore down, he calmly suggested I move into the warehouse.

"I don't think I've ever shown you my father's secret dwelling. There's a separate entrance on the ground floor. It is kind of dark. No windows. But cozy."

I didn't ask to look at it; I knew it was the right and only option, if potentially self-destructive (moving into the extraordinary from the ordinary). Staying in the healthy and ordinary life on the hill was the sensible thing to do but would have probably, irrationally, drove me into insanity.

I left most of my stuff at Michael and Linda's, and told them I wasn't moving out, just spending more time at Jack's. The apartment was a cement cell with no windows. It was clammy. If I left paper on the floor, it would roll up into a scroll. There was one electrical outlet. I had a portable toilet, the O Johnny O. Jack supplied me with a 50-gallon drum for water. I got out my Alpha wave machine and tape recorder. I was going to lay there in the dark until I no longer knew the difference between night and day, record everything I was thinking and dreaming. It was my metaphysical protest. Like the one I imagined as a child when I told my friends I thought we should all just kill ourselves and then see what God would do. And I do mean everyone. Everyone on the planet would agree to kill themselves at 12:01 pm. We would warn God of our plan. Then do it. See how he liked complete silence. But there was always a fatal flaw. One person, just one, that's all it would take, would hide out in the jungle or more likely in a walk-in closet in the Hamptons, and the total mess would start all over. Well, at least it would if he found a woman in another closet.

I learned to hang out between wakefulness and dream state for hours at a time. I still have a box with cassette tapes and another box of spiral notebooks filled with stream-of-consciousness wanderings that might as well be ancient texts without the Rosetta Stone.

I received letters from Kathleen delivered through the Crying of Lot 49 postal service. Well, indirectly. Roger had shot a Lot 49 carrier, who was a member of the VonuLife post apocalypse anarchist collective; an unsuspecting Viet Nam vet with post-traumatic stress syndrome, set back another few years by the encounter. So, we changed the drop off to a minute mart in Silver Lake. We could have used the regular mail service, but I enjoyed getting special deliveries from the cute messenger dressed in roaring twenties cigar girl costume.

Kathleen's first letters were factual. The big events were figuring out how to wash her hair with icy water from Agency creek, a creek they had renamed, Blue Crane.

I think I continued to be the most constant and closest person to Kathleen. I was the one who waited in the chemo waiting room—the kindergarten detention room. We didn't believe it helped, except maybe like control burning in combating forest fires. And, Kathleen did it so she wouldn't have to listen to her family and friends ask her why she refused to do anything about the cancer. If she said she was meditating or listening to the raven and doing radiation, then that was acceptable.

She lived several years on the barge. Wildlife, including bald eagles treated them like they were a part of the landscape. The boundary between civilized man and noble savage was a fine and wavy one. Sometimes the Harley aspects of her new life were disconcerting. Her letters seemed to reflect a decent into desert redneck. I would picture them riding the back roads of desert and high country as a gang. They took peyote and psychedelic mushrooms. They had arguments and sometimes it seemed Kathleen was just the blond Harley babe of a motorcycle gang. They did laundry, crafts, scored good firewood, lived off Kathleen's parent's money, prepared foods from the wild, deer and Salmon, wild berries. It was as though she had transposed one form of the ordinary for another. It was also ironic that she had returned to our dream of living on the land, but in a more extreme rendering.

Then I remember thinking that she was floating off into her own version of a cult. Roger with dictatorial powers, passing judgments about her behavior, and the right ways to become a worrier. Maybe I was jealous too. Isn't that what I had asked of her too, to be a worrier? While they were supposed to be just teacher and student, it didn't always work out that way. She felt dependent on him as she was on me, tearing her hair out when he just walked out, to come back the next day, out drinking in the local bar, where she was only sometimes allowed to go.

I remember listening to her describe her life in Klamath. It didn't seem like the Kathleen I knew. When she would tell me about some of their experiences, crows talking to them, nights when whole Hollywood sets emerged and disappeared in the flicking of the firelight, or times when she could literally feel the white cancer cells leaving her body. Now I was asked to believe in this as much as I had in the therapy of the ordinary.

I begin to just listen and not respond, afraid to poke any holes in Kathleen's life. Part of me didn't want her running back to me; part of me sincerely believed that believing in anything for Kathleen was very important. If it stunk a little of righteous and lightheaded fantasies, so it goes. To see her revved up over these things they were doing was astonishing. She also talked like a redneck. The hypnotic world they rode over was fragile. Just on either side of it they were as different as night and day; but Kathleen, always one to take direct chameleon action, just adapted a lot of Roger's biker mentality along with the Don Juan stuff. She started bad-mouthing environmentalists and making fun of all the things she used to think were so important. She was burning bridges right and left. And I think she fell away from the spiritual reasons she had left and just created another home. She was like a dazed pigeon still trying to build a nest on a freeway overpass when all of her children have been smashed by a semi.

Thanks to a common friend, they secured land in the high desert. A remote site with a road that was only passable by 4-wheel drive and even with that sometimes in the winter they were isolated for weeks at a time from the world. I visited several times. Kathleen lived in a teepee. They had moved a hospital bed from a Klamath hospital. She gave up radiation therapy but was given heaps of narcotics. Sometimes when I visited her, the last couple of years, I would panic. I had to fight back an urge to tell her to move back to her ordinary life in Portland.

I had been in a hypnagogic state for 48 hours when someone knocked at my door. I tried to ignore it. It went away and then a half hour later (not that I knew exactly) the knocked returned. It sounded like "hang down your head Tom Dooley." Irritated I ripped off my alpha wave machine headgear, turned off my tape recorder and went to the door. I could only imagine being pleased if it were Don Juan or Marilyn Monroe. The door stuck, so by time I jerked it open I probably looked even madder than I was.

Shit. They were back. Like Peruvian music groups, religious fanatics seemed to follow me. It was a Jehovah's Witness. I let him have it with an uncensored stream-of-consciousness blather that forced him to back off step by step until he almost fell off the curb. Then told him the story of the day JW arrived along with Jack Ainsworth and Hearing Aid sales agent and my junk drawer epiphany.

I learned that day the technique of nonstop gibberish that gives you the upper hand. You can't pause and you need to have good eye contact, be sincere, don't flinch, look like they can't get away you will follow but you don't swear. A young couple loaded down with Nordstrom shopping bags watched us along with a wino drinking from a sack. I brought them into the conversation. "This might happen to you too. One day you have a platinum Visa card, the next you're living in a warehouse without plumbing connected to an

Alpha Wave machine, surfing the ebb and flows of your memories like the Tambourine Man."

I had barely gotten resettled into my alpha wave machine couch when someone else knocked at my door. I wanted to break heads. Then I heard Jack's voice, "You got to move. Someone complained you threatened them. A Jehovah's Witness I think."

But Jack had another place for me. So, I moved again. Easily since I only had the clothes on my back. I had stuff everywhere: The Shire, the warehouse, Michael and Linda's. I moved into an old Victorian house only a few blocks from the warehouse by dinner time.

I have little recollection of the place. I wondered if crazy just followed me. There was this time when a local TV news crew showed up to interview a roommate about a plan to save the plant Wapato on what used to be called Wapato Island, Now Sauvies Island.

I have a diary entry of the event.

The first thing my other and loony roommate said to the news crew:

"why the fuck do you think I went to the trouble of getting rid of all my identification. You know my ID. My ID. My ego. My super ego. Everything. There will be no trace of me or I will die trying." He held out his wallet, which was completely empty. "Do you see anything there? Do you?" He shoved it into the cameraman's face, who reflectively covered his camera lens.

And later. "do you think I wouldn't know you were coming? Do you think I wasn't prepared?" He paced the floor and grabbed the video camera. The cameraman quickly yanked the camera from his grip. "And you, you think you will have footage when you get back to your black lord celluloid melt down studio?"

He directed some of his anger at me "And you fuckface, how dare you bring these mutants into our house. The one place safe from the array. You will thank me. You'll see!"

One more time he stared at me as he turned toward his door, "And you touch my fuckin yogurt or bean sprouts in the regenerator anymore I'll..." he stammered, "and I will give you nightmares for the next six months that will make you wish you were dead."

1. Joan Baez is an American singer, songwriter, musician and activist. Her contemporary folk music often includes songs of protest or social justice. Baez has performed publicly for over 60 years, releasing over 30 albums. She attended high school in Palo Alto, California. https://www.californiamuseum.org/inductee/joan-baez.

THE FUNNY FARM: LAST STRAW ON THE CAMEL'S BACK

Preamble

I wasn't about to trust Jack's recommendation for another new domicile, but fortunately Uncle Gus came along and told me about an amazing deal that made me think God was looking out for me. There was an 80-acre estate west of Portland that had been donated to the local Parks district that needed a caretaker.

I was homeless so I couldn't be choosy. Just an ordinary life with my wife dying; but who had run off with a motorcycle gang. At my present home, run off by Jehovah's Witnesses or sacred shitless by a guy who wanted to be a psychedelic Cheshire cat. Or, I could be grounds keeper on an English estate, at least in photographs, that had landed in suburban Portland, part of the collusion between *A Wrinkle in Time*[1] and the *Wizard of Oz*.

Moving was simple. While negotiating with the Parks Dept. wasn't; fortunately, one of Jack's friends went to bat for me; someone he said who was "old wealth". The Park's director would probably rather have told me to leave the country along with all the other hippies, but clearly was powerless to resist Jack's patron. It took me 3 hours. 2 to pack and 1 to get there.

My house was in a wooded area away from the more manicured part of the estate, which included a graceful English hunting lodge mansion with 7 bathrooms and several outbuildings, including a run-down stable that at one time had 20 horses. They orchestrated the gardens like a Disney time-lapse movie. Varieties of plants and flowers would emerge, as others declined, creating arrays of color coordinated displays.

Gus didn't tell me much about the estate. I found out from the Parks district liaison that it had been sold to the Parks and Recreation District by a gay interior decorator, Edward someone, who had inherited it from a rich spinster. Part of the deal was that Edward's parents, Mrs. and Mr. Oglie, could live in the hunting lodge until he had a home built for them in a tract home development several miles away. Edward had moved his parents from the Ozarks when they retired and he came into the inheritance. I found out it was more complicated than that. Edward had inherited from one of the Ainsworth's. He was much younger than her; she was a known as a spinster but there was talk they had an affair.

The first day in my new home, a loud noise in the kitchen woke me. It sounded like someone had broken down the outside door and was running full tilt through the living room and headed toward the bedroom where I was sleeping on a mattress on the floor. And it was. Not a person, but a St. Bernard. The next thing I knew, the dog with the head the size of a beach ball was standing over me drooling. He shook off his drenched fur, sat back on his hunches and let loose with a series of playful thundering barks. It was as though we had known each other for years and I had forgotten our play appointment. It was cold in the house. The woodstove I was going to use for heat wasn't installed. I had gone to bed wearing all my clothes. I got up with Thunder Drool following me and went into the kitchen. He had had knocked the door down, which had fallen on the kitchen table and taken a box of plates with it. Big dog, but also an indicator of the shape of the house.

Thunder knew exactly where we were going. The hunting lodge

and sweeping lawns and gardens seemed more imposing than I had remembered. When I visited the estate with the Parks district manager, he made it clear that this part of the place was not my domain. I was going up in the world but only slightly; from homeless squatter to servant class in a Jane Austen novel.

I went to the front door and knocked and then hit a doorbell but got no response so I went to the back door, which was difficult to find. I later found out it was the entrance to the servant's quarters. A scruffy man came to the door with a filter less cigarette hanging from his mouth. What the heck was he doing in the lodge? He looked like he was part of my menial class and first suspect if there was a serial murderer on the prowl.

Thunder Drool instantly recognized him and dashed for the open door. The man blocked him with a curt, "Fuck no. Don't even think about it." He turned to me, "what do you want?" I explained I was the new caretaker living in the farmhouse. He stared at me while holding a leg out to block Thunder, then shut the door. Just before the door shut, I glimpsed Bob Benson's famous map of the Cascadia bioregion. One of the few remaining original ones in three colors. I stood there for a few minutes trying to figure out if he had just left me there.

Then a woman came to the door. "Sorry about my husband," she said. "He doesn't want to be here. "I'm Mrs. Oglie." She motioned for me to come in. We went through the kitchen, which while imposing —an industrial strength stove, two humongous refrigerators—was unkempt. A box of cereal on a card table, a sugar bowl with a trail of ants leading down the side of the table and across the floor. "This is Sam's part of the house," Mrs. Oglie explained. We went down a dark hallway and then when she opened a door, we entered her world. The blue-blood dominion. Richly paneled walls and hardwood floors, oriental rugs, ancient looking furniture, old growth house plants, credenzas filled with plates on display.

Mrs. Oglie and I talked for a couple of hours that day. Well, she talked, and I listened, feeling honored to be accepted in the landed gentry life. After that, Mrs. Oglie and I established a daily ritual. She had the local paper delivered, but they had refused to deliver directly to the house, a quarter mile from the road. So I would pick up the paper sharply at 9am and then spend an hour with Mrs. Oglie (I never knew her first name), talking about her plate collection, stamp collection, pressed flower collection and the history of her family that she could trace back to 500 AD, "they had a castle, just like me."

I would come get Thunder and take him for a walk around the place where he would take Bear-sized dumps. Then I would shove Lucy (thunder drool's proper name) into the servant's quarters. I could almost always see Carl sitting in his worn-out plastic recliner watching television, always with a Lucky Strike cigarette hanging from his mouth or burning in an over-flowing ash tray. I would then walk to the magical door that led back to Victorian days, and Mrs. Oglie and I would have tea. I looked more Beverly Hills hillbilly than English domestic help, but maybe she had a good imagination. We arranged for me to do more around the lodge. I slowly became her servant. Mostly she only used the living room, one bedroom and a bathroom. She infrequently used the kitchen since once a week her son would arrive with neatly packaged breakfasts, lunches, and dinners. She never went upstairs to the library and billiard room and additional bedrooms, but she still had me clean them. I did not have to clean up Carl's quarters.

Edward called me one day to tell me he didn't want his mother to drive anymore, and that he would pay me extra if I could do their shopping and errands. Mrs. Oglie told me about the plan the same day, a little irked her son didn't trust her driving but willing to go along with it. She handed me the keys and told me her car was in the horse barn. I didn't expect what I found. A 1954 black Cadillac in mint condition.

I drove the caddy around to the front entrance. Mrs. Oglie came out, dressed in something that appeared to be like white doilies so faded the edges looked burned from a bad ironing. That day she reminded me of the Faulkner story, "A Rose for Emily."

We drove to the closest shopping mall. I wish I had a driver's cap, but I was a hippie in overalls. Maybe people would think it was the driver's day off and I was the gardener. We walked baby steps through the parking lot and then more baby steps in the store, filling up two shopping carts.

On the way back from the grocery store, we drove past the State Unemployment office where I had been earlier in the day applying for my tiny benefits; struck again by the incongruity as I imagined explaining to my job counselor how I was Mrs. Oglie's chauffer, whose ancestor had a castle in 500 AD. I wondered what my case worker would have thought about me being a chauffeur. Should I report the income?

It was one of the driest winters on record when I was at the estate. Usually storms off the Pacific roll in one after another from the third week in October until June. But day after day it was sunny. The estate had the oldest water system in the county. There was a 50,000-gallon water tank. I imagined if things got worse the suburban peasants would storm the estate and we would have to stand them off, me, Thunder drool and Mr. Lucky Strikes.

The estate was also on the edge of Portland's urban sprawl. From one vantage point I could see sprawl washing against the bottom of the hill; in the other direction there were pastoral hills and farms. I could see the visual difference, but it was the acoustic characteristics that were the most astounding and irksome. Standing on the highest point of the estate if I turned east there was a roar, the heartbeat of progress. On the edge and facing west there were more individual noises. I could count how many chain saws or weed whackers were operating. On the roadways in the borderland on the sometimes paved, sometimes only, graveled roads teenagers in Dodge Chargers flew past old timers with triangular slow signs on the back of tractors.

To the north there was a dog kennel. On weekends and holidays the muted sound of dogs whining and barking turned into a zoological amateur orchestra tuning up. I waged war against the kennel. First, I tried legal means to report them for violating noise levels. That didn't get anywhere, so I started rumors that animals were being mistreated. Still nothing. I drove by and tried to find other violations. I tried to find any infraction, things like the height of their mailbox. The noise raged on, so I went vigilante. I called them at all hours. Heavy breathing. It was before there was a star 69 function.

South of the estate was an even more troublesome issue, a rock quarry. I tried all the regulatory processes I could think of. I drove to the parking lot and took photos. I thought maybe I could find sympathetic workers, start a union. I sometimes sat for hours staring at the quarry. Imaging for how many centuries man had been doing this. I wondered if it was a front for something else. Or maybe I could spread a rumor. I spent an entire day crawling through the woods, up and down hills and cliffs, getting photos.

A few days after I sent Jack the second package, Parks department staff arrived. It was Mr. Simpson, my contact, along with two burly and surly looking guys wearing gardening crew uniforms. Mr. Simpson stood at the door while the other guys hung back at a distance with their arms folded, dark glasses.

"As prescribed by law," Mr. Simpson said formally, "I am giving you 48 hours to vacate the premises. We have complaints from neighbors. I can detail those charges if you wish?"

"Ok, well give me the ten cent version." I leaned over to grab my cup of coffee. The body guards moved toward the door. "Cool it," I said, " just my cup of coffee."

"The owners of Pet Paradise kennels have evidence you repeatedly called them and hung up. The owner of the rock quarry spotted you spying on them and allege that you were carrying a machete. A family reported they spotted you by the road. While peeing or doing some kind of exposure in public thing. And finally, Mrs. Muir said she thinks you stole some of her stamps. But isn't sure and doesn't want to press charges. You want any more?"

I racked my brain. How could they know these things? I had never seen a car go by while I was peeing and I only did that when I was well hidden or it was very early or very late. Short of a police tracing, there wasn't any way to trace a call in those days. And I was far away and well-hidden when I spied on the quarry. It was Jack. In passing, I had told him about all these things. My war waged against the Kennel, but how nice it was to have the outdoors as my outhouse. Some things Jack did made more sense than anyone in the world; on the other hand, he could be infuriating. Life wasn't always a game. People got hurt and killed. There were consequences. There was a reason for truth and scientific method. Something in that moment clicked. I turned off. I no longer wanted to play games. My wife was in unbelievable pain and dying. And I was dying too, eventually.

"Fine," I said matter-of-factly. "I will be out by tomorrow at noon." Mr. Simpson stared at me, I guess expecting resistance or something. "I've got lots to do," I said and politely shut the door.

On my walks between my hovel and the estate lodge, I found things. Some things that should be there like the rusty head of an axe, the moldy part of a horse's saddle, bottle and cans and a Colt 45, along with a nearby cash register. Ok, the last items were odd. But I also found a wooden comb that I found out was likely Peruvian; a stash of moldy Olympia 4-star Olympia beer labels, and lastly pieces of an Apple IIe computer with an oddly readable floppy disk. Well, partly readable. The only text I could discern was "Jack was a bitch," and part of a spreadsheet for the Apocalypse Reconstruction Company, who at the time appeared to have $325.70 in its account.

Hiding the Secrets to the Meaning of Life

I resented how I felt gleeful while hiding the Ainsworth Chronicles. A part of me wanted to send jack a cleanly written manuscript in a registered mail package. What would I get back if I sent it with returned receipt form? No comments or a boiler-plate official-sounding-like memorandum showing with precision how I had fulfilled elements of our contract. I thought about this process for over a week. And again, resentfully, I laughed out loud. The ultimate existential con-man had bested me no matter which way I buttered the toast. The one thing I couldn't do was extinguish the whole thing. He knew that. He knew no matter what I felt, I could never destroy the manuscript.

Maybe this part was spiteful. So be it. I went back to the warehouse and hauled off 25 boxes of stuff I had collected about the Gertrude Stein history. Back at the Funny Farm, I spent several days hiding the boxes. I mixed and matched and numbered the boxes in random order; seemed fitting.

I know where I left my manuscript, as per our agreement. It was inside cotton dresses inside plastic bags inside metal army storage box inside the largest western red cedar stump, about 5 feet across, about fifty feet south of the 20-foot-high pile of steering wheels.

There was also a calligraphed note, "Author's official finders keepers' notation: Box 1. File folders 1—36. Found by Jack Ainsworth in the metal box on the Ainsworth estate. Found 1978 after a 15-month search following obscure clues left by the author. Found in a box that had no bearing on the content."

The documentation I left behind at the Funny Farm was only partly organized. I didn't know my tenure was going to end so abruptly and completely. I kept monthly roll call records of all the tenants. I did this to collect rent, but we also used it to document activities and evolution of the planet. I also wrote up more impressionistic accounts of the residents and life at the Fellowship Club. I had imagined I would put this all together in one comprehensive and imaginative document capturing a tiny raindrop of planetary history. I ended up with 2 boxes of somewhat organized material.

I'm not sure where I hid all the boxes. Neither Gus nor I know how Jack found the stuff, or even if he found everything I left behind.

As far as "The Ainsworth Chronicles," if I had to estimate, I would say 60% of the content is mine.

The next section, "My First Days at the Gertrude Stein Fellowship

Club," I think is my writing with only subtle editorial changes—I didn't have time to edit, check spelling, etc.

Now to the most egregious Jack action. The Henry Sycamore document. As far as we know there never was a Henry Sycamore and the document is mostly mine. Can I prove it? No.

---

1. *A Wrinkle in Time* is a young adult novel written by American author Madeleine L'Engle. First published in 1962.

TO THE ENDS OF THE EARTH

Preamble

G us told me Jack felt sorry for the things he had done and wanted to make it up to me. What things exactly? A litany of deceits, disappointments, disenchantments followed by a feeling of how shallow I was or easy to deceive burst into mind, but Gus didn't let me unleash. "So, he wants to create an identity for you that will allow you to travel around the world for free." There were only a few things that might counter my anti-Jack stage, but this offer sounded like exactly what I needed. But then I would be more indebted to Jack. I pictured going everywhere haunted by people who knew him, owed him something and allowed me to see the world in a way not even a travel agency for the rich could have arranged.

I had a skill set and perspective about small computers that was rare and on the groundbreaking at the time. I realized, having been around computer nerds during the Gertrude Stein Club days had provided me with skills and knowledge that would allow me to pass as an expert. Jack had also arranged it so that I could have a hidden mike that fed me messages from him and others via a connection of local computer networks; translated by some invisible and funny translator.

It all happened quickly.

The first trip arranged was to help certain tribal groups in the headwaters of the Amazon fight back against oil and mineral corporations who were stealing their land. My job was to bring donated computers (Apples) to their villages and through elaborate connections between local computer networks link them up to information and organizations battling the same corporate theft in different parts of the Planet.

Later in Australia I followed in the footsteps of Lorenzo Miliam, who had created community radio and TV stations in the outback. I was to distribute digital cameras to remote villages and use the networks Lorenzo had established to help Aboriginal Families find family members separated from one another through 19th century colonial policies.

Finally, the trip to Japan that lasted far longer than I expected is harder to explain. They honored me wherever I went, drank a lot of sake, and felt like I was on the fringe of something very exciting even if I couldn't define it. One of the most important things I did was networking. Jack and the nerds at the Gertrude Stein club fed me the latest information about the birth of computer networks, cutting edge technologies-like at one time I conducted workshops on how to use Apple's HyperCard to create social change. Almost everywhere I went, I discovered I had published a small publication about the coming personal computer era.

In the Headwaters of the Amazon: Am I supposed to Hurl?

All I remember about arriving in Quito Ecuador is hundreds of people behind a chain linked fence, waiting for loved ones. It reminded me of cattle cars in Nazi Germany. Then there was a familiar face, Ginger waving. I was going to a village in far east Ecuador, the headwaters of the Amazon, to help a village fight oil companies stealing their land and resources.

Ginger. How I met Ginger was: (1) Just coincidence (2) Random, but in Dr John's random universe (3) Jack planted plot. We met up at one of those tiny dilapidated shopping "mauls." I think there were 4 stores: a connivence market that smelled like dried out pizza and lottery tickets (2) a hair salon, and (3) a junk store which is where we met. She was attractive in a sloth-kind of sexy belly dancer body. I was looking for anything to fill my empty house on the estate I was caretaking and she was looking for a particular blue braided rug that she had grown up with. She had been to over 100 of these junk stores. She had many other things—some which she had sold for a profit. She was also a translator, fluent in Spanish and some obscure tribal languages in the headwaters of the Amazon. We went back to the estate together and made love. She translated every expression of joy in at least 3 languages. It was also when she confessed to stalking me. Well, minor stalking. She had seen me chauffeuring Mrs. Oglie and got curious. It was an interesting plot, if not an insidious or demented one. She had followed me back to the estate. She hid in the woods and watched me as I walked from the estate house to my domicile, followed by a giant St. Bernard. So Amazing really, *and here we are together naked.*

As she dressed to leave she casually described her upcoming trip to the Amazon to help Charlie, a white activist who was trying to help tribes fend off Oil companies from "purchasing" their land. And, where she was going to have an ayahuasca experience with a well-known Shaman and his family. She offered to pay for all my expenses if I could raise money for airfare. Seriously, how could you say no.

I had read about ayahuasca years earlier when I became obsessed with William Burroughs. A thin edition of letters between Burroughs and Alan Ginsberg[1] documented their experiences with ayahuasca. It seemed that Burroughs and others, including Timothy Leary, were brave explorers of the new world. They were like Ponce De Leon or Magellan exploring the edges of the known universe, encountering strange unknown species and facing fears about the unknown head on. They went into uncharted areas that had both the lightness of Shangri La and the darkness of Conrad's jungle. I didn't think of psychotropic drugs as party amplifiers, but like giant flashlights on the bow of a ship in a sea of wonder and perils. If I walked south 200 miles, I would be where Burroughs had taken Ayahuasca. Ah, two degrees of separation.

I also had preconceived notions of what the ritual would be like: feathers, drums, exotic costumes, talismans. Of course, I also imagined the Amazon rain forest differently, probably from cartoons or *National Geographic* specials. Our part of the rain forest had been clear-cut, so it was a tangle of small trees, bushes, vines, and most of all mud. It was never hot, just mild, humid and most of all mildewed. I also imagined that the Shaman might put a hand on my forehead, unleash tiny minions who would run around inside my brain, igniting brain cells like they were street lamps or fire crackers.

We had been in the village for a week when the Shaman invited us to take part in an ayahuasca ceremony. He told us this while we shared breakfast with his extended family of twenty in the kitchen which was also the village's living room. For breakfast we drank a tea that tasted like chamomile tea and old socks. The tea was to help us remember and share our dreams. Listening to everyone share their dreams, I imagined breakfast time in an American suburb. "Here, kids drink your illegal hallucinogenic tea and finish your pop tarts. We need to hear everyone's dreams so we can go to the Mall and get school clothes for fall."

The invitation was for me and Ginger and Charlie, who as yet had not said a single word. Ginger kept telling me that my mission would be revealed through the ayahuasca. We had 24 hours to prepare for our *trip*. I'm not sure how I was supposed to prepare, but we had to make a torturous 50-mile road trip to the nearest cyber-café. There had been flashfloods in the region so the trip would easily take the entire day and we might even have to stay in town overnight. We had to go to the cyber-café to research a potential drug-interaction problem. Ginger had periodical depression cycles and was taking Prozac. She had heard about possible "bad trips," when mixing ayahuasca and anti-depressant meds. Unfortunately, what she remembered was vague. Charlie had heard ayahuasca helped people with depression. it was amazing that all we had to do was take a 50-mile trek in a broken-down pickup truck to re-connect to the world brain. The village's direct connection to the "civilized" world was an electric line that ran two light bulbs and a radio. Once a week a neighbor came by with a mobile phone.

The three of us prayed to the God of dilapidated pickup trucks and left for town. We started with five people but by the time we got to the town there were ten of us. Any car or truck was de facto public transportation. Miraculously, we only had one flat tire, lost a rearview mirror, and had one near-death occurrence when we had to gun it to get through a gushing creek, almost hit a small child and then ran the truck into a log to avoid putting too much stress on the failing brakes. Oh, right, and when we started the engine, the ignition wires briefly caught on fire.

Back at the Village

Rodolfo focused on the fire. He kept re-arranging the wood. It didn't seem to help. He created more smoke than heat. I had wood heat all my life; it was hard not to intervene. He seemed to not like flame. Every time a flame kicked up, he quickly squished it and spread the small pieces of wood around. Finally, I had Ginger ask him if the fire was important. He didn't respond right away as a firefly distracted him. Ignoring our question, he grabbed a jar and started following the insect around the room. He captured it and then put the jar in front of his father. He looked at me and said, "No."

"No, what?" I asked Ginger, a little irked. The shaman was still talking about the pickup truck.

"No," she said, "just not important."

There was a hole in the ceiling, no chimney, which always struck me as odd as the room filled with smoke. Maybe the firefly was important. But no one paid any attention to it. Was this like the holding pattern? It felt like I was at a college party making small talk while waiting for the party drug to take hold It was also difficult to take the Shaman seriously since he was wearing one of my red plaid shirts. I had left it in a bin at The Gertrude Stein just before I left town. But how could it get here? Oddly when I thought of that I felt like I traveled quickly to the warehouse and people were moving around in what felt like real time. The shaman's son said, as translated by Charlie, "where did you go?"

They passed the Ayahuasca tea around several times. I wasn't sure how much time had gone by. Fifteen minutes, maybe. Or maybe longer. Charlie's rough translation from the Shaman said, "Time is like Jell-O," which made me think of Jack. I felt the first wave of something. It felt a little like the flu. When my eyes were closed, I could see an aerial photograph of South America. I heard my name several times, so I tried to look interested.

Ginger turned to me, looking a little sick, and maybe even frightened. "He wants to know how you are enjoying it. Do you feel sick?"

I smiled. "Am I supposed to throw up? Don't tell him this, but I'm a veteran of the 1960s, so I'd say this is somewhere between a mild LSD, peyote or good marijuana... tell him I was flying over the jungle, and then higher until I could see the globe as far north as where we come from, and saw migrations of people going here and there over centuries of time." I paused, looked at the Shaman who was looking at me like a host, wanting to see how I liked the appetizers. I felt uncertain. The drug wasn't strong enough to overcome my ego. I was firmly planted in my personality, unlike my experiences with LSD when I disappeared. As Ginger translated, I added, "Tell him I think there really is only one person on the entire planet but he manifests himself in a billion forms and lives billions of times, billions of lives, and manifests actions across billions of planets." Ginger looked at me, smiling but with disapproval, "I told you it's hard to translate sidebars."

"Maybe life is the sidebar and everything else is reality," I said. I realized everyone in the kitchen was staring at me.

Shit, why did I say that. But something else was different. The light, smells, and right the people. Ginger wasn't there. In fact, no one I had started the evening with was there. When did that happen? I thought I was just waiting for Ginger to complete the translation of the last thing I said. Now everything had changed. I only recognized the Shaman's wife, who nodded at me with her usual polite befuddled look. There were shirts drying on the clothesline. Shit, wait a minute, wasn't that one of my plaid shirts? The shirt made me feel at home. I have never loved a shirt or piece of clothing so much. It was part of my offering along with the equivalent of $200 USA dollars. A pile of bills that either looked like monopoly money or drug money, which I suppose it was in a way since I was tripping my brains out. And just then the Shaman reappeared, naked from waist up and as though on clue, put my plaid shirt on. Will miracles ever end?

The sun was rising, the usual gray had turned to a brighter gray. So somehow, between my response and the sidebar, several hours had gone by. Ginger turned to me, looking sick, and said, "He wants you to know that he had a vision of who you are." She got up. "Excuse me, but I have to throw up." On the way out the door, she added, "He wants you to know your guardian is a white wolf."

I smiled at the Shaman and repeated to him, "White wolf. That's interesting."

Rodolfo got up and went outside. I heard him talking to Ginger while she continued to throw up. He came back in and said the most English I had heard from him: "Ginger is a mermaid and you are White Wolf. Very good." I walked off thinking where the hell did they experience wolves and mermaids, neither of which were as far I knew indigenous to the Amazon. But I pictured a mermaid on a log raft with a wolf staring at her from the shore, and it was thousands of years ago.

After the ceremony, Rodolfo followed us to our cabin. Ginger and Charlie nestled into a roach-proof screen tent. Without explanation, Rodolfo settled in next to me. I wrapped myself inside mosquito netting, not protecting myself from mosquitoes so much as roaches. They crawled inside your sleeping bag, trying to find warmth. When I finally had what I thought was a bug-proof cocoon around me, I could see Rodolfo in dim moonlight. Lying on his side just a couple of feet from me, his eyes were wide open and not blinking. It was like lying next to a dead body. If I tried to turn over, I would likely create holes in my cocoon. So, I had to stare straight at him just inches away. I would close my eyes, try to sleep, then open my eyes. Countless times throughout the night. His eyes were never closed. At one time he was humming. In one vivid dream I was laying with Kathleen and we were in her Oregon encampment. She whispered in my ear, "I'm glad you are a part of my life."

The sun never reached our tent cabin until mid-morning, which is how I knew I had overslept. No hangover from the trip, except I didn't feel I could move, as though my body was made of lead. Also, the sun never really came up or went down. In fact, I hadn't seen the sun in a clear sky the whole time in the village.

The village was waking up. There was a baby crying; someone hammering something; someone else singing; a short laugh followed by another cry. I smelled something like bacon. Grubs, maybe.

Rodolfo came to the cabin door, smiling. In English he said, "White wolf."

Electric Carrier Pigeons

While in the Amazon, I received letters from Kathleen delivered through the Crying of Lot 49 postal service.[2] Well, indirectly. Roger had shot a member of the VonuLife[3] post apocalypse anarchist collective; an unsuspecting Viet Nam vet with post-traumatic stress syndrome, set back another few years by the encounter. We could have used the regular mail service, but I enjoyed getting special deliveries from the cute messenger dressed in roaring twenties cigar girl costume.

The Cyber-café had two computers. Fortunately for us, one was working and the Internet connection was relatively strong, which meant the bit rate was about what a first year typing student might type. It took us three hours to find what we were looking for. For Ginger, the news wasn't good. Warnings from a reputable pharmaceutical website confirmed the rumor of mixing ayahuasca and anti-depressant meds.

Just as we were leaving the Cyber Cafe, a geek handed me a computer printout. "You are White Wolf, right? It came in on my email account. How did they do that?" It was a message from Kathleen. You got me I said, although I doubt we meant the same thing. He wondered how someone got a message to me via his email account I was trying to figure out how Kathleen had access to a computer in the middle of nowhere. From the middle of nowhere to another middle of nowhere. I scarfed a couple of tiny bananas as I read.

> "We've had lots of guests who all brought food. It felt like a potlatch. I didn't expect the one guest, Steve. You know I think I told you about him. He fancies he is in love with me. He's tall. And I mean tall. weird being around him like you and what's his name who weighed 250 pounds, and you were always afraid he might just fall over and crush you. Well, Steve is 6 feet 7. I'm not sure he loves me so much as he loves that I am dying. I know that sounds strange, but he's like the peanuts character with a black cloud over his head. He keeps repeating, "how can you be dying and you look so beautiful luminous or is it because of that?" Did I say he reminds me of a praying mantis? I don't mean to poke fun at him. He is a welcome relief to the plethora of rednecks. He waits on me hand and foot; reads Yeats and Emily Dickinson poetry. Brings me gifts."

> "He was here for a week. Roger tolerates him because he is tall and strong, so we have a gigantic supply of firewood. And he whittled me this totem of a raven for my teepee. A raven the size of a grizzly bear. Also, nice to see Roger jealous, making up for the times I could hear him and the Starling bitch he tells me just wants to find her spirit guardians. Or like Steve's brother (the guy who gave us a new engine for the Volvo) who shot his girlfriend's lover eight times when he tried to come through the roof. Don't ask me. I don't know how or why you come through a roof and I don't know how you

can shoot someone eight times, including once in the you know
what, this all according to the Starling Bitch. I tried to comfort
Debbie, his girlfriend, when they hauled him off. On a more positive
note, we got some very good vitamin C (ha ha) if you are still
looking. Come to think of it, where are you?"

"P.S. Thanks for sending New Model of the Universe. I've been
trying to read but it reminds me too much of philosophy class you
know those ultra-rationalist linguistic analysts. I did like the
chapter, which included the passage about how a man can go made
from one ashtray. That reminded me of you."

By the time I finished reading Kathleen's letter, I felt like I was
going to throw up. I could feel the pain in her arm, like a phantom
limb sensation. I wanted to run further into the jungle and become
green; where I would find her and we would turn into an
underground fungi that would eventually fill the jungle.

From the messages I gathered, she continued her radiation
therapy sessions. Michael and Linda and Kathleen's friend Jude
alternated trips to the hospital. But there was a point when the
exhaustion of the trips from Klamath Falls and ambiguous outcomes
just made little sense. But more disturbing to me was how the hell's
Angel karma of her choice to live in the desert seemed to overcome
the spiritual.

She was surrounded by buffoons often. Lewd people. She told me
about a woman Roger took in who they picked up hitchhiking. She
became part of his entourage. And they slept together and spent
more and more time with each other. Roger had Kathleen move from
their new tiny cabin to a teepee. He made it sound like move toward
god. She was livid. She told me she would literally tear her hair out.
After a couple of days she felt more at one with the universe and
could see how Roger had helped her. This woman, Cindy, was
younger and beautiful, and from Kathleen's point of view, ignorant
and crass. She had two states of mind: pissed off boredom and utter
distaste for everything. In town—Ft Rock, there was an unwritten

rule that she was be in toe, submissive like he was a cult leader and she was a follower. Well, more than that. She had to make sure her blonde hair was out and blowing in the wind, that Roger could grab her butt, that she would fetch beers for the boys. She just said to me that "Keeping my mouth shut most of the time is the best policy."

I remember the last time we got together in the Pancake House in Eugene (a place she used to avoid) and her language and body language seemed to turn red neck. I stared at her like watching a cinema flashback. The redneck cowgirl in front of me and the young, beautiful blonde, classmate of Joan Baez and the one who had an affair with a Stanford University English professor.

But the language she started using starting going over or around my head. This is a new person. And the crassness, learning to shoot a gun—and she was packing one, seemed commingled with a cult like spiritualism that was disturbing. His small gang treated him like an undisputed leader, as did Kathleen. And I knew better than to doubt him or his beliefs. When she would tell me about some of their experiences, crows talking to them, nights when whole Hollywood sets emerged and disappeared in the flicking of the firelight, or times when she could literally feel the white cancer cells leaving her body.

During our last visits I had just listened, afraid to poke any holes in her life. Part of me didn't want her running back to me; part of me sincerely believed that believing in anything for Kathleen was very important, if it stunk a little of righteous and lightheaded fantasies, so it goes. To see her revved up over these things they were doing was astonishing.

The hypnotic world they rode over was fragile. Just on either side of it they were as different as night and day; but Kathleen, always one to take direct chameleon action, just adapted a lot of Roger's biker mentality along with the Don Juan stuff. She started bad-mouthing environmentalists and making fun of all the things she used to think were so important. She was burning bridges right and left. Also, the number of drugs and alcohol was phenomenal. She was given unlimited access to morphine and other pain fighting drugs, while Roger and his friends had unlimited access to peyote and mescaline and mushrooms. And they often drank their meals, long into the night.

Knowing a Place like the Inside of Your Hand

The day after our ayahuasca adventure, the Shaman's 14-year-old son, Pita La, led us through the jungle around his village. He knew 2,000 plants and their uses. We snaked our way through the jungle. He would say things in his native language which Rodolfo would translate in Spanish, which Ginger would translate into English. We stopped at one point to have lunch at a stump that was filled with big creamy grubs. Ginger swore they tasted like lobster tail. He then crushed up leaves and showed us we should chew them. I hesitated. Ginger explained, "he says remember the snake in the village he had in a jar that could kill you in 20 seconds."

Yes, I remembered it well. I had imagined what I had to be fearful of was gigantic boa constrictors, not snakes the size of a night crawler. Well, if you chew the leaves, you will sweat and that will drive away the snakes. I chewed the leaves. We continued on until he stopped again. This time he cut down palm tree leaves and showed how we should hold these over our heads. Remembering the dire consequences of the tiny snake, I immediately held the leaf over my head. Why? Well, because we will soon pass under certain trees, and if the pollen from these trees fall on your head, you will go bald.

I wondered how many generations of dead and bald people did it take to figure all this out? When we stopped for a break of more grubs and grass that we sucked juice from, Rodolfo sang a song. Ginger told me it was a song that was passed on to small children. The song was about a small child who got lost in the jungle. Each element of the song contained vital information that would help them survive. At the base of a tree with purple flowers grew a blue lichen that was sweet as honey. Eating it would keep one from getting mosquito bitten lips and be laughingstock of the village. Ginger wasn't sure, but she thought it was a planet that in effect reduced your need for water, and from getting dehydrated. I imagined the knowledge we passed on in schools in America. What did we pass on? It seemed to me the basic lessons were to get a job, let someone else worry about everything else, and know how to get to the mall.

Bokonon's Next Marching Orders

We were going to leave via Quito. It is a big city but from the minute I arrived at the airport I felt like everyone knew who I was; maybe a fallout or insight from my ayahuasca journeys. It was one thing to have Jack or Gus repeatedly remind me we are all only a few degrees separated from each other, but sailing through the maze of life, as though God were constructing a cat's cradle of my life; well the image stayed with me. I kept seeing it. People all around me had delicate fishing lines connecting them to everyone else. Do you know how many lines of connection 5 billion people create? And then add to that the ghosts of another 70 billion who have lived on the planet throughout time. Well, it takes something more than the best MIT or defense system computer to process it. But, in Dr. Ainsworth's world, that unfathomable intricacy is reduced to a few explicit instructions if you know what to look for.

When I walked into the Magic Bean, everyone stopped to greet me. The hotel manager, a Belgian who spoke perfect English, said as though it was nothing special, "the man in a black suit has been waiting for you now 2 days. We put out sandwiches for you. Trade Jack (Jack to me) told me you had saved aboriginal's life. Thank you."

I'm not sure why I accepted the mission. It seemed futile to resist. The anger I felt over my discoveries around the Funny Farm seemed distant, and the bleak homeless feeling I had the day I ran into Ginger seemed like another person. I could check my bank balance. Maybe it validated a Dr John's theory. I entered Ecuador with $500 and I was leaving with that much. I had spent money along the way and not put anything in, although Kathleen had, because of our rental property. I was pondering this. There may be some kind of requirement to enter Australia. so how do I resolve it? I had spent money on in—six months was my stash of chocolate waver cookies. I laid in bed, listening to the hotel noises: noisy water pipes, some screaming in what sounded like French, the clunky elevator and the sound of motorcycles and cars outside. I fell asleep holding the airline ticket and an envelope. My James Bond contact had told me there was everything I would need in the envelope. I hadn't realized until after he left that there was $500 in $100 bills, along with simple directions:

> Should you decide to *accept this mission, Anthony Chamberson will meet you at the Canberra International Airport. Your mission will be to distribute digital cameras to Aboriginal communities so they can create Web sites as a way of finding family members separated during colonial days, when Aboriginals were separated and their children sent to church institutions to be converted from pagans to Christians. Anthony is Director of the Preservation of Aboriginal Culture and Language (DUCK for short). He is a reformed motorcycle gang leader modeled on the Hell's Angel. A Sweet guy who married an aboriginal who is part Japanese and as "crazy as a snake on glass."*

The other reason I took jack marching orders was that I wanted to travel horizontally across the southern hemisphere.

I found on my bed a tiny package that looked like it had been lost, opened, closed, lost again and yet somehow got to me. The letter itself on parchment like paper and in Kathleen's tidy script looked like it might have been found inside a 19th century first edition book.

"Thanks for sending the money. Really needed it since Roger's 40-year uncle who nobody had seen in 27 years suddenly showed up. And I mean at our encampment. Roger heard him coming and had his gun. He went to the high point while I hid behind the toolshed. Roger shot a warning shot. He stepped out of the car, "Hey Roger, it's your uncle, you know the black sheep of the family." Well anyway, he eats like for three people. Roger found out from his mom in Maryland that he also stopped there. He was like a puppy, someone just walloped. His lady friend of 10 years disappeared. Just leaving a used rubber with a note, "Fuck you." It was rough at first but Roger and he hit it off and talk late in the night, although they don't like me being around. Thing is, they don't listen to each other. like having a TV on at the same as a radio.

Uncle Ben went to Bend and came back with a pet Margay. Unbelievable animal. He is in constant movement.

Finding Dreamtime in the Australian Outback

I met Anthony in Canberra. He was an odd duck. He had long legs, a large butt, and red hair that was sometimes braided, but most of the time disheveled like a bird's nest. His eyes were almost closed shut; maybe blue, but hard to tell since they were always bloodshot. He met me dressed in a Hawaiian shirt, high-water pants, and old fashion lace up tennis shoes.

At first, I didn't think he spoke English, at least not any dialect of English I was familiar with. He stuck out his hand that went limp in mine and said something like, "there's a Louie died in your dog and your abs frozen into a suckegg mule but partying the visa yours are the biggest in the world. So, no worries, mate." The problem was that he spoke a dialect of Scottish, Aussie, Kiwi, Aboriginal, along with feral hippie jargon. what I heard was "no worries, mate," which over time I learned meant everything and nothing.

What I finally figured out was that I had arrived just in time to be in the largest aboriginal Land Rights demonstration in Australian history. Not even time to unpack. Anthony was friends with one of the national leaders, so I found myself at the lead of protesters that snaked through the capital. It differed from the March on the Pentagon. Didgeridoos led us. Before marching up the steps to Parliament building, we spent time in the Aboriginal encampment which had been there for several years. That's where I met Rob and Elvia, who would play an important role in my down under experience.

Anthony was daft—his own description—kindly, eccentric like the seed of a family with too many brilliant inter-marrying cousins.

He had married into an aboriginal family, but he seldom saw his wife Lucille anymore. They broke up because she was as crazy as a snake on broken glass. They were still legally married, a status that provided him privileges useful for our mission.

Sitting in front of a campfire with the sparkling new Australian capital in the background with Rob and Elvy and their extended family, basically everyone we met were family. I forgave jack. Did truth really matter? Knowing Jack had brought me here. What would my carrot head high school teacher think of this outcome? How did I get here?

It shocked me to hear Rob was 15 years younger than me. I was thinking he was old enough to be my father. Anthony later explained that like Native Americans many aboriginals, especially men, adopted eating and drinking habits of white Australian, and their bodies were confused. They often died in their 40s and 50s. This was confirmed later, when Rob was rushed to the hospital when we were in Alice Springs, his fourth stroke. And he and Anthony treated it as though he had just run to the video store.

Rob told me stories from his youth. During the week we were in Canberra, he and I got in the habit of sneaking away to a nearby pub. He was not supposed to drink or smoke, but did both while we were in the pub. I was his first American. He was intrigued and mystified. I think in part because I was small and quiet.

At the Stuart Arms bistro Rob ordered bush meat dishes while we drank beer and bourbon, "It's from Kentucky, America. Are you near there?"

I tried to eat kangaroo (tough) and then Australian camel, (even tougher). I had a piece of that in my mouth for a half hour and finally had to spit it into my napkin. Rob told me about his days prospecting for gold and the time in the Indian Ocean when he barely escaped with his life when he was caught in bed with the Yugoslavian captain of a fishing boat. The captain chased him around the boat with a meat hook and then shoved a jib boom at him, which tossed him like driftwood into the sea. He swam a mile to shore where he would have died if it hadn't been for a cousin who found him unconscious on the beach with shark bite marks all over his body. Rob was supposed to go home from Canberra but decided he wanted to come with us on our expedition across Australia.

We were getting up to leave the Bistro when a conservative-looking businessman came toward us and without hesitation first hugged Rob and then Anthony. I felt like it diminished my special status as friend to the oppressed. They immediately talked in code about friends and events and issues, and experiences, leaving me on the outside. They were into their conversation for 15 minutes before Anthony introduced me.

"Fred Norris," Anthony said proudly, "CEO of Australia's third largest mining corporation, Bentham Hills. We go way back."

While telling a story about an expedition that he and Rob took along with several others, all part of a gold prospecting group, which sounded more like a rationale for drunken mayhem in the outback, he got out his checkbook. I watched while in astonishment he wrote a check to Anthony for $20,000. He then stood up. They all hugged again.

When he left, I glared at Anthony, "what the fuck was that about? $20,000?"

"Ah, you noticed that ah?," he said, winking at Rob who downed a shot glass laughing. "Guilt money," Rob said, "Fred raped an aboriginal teenager that lived at his station house. They threw him into the back of a Chevy Malibu in the sun until he promised."

"Was it a Malibu?" Anthony said "I thought it was an Impala."

At the hotel lobby we got caught up in an ugly shouting match between an aboriginal man and woman.

"They are sister and brother" Robert said. They were speaking English, but I could understand very little of it.

"Fine for you," he said, and threw a bundle at me as though this whole fight thing was my fault, and in one sense it probably was since all their plight came from White colonists.

Back to the Crying of Lot 49 message from Kathleen, or a facsimile of her Jack had created. It seemed like there was a missing page or more. A fragment of Kathleen's life. But also, a confusing chronology since the actions and players were from different periods. I remember the laetrile mission, but that was before Kathleen moved to eastern Oregon. It almost seemed like someone cut and pasted diary entries or letters from different sources and time periods.

In the letter a drawing. While she was reading Don Juan, a giant wasp landed on her knee. she draws a picture to show how big it was and she just let it sit there, even though bees freaked her out.

On a separate sheet she wrote, "So we made the laetrile connection. It felt a little like connecting with Mexican Mafia. Did I tell you Linda's mother helped on this? Imagine this elderly woman from an upper-class Boston family driving me around getting illegal drugs, and then we had to go to a vet supply place to get the right size syringe. Then back to Roger's ex-wife's house. Remember, she's a nurse, so we all tried to figure it out we got the needle in fine but the shit wouldn't go into my vein. And we had to figure out some way that Roger and I could do it when we're back at our place. So, ended up doing a butterfly syringe, which means I have to walk around with a needle sticking out of my good arm. Just for two months. Please don't mention any of this to anyone. Remember what happened with Dr. Weddle and the acupuncture."

Into the Zebra Tree Forest

We traveled around Australia in Anthony's 1959 red Ford Fairlane. Anthony's drug of choice was marijuana. He toked whenever he got into the Fair lane. He toked when he got out of the Fairlane to pee at the side of the road, and before breakfast and after dinner, for dessert, or when he prepared to talk politics, the coming of the world brain, and our mission.

We had to spend several days in Alice Springs in order to get permission to go to the aboriginal community. I figured there was an office somewhere; we'd fill out a form and be on our way. Instead, we wandered around the town. All day in the blazing sun. We spent a lot of time in the dry riverbed in the middle of town, where many of the homeless, or nearly homeless, aboriginals lived. They had gathered in the riverbed from time immemorial so they naturally still did, even though now it was filled with litter and their homes were shanties built from debris and broken cars and trucks. Anthony would disappear into a shanty and come out later smelling like marijuana, and we would move on. They never invited me in. He came out one time with a package of Hostess cupcakes. We stopped to talk to a very old Aboriginal with a gray beard halfway down his chest. Anthony and the elder never looked at each other. They looked up to the sky or down to the red sand and rock. Anthony said,

"So, Johnny doing OK?"

"He living in the Chevy on Baxter road. Broken you know for long time."

"And did the Yanks give you back the lumber?"

"Thanks to you."

"No, just a thanks back to you. Or Lucille would still be in jail."

We moved on. Anthony was smiling but said nothing about the encounter, just, "It'll be getting hot soon. We should go inside and have a beer." As though it weren't already hot. Two young white guys we had met in Brisbane stopped us.

The tall one said, "So I hear you got permission to go to tenimie. That mean things OK with you and Papa, I suppose?"

"I suppose," Anthony said, and turned to me, "So might as well go, right?"

We left the next morning. We roared along endless primitive roads going 140 KPH. Emus in small hoards would suddenly appear in the shrub forests, almost pacing us. Then they would just as quickly vanish. Besides killing an occasional lizard or snake the size of a fire hose, and Anthony's habit of driving at high speed while talking at me like we were sitting across from one another at a table drinking beers, something else bothered me. The graveled road, even with occasional tarmac, was fairly smooth sailing, except occasionally we would suddenly dip below the plane of the landscape into creek beds. Sometimes there would be water in the creek bed. Anthony wouldn't slow down. The wheels might spin, slightly hydroplaning in the rear, but we'd sail on through.

I wondered. How could he tell we weren't about to hit a bona fide stream, raging with water, or quicksand? He had showed me the deceptive nature of ground one day by throwing a large rock into what looked like solid ground. The rock had sunk and disappeared, leaving only a tiny dimple in the ground.

Anthony had been on this road many times. His wife Lucille was originally from a village nearby. Maybe he knew the road that well. But then again, how would he know if there had been recent rain and flash-floods?

At one point he was pontificating about the power of the Internet to change the world. I interrupted him, "So, Anthony, how do you know about these streambeds...." Suddenly we were going downhill into one.

"What's that, mate?" He said, turning to me. Too much eye contact. Look at the road. Shit. The car went from 100 kph to zero with no hydroplaning. I could feel the car slowly sinking. The engine died. "Fuck!", Anthony shouted. "Ah fuck fuck." He hit the steering wheel, turned to me with his stoned smile, "But no worries, mate. I've got Anthony's special breadboard kit in the trunk for just these circumstances." He reached into his pocket and pulled out a roach the size of a Cuban cigar. "time for a toke or two." He went to open the door, but the mud was high enough that the door wouldn't open. Same on my side. "Well Fuck again." As I climbed out my window, I heard him say, "ah it's not bad. No worries. But, say mate, I need you to do something. Can do?"

One of my shoes caught on the door and I hit the soft wet mud with my face. The mud was very soft, so it didn't hurt. I wiped the mud off my face, and optimistically responded, "Sure, what ya want me to do?" I looked around. This was one of the larger stream beds we had driven through. In fact, we were far enough below the horizon that all you could see were uniform trees that looked like zebra legs in all directions. Rather oddly, all the trees seemed to be of the same size and shape, and they were equally distributed. And now, without the car engine, it was silent. I've been in quiet places, but this was another level of silence, like a black hole. I noticed that even if I walked 20 feet from Anthony, I couldn't hear him. Weird. How could I not hear? He was right there. But sounds seemed to get consumed in the vastness.

I went from panic to calm to panic. We were nowhere. The last car we had seen was at least two hours ago. All we had to eat was leftover fish and chips that we had picked up at a store in a rusty trailer from someone who looked like Crocodile Dundee on meth. We had water in a gunnysack plastic gizmo tied to the front bumper and a warm coca cola in a big gulp size plastic cup.

Anthony was intent on his weed. Puffs of smoke wrapped around his head. His red hair looked like it was on fire. "Flat rocks are what we need," Anthony said while inhaling. "they're big but light." I looked around and went up the creek bed. After-all streams and rock go together. "I'd stay clear of the creek bed if I were you. You sink, you know."

I corrected my path and headed into the zebra tree forest. Even though I had not smoked, I had a contact-high. When I first entered the woods, I could hear Anthony rummaging in the trunk, the sound of metal on metal. Then nothing. No wind. No insects. Nothing in the sky. I walked for a few minutes and found a stash of flat rocks the size of doormats. I moved on and discovered as Anthony had said; they were light. I figured I could carry three at a time. I piled them and then stood up to return to the car. I had a feeling of vertigo. There was no direction. Every tree looked identical. No sign of which way I had come. I looked for footprints. There were none. I yelled for Anthony. My voice disappeared.

As I made what felt like a complete circle, I realized there was someone or something staring at me. I turned around and came face to face with a very large Ram. I stared right into his eyes. One of those inter-species moments of recognition. His horns curved away from his head, the size of heating ducts. He didn't move, and neither did I, still holding my rocks. I tried to remember my wildlife preparedness books. What was it? Do run? Don't run? Do make eye contact? Don't? I backed away, a step at a time. He followed. Never closer. Never further away. He made a small guttural noise.

Then I heard Anthony calmly say, "Fuck, there you are. I was going to send out a search party but couldn't find anyone." He laughed. Ha. Funny joke. I turned around. He was sitting on the hood of the car, now out of the creek bed. "Guess we won't need the rocks. The old breadboard worked." I expected him to say something about the gigantic ram. I turned around. There was nothing but zebra leg trees.

In the car, I described what happened. Anthony's comment was, "Fuckin A, you found your guardian in dreamtime."

We drove past miles of serious barbed wire, and just over the horizon a tower that looked like a Star Trek movie set. "US military," Anthony said.

We climbed a gradual slope and arrived at a plateau. I couldn't make sense of what I was seeing. At first, I thought it was a dump. Piles of colorful plastic, wood, blankets, broken-down cars. As we got closer, I could see people moving about like ants. Small fires.

"Anthony, what is that?"

Anthony looked around like he wasn't sure which "that" I meant. "Oh, that," he said, toking. He explained it was where mostly male Aboriginals lived who for one reason or another couldn't live in the village. Some of them were addicted to fumes (gasoline), or had beaten their wives, or stolen from their neighbors, or were just down on their luck," he said.

"We call it the suburbs," he said matter-of-factly.

Which is why a Rastafarian Drives a Chevy Fairlane

We arrived in the village. The Colonials built it as Anthony called any white Australians, past or present, other than people like himself. Someone had described him as a feral hippie. There were several substantial buildings, and many ramshackle ones. Junk everywhere. Piled along the road in front of houses. Houses with rusty metal roofs or blue plastic tarps; unattended fires in 50 galleon drums. As we drove along the one paved road, little quick tornados of wind picked up litter and tossed it here and there. Everyone, including the kids, watched us as we drove slowly toward the largest building. It was in disrepair on the outside, except for right in front where there was a neatly landscaped and incongruously green courtyard.

We walked through the courtyard. First thing that caught my attention was a health clinic.

I pointed and said, "well that's good, right?"

"Not really," he replied, "the guy's not that good. Almost killed himself biting the head off a snake." Then the name struck me, familiar, "White Knight Health clinic." Just then Dr. White came out. He talked slowly and was really boring. Excited to meet someone from his home state, Oregon, he said like I was his first tin of spam. First time ever. I told him I might have known his father.

He said slowly and bored, "I won't bother you with the whole details, but in short, yes that was my dad who ran the clinic in Albany but he was kicked out and arrested for doing surgery while he was drunk, severed a guy's ear. So he moved here to start a new. So imagine I figured I would never run into anyway from Oregon, but here you are. I loved my father, so I kept the name of the clinic. But we're going to change the name; some think it's racist."

Further on, announced by a larger torn banner, was a radio station, KXAY. Another sign further on pointed to "Multi-Media Center." A strikingly unusual and beautiful woman sat at a barren desk. When she saw Anthony, she stood up, and with a weary smile on her face, she moved toward him and gave him a cursory hug.

"So you come back. For what? Run out? Run away?" She looked Aboriginal and oriental, a combination I had never seen before.

"This is my friend. He just discovered his dreamtime. We are here with digital cameras. You know, I told you about it." He kept looking nervously at a door labeled Multi-media Director. "And this is Isabel, my Madeline's sister." He turned to me, "But, you realize all Abs think all other Abs are their brothers and sisters."

"Better than your ways of thinking that an entire country is made up of your children you can subjugate," Isabel said as she motioned for me and Anthony to follow her. She led us to the radio station door and knocked. A young aboriginal opened the door, and for the first time I saw someone greet Anthony with enthusiasm.

"Anthony, Anthony, we've been waiting. How you been? And, guess what, just like last time you are here..." he looked at a large fancy watch, out of place with his Rastafarian garb, "in ten minutes a simulcast with Broome."

"Wow, what's the odds of that?" Anthony said as he looked around at the room, jammed full of equipment, some functional looking, more broken and frazzled. "My friend, from America," Anthony said, pointing to me. "This is Dung."

As I put out my hand, he raised his to hit a button.

"Just a second, I have to change the tape."

Isabel stuck her head in. "By the way," she said, handing me an ornate envelope, "package for you delivered by a fucked-up ab teenager high on petrol on a motorbike there's no way he could he afford." There was the Entropy Evasion League postmark. Just how the hell did they do that? A letter from Kathleen. Impossible to explain this and no one seemed to think it was strange.

"How did you get all this equipment?" I asked.

Dung finished hitting buttons and looked back at me pleasantly, but slowly. At least it seemed so. I guessed another pot smoker, which would explain his good welcome for Anthony. Finally, he said, "Years ago, a strange man came from your country with a radio station in his classic Chevy station wagon. He left behind the wagon which I still drive, and the radio station. Taught us to use it and then we never see him again."

I felt a pleasant shiver down my spine... Is this too part of dreamtime?

"His name was something like Armsworthy."

"Jack Ainsworth?"

"Yes, that is it."

Yes, I thought this was astonishing; but it was now commonplace for me.

We watched part of the live video cast of a dance performance near Broome, at the far west and north side of Australia. During the performance, enormous faces would suddenly nearly fill the 10' X 12' screen and ask to talk to someone or another. Dung would open the door and yell out a name. Sometimes someone would come, sometimes not. It was a video wormhole in outer space.

We had a small cabin to ourselves. Very Run-down. Anthony turned the kitchen water faucet. The water looked more like oil than water. I was on sensory overload. It felt either like I was coming down with the flu or on LSD. In the tiny bedroom there was a wrought iron bed. The mattress looked like a giant piece of moldy cheese. I was too tired to care and glad I had a sleeping bag. Even though it was 90 degrees in the shade, the sleeping bag was comforting.

I pulled out my Entropy Evasion League package. I realized how much I loved Kathleen's handwriting. It gave me an icy stab in my chest, remorse, mystery, guilt.

"Roger and I tried to find the sacred place we heard about when we were at Rolling Thunder's[4] encampment. It felt like we were definitely going somewhere magical. It was dry and dusky (is that a word?) everywhere then suddenly there was a meadow of wildflowers and a box canyon that looked like the kind that Hopalong Cassidy had his secret lair. You know where he would ride through a giant waterfall into a hidden canyon. Anyway, the gravel road turned to dirt then to a trail. We walked but I couldn't do it so waited while roger forged ahead. It started getting dark, and I freaked out. I worried. What if Roger was injured what the hell was I supposed to do.? I can drive an automatic but really hard with one arm to drive the jeep. I thought rather resourcefully I could get a fire started just when it got dark. Then I listened to the most amazing crazy orchestra of Coyotes. It sounded like they were all around me. It reminded me of what you said about Morgan when you sat around the fire and you looked to woods for danger and he, more rightfully, watched the road which is where, man, real danger might come from. I didn't feel unsafe but still kept myself awake and the fire going. That was good because Roger had

gotten turned around but he smelled the smoke and then could see the fire."

It occurred to me that we were worlds apart and yet we were both in the hands of indigenous people or culture and the landscapes were similar. When I woke it was dark and I was drenched in sweat. On my pillow, a giant roach (the insect type). I sat up quickly and was going to swat it when I realized it was dead.

Anthony yelled from the kitchen, "there's fish and chips in the Esky."

I wanted water desperately but didn't dare take it from the tap. Beer in the cooler. I am not a beer drinker, but it was cold and was the best beer ever. I could hear Anthony and Dung out in front of the house. Otherwise it was quiet. So quiet that I heard someone drop a utensil into a sink in the next cabin, 100 feet away. Not quite ready for the boys, I went out the back door. The sky was dark, no moon but billions of stars. The Milky Way looked like a white carpet runner.

Deafening music suddenly broke The quiet. My stereotypes took hold of me and I imagined natives preparing for war. I couldn't tell where it was coming from. It seemed to be everywhere. I walked quickly to the front of the house, trying not to look alarmed.

"What's going on?" I said as calmly as I could. They both looked at me as though I had asked them about the origins of life on earth.

"Oh, that. Disco night," Anthony said with a pot filled smile. Dung smiled. "Come, let me show you." He pulled on my arm and then never let go of it even though it meant as we went in the dark, I tripped repeatedly on stones, and even a dog and a giant rat.

"Anthony tells me you had a dreamtime experience," Dung yelled at me over the deafening music. Then directly in my ear, "I doubt it but tell me your story."

I tried the best I could to tell the story of my Ram while keeping my balance. As we walked along Dung motioned to others, who joined us. When we arrived at the building where the music was coming from, Dung stopped me, stared at me, and said, "No mate, sorry you ain't had dreamtime yet." Then he laughed, "there are no animals like you describe here. So, you couldn't have seen one. It just wasn't real." He laughed more and then opened the door.

Inside were dozens of young people in the middle of the floor dancing wildly. Along all the walls older men and women stood quietly. Many of the young people held flashlights in their hands or fastened to their heads, giving the dance floor a kind of Saturday Night Fever appearance. It was then I realized that the music was Michael Jackson.

In Alice Springs we met up with a group of idealistic young geographers and planners who worked under contract with the federal government to help aboriginal communities inventory their land holdings, substantially increased under the Land rights Act. Some Aboriginal groups had been victims of speculators and developers. The hope was that the specialists, equipped with new technologies like GIS (although Beta versions) and AutoCAD, and mountains of geographic data, could help the aboriginals determine the extent and value of their resources.

They put together data and maps and journeyed out to a remote Aboriginal community. They were discombobulated by the community elders who, after a quiet examination of their maps, made corrections and added "data." They corrected features such as the extent of floodplains.

The team was astounded upon return to their research facilities, to find that their data was wrong, and the Elder's was correct. The Elder's knowledge, for example, about floodplains, was based on generations of experience, while the scientific data had a much shorter shelf life. In areas where some plants, because of a shortage of rain, might only emerge every few years, having long term experiential knowledge is critical.

They returned to the village, apologetically. Hoping to make amends, they asked what they could do that might allow them to integrate the Aboriginal data and their "scientific" data. With little explanation, the elders instructed other residents, in particular young people, to collect a cacophony of objects and distribute the items in an acre plot in front of the community center building. There were old tires, road signs, rocks, boards, boxes, rope and string, and branches and plants strewn over the plot of land.

The process took several weeks. At the end, they announced, "Now we have a sand map." They explained the acre was a representation of their land, and the found objects were map legend symbols. At one point one of the teenagers declared to their elders, "Why didn't you tell us about all this before?"

Back at their lab, the "experts" could construct maps that integrated the Aboriginal experiential knowledge and the scientific data. Also, the map making exercise had become an interactive storytelling tool, allowing the elders to pass on knowledge to the next generation.

Dizzy with the Weight of Life

Just before I left for San Francisco and then Julie, one of the Gertrude Stein Fellowship Club's faithful organizers, died giving birth to twins. It gave the trip a kind of surrealistic element. what am I saying? All the other trips were, in my mind, surreal. I didn't know her all that well, but she haunted my dreams night after night.

Julie, at first impression, was sweet, normal, and shy. She often seemed far away. She told me in high school kids called her horsy because of her long face. I could see the horsiness, but only when she was far away. When she came back from wherever she was, and smiled, the horsiness disappeared and I noticed her beautiful brown, but sad, eyes. Like a sad-eyed lady of the lowlands. If Julie were alive today, she'd be on Prozac. She seemed to be living part of the time in a dream world where virtual people were trying to get her attention.

My impression of Julie changed over time as she told me stories of her growing up. Her father had left them when Julie was very young. He was an alcoholic and died in the burning sands of Death Valley when he ran out of gas and no one found him for a month. Her mother was a fortune teller who had many lovers and carried Julie from town to town. They would live with a man for a while or other extended families, and something would inevitably go wrong, and they would move on.

More than anything, Julie wanted to have a baby. Doctors had told her it wasn't possible, or at least not a good idea. Her cervix was small, and she had a chronically low white blood cell count, and might die giving birth. Through the salons Julie met Nick, a wispy hippie with long blonde hair. He was a Salon groupie, one of several hippies who hung out at the warehouse with nothing to do. It was large enough that people could hang out there without getting in the way. In fact, it was chaotic and lose enough that someone could probably live there and no one would raise an objection. Which in Nick's case is exactly what happened. When I noticed him two days in a row coming out of the bathroom with wet hair, I asked Jack.

"Well, maybe so," he said casually, "but he's useful."

I think he was perpetually stoned. Which meant you could give him a task like sorting flyers by zip codes and he would keep at it until he was done. All day, all night. Always smiling. He seldom spoke, but often giggled. Everything seemed to strike him as funny— our meetings, advertisements in magazines, newspaper headlines, and the ants that created small freeways in the kitchen. He would tell us everyday something new he had learned watching the ants like, "they don't have leaders but they know what they are doing all the time... you know. They never get depressed or worry about who they are... great, isn't it?"

Nick was passionate about painting. He had a theory about painting he tried to explain to me one day. It had something to do with how painting took a wrong turn in the 18th century that led to Picasso and what he called Scientific art. The only drawings I ever saw looked like billions of multi-colored worms inside decaying people, with strange titles or embedded script like: "If you think, it is too late."

Julie had tried to get pregnant several times in her life, once by a friend of her mother's, an older man who promised that he would support the child. But after they tried several times, nothing happened. So, along comes Nick, her best chance in years, and her seed finally takes hold. For months, her depressed demure disappeared. Now when she was far away she was listening to the new life inside her. Throughout her pregnancy, she followed an extreme nutritional regime. Her primary sustenance was a green nutritional supplement drink of vitamins, brewer's yeast, and wheatgrass.

I had just had flowers sent to Julie in the hospital on the day she gave birth, when Jack called and told me she had died, giving birth to not one baby, but twins. I was told she knew she had twins, had smiled, never got to see them, and then died.

It felt very unreal, especially since I was packing to go overseas. I couldn't imagine what Nick was going through. Barely able to take care of himself, now he was the father of twins.

The day before I took off, I talked to Nick on the phone. He seemed normal, that is stoned. "well you know," he said, "what was supposed to happen does...(long pause)...you know, after all, everyone knew she wanted to have a baby...." We arranged to meet up at his place.

When I arrived at his apartment, about 10 in the morning, there was the smell of marijuana in the air, and Nick was sitting with both babies on his lap. All three looked like they were stoned. Nick's mother, Sylvia, had just arrived to help her son. This seemed like a hopeful sign until she came out from the kitchen. Dressed in a worn out bathrobe, she had bleached blonde hair and too much makeup. I thought she was carrying red juice for the babies, which I thought was odd considering they had only been home from the hospital for two days. Then I realized it wasn't juice, but red wine.

We were introduced and then she lurched toward the babies, "Here, let me pick up one of the little buggers." She grabbed at Nick and almost put the glass of wine in his face, spilling some on the twins. "Do you have any children?", she said to me as she grabbed one of the twins, and then fell backward off balance, landing by coincidence on a dining room chair.

I stayed for about an hour, and by the end felt faint. The more I grasped the plight of this family—Nick perennially stoned without a job, an alcoholic mother, a disappearing mother-in-law, last reported to be somewhere in the Caribbean. It all seemed so impossible. I felt dizzy with the weight of life. It can be so brutish, so uncaring or experimental. Is someone playing with us: Here try this combination see how long it survives, with suffering as the catalytic chemical. Sartre describes a similar sense of nausea in his book by that title, just watching a tree grow through an impossible jungle of cement in a park, with such tenacity, a dumb will to survive, incapable of committing suicide.

Land of the Rising Sun: How did I get Here?

I was in Japan and like in Ecuador I had handlers. I was passed from one group to another like a baton in a relay race. But more astonishing was that I awoke one morning on a futon on the floor. The smell of tatami mats and that indescribable smell of Japan that I knew like the perfume of my mother, even though I didn't have the name. I moved my eyes around, still under the covers, expecting what? I was a prisoner? A computer network consultant? A 16-year-old kid with shaven head thinking out loud in Japanese; wondering what I could say to make Kyoto love me. But the crushing Deja vu was the noise that came next. A loud sucking. But I wasn't fooled like I was when I was a teenager. It was the honey truck cleaning out the toilet. But this was 25 years later, and I was where? Someone who still has no flush toilet?

My handler, Katuko Nomura, was like a female Mr. Phelps in *Mission Impossible*, or Charlie in Charlie's Angels. I never met her in person. We talked on the phone. Messages were relayed via our patched together computer networks, and often I was greeted at hotels with beautifully written messages from Nomura-san informing me of my next mission. I tried many times to find out more about her or meet her, but no one would help, either refused or like me were in the dark. I found out once that I had been within a 1/2 mile of where she lived, a converted Christian church north of Tokyo where she lived with her grandson. She was on the short list for a Nobel Prize.

There was very little downtime. Apple paid for the trip. I never figured out what Nomura-san's relation was to Apple. But she knew everyone.

My task was simple. I was to create the Japan part of the world brain. I pictured the brain module like the bullet train whizzing through perfect Zen like rice fields. I had 15 computer networks to distribute. They designated thirteen groups who had submitted proposals. I also had two packages that I could grant to networks of my choice. The packages were 5-6 Macintoshes, printers and network software and wiring for local networks. My role was to set up the systems, provide training, and create networks between the networks, using rube Goldberg bridging technology and willing mini computer operators so that one network could be connected to another. It was a strange period in the evolution of technology. The most dominate device in Japan at the time was the fax machine, in part because original signatures and stamps were important to Japanese businesses.

I had two other constant companions: Aki-san and Masako-san. They handed me off from one to another. I rarely knew what to expect. Aki would disappear and Masako would reappear. Aki was known as Mr. Computer Network in Japan, and Masako as the first of a fresh wave of young activists.

I visited 40 nonprofit organizations in three months. While I was god like when I came bearing computer gifts—and I was expected to bring the newest and latest in computer and social networking. When I looked back on the journey many years later, I realized I had been viewing nascent organizations and innovations that I didn't have a way to catalog at the time.

In the basement of the Imperial Hotel, designed by Frank Lloyd Wright, I set up a computer network for a group whose name did not translate well, "the against the throwaway society network." While I messed around with wires, people came and went picking up milk, vegetables (radishes that looked like erotic Portuguese man of war), eggs and bread. Yes, they explained, it is a kind co-op. There is a marriage between the farmer and the customer. They own the food and the risk together. There are 250 families who pick up their food here. The food is all made without pesticides and chemicals.

Then Masako took me aside to another room that was locked. The room was filled with hundreds of sacks of rice. When he saw he had gotten the amazed expression he hoped for, he made the universal motion for someone smoking marijuana—a very un-Japanese gesture on many fronts. He said in hard to understand English,

"Mary jane," he said smiling.

"Mary jane, who's that?" I asked innocently.

He put his fingers to his mouth, "you know you smoke it."

"You smoke rice?" I asked.

Then I realized he meant it is that valuable.

There are many groups like this in Japan. They started with resistance. This group was first against nuclear power, then against pesticides, and that grew into developing an alternative way of working with farmers to grow organic food. They want to network with other groups in Japan and around the world.

When the Apple tour was officially over, they took me to a traditional Inn near Ueno Park in Tokyo where I thought I might just stay a few days before returning to home. But, as with much of my trip, I rarely knew what was in store for me.

At 7am a voice awoke me. Rather freaky. I couldn't tell where it was coming from. I had heard it my sleep; I think. Then it seemed louder as it repeated, "your guest waiting for you." I put on my warm bathrobe and went to the lobby.

It was Masako, "are you packed?"

For what? I thought. Airport? One more organization to visit?

Masako spoke good English, but it had an odd rhythm. It was like she was pretending to be fluent and slurred words to make it seem natural. But to me, every other sentence made little sense. As we walked to catch the train, she said something like, "Today you will undergo metamorphose. Is that how you say it?" She didn't stop to get my approval.

We took the train to Yokohama and there we went up a long hill, past a cemetery for foreigners to a bluff overlooking Yokohama Bay, and a monument to American Commodore Matthew Perry. Under the caring arms of Perry who opened up Japan to the west, one after another of my comrades for the day arrived.

Kataoka-san arrived first. "Sensei, we met. Do you know Dana Space-san and Microwave Spin Surfer? I'm just on a break from Cambridge. You know the university?" His English which was fast and fluent and difficult to understand. He had blended Oxford English with London street jargon and went back and forth between English and Japanese, usually talking to 2 or more people at a time. Kuma-san, definitely a post-world war II Japanese, was a head taller than me. Impossible in the Japan of my youth. But he was quiet, almost shy.

Then, finally, Kuroda-san, who turned out to be the leader. Of what, I was never sure, but everyone deferred to him.

Masako had explained that the group we were to visit south of Yokohama, near Mt. Fuji, were futurologists. "You know," she added, as she often did. Masako told me, as though I would know exactly what that meant. Once we're on the train, everyone in our group spoke Japanese. I understood enough to know most of the time the topic, but the drone of Japanese and wonderful sound of the speeding train lulled me to sleep.

"I'm afraid you may not have underwear, yes?" Masako said brightly, as she softly shook me awake.

"No. Why?"

"Well, we will stay there. But don't worry, we have hotel send you your suitcase. But I think you will need some underwear so we will go to the shopping mall before we go. It is about a one-hour train trip and we will be back tomorrow."

"But my luggage?" I asked. "I have to be in Kyoto the day after tomorrow."

"Don't worry," she said, "the hotel will send it to the Inn you will stay at."

When we arrived, Okada-san, the leader, handed me his business card, with the group name, Metamorphosis. Oh right, now it made more sense. It was futurologists who go by the name of Metamorphosis.

Okada-san spoke an interesting English, three years in America, three years in England. He was more difficult to understand than the Japanese who had never traveled overseas. He interspersed out-of-date English and American slang with 19th century diction. He talked fast and sometimes his body language wasn't in synch with his content, like an out of step Karaoke act.

I asked him the obvious question, "Ah, Kafka, huh?" He looked dumbfounded.

I tried to explain the plot of the Kafka story. "This person wakes up as an insect."

Masaka added, "Oh, like Godzilla?"

"Not really."

Thankfully, Okada-san changed the subject. He described his grandfather who was a religious leader. He called it a cult.

"OK. Is cult a good thing in Japan?"

"Excuse us," Masako said, "we need to converse in Japanese."

While they talked, I tried to figure out what was billable to Apple? Nobody had mentioned computers all day. I didn't think Apple was interested in creating a computer network for a cult.

With the underwear crisis resolved, Masako and Okda-san told me of our plan.

"We are taking you to the Metamorphosis world headquarters.

Okada-san added, "It is very wonderful place, an abandoned hot springs town that my grandfather bought. We can take baths and drink much whiskey."

The Metamorphosis world headquarters was unique. At one time the town was quite prosperous, a destination for swell to do Tokyo businessmen. But something had happened. I never quite understood. Corruption? Or corruption in the pipes and disease. At one time there were 5000 people living in the town; now 200, not including Metamorphosis staff or cult members. But the town was very tidy. No people but nicely kept yards. Even the windows in deserted shops were spotless. It was like a Hollywood set. The

Metamorphosis headquarters was in an abandoned hotel with 100 rooms.

It was 10pm by the time we arrived and we went directly to a fully stocked bar on the ground floor. Basically, it was a wet bar since the hot spring gushed through it. This is the hot tub, Okada-san said, smiling. Yeah, a hot tub the size of an Olympic swimming pool.

For the next few hours we drank while snacking on sushi, dried fish, cold French fries and then a proper meal of strips of meat and a wild array of unknown vegetables. All the while either sitting on the edge of the hot tub or floating in the scalding water. I only fully understood the location of the hotel when I wandered down a long hallway trying to find a bathroom. I opened a door and almost fell into the hot springs. The hotel was built over the top of the hot springs river.

By time we spent an hour dipping in and out of the heated pool I was ready for sleep, but we began to work. It felt like finally I had some time I could legitimately bill to Apple. They pulled out a pile of scrapbooks and explained the work of Metamorphosis, Akada-san's grandfather cult, and a half dozen other NGOs. The Sake and beer didn't help much, but I found it difficult to distinguish one group from another. In the photographs groups of people were planting trees, or demonstrating or praying for peace, or growing food. They all drank beer. One of the Metamorphosis members who had said nothing all night told me he wanted to show me their most important work. He pulled out a scrapbook that was titled: UXP, Unexplained Phenomena. Photographs of strange lights, flying machines, people who could stop their heart from beating a rather gruesome photo of a man pulling a diseased liver out of a small girl. And, finally in one photo a young Japanese man wearing a UFO tee-shirt in front of an Apple computer.

Kataoka-san was upstairs in his living quarters when we arrived, so we talked with the next best English speaker, Toshihiro Tsubo, one of 9 members of ICPC. Tsubo-San was most knowledgeable about the computer communication experiment ICPC took part in. He explained ICPC could not physically attend a conference held in

Vancouver, Canada, so the groups worked out an arrangement by which ICPC could participate remotely using The Source, the computer communications/Information Utility based in Virginia.

Kataoka-San came down the stairs, wearing a fairly thick white sweater. He looked like a frumpy professor.

We all gathered around a round table for lunch. Kataoka explained they decided only a short while back to all cook and eat lunch together to enjoy each other's company, save money, cut down on their excess eating, and controlling the food to prevent consumption of bad chemicals or food that exploits people or the earth. I could see that this Citizen's information Center is in the integrated-concerns model of which I will see several other examples, though mostly not in the Tokyo area.

The philosophy is basically that to create social change one has to act on an individual, and community and global perspective. ICPC worked on several issues at any time which might be environmental, consumer, or social justice oriented, but they were also working on their own personal roles in the world and within the group. Kataoka was the only group representative who volunteered a description of how the group made decisions. It was consensus decision making, and it was one thing they were working on. They cooked the lunch at the table, clear broth with vegetables of many types, including very large and soft mushrooms and a small amount of chicken—and of course white rice, the only thing more common than 7-11 stores. Each person introduced themselves in English or Japanese.

After lunch we went into the second large room. I met Nomura-san.[5] She might be called the librarian of the citizen's movement in Japan. She is the one who answers questions from citizens, with answers either in her head, or by knowing where to locate it in this room full of books, reports and periodicals. They received and kept over 800 newsletters produced by Japanese citizen groups around the country. We understood each other. By the few questions translated by Masako for me, they understood that I've spent much of my life doing exactly what they did, organizing information and answering people's questions.

Finding my Way Back

The Metamorphosis workforce waved goodbye to me at the train station.

"Just stay on the train until you reach the main Kyoto station. Everything else will just happen", Masako said, followed by a pot-pourri of hand signals and broken English instructions about when we would next meet, what we were going to do together to change the world, and who would wait for me in Kyoto. My hangover was concentrated in the place reserved for my third eye, and I couldn't get enough water.

One of my favorite memories from living in Japan as a teenager was eating a bento lunch, gliding through the tidy Japanese landscape on the bullet train. And the Bento women with their carts. They entered each car, bowing and the same when leaving. The bento boxes at train stations were revealed by plastic models, but not on the train so no idea what it was but the box and wrapping was worth the price: bamboo box with a sliding lid, tiny can opener, tiny napkin, tiny straw, tiny handi-wipe. I fell asleep before I ate anything.

I only woke when we approached Kyoto. I was looking forward to two days to myself before meeting up with other NGOs. I needed time alone, precious in Japan, and I wanted to write up my notes from the journey for Apple.

At the train station there were three Japanese men holding a large sign, "American Sensei wanted." What was that about? They forgot my name? There was a good reason. My host in Tokyo had received an urgent phone message from America. I needed to call home because my father had been rushed to the hospital.

"He is dying sick," one of my greeters said.

They whisked me to a Japanese Inn. I tried to think. Sick? Dying? My father always swore he was going to live to 100, and most of us believed him. He was only 79. The Inn was just past the Geon district, not far from Kyo-Misu. My hosts got me settled and thankfully left.

It would be 8pm in Portland, a good time to call my mother. It wasn't easy to make a long-distance phone call in those days. I finally had to get help from hotel staff, which meant I had to talk to my mother, hard of hearing, with a lot of background noise.

My mom didn't always remember names, even her children, so I said, "It's your youngest child. You know, the one who can eat a spaghetti with his feet. The son you sat with in that gigantic Sitka spruce on Orcas Island."

Finally, she understood what was going on. "Are you stuck in the tree?" She giggled.

I explained I was in Kyoto not too far from where she and my father lived 20 years earlier. Time flies. I was a teenager than with all my life ahead of me, and now I had a wife who was dying in the high desert of Oregon and maybe my father.

Sobbing quickly followed my mother's giggle, and then a panicked question: "Are you coming home?"

I hadn't decided or even thought about it, although as soon as I heard her question; I knew the answer. "Yes, I will be back as soon as I can get a flight."

Her sobbing disappeared, and she gave me the basic facts. He had prostate cancer. He was home now. He could get around on his own. But he was in a foul mood. He kept repeating that his "body had betrayed him." The cancer had advanced beyond his prostrate into his liver. There was nothing they could do. He refused to take pain medicine because it gave him nightmares. Not to worry, friends and neighbors and my sisters were there all the time. And there were hospice nurses. She like them all, except for the one who kept asking her if she had thought about funeral and burial options. She made another joke, "I think we should bury him on top of Uncle Telmer and Aunt Dodo." She was referring to the family's cemetery plot and how when the family had run out of room so they put one body on top of the other: Telmer known as the family's hippie from the 1920s and Aunt Dodo, the battle-ax old maid of the family. Teenagers who hung out in the cemetery reported they could hear a man and old woman mumbling poetry after midnight at our family site.

After I talked to my mother I walked up to Kyo Misu temple. It is one of those Japanese gems, wild and yet tamed like a circus bear. It was special to me because when I lived in Kyoto I had made friends with several of the monks. They knew Japanese girls called me "kawai baby," so that is what they called me. One in particular, Ueda-san would tell me, "Today kawaii baby, tomorrow Sensei."

I found my way to the tiny "secret" entrance. Amazingly, it looked the same. An elder monk smiled at me, but held out his hand in a stop gesture. He asked me in English if he could help me. I tried to explain in Japanese-English about my childhood experiences. I ended my story with lyrics from the song that teenage girls had sung to me, "Kawaii Baby," and pointed to myself.

"Me, Kawai baby," I said in Japanese. I expected polite confusion, but...

"No. Kawai baby!" he exclaimed, sucking saliva through his front teeth. "No. Kawai baby!" He immediately led me down a path to a tiny meditation sanctuary. Inside I could see the back of a monk with bald head, gray hair. My guide was excited. I heard "kawai baby" several times. He stood up and then over to me doing a half bow, which I returned.

"It is me," he said in English, "Ueda-san." He remembered me because he was only a few years older than me when I lived in Japan, and I was the first American he had met. And stories of my sojourn there had become mythical. How I dropped my wallet in the outdoor toilet; my other nickname, "the crow who ate strawberries" (I don't remember how I got that name).

I told Ueda-san about Kathleen and my father. He showed no emotion, but I knew he was not heartless. In fact, I felt relief in telling him as though someone were hugging me closely or had pulled me from the ocean on to the deck of a ship.

"I told you someday you would be sensei. And this is how. Do you see?"

I told him how for years I had been crying to God or some power in the sky to tell me the meaning of my life.

He replied, "Hmm, maybe you shouted too loud. But this is the answer. By caring for the people, you love you will learn meaning."

Then he showed me a meditation. He poured water into a wooden bucket.

"Full?" he said when it almost reached the top.

"No."

He put more in. "Now?"

"No." It was almost to the top. He then dropped water in a drop at a time and with each drop.

"Now? No."

"Now?"

"No," I laughed. Before he could say no, I said no again. Then he didn't ask me as he let one drop fall.

"It is full now," I said, as I could see it was at the top. He kept adding drops and still it didn't overflow.

"How many? Count."

I counted in Japanese. At 23 it overfilled.

"So," he said, "you should think about what is important that long. You will know when it is enough. Stay here as long as you want. I will come back later and we will have Ocha."

After Ueda-san left me, I tried to meditate. It should have been easy. My father was dying, Kathleen and my mother were in great need. But I kept thinking of practical things: telling Apple I was cutting my trip short; appointments in Japan; getting a flight. I would focus on things I could kind of control. On the phone, my mother had gotten angry. A very rare occurrence. Typical of that generation, she often turned her anger into depression. But still she was saintly. When I told a neighbor, I thought she was saintly, she had said, "well she had to be to put up with your father."

But on the phone my mother had blurted out: "Damn him! It's your grandmother and her Christian Science crap. He had the cancer for six months before I knew, and he wouldn't let me tell you or anyone about it." I then remembered my father had told me he had been feeling exhausted, and he thought it was chronic fatigue syndrome. Something he read about the syndrome in the Saturday Evening Post. I tried to hold my father in my mind or heart. I could see him blustering through the house in his tattered red bathrobe, with a mauled and unlit cigar in his mouth singing, in a false baritone voice, Swing Low Sweet Chariot. I thought about working with him on the place he loved, the shire, and how we would never do that again. His delectable spaghetti; his love of books. The time he cut his finger off on the riding lawn mower. I felt tears well up when I remembered settling in for the evening in his Walden hut, reading Don Quixote, the smell of the mildewed sleeping bag.

But, no matter how much I tried to keep him in mind, I kept coming back to my mother. I stopped fighting it. I understood. Of course, when I returned, assuming I returned in time, I would need to do what I could to make his last days at pain free and I would want to tell him how I loved him, but my mother would be left alone. The living needed my support more than the dying.

My mother's love was almost too easy to achieve. With my father it felt like you had to earn it, and you gained it or lost it every day, over and over. If you did the right thing you gained some points; do something wrong, or something that impeded his happiness and contentment, then you had to struggle to regain it by doing many things just right. It was as though there was a complicated algebraic formula that only he knew. Sometimes I don't think my sisters and myself or even my mother wanted his love so much as that mythical book in school, the teacher's copy that had all the answers, so we would know what to do and what not to do.

I could hear the distant sounds of tourists and monks chanting; and I realized I was crying. Wailing. The wailing was in synch with the tone of the monks' chanting. My father was disappearing, my mother couldn't be too far behind. I was crying for myself too. Soon I would stand on that cliff, with no one in front and all the unborn and younger behind me, telling me to get out of the way.

My mother tried things as a parent that when I thought of them, it was the ordinary or botched parenting that made me most sad. When we purchased our first freezer she relentlessly used it to achieve Betty Crocker excellence. She froze my father's vegetable garden for the winter and made lunches for us weeks in advance. The frozen peanut butter sandwiches on white bread turned into a concoction that could be squished into a piece of dough the size of a marble. The lunches were so bad that in grade school I dumped them into an empty locker until the stench alerted my teacher. The contents filled an entire garbage can. But her love was so unequivocal that I could never criticize her. If she got me the wrong present for Christmas or my birthday, I accepted it and only cried or got angry in the solace of my bedroom. If she brought back an utterly stupid souvenir from a parent-only vacation, I made sure she saw me play with it or wear it.

I had tears for my mother mingled with anger, toward my father and his intellectual friends. They were cruel. They didn't think of it that way. Academic dog eats dog world. Everyone else in the circle had PhDs., even most of the women. I found cliff notes[6] on American and English classics hidden in my mother's closet. She wrote a column for a coastal newspaper and occasional brief articles in the Oregonian. They humored her. Charming, they said. Code word for cute, like how one commented on a high school production of Hamlet.

When Ueda-san came back he had drawn a picture of me as kawai baby, super-imposed with a picture of me now, and one of me as a very old man. I told him what I had been thinking about.

He said, "Well, I think your neighbor was right. You don't become a saint or learn the meaning of life by having fun and no pain. You learn it through pain and giving with expecting no reward. Think of your opportunity. I am sure you will know the meaning of your life."

All The Animals in the Zoo

The last time I came back from Japan, I had metamorphosed from a caterpillar (a delinquent) to a butterfly. Well, at least the aspirations to become one. Now I was coming back, about to face the fact that I was the next one to stand on the cliff of mortality.

When we came through customs at SeaTac, it was like we were staring into an exotic zoo behind glass. While Japan is filled with as exotically unique people as anywhere on the planet the basic body types are a narrower range. Dark hair, few people overweight, not as much difference between short and tall. I felt the nausea Sartre described watching roots forging through the earth. Too much fecundity. Hippos, Duckbilled platypuses, Giraffes, lions, tigers and bears. I felt dizzy and grabbed the shoulder of an American businessman who turned around at first annoyed and then stared at me,

"Hey Nature Boy!"

Ah, shit. What? How could I know someone here?

"You don't recognize me, do you? Gerald Gumbert. You know Cleveland High school?"

The focusing lens of Disney time-lapse camera. It was him. But not. It was a Gerald who had turned gay. Or at least that was my assessment.

"Right," I said, trying to get to the heart of something. "You remember how in third grade we put up Christmas decorations. I was thinking of that the other day... how weird you know you're Jewish, Right?"

He laughed. "Not only that, but I'm a gay felon." He put his hand on my shoulder. "Not of the axe murdering type. I got caught up in the—you remember him, Doug Glancy—junk bond scandal."

We moved forward. Other people were listening.

"What else was there to do. I got six months and six months of voluntary service. And guess who that was with? You remember Cathy? (yes, the Cathy I would pray to the Gods of Fallen trees to, so she would notice me falling in the primeval forest)." She's a Buddhist and works for a soup kitchen with no worldly belongings."

That was way too much for me. I described my life in a nutshell. Something like...."I work for Apple. Training weird groups like Metamorphosis in Japan. My wife is dying of cancer in eastern Oregon and my father doing the same a few miles from here... And there is a warrant for my arrest for refusing to go to Viet Nam. But, I'm heterosexual."

Now people turned deliberately away. One guy in back of us said loud enough for others, "fuckin weirdo!" I gave Gerald my business card, an old one with wrong information. I caught him looking at me now and then. With one horrifying image from growing up, I hadn't had since. Gerald had started a pornography ring, using his basement darkroom he had taken pictures of me so I looked like a sexy teenage girl. We could sell naked photos of me to small kids for fifty cents each.

On the short flight from Seattle to Portland, my stress level increased. I wanted to be at Kyo Misu. I didn't want to be at my father's deathbed. I wanted to be there for my mother. I wanted to say everything, or at least the one perfect thing I should say to my father. I wished Kathleen and I were back together. Couldn't we just go back to Cascadia and be pondering tasks for the day like cleaning the latrine or smoking Panama Red and bathing in the icy waters of Dobbin creek. Grow old like everyone else. Maybe even slowly become retro-red necks; so slow that we didn't even notice.

I had told my mother I would move into my uncle's house. My father and I had spent countless hours cleaning up after my uncle. I realized my father probably had cancer then. One day I spotted him sitting on a stump smoking one of his stinky cigars. I hid and watched him. He got up and moved 100 feet and sat again. Twice. I had smiled thinking he was pondering Santayana or something. In hindsight, he was ill. He had been probably telling my mom he was off to go work in the yard and then found places to hide and then would go in for lunch as though he had put in a day's labor. I had asked him what I could do, and he told me the Walden hut needed some roof repair.

I hadn't been in the hut for some time. When I went inside my foot went through the floor. Almost the entire floor was rotted out. When I looked up, I could see that the roof likewise was rotting. I quickly exited. The hut was a goner. But, I couldn't tell my father so I shored up the roof with some 2 x4's and when I was finished I told my father I had fixed it. I knew he wasn't using it anymore. My uncle's house, 20 times the size and with running water and electricity, was his new Walden hut.

Just before I left for the Amazon I had found him sitting peacefully on the A-frame's deck. He was at peace; it seemed. Finally, he didn't have to look over at my uncle's chaos, the poor man's laboratorium, the dilapidated deck. He had been victorious. But also maybe not at peace with himself. He talked obsessively about my uncle. His obsession with Thoreau or Santayana had been replaced with memories and pondering about my uncle. He had a journal devoted to memories and sayings, like "Ken, you know you can't dig a hole with a pen."

I snuck into the compound via the back road. It was late, and I didn't want to disturb my mother. But I also just wanted to ease my way in. I figured if maybe I could sleep for ten hours, I might shake off jet and culture lag and develop a strategy for how to cope with this stage of life.

When I finally felt like I had created the appropriate and robust persona, I walked slowly up the trail to the main house. I tried to stretch time so that my own life felt long. My earliest recollection was when my sister had "accidently" shot an arrow in the sky, and not knowing where it landed, it landed in my eyebrow; a half inch lower and I would have been my one-eyed lady wrestling teacher's pet.

Nothing could have prepared for the scene as I entered the house. There were 5 cars in the driveway. A large woman greeted me at the door who might have been an understudy for Nurse Ratched in *One Flew Over a Cuckoo's Nest*. My oldest sister, who upon seeing me, burst into tears, then my other sister who said in her most officious and loving tone, "Well thank god. Your father is being a royal pain in the butt! One nurse won't come back and I've had it. I've got an actual job." With that, she grabbed her purse and was gone.

The kitchen was full. Who the hell were all these people? My sister introduced me. Nurse Ratched, hospice nurse #1, Sylvia, a social worker. John, a lawnmower guy hired after Phil had left because of a parole violation. John, a neighbor I had never met, who just kept saying your father is a great man.

---

1. The *Yage Letters* by William Burroughs and Allen Ginsberg, City Lights Books, 1975. A collection of letters between the two, written while they were traveling in

the Amazon river basin. One of their aims was to experience the native hallucinogenic plant, Ayahuasca.

2. *The Crying of Lot 49* (1965) is by American author Thomas Pynchon. The narrative follows Oedipa Maas, a young Californian woman, who embraces a conspiracy theory as she possibly unearths a centuries-old conflict between two mail distribution companies; only one of these companies, Thurn and Taxis, actually existed (1806–1867) and was the first private firm to distribute postal mail.

3. Vonulife was an underground mail service and support network focused on returning Vietnam veterans who could not cope living in urban areas and lived in the wilderness of southern Oregon and Northern California. See: *Transformation of Civic life in Portland Oregon*, Steven Reed Johnson.

4. Rolling Thunder (birth name: John Pope, 1916–1997) was a hippy spiritual leader who self-identified as a Native American medicine man. He was raised in Oklahoma and later moved to Nevada.

5. Katsuko Nomura, https://nader.org/2010/08/27/katsuko-nomura-consumer-champion/

6. Cliff Notes are study guides to literature and science topics. Originated by Clifton Hillegass and Catherine Hillegass in 1958. Today there are about 180 guides and many similar series.

NO PLACE LIKE HOME

Preamble

When my father and then my uncle died, I realized that my life with Jack was a separate reality from my tribal one. Jack met them both twice but his response, I thought, to their death was on the level of "sorry for your loss." But then we found some unfinished pieces Jack wrote about both of them. Not about their deaths, just who they were. Again, not always sure what I wrote, and he did. For example, I am pretty sure jack wrote this about my uncle:

"He loved old movies, in particular Charlie Chaplin and W. C. Fields. When I was in grade school, he would take me to the movies. He embarrassed me because he laughed loudly and repeated the lines out loud. But he got me popcorn. On the way home he would say over and over, "No, sir. They just don't make movies like that anymore." My uncle didn't watch old comic movies. The only connection point between Jack and my uncle is a junk drawer item; a photo of my uncle's poor man's greenhouse. The thing is, it seems so like my uncle.

Likewise, in the story references to my father's love of Thoreau; a photo of his Walden hut in the woods at the Shire. But Jack wrote this:

"Sometimes when he got angry at me, he would later apologize. He wouldn't tell me he was sorry. But, he might give me the larger piece of meat at dinner. I was supposed to read the subtext... something like: I am the alpha male. I am giving up my bigger piece of meat to you. I have unresolved issues from my childhood. Your Uncle, my brother Ron, was always better than me and he always got the best of everything. And I would have been happier if women had desired me like a Chippendale dancer. Sometimes I'm not angry at you, you are the closest male with less power. I can't seem to control my temper, and I'm not sure I want to. It feels good. The piece of meat was like a red wheelbarrow in the rain or a haiku. I could easily see my father acting this way."

Not sure why, but Jack left only my journal entry about our reunion. I found two fragments from may have been a longer equivalent journal entry. He had made it look like it was mine, but never completed the deception. He might have done this on purpose, but keep in mind, unbeknownst to the rest of us, Jack may have been ill.

There was a partial description of a remodeled Gertrude Stein warehouse. Back story was that Fire and Police and Planning departments had all but closed the place down, but Jack's benefactor had come through and saved the day. He described a classroom full of unopened new computers and printers, like "a social change agent if it was created by a trust fund baby."

The Poor Man's Greenhouse

The police had to break down my uncle's door when he failed to respond. They found him sitting in his lawn chair with the television on and a TV dinner on a 1950s style TV tray. He may have been dead for three weeks. The police told my father there were maggots in the TV dinner. Why did they provide him with that detail?

My uncle lived alone all of his life; most of those years in a house he built in the dark woods a few hundred feet from the house I grew up in and where my parents were living when he died. In the last couple of years, other than my father, utility meter readers, and occasional vandals, I was my uncle's only visitor.

He never had garbage service. I found him one day pitching tin cans into a fire pit that was all embers and no flames. There were three old fans with extension cords leading back to the house. "I can get the temperature in the pit to over 1500 degrees, enough to melt everything," he explained.

He loved old movies, in particular Charlie Chaplin and W. C. Fields. When I was in grade school, he would take me to the movies. He embarrassed me because he laughed loudly and repeated the lines out loud. But he got me popcorn. On the way home he would say over and, "No, sir. They just don't movies like that anymore."

He was always at our family Christmas gatherings. For years he gave lobster tails as presents to everyone, even us kids. He handed them out, still frozen in white butcher paper. He also got inebriated. My father gave him the task of bringing alcohol for a punch. He would sometimes bring Rum, one year 150 proof. That was the year my father was living in Japan and my mother had so much punch she forgot to turn the oven on for the turkey and my nephew had to go find an already cooked ham. While the family was all in the kitchen trying to mend the disastrous dinner, I found my uncle in the living room. He was hugging the family cat and crying.

My uncle was always trying to demonstrate that my dad's liberal arts education (Reed College), and Master's degree in philosophy from the University of Nebraska, didn't give him any real knowledge. He would tell me, "you know you can't dig a hole with a pen." He had a degree in engineering and he knew you had to use a pen, but he surveyed roads for the BLM. Real stuff. One day he heard my father yelling for help and found him caught up a tree. His ladder had fallen over. He finally had a teachable moment. My uncle stood below him and gave him a lecture about how to secure a ladder. It must have been a decisive moment for my uncle. His older useless philosophy major brother hanging from a branch.

He loved to ski. In World War II he was in the Seventh Mountain Division. In letters he described his tasks as a soldier in the Italian Alps, taking out remote German outposts. On one of those treks he came across an abandoned monastery. He found an 18th century Vatican papal decree. He brought it back to America as a gift for my father. Years later, I attempted to return it to the Vatican library. They told me they didn't have a copy. I almost took it with me on a trip to Italy but change my mind, thinking I might end up in prison.

My Uncle took care of ducks on his pond. Sometimes when I visited him, he would be striding around with nothing but swimming trunks on and a silver hardhat with 30 or more ducks following him. It was touching, a BLM version of Dr. Doolittle.

There was a particular ritual I used to announce my visit. You couldn't easily get to his front door because the front porch had rotted out. There was a plank that led across a small marsh. To get his attention, I would walk around the pond in front of his house pretending to do something: looking for salamanders; examining one of the dismantled lawnmowers. If he wanted to see me he would come out, often with an extra cup of instant coffee, sometimes a jelly doughnut.

The last time I talked with my uncle was about a month before he died. I paced around in front of his house, then pretended to be clearing out one of the many pipes that fed water into the pond. Finally, he came out with a gruff but endearing welcome, "What you doing there?" He didn't like people fussing around with his intricate water system. He loved pipes. and fixtures. He could have opened up a pipe fixture store. He made his way carefully down the wobbling plank from his front door, with an extra cup of Nescafe, and a jelly doughnut. The coffee tasted like beef bouillon and there was a dead insect floating in the cup.

My uncle always had projects, always in progress. He showed me his greatest achievement, what he called the poor man's greenhouse. To the indiscriminate observer, the greenhouse might look like a pile of rubble. He built it out of road signs and plywood collected from the nearby creek. He covered the top of the greenhouse with clear plastic to let the sun in. One of the greenhouse's innovative climate control features was 15 down sleeping bags in large garbage bags. The greenhouse was heated by 3 heat lamps and 1 space heater. He also had 2 flood lamps that lit up at night. The heat lamps were on all the time. The space heater was on a timer. He could control the system from his lawn chair inside the house. Sometimes, at night, he turned the floodlights on and off to see if it was working, surprising night creatures like a Great Horned owl.

"Look at that," he said, boastfully, pointing to a gigantic thermometer in the greenhouse, "70 degrees!" Another thermometer on the outside revealed it was 40 degrees. Inside, I could make out several tomato plants with red and yellow tomatoes. Impressive considering it was almost Thanksgiving. There were also a dozen stalks of corn. I told him about tomato plants I had seen near Klamath Falls that were five or six years old that ran the length of a greenhouse with vines that were like tree limbs. Old growth tomatoes, I said, heated by geothermal wells. "Oh," he said, as though a great mystery had been solved, "You can do that if you got geothermal."

We surveyed the growing number of partially dismantled lawnmowers. I counted ten. Four more than last time. Without irony he said, "You know some people take these things apart and can't ever get them back together." Then he took me to a cluster of beat up ice chests. "Refrigerator quit on me, so I've been using dry ice. Still have some Coho that Smoky and I caught. He opened an ice chest to show me the salmon. Inside was the rotting body of a large salmon. The stench almost brought up the Nescafe and jelly doughnut. I tried to make eye contact. Could he see what I saw, or smell? Nothing. No sense of irony. He seemed to not notice the smell nor think there was anything amiss. There were maggots crawling in and out of the eye sockets and mouth. "OK," he said, I have to get on. I'm sorting slides from the Squaw Valley Olympics." With that he walked off up his plank and disappeared, leaving me staring at the rotting fish.

I went back to my life across town but obsessively worried about my uncle. When I tried to go to sleep, I would see the ice chest with rotting fish and the mountains of junk surrounding his house.

A week after the rotting fish episode, I went back to visit him. I conducted my usual ritual. Back and forth in front of his house. Nothing. I moved some copper pipe around, thinking the noise would stir him. I thought about even going up the treacherous plank leading to his door, but turned away and walked slowly back up the hillside. Half way up I paused, looking out over the creek, thinking maybe I should go back. Then an image came to mind. I saw him sitting in front of his black and white television dinner with a TV dinner. His head was bobbing up and down, in and out of sleep. I realized I was my uncle's best friend.

After his death, my father and I had to clean up the place. I knew my father, who died only a year later, could not do it alone. We could barely get into the house, piled with junk. There was a pathway through the junk that led from the front door to the kitchen, and one to the bathroom, and to his bedroom. He slept on a mattress on the bedroom floor. Piles of National Geographic, his favorite magazine, next to his bed. In front of his bed on an apple crate was a photograph. I recognized the woman. I think the only love of his life, a woman he had met when he took Author Murray dance lessons. I later found a photo of the two of them in a dance studio, with my uncle holding her in a kind of Tango move. He was smiling.

It took my father and me six months to clean up my Uncle's place. We hauled off 18 truckloads of junk. When I first started shifting through mountains of junk in his house I was methodical, thinking there might be things of at least nostalgic value. Then I realized it would take years and began instead to be ruthless. Until one day I picked up a box of moldy jelly doughnuts and noticed an official-looking piece of paper stuck to the moldy doughnut box.

It was a deed to two acres in Sun Valley, Idaho.

My father sent me off to Sun Valley to assess the value of the land. At the time Sun Valley was in a slow decline. It had been a prime destination spot, but Colorado ski towns like Aspen had taken predominance. There were still many vacation homes the size of small department stores. When I was being guided about town by a real estate agent, I noticed one home in particular, on top of a spectacular promontory. I commented on the size of the place.

"Funny thing about that one," the agent said. "Awhile back the security alarm went off on it and it took the police quite a while to track down the owner. They finally found him in upstate New York. They explained the situation about his house."

He at first told them they must be mistaken, then he admitted, "Oh right, that is my house." And angrily, "I built it for Cynthia, and she left me for a fuckin' musician."

"Imagine," the real estate agent said, "being so rich you don't remember you have a $15 million home in Sun Valley."

So, here is the strange thing about my Uncle's life and legacy. The story of my finding a deed to acreage in Sun Valley was passed around and transmuted into a legend of treasures he hid at The Shire. There were rumors of boxes of gold coins, sets of precious china, German Nazi diaries (he had this, really; never found), a small gold dragon sculpture. The only things anyone found were three fifty-gallon drums of gasoline and several boxes of World War II army uniforms and rations. For years people wandered around with metal detectors. We had to call in police once when two guys got into a fight over a fragment of china.

Damn It Not That Way

My father often lost his temper, and his moods dominated our home. If he was in a good mood, so was the household. When I came home from school, I would review what I had or had not done. There was always something I had done wrong. Instead of feeling like home was the one safe place, it could feel like one more place where I didn't live up to someone's expectations.

One of the things that upset my father was how I didn't put things back where they belonged. The problem was he didn't have an organizing scheme; no tool cabinet or peg board. Things belonged where he last put them.

I have fond memories of my father. When he was in his Walden hut reading he was satisfied with his life and wanted to be a good father. We sometimes stayed in the hut overnight. After dinner we would walk down the winding trail to the hut. A long skinny flashlight (with 5 batteries!) led the way. The trees were so thick in those days that the light could only shine a few feet before meeting the impenetrable. If you didn't look in front of you on the trail you would step on gigantic orange and olive-green slugs. The trail was their slow motion highway.

From the hut you could hear the nearby creek and several springs. From most anywhere you could hear frogs, and in late summer, crickets.

When it was cold and rainy, we would light a fire. My father would get out the old brown sleeping bag from a cedar chest. The bag would be cold at first, but as our bodies warmed up the inside, it would give off the comfy smell of Oregon mildew, Johnson bodies, cedar chips and flannel. Sometimes we would have a small snack, most likely hot chocolate in a thermos and cookies. Then he would read stories out loud. He was a good reader in part because he knew the stories so well. To prepare for his classes as an English professor, he had read some stories countless times. I figure in his 35 years of teaching the same American literature class he read Turn of the Shrew and Daisy Miller 150 times. I listened to him and watched the fire or the hypnotic neon glare of a Coleman lantern. Now and then I would drift off and sometimes fall dead asleep. My father's loud voice would come cascading down halls of sleep, taking forever to reach me, "are you awake?" Most of the time I thought I had been awake, but when he posed questions to see if I was following the story I realized I had combined plots from several stories along with my own dreams.

The stories my father read me tended to be adventure stories, and curiously they were all asexual heroes: Robinson Crusoe, Don Quixote, and Natty Bumppo. Later, when hippies dropped off the grid, myself included, it seemed very natural. Doesn't everyone want to be self-reliant, drop off the grid and set out on quests?

We moved my father from his favorite living room chair to his library room a few days before he died. It was an appropriate place for him to die, surrounded by hard bound books. Just above his head, the complete works of Santayana, the subject of his master's thesis. We had ordered a hospital bed through the Hospice program, but it hadn't arrived so he was lying on a narrow futon bed.

The last week I camped out in the bedroom next to his library. One of my duties was to administer the morphine. It occurred to me that I was killing my father. The hospice nurses provided broad clues, like give him whatever you feel is appropriate. There was no law in Oregon, as there is now for assisted suicide. When I gave him morphine in a dropper under his tongue, I remembered wishing him dead when I was growing up. From my father's point of view, I just never did things the right way. And now I was killing him. He was the lost and confused child, and I was the adult. Now and then I had to roll my father over so he wouldn't get bedsores. The last time I did this, I reached under his chest as I had before to turn him, and he shouted out in pain, with that scary voice he used when he was angry at me, "God damn it not that way." That was the last thing my father ever said to me. In the Hollywood versions of our life with Pachelbel soundtrack, our loved ones say the perfect thing that will reconcile the hurts and confusion or an enduring comment that we could always remember with fondness. But funny thing is I do often remember his last words and when I tell others, they often laugh and find twisted solace.

Jack and Narrator Reunited

I did not want the world to tell me anything new. I screened my phone calls, which was tricky. My phone was a hotline dedicated to helping my mother die. But, because she was losing her facilities by the month, including her hearing, I couldn't rely on my phone machine. She got stage fright and would hang up. I also had to accept all calls from her helpers: doctors, dentists, nurses, social workers, gardeners. I spent as much time with them as I did with my mother.

I continued to get odd postcards and packages from Jack, but we hadn't talked in months. Then one day he called 5 times in an hour.

"Jesus pick up, I will not hurt you. I can hear you breathing. I have $10,000 for you, and beauty or truth whatever comes first."

So, I picked up. He was living in the Gertrude Stein warehouse. He was embarked on what he called the Last Roundup. He had taken over the third floor and was organizing everything he had accumulated during 40 years of networking. He was returning stuff—papers, letters, sculptures, paintings, posters, flyers, newsletters—to the receivers, the original owners or people he thought might need the stuff, or sometimes people picked randomly from the telephone book. Jack was living in his junk drawer! which took up an entire floor. He had 15 boxes for me.

The idea of Jack still filing and refiling mountains of papers that documented invisible fringe people, or reclaiming stuff that documented naïve exploits from my youth, was not very appealing. But I decided to reclaim my boxes.

I had never been to the 7th floor in the Gertrude Stein warehouse. Above the 5th floor, the elevator made strange noises like a raccoon in heat.

When I opened the elevator door, I almost left. It was like being in Willie Wonka's chocolate factory on a hangover; instead of chocolate, it was filled with information. A gigantic space; large enough and dark enough that at least in one direction there seemed to be no end. The space was dominated by row after row of cinder block shelves with neatly arranged boxes. Along almost every inch of the outside walls there were paintings, sculptures, maps, enormous posters. At the beginning of each row of boxes there was a small table. On each table: marking pens, tape, staplers, empty file folders, and envelopes. In front of one row was a heavy-duty weighing scale, and a very large and battered US Postal service zip code directory.

Jack's living space was an island, surrounded by the tide of boxes. A large round braided rug defined the living room with a stuffed couch and two worn reclining chairs. There was a dining area with a large wire spool surrounded by stumps with pillows nailed to the tops. The kitchen had a 1950s vintage refrigerator and a two-burner electric hotplate. There was a large ornate canopy bed next to a stained-glass standing lamp.

In the middle of the spool table there was a delicate flower arrangement in an elegant crystal vase. Like the canopy bed, out of place in this world of boxes and museum still-life, archive, or theater deep storage.

Jack was there to greet me. It was good to see him; like seeing a favorite uncle. His hair had turned from gray to white. He had a new hairdo. He caught me staring at his hair as he held out his hand, "My niece calls me the last of the Mohawks." No hello, no how are you, he just pointed to the flower arrangement. "Funny thing about the flowers," he said as he handed me a cup of tea. "you should try this. It's the last of my sanpaku tea." On the teacup it said, "I was there. Were you?"

"Once a month I get a call, telling me to leave." He smiled in his inscrutable way that always made me wonder if he was telling the truth, followed by wondering if it mattered. "And when I return there is always a flower arrangement"—he pointed to the flowers as though he were on the Price is Right showing the prize behind door number two—"and sometimes a poem or a letter, usually from famous people —I mean the real McCoy, like a letter from President Taft to Eleanor Roosevelt." He handed me a thick envelope. "This time was the biggest one. $10,000."

I had never held $10,000 in hundred bills. It reminded me of handing over my donation to the Shaman in the Amazon. If it were anyone but Jack, I would have asked questions. Who? Why? But it was jack.

We talked about this and that. He had killed off the Gertrude Stein Salons. First, he brought out a ratty journal. It was a listing of what had happened to many of the groups who had been tenants at the Gertrude Stein Fellowship club. It was like high school reunion, where are they now report.

Where are They Now (1990)

Abundant Life Seeds—became seeds for Jesus. reborn
Academy of Socialism—merged with Far-Left hand Socialist alliance
Apocalypse Reconstruction Company—when world ended they disbanded
California Green Lace Wings Collective—have an impressive line of Tofu products
Captain Compost—in prison for rape
Coalition of International Cooperative Communities —vanished
Continuum Limited—vanished
Dana Space Achley—had sex change
Dicelife Foundation—It was only Slim really, and he operates a water witching service; drives an Edsel with large mountain goat horns on his hood
Dildo Press—last booklet, *Liberating Masturbation*
Dr. Gus's Irregular and Uncertain Health Clinic—he became a proper doctor. Works in Albany, Oregon
Earth Reassembly Factory—merged with Apocalypse reconstruction company
Emma Goldman Collective—disbanded after the movie Reds came out. People thought they were friends with John Reed, or that is Warren Beatty.
Esperanto—gave up when they saw the world wide web came into being Experiments in Art and Technology That was always just one guy in Toronto who died of HIV infection
Fallen Arches (anti-Macdonald) —totally disbanded. Just left some Big Macs for their last rent.
Family Circus—joined with some larger circus group
Fat Chance—vanished
Fields of Merit—vanished
Firebrand Commune—bought land had their communal

dream but someone offered them shitload of money for the land. They used the money to start an organic food market.

Float Town—Their boat sank

Friends of Henry George—Bob Benson carried out their work until he died.

Frog in the Well Collective—vanished

Futures Conditional—Last I heard, the leader was big into Reed College alumni activities

Great Western Radio Conspiracy—vanished

Here Comes the Sun—Still living on revenue for a solar collector

Imagebank—that was always Jack. Mr. Peanut Head, our mascot is still on the warehouse.

In a Nutshell—vanished

Jaybird Information—changed name to White Eagle

Koinonia House—Now Safety Security Office, Portland State University

Living Systems Institute—Founders died

Madame Blavatsky Study group—an interesting story, but I can't divulge it.

Main Street Gathering—There is an article in the Oregon historical Society Quarterly about their place in history.

Muddy Duck Sound—moved to Seattle. Work with surviving members of the Random Lot

New Life Environmental Design Network—got involved in alumni association Lewis and Clark College

North Paranoid Climbing School—Founder has Parkinson's

Observations from the Treadmill—vanished Pomegranate Design-Founder has Parkinson's

Portland Community Warehouse—Helped start Food Banks in Portland

Pot Walloper—Help run a barter festival in Okanagan

Pragtree farm—still in northern part of the state of Washington

Quicksilver Messenger Service—Got involved in CompuServe

Reality Library—changed their name to The People's library

Science in the Neighborhood—went back to speech writing after founder's experience doing that for Barry Goldwater

Service Exchange—taken over by a tool lending library in North Portland

Society of Strangers—founder had a heart attack

Sonny Blue Boy Astrology— popular national column for a while but wife abuse charges kept circulating around him

Stone Mountain Trail Institute—vanished

Sumerian World Improvement Association—vanished

Talking Leaf Association—vanished

The Rap Line—vanished

The Wastebin—Merged with Cloudburst Recycling Inc.

Universal-one Center—Founder in prison for fraud

Webfoot Postcard Collectors Society—the last of the collectors, Mrs. Oglie, died just a few years back

STALKING THE WILD KATHLEEN

It was like telling me a Ford pickup was in love with Joan of Arc

The discovery of Jack's real and virtual love affair with Kathleen was like a grieving process. Several milestones. When I finished reading *Falling in Love while still being reconstructed* and *Wormhole between the Shire and New World Order* I realized I could not distinguish between reality and fiction. Was that really how we met? But maybe more disconcerting was how I liked the fictional version more than the real one, or maybe closer to the point; the fictional version seemed more like the real one, as though Jack had tapped into an alternative universe. I got lost in that thought for an entire afternoon. Wondering why if that were the case, why did Kathleen have to die? Or maybe it was me writing the story about Jack and Kathleen; I was the outsider.

Jack Ainsworth stole my stories, and in effect stole my life. But, it's like a thief broke into your house and fixed everything, bought new things, created organization where there was chaos. I was sitting on my perfect couch in my perfect home with the perfect view, and when my family came home, they were quintessential versions of themselves.

It started out as fun and games. And not cheap thrills but games like only God can create, or in this case Jack Ainsworth, who I held almost as high as the big Kahuna. After all these years, and the pain he created in my life, I still love the guy. I know he changed my life. Sometimes it is hard to acknowledge the change, like the butterfly thanking the larvae.

I never saw Jack angry, and I saw no one else angry at him, including myself. To be clearer. I never saw people *exhibit* anger toward Jack. I was angry at him for many things, but whenever I had the opportunity to confront him, I was speechless. Here is my theory. Jack acted like an innocent youthful prankster, even when he was old. In a more elevated status, he was like the prankster Coyote. What he did might prickle or confuse you, but he did it for your own good. The action I could have the most anger about was his relation to Kathleen. But what did he do? He never touched her; never really stole her. He did some creepy things like spying on her. But even that was rather innocent. He liked to watch her boil water or pull her split ends, not undressing or making love with someone else. Also, most of the time people didn't even know what he was doing or didn't understand that he caused a revelation in their life.

On some days I went from complete trust to total mistrust.

Imagine having onset of Alzheimer's at the same time as global warming triggered tidal waves that erased 1/2 world's population, and they arrested our president for stealing bubblegum from a 7/11. That's how well I remember the day my life changed. I met Jack Ainsworth on the phone and began a slow breakup with my wife, Kathleen.

Sometimes the very thing that sends us head over heels in love ends up drives us crazy and out of the relationship. Right? Well, that's been a theme in my life. Kathleen's desire to be born a deer or eagle instead of a person was infatuating when I was in college. But I didn't know she really meant it.

Sometimes my entire life seemed like a succession of Deja vu. Sometimes I would have a rush of images and experiences that rushed forth from the depths like water churning up from the sea in the Devil's tunnel. Or paranoia would set in and it seemed everyone was in on the joke except me. I was standing in a party with a spotlight shining on me and everyone staring, but I hadn't noticed. Meanwhile, my biggest concern was that I had spilled beer on my white pirate blouse. There were billboards on highways forever... How could you not notice?

Let's start way back. Why wouldn't I notice that one of my best friends and mentor had kidnapped my wife?

Just how smart we are in hindsight. Duh. Right. The first clue was how dis-interested Jack was in Kathleen. I figured they might be like oil and water. Jack drilled people with Rasputin eyes and a mischievous aura that would put Kathleen on edge. She looked away, and since becoming beautiful and being deceived many times, she was shy and mistrustful. Her response to Jack is about what I calculated. It was Jack's that should have cued me in. He was too disinterested. He was always interested in people, at least for a while. With Kathleen, he seemed bored and just polite.

Then there was the junk drawer process. About the same time, we discussed the Japan anomaly, Gus and I both noted the same thing about Kathleen. Of course, there would be many junk drawer items related to her in what was our junk drawer. But there were some things that were found that seemed out of place. Why would Kathleen have had so many things in what was otherwise mostly my junk drawer? Look at this list:

1 carved wooden comb
1 torn baby picture
1 blue polished agate
5 bobby pins
A broken ear ring shaped like heart
Several rubber bands
An old photo of Adlai and Estes
Perfume stick, "occur"
Thermometer
Angel face compact
Matches from Hotel Olympia, Indonesia Raya, Eddie Mays

Free sample Dial deodorant
Gold painted Santa Claus head
13 bows (blue, white, Gold and silver)

Jack had a Kathleen box. It was a very new banker box filled with letters, grocery lists from our refrigerator, photos of beautiful animals, mostly Robinson Jeffers and sierra club photos. and some of Kathleen's photos. He had saved more of Kathleen's life than I or anyone else had. To me the longer the distance from when she died the briefer her life seemed. My memories of her seemed to be etched in parts of my brain, repeated so often that I rarely had a unique image or memory. There were many surprises in the box, including artifacts that I don't think were Kathleen's but might have been in an alternative universe, like a small set of deer antlers, partly configured to carry electricity. I took several hours to examine the box's content. One disturbing observation was that some items matched ones that were supposedly stolen by a stranger when she and I shared a house. Was Jack the burglar?

There are so many analogies in this story to what I felt like when I figured out that Jack stalked Kathleen for at least 10 years. He had written himself into being me all the way back to college days when we met. His most intensive re-writing projects were about when Kathleen and I met. I figure he figured if he claimed the beginning, he could erase me like the Cheshire cat.

The pieces didn't fall into place until recently and it was, of course, by coincidence. I was sitting at Gus's desk waiting for him to return from a meeting with the Gertrude Stein bookkeepers. He was late, and I happened to see a pile of exchanges—computer printouts —between me and Kathleen. But they were not the ones I had sent or received. I only got to read a line before Gus arrived.

"I can't wait to come out to the desert. I will love what you call your lobster arm as I will all other parts of your body."

I never wrote that. It was not quite my style or wording and Kathleen and I, if when we meet, we gave each other an awkward hug. While by then I don't think Roger and she were physical,

Kathleen always treated anything physical from me as something to hide from him.

I didn't know what it meant, and wasn't sure if Gus was the ghostwriter, or at last co-conspirator—in what exactly I wasn't sure. But I thought my best course of action was to pretend everything was normal and then come back and steal them. They were after all in effect mine.

I ran out of exclamation phrases. Astonishment, stupefaction, bolts from the blue. We started making up our own, bolts from black holes, eye socket blow outs. I purposely came up with new phrases and emotional states, in part to keep Gus side tracked, allowing me to stare at him to see if he was hiding something; a part of the plot to erase and recreate me.

It didn't quite make sense. Jack in love with Kathleen, like telling me a Ford pickup was in love with Joan of Arc.

I always thought Jack was a virgin. That is important to understand in my discoveries. A lot of cuddling. He laid next to women he loved. Even once, rather creepy, he laid next to Kathleen while she was asleep and apparently she didn't know it. That is important to know because he stole Kathleen, but he didn't rape or pillage her. I think he remained a virgin until his death. In his recounting of the Jennifer story, they hug, they cuddle, spend nights together but there is no mention of making love or sex.

I was spending my days cleaning up my uncle's house, which was liked being assigned the task of finding a wedding ring in a city dump

I was numb or unbelieving at worst. I should have felt deep anger, right? But I had already discovered how much Jack had taken from me; this was like being at the bottom of an avalanche when one last large rock hits you in the shoulder. The first things he wrote about made little sense. I collected all the boxes marked Kathleen. I bought some special color pens and file folders. I was going to color code record boxes and files with pain and crying each one induced.

Most of the stuff I can throw away without much loss. I was writing things like "I went from love and admiration for Jack. He changed my life more than anyone else. Then during the Gertrude

Stein period, I researched his family's history, his own, and Dr. John. And I admired him and them even more. A factory of improv artists. As someone said, "you can't write a biography of Jack, he rewrote history as he moved through life."

I found the three pieces that mark the beginning of my relationship to Kathleen when we were at Lewis and Clark College. I found all three to be moving, insightful. Mid way through, I forgot it was really me. But then again, it wasn't me. I'm still not sure how Jack constructed these stories. I know he had my journals and junk drawer stories. And I found out he had interviewed our classmates at Lewis and Clark College and neighbors. Even an FBI report about a friend who was being investigated at a draft dodger. In the report, the dean of Students was quoted, "John (our mutual friend) and Cathy (the name she went by then) were found by the swimming pool way past the petting stage."

And then there was a moment; a passage was especially poignant to me, but it wasn't just that. I suddenly loved this life. I loved myself and jack and Kathleen. The truth didn't matter. It wasn't that far from truth.

I spent days and burned up many brain cells trying to figure out what was my writing, what was Jack's and what was fact and what was fiction. I entered the Betwixter quandary. If I kept reading and re-reading the Kathleen stories, then anything real was displaced. Similar, I suspect, to what has happened to my memories; the actual ones replaced by a few photographs. But, if I never read the stories again or if I destroyed them, then whatever stood out in the last reading would become the most real.

There were many stages of grieving and reconstruction. One was of loss. Or that I had missed out on something. Kathleen drew men to her. Like a moth to a campfire. Not a moth to Bic lighter, or Moth to forest fire.

The thing about Kathleen was that she was beautiful, but it all came on over summer before she went off to college. She didn't understand, or did not want the attention. She didn't understand the effect she had on men, and even women. But when she did, then she was mistrustful. All men wanted was to conquer her.

Why didn't I notice that about Kathleen? That men fell for her. And she never tried. Seldom wore makeup. Maybe she flirted, but not really. She made you feel everything would be alright if you could wake up beside her in the sunshine, her blonde hair on white sheets. But the deeper thing was that at some point you felt totally in synch with her. She brought you a Be here now state of mind. It felt like she knew exactly what you were going to say or do. No gaps. There was always just one thing to do next forever.

She was shy, but guys viewed that like she was a butterfly with fiery loins. Men sought to make her smile or laugh so they could see just how pouty her lips were. They wanted her to walk away so they could see her blonde hair fly loose like a small unleashed blonde waterfall or catch a profile angle that revealed her perfect button of a nose.

When we were homesteading practically all the men—there were only a couple hundred in the town, stopped dead in their tracks when they were face to face.

Two cowboys in effect kidnapped us, but we were saved by guy with a limp who pulled out a rifle and chased the guys off. He wanted to protect her. He probably would have sacrificed his life for hers even though they had only known each other for 6 hours. He was also one who could not imagine soiling her. Another pedestal-platonic love. There are several people that fall in love with Kathleen. jack obviously, but also I noted the director of an environmental group, and the outlandishly tall guy at the coast. They fell in love before and after her illness. The ones after or still in love during her illness were in love in a twisted way. Their meditation was: why did bad things happen to good people; and good things happen to bad people?

But this is how stupid and limited I was in the days Kathleen and I met. The most important thing to me as a mousy immature pretentious asshole was that other guys were jealous of me. That I—for the first time in my life—had something that they wanted. They also got what I wanted through some mysterious process that was invisible or a mystery. I did not understand if was attractive to girls. I knew that no girl I was attracted to was attracted to me. I was as moved by walking across campus and watching guys with obvious and furtive glances, wondering how this dork or nerd or hippie could have landed this babe. That was as important to me as how we made love. I call Jack's love for Kathleen—and maybe others, but she is the epitome—Pedestal platonic. He held her on a pedestal in astral plain glow. He might hug, but anything beyond that would be desecration.

Jack drove 200 miles, and then down 15 miles of dirt, deeply rutted roadway, leading to their encampment, past bear traps and spotlights, and past Roger's vigilant watch with knifes pistols and rifles.

Jack wrote, "I watched her tonight from my vantage point in the woods. I know this may sound deviant. but not. If you had a chance to watch Cleopatra as she disrobed to a thin, almost invisible silk gown; wouldn't that be enough? I just watched her everyday moves: boiling water, or pulling at her long blonde hair to find split ends. It was the split ends or sensuous of her hair that entranced me but also the pauses. She would hold some in her hand and not move. I wanted nothing more.

Falling in Love while still being Reconstructed

During this period of my life I deconstructed and reconstructed myself from ground up. I think it was more of a renovation job than my father had when he went from working with his father, who never wore a suit in his life except for weddings and funerals, to lounging around with communist sympathizers and intellectuals at Reed College. He told me how by the end of his first year in college he had to fake it with his father. They were no longer from the same class. His father had paid his way out of the proletariat into the intellectual class and there was no turning back. But mine was more fundamental. While my father continued to harbor conspicuous consumption envies, irrational anger about trivial pursuits, and used his intellectual capacities to rationalize self-centered behavior I didn't have a choice in such matters. In some ways I longed for the simpler days when all I did was drink and cruise for chicks. But there was one arena that even with radical surgery I had not overcome infantile desires.

I was still lonely and attached to what I knew to be primitive and immature ideas about love and attraction. I could see it for what it was. But I still couldn't control myself. An attractive woman could make me weak in the knees and hopelessly depressed when I realized how microscopic my attraction aura was. I felt like I was a praying mantis wearing Old Spice, or on good days, Kafka's insect with no hope of waking up from a dream. I found a note in my journal I used as guideline when it came to this part of my self. If you look too hard for something you won't find it.

I also think I had made progress on creating an authentic self who could hold his own in intellectual banter. I gauged my progress relative to one particular intellectual snob, Bill, a gifted musician who was probably a geek or bookworm even in Kindergarten. He glared at me as though he could see through my facade. The only thing that held him back was his respect for my father and a common friend, Peter. Peter could take my pedestrian insights and turn them into intellectual stances. I brought a 45 record to a term end party, *Bird is the Word* by the Trashmen.[1] I just thought it had a cool driving beat. Peter developed a multi-tiered camp interpretation of the Trashmen. Nothing I understood but went along with. One party was dedicated to Surfing Bird. We played it over and over, each time discovering yet another way to hear it. I did not understand what they were talking about, but it made me the center of attention. I felt like Madame Blavatsky when she brought eastern philosophy to William Yates in the 19th century.

But with attractive women, I was still a mess. There was the hormone issue, but now it was more complicated. The ones that just shot lightning bolts straight to my gender, I could overcome by simplistic sheep counting games. I might look the other way, hum songs, immediately open a book, focus my energy on things that worried me sick, like preparing for exams or the fact that I would be dead soon, relatively speaking. I had also decided to not care. I would follow my first note to myself. By actively not looking for a woman I could call my own, I would find one.

My stupid insight proved to be kind of true. I walked into a fairytale romance with a princess. Beauty and the Beast. We met in a French literature class. Well, we had met briefly at a party before that. She was there with a friend, John, and my small self was jealous. John didn't seem worthy of this princess. When I saw a star jock with perfect genes with a babe, it didn't bother me. I was used to sitting outside the cave chewing on the left-over saber tooth leg bones. Kathleen was, I assumed, out of my reach. But over the coming few months. I realized yes, Dylan the times they were changing. Even the jocks and fraternities got it, for a while. Things were beyond their control. For the first time in history, some attractive women were not automatically owned by powerful males.

She had Long blonde hair. Deep green eyes. She had more of a belly dancer body than an anorexic ballerina. Her hippie clothes were not off the rack. She seemed to have made them up herself. She often wore tall soft leather brown boots, peasant blouse, no make-up. She didn't need it. She had as a friend said, perfect insect bitten lips, a Californian tan but not like she baked in a shake and bake but because she spent as much time walking in the woods and meadows as she did on city sidewalks.

I had noticed her in the French Literature class. I watched her pick out split ends and take notes in green ink with handwriting I could read from a row over and behind. And I had noticed she didn't just take down what the professors said. She seemed to write questions more than statements. Her beauty struck me, but I was still in my acid being, and everyone and everything was beautiful or strange. Funny thing about the truth serum acid, it made you doubt everything. If everything was beautiful how did you know if it "really" was?

One day we stood outside the class. There were other people she might have spoken to, but she said something to me. I did a double take, resisting the urge to look around to make sure she wasn't really talking to some stallion higher up the gene pool ladder. She had a soft voice, and I had to ask her twice to repeat what she had said. Finally, I understood she said she had a funny story about Dr. Brown, our instructor. I knew Brown, since he was a family friend, as most of the professors were on this small campus.

Dr. Brown looked like an old testament figure. He was tall, angular, with gray hair and beard. As she said, he looked like El Greco painting of old Testament character. He even wore a red cape sometimes. He walked across campus with giant stride always lost in thought. He hardly noticed anyone around him. My father told me he usually had to stand in his way to get his attention and that he had once offended the university president by walking right past him with one of the university's largest donors leaving them both staring at him as he continued to stride past them. Often he strode into class and just started up as though we would remember the exact point we had left off the week before. Or sometimes he came in and then stood there glaring at each one of us, one at a time (it was a seminar so only 10 of us). His glare would drill way right to your core. He was like Santa Claus: he knew if you had read the assignment or were good or bad. If you hadn't it was like he sent a lightning bolt to your spleen. Sometimes he would just read a passage, sometimes in French, sometimes in English. He would finish the passage and then stare pleadingly, beseeching us, almost shouting: what does he mean? What does it mean? what should we do? Will we ever know? Is it worth it or should we just play bridge or Frisbee and let the Pope decide? Anyone? Please! He had been a preacher before he was a professor, so his lectures were more like sermons. His voice was loud and forceful. It was an 8 am class, and hung-over students, or students coming down from psychotropic experiences either looked sickened and close to upchucking or some would smile as though they weren't sure if this was still part of the acid trip.

Kathleen told me how she had seen three sorority girls walk with him after class. They could barely keep up and he listened, even smiling in a vacant but polite way. One girl tried to explain how their sorority was raising money for an upcoming event on campus to introduce foreign students to the sorority system on campus. The others would chime in now and then with statements, like, *oh last years was so sweet. One Japanese girl got to have her first real hamburger, not from MacDonald's.* "Oh, right," the other chirped in, "*and that's how Hannah got involved in becoming a member of the tennis club.*" Then they made their plea. *So, we were wondering if you might want to come with your wife. We like to have some professors come and thought it would be really neat if you could.* Dr. Brown stopped abruptly. Kathleen a few feet behind had to also stop since the trail was blocked. He stood there staring at them. It was probably less than a minute, but it seemed to take forever. The girls smiled at first expectantly.

"He looked at them like it surprised him they were talking to him," Kathleen said, "as though a Monarch butterfly were suddenly reciting the evening news. The girl's smiles evaporated. One dropped her books, then quickly picked them up. He said nothing. They finally snuck around him, never looking back. He spotted me and said, 'That was strange, wasn't it?'

During the story, I could feel my big and small selves open and close. I was attentive and listening, then I was lost. She was beautiful and talking to me. My censors and my sub text translators were furiously searching for clues. Was this just by chance. Was she just passing the time of the day? Did she know who I was or ever thought of me before? Was this it? Knock knock knock on heaven's door? Could she possibly be interested in me? How stupid and intrusive and simple minded of me. We were classmates. This was a chance encounter. Make nothing of it. But as the story ended, and I was genuinely (I think) smiling and laughing, I was also desperately trying to think of what to say. It would be up to me. I knew she was shy. Not sure why I knew this. I had noticed her in class and on campus. Most of the time she was alone. The one thing I remember my friend Dave who had dated her said about her was she loved animals more than people and sometimes slept by herself in the woods behind the dorms. My stupid self's response was, "That's funny. He is pretty intense..." pause... "so what did you think about

Robbe-Grillet (this week's reading)?" Then that same self-thought about impressing her by telling her a personal story about Brown that only I could know like the time he read the instructions for badminton when he was at my parent's annual 4th of July picnic and even that sounded like it was Old testament. That seemed pretty good. But I knew it would come from the desire to impress her. That it would give me points. Shit, I might go right from that to, "want to meet for coffee", to getting her in bed, all in 24 hours. Thankfully he arrived and all I had to say was, "That's funny."

The class was a blur that day. I watched her every move. I watched how she listened. I saw how her blonde hair glistened when sunlight reached the classroom. Her blue spiral notebook. I waited for any clue. Then when the class was over, I timed my exit so I could leave immediately following her. I had excuses for any direction she might take: I'm on my way to the bookstore; the library; the student commons; a place to study near the rose garden; the dorm to visit a friend; the romantic reflection pool. And I had multiple conversation starters. I imagined us by the abundant swimming pool and I would have the perfect thing to say. But it was all shattered as soon as I walked out. She was greeted by Jim, who I kind of knew, and thought might be her boyfriend who I had always thought was a kind of pretentious twerp but now knew it with a vengeance. I didn't want to be forced to walk with them. I wanted to pretend it wasn't happening. I went to the library and mopped. All the progress I had made with creating my new self-dissolved. The only hope was to pretend I was that person no one paid any attention to or had any expectations for in college but who would write the great American novel with fellow students just acting surprised, "a quiet guy. Stuck to himself mostly." But they would also want to claim a right to be a footnote in his bio. I went early to meet my father at his office for my ride home—even that felt sad. It was like I was in high school and driven to and from school by my parents. Pathetic.

But then, oh thank you, God. I sat outside my father's office. Finally, the door opened and Kathleen walked out, followed by my father. Everything came together. Life was good. And then I noticed my father eyeing her as she left as he was casually greeting me, he was also sizing her up. It substantiated his reputation as one of the womanizing professors. Was he oblivious to how obvious he was? My anger almost overcame my desire. I wanted to yell at him for all the irrational times he had been angry at me and tell him it embarrassed me to be his son. But Kathleen greeted me with a bright smile.

My father said to Kathleen, "Do you know my son. He's an English major too."

It was weird. He hesitated as though he had forgotten my name. It was only 8 seconds or so, but made me wonder. Did it matter he was lecherous? God, maybe he had even made a pass at her. Maybe they were having an affair.

"Yes," we both said almost simultaneously, "we're in French lit together."

My father said, "OK, then Kathleen let's talk again soon," and went back into his office, leaving the two of us with yet another awkward moment.

"Well, I have to run," Kathleen said. And it seemed her face there was a change of complexion. Wasn't that a flush? She quickly turned, looked back one more time with a slight smile.

It was all I could think of for days that followed. I found out where she lived. I found out that Jim was not her boyfriend. And her phone number and where she came from, Palo Alto. I schemed countless ways to call her. I stood in my father's library at home countless times, phone in hand. But I couldn't do it. I was happier in a state of uncertainty, just imagining she might be interested and say yes to wanting to go for a walk or meet at the library, or get a cup of coffee, or get a beer. then it was too late. Christmas break and I figured she had left to go home for Christmas.

New year's Eve. And I was alone, again. It was a quiet, dull, and gray, not like the previous year's tumultuous windstorm. Things were so bad I wished to have a kidney stone so they could rush me to the hospital and I would get a hit of morphine.

My parents were out at a party, so it was just me and my faithful cat, Yasi. Just before midnight the phone rang. I figured it was my parents.

Instead, "Hi this is Mary you don't know me." I could hear giggling in the background. Oh, great a prank call or wrong number. "No, really don't hang up. My housemate is too damn shy to call you and she wants to wish you a happy new year."

"And just who would that be?" I said, trying to imagine who it might be like Cheryl or Linda, two girls that came to mind that friends had tried to set me up with who I had absolutely no interest in.

"Well, happy new year from Kathleen, you know from your French literature class." I heard Kathleen shout it out and then they hung up.

With that, my life changed. She left the next day for a week in Palo Alto, but I ran into her the first day of classes. She was sitting by the reflection pool on the stepping stones. I looked at her from a distance. In either vein hopefulness and a genuine sense of fate I knew she was the next big thing in my life. She was looking at Mt. hood at a distance, which had the only cloud in the sky almost like a halo. She turned toward me before I was even close, and when I got closer, she said, "I was waiting for you. You're late."

I thought she meant it at first. Had I promised something on New year's—then realized she was kidding me.

I said, "Funny. There is a photo of my father sitting where you are the first year he arrived here to teach. He was wearing classic 1950s intellectual gear, surrounded by books. He must have been so happy." I avoided looking directly at her, afraid I suppose that it might reveal something like, you know, I'm just looking for a friend, not a lover. Next to her was a tiny algae filled pond.

She looked in the pond, maybe also averting her stare, "God, so full of life, especially tadpoles."

I told her that my childhood friend, Kim Stafford[2] and I used to collect the tadpoles from the pool and take them home. The game was to see if you could collect them in all different stages so you could watch them go from fish-looking to fish with legs and then frogs.

We never went to class that day. We walked around in our bubble. She told me how she was living on borrowed time. When she was six months old, she had suddenly stopped breathing and had to spend a month in the hospital. The doctors didn't know what was wrong and that it was a miracle she survived. She thought it was because she was supposed to be a deer or an eagle.

"You know some poor heavenly gate's clerk got his pay docked for that one," she said.

Wormhole Between the Shire and New World Order

After Fred Jett and I got out of the Clatsop County Jail, I went to the shire and never left until school started three weeks later. My parents were in Europe and would be back the same week school started. I knew I would have hell to pay. But I had it figured out. I would be contrite. I knew my uncle wouldn't say anything. I even had the exact moment figured out: after they had given me their European presents and showed me the photos they had already developed, after my father had walked the grounds and realized I had done everything I had asked him and then some. I would tell him about my classes and how I was excited to be in college and had several family friends as teachers. Then, *I have to tell you something I would say; I got in trouble while you were gone. But over I've learned my lesson.* I would explain how I owed my uncle $500 for bail and I would sell my car to pay him, and it would never happen again. I would do nothing but study.

It kind of worked, although my father had to repeatedly to say, "what the hell's the matter with you," and my mother looked hurt and scared, as though I had told her about a near-fatal car crash. I even had my cluttered room re-arranged, so it looked like what I thought a college student's dorm room looked like. I had removed high school icons (neon Hamm's beer sign; an Everly Brothers' poster; comic books, and even thrown my *Playboy*s away, which they didn't know I had, but it felt like part of the purging process. I had retrieved a desk from the basement, constructed a long table strewn with college textbooks, blank notebooks, rulers, pencils, and pens; above my desk a large photograph of Bertrand Russell.

The small liberal arts college was only 5 miles from the Shire, but to get there you went through a wormhole in space to a different planet. The college had been the estate of one of Portland's founding white guys, and it was referred to as the country Club on the hill.

I understood I created the self that moved my body and spirit through space, and I knew the shallow, angry and thoughtless me was a charlatan, and that I had discovered a bigger me, the real one in Japan, but I did not understand how to further develop the new one. I lived in two worlds: one foot still in the American high school terrarium and one in a world of ideas and myths and a role in the planet's history and accurate instructions and operating manual for my time on earth. I could think about it and had moments of clarity, but it just wouldn't come into focus. In some ways it was easier in high school. At least, I understood the rules. I was average, an outcast, or just hung around the outskirts of the in-crowd, like a crow waiting for the larger predators to finish eating road kill. In college I was a pretender and sure they would recognize me as a charlatan. There was one guy in particular who worried me. He had the piercing uninhabited glare of someone who had always been bright, always an outsider because of that, and had no problem staring at you until he glared you to death or exposure of your puny act of intelligence. The crowd I hung out with could read a novel in a night and summarize or critique it by morning. They talked fast in some kind of existential code. Where the hell was the dictionary or handbook? Then I thought I figured it out, Cliff Notes. Not what they used, but what I might use to keep up. But I knew I couldn't buy them on campus, so I drove half way across town to another college campus. Even there I disguised myself with a hat and sun glasses to make sure no one recognized me.

Without a car, it meant I had to wake at 6am every day and drive to the campus with my father, which wasn't half bad. He had a red jaguar and look so professorial, with French beret and pipe. The first months I spent all my time either in classes, the school library, or my room. I went to the school commons for lunch and sometimes hang out there, but that felt dangerous. The Commons is where the commuters hung out, along with students that my intelligentsia friends made fun of. They were fake hippies or brainiacs or losers who would never make it through even their first year. If I hung out there I felt like an alcoholic tempted by decorous friends to travel back in time to high school drinking and chicks.

Also, I was an outsider. Commuters were in the minority. The on-campus life seemed glamorous. I watched other students enviously as they went from dorms to classrooms in packs. I tried to be a good student, but the trouble was I was illiterate. I had never listened in class and usually found ways to cheat my way through to passing grades. I begin to think that my last term of getting mostly A's in high school was a fluke. I didn't know how to do this. I could read a page of college text and by the end not remember the beginning of the page. It probably didn't seem so bad from the outside. I ended up getting B's and C's. But just to get those passing grades meant I had to study 10-12 hours a day. I was alone and miserable.

I tried to live in both worlds, but I was a fraud in both. If I returned to the old world I had to pretend to have found a way to get grades effortlessly or by cheating and talk about the hot chicks I was scoring with. I could only exist in the new world by studying all the time and memorizing Cliff notes. I spent hours changing Cliff note text into my own. I discovered a pallet of stock phrases and questions like, "Do you think Salinger is much like Holden Caulfield?"

My junior year, I talked my parents into a deal. If I could get at least all Bs by the end of the year I could move on to campus. To just do that, I became a hermit. I stayed up all nights and begin to not care what I looked like. I didn't realize it until one night I pulled into the Whiz Burger, one of my high school hangouts with a campus friend who looked like Maynard G. Krebs.[3] I was recognized by a jock from my high school, and not just any jock but one of three brothers who probably weighed 800 pounds.[4] The oldest one made it to the NFL as a tackle. The jocks took one look at me and said, "Fucking Christ, Johnson what happened to you, you look like a fuckin hippie."

348

Without even meaning to, I had crossed the line, stepped off the cliff into the world of the others.

---

1. Bird is the Word, song. Trashmen. 1963 "A-well, a bird, bird, bird, well-a bird is a word ...A-well, a bird, bird, b-bird's a word... A-well-a don't you know about the bird?... Well, everybody knows that the bird is a word."
2. The son of poet William Stafford. Since 1979, he has taught writing at Lewis & Clark College in Portland. He has also taught courses at Willamette University in Salem, at the Sitka Center for Art and Ecology, at the Fishtrap writers' gathering, and private workshops in Scotland, Italy, and Bhutan. In July 2018, he was appointed Oregon's Poet Laureate by Governor Kate Brown. He is the founding director of the Northwest Writing Institute and is the literary executor of the Estate of William Stafford.
3. Maynard Krebs is the "beatnik" sidekick of the title character in the U.S. television sitcom "The Many Loves of Dobie Gillis", which aired on CBS from 1959 to 1963.
4. Ken Patera was a strong and extraordinarily athletic. His brother, Jack Patera, played football for the Baltimore Colts and was the head coach for the Seattle Seahawks from 1976 until 1982. His brother, Dennis Patera, played for the San Francisco 49ers. Ken played football at Cleveland High School in Portland, Oregon. He was also friends with Andre the Giant. https://www.youtube.com/watch?v=dYjVmQPhLm8

WHAT REMAINS

Jennifer

Preamble

J ack had several lovers in his life. He mentions Lilly and Polly as prior lovers. But I think the most important love in his life was Jennifer. No one ever saw them together. All we have is Jack's account. But in his account, Jennifer is my lover; an answer to my existential crisis.

Jack found several of my most plaintive journal entries in which I pray or yell at God to tell me the meaning of life. He figured he would answer my prayers with the love of my life, Jennifer, a short circuit life with intensity, joy, pain; and who would reveal to me the meaning of life.

I tried the best I could to piece together all the pieces he wrote about Jennifer. The following three chapters: *Knowing There is a Fatal Crash Ahead; The Answer to My Prayers*; and *It's mobular*. The stories were mostly complete. I had to fill in some gaps from Jack's files and journal entries.

Also, the fictional Jennifer had a daughter, Rose. From the various descriptions, she is somewhere between five and twelve. It's the first time I can remember Jack even acknowledging children. Also, in notes he describes Jennifer as a "gypsy." She would mysteriously disappear; and just as mysteriously reappear with no explanation. Jack never seemed to settle on where we lived. He had us living at the Funny Farm; the Shire; the Gertrude Stein Fellowship club—a very cool sounding suite of rooms behind a fake fireplace. In that suite Jennifer had us build a fort. She insisted it was for Rose; but it seemed as much to give her a sense of her own home inside out larger home. Apparently it didn't seem at all strange to Rose that the fort occupied most of the living room. We were like squatters in our own house. Did she wonder why other people didn't have forts in their homes? We had used our dining room table and chairs, every available blanket and table cloths. Electric cords ran this way and that, powering a television, VCR, even my coffee grinder and espresso maker. To build the extra room I brought in the boxes from Jack's that had been sitting in the car for weeks. She had rules about when I could enter. It is where the "Its Mobular" experiment took place.

He also dropped a piece about Jennifer's upper-class status. I thought it was interesting and revealing; but maybe he didn't want her to be aristocratic and more down to earth:

"When we got back to the car, she scrambled around looking for something, and then calmly said, "I think someone stole my purse." I looked at her, disbelieving. She left her purse in an unlocked car? It hadn't occurred to me to check. She started the car and told me what was in her purse. "Let' see pearls that belonged to my grandmother that makes me sad. And there was some hashish that might have been nice at your place. And darn, I forgot there was more jewelry, including my wedding ring. That was stupid I just didn't want to wear it anymore and took it off when we were at Powell's." She looked over at me, "It was just time to do it...Oh, I think there was $1,500 in cash and another $1000 in traveler's checks. That was about what I earned in 3 months.

I looked at her, thinking she might be kidding. As she pulled onto the road, "Oh shit, and I had the Portland share of the Grateful Dead's Osley acid for the country fair. 2000 hits, I think."

Here is how Jack described my existential crisis:

"There was a time in my life when I pleaded with the almighty to tell me the answers to lives' persistent questions. I expected he or she might just direct me to a good book or guide me to dazzling insights. I shouted and bellowed and drank and experimented with hallucinogens. I ignored basic physical limits to my body and scientific principles governing immoveable objects. I spent several months in a garage with an alpha wave machine, a portable toilet, subsisting on peanut butter sandwiches while recording my every thought and dreams. I learned to hang out between wakefulness and dream state for hours at a time. I still have a box with cassette tapes and another box of spiral notebooks filled with stream-of-consciousness wanderings that might as well be ancient texts without the Rosetta Stone.

The Creator answered my supplication. But it was like a classic deal with the devil. I had to lose, not my own life or soul, but others around me. In a ten-year period, I lost ten people I loved. By the end I was shouting back, "OK, alright. I get it. Enough with the lessons."

During this time, I was trying to focus on what I called the attentiveness mantra. It wasn't a structured practice, just my own. I figured God was always trying to point out the obvious to me, about what to do next or the meaning of life, but I couldn't see it because of the blare of my interior monologue, and urgency of to do lists.

According to Jack, Jennifer taught me many things. One important one was that when we give completely of ourselves, with no expectation of reward, and are fully attentive to someone we love, then we know with certainty exactly what to do or say. You enter a state of absolute free will. Dr. John's theory of randomness does not apply. I had always enjoyed the rewards of giving someone something, a gift or doing a favor, but this was beyond that. I didn't exist, and yet I could experience the life force within me. No ego, just a state there are no alternatives. Instead of a jumble of rational and irrational choices, there is only one. No fork in the road. No Cheshire cat in the tree. It wasn't about saying something clever, and it wasn't based on wanting to be the best storyteller, or the hit of a party. There was only one thing to do. I realized for most of our lives we are presented with endless possibilities and choices. My meditation on the importance of attentiveness culminated here and now. There was no other state to be in; and giving completely and without reservation or egotistic intervention of the buzz of my interior monologue was almost nonexistent.

I was exhausted. Jennifer had been fighting cancer for a year and it felt like I had been on a battlefield waging war and hoping for peace, while praying to God on a desolate planet.

The Answer to my Prayers

When Jennifer showed up at our office, which was also home for me and a close friend, the attentiveness mantra wasn't working too well. If God was shouting at me to pay attention, he couldn't get through my self-imposed haze. She struck me as beautiful, and Eastern European or Russian, Dark hair, olive complexion. She seemed self-composed and, although I didn't think often about these things, upper class. Most of all, she struck me as serious and intense. She had penetrating eyes. I avoided her stare like I might with a recent convert to Scientology. A true believer. When I held out my hand, she hugged me. I ordinarily might have shied away from or felt awkward about a hug at the first meeting, but Jennifer's hug was comforting. I understood hugging for the first time in my life.

There was a moment that I remember as the beginning of our relationship. I was climbing the stairs to my personal space and met Jennifer coming down.

She said, "I was looking for you."

Which struck me as more than the immediate statement of fact. She was looking for me. I remember thinking, *oh my God, this is the next big thing in my life*. Not that I had fallen in love.

When we went back into the work session, I thought I would be too distracted to continue, but it felt like I was attentive. Not to Jennifer, but to the process. It felt like there was very little lag between what I thought and what I said. Whenever I glanced at Jennifer, I was met head on as though by the light from a Lighthouse. Our glances seemed orchestrated by cues from off stage prompts. But the moments didn't seem to rob me of concentration, but fueled it.

About two weeks after our first night together I took her, as I had several lovers before her, to Twin Rocks, a hardscrabble coastal town with one of the last Natatoriums on the Oregon coast. Family friends owned a beach house at the eat the end of a dead-end road that led directly to the ocean. There was an unruly sand dune area between the cottage and the ocean that was littered with driftwood and makeshift forts and windbreaks. It was easy to find a secluded place to set up an informal camp.

By then I felt the familiar patterns of new love. I was no longer alone. The universe seemed both small and large. I didn't want to spend a moment without her. Everything was right. But there were also feelings I had not felt before. It felt like I had been chosen to catch a small child falling from a burning building. I had been chosen to save a life. And with that feeling, there was something disquieting. At the bottom of the well of love there was also a sense of annihilation. At the time I thought it was yet another element of true and complete love in which the self is erased or enlarged to incorporate another. But it was also a very strong visceral feeling, as though I had taken LSD cut with speed (the best metaphor I could use at the time). It felt like terror and a paper-thin wall separated love.

We found the remains of a driftwood fort that may have been one I built many years before, that had been added to and modified by many people in between. But there remained a piece of wood that still had visible letters: a-d-r-e-n-a. As a teenager I had decided it was a sexy mermaid name, Adrena. Jennifer decided it was probably from the name of a boat, the Adrenaline. I told her how I had fallen in love with Clara, a French foreign exchange student. How we played Del

Shannon's Runaway over and over on the jukebox in the local hamburger joint.

We re-arranged what remained of the fort, gathered driftwood and started a fire. The fort protected us from the breeze off the ocean. I climbed past the fort and over a ridge to pee. I quickly lost body heat. When I came back and cuddled into our blankets next to the fire, the heat of Jennifer's body was magical. I was instantly warmed. We tore pieces of bread from a sourdough loaf with Tillamook cheese and shared a large crab cocktail while we drank red wine. We were often silent, which also struck me as unusual. Whenever one of us started up again, it seemed like we had been talking all the while and never wandered from each other's orbit.

The last thing I remember her saying before we fell asleep was, "Do you really think that moon effects the ocean? Isn't that a stretch?" She held up her thumb between me and the moon, "Look, it's not bigger than my thumb and the ocean is much bigger."

"I don't know," I said. "I can't see the ocean."

"But you can hear it, right? And you can't hear the moon, can you?"

I laughed lightly and felt her pull herself closer to me. Before I could answer I fell asleep. It was one of those falling asleep that feels like you are falling. No foreplay. Just gone. I woke up minutes, hours, or years later. The fire was just a few glowing embers. Sleep in my eyes was mingled with sand. It felt like I had been with this person forever, even though it had only been two months, and less since we first made love. Then for a split second I couldn't remember who I was with or where I was. I thought about how this relationship was going to be perfect. Whenever it ended, and it would, that we would have nothing more to say to each other, nothing more to declare. Of course, there would be great pain and pleasure, but I would learn through this person how to give of myself, completely and without reservation. I also knew that nothing could ever harm me. I looked up in the sky. The moon had come out. Almost whole and white. Then I remembered what Jennifer had last said:

"Can you hear the moon?"

I turned. She was awake and turned like I had from the moon to me. Then she motioned to me to look back at the moon. A cloud was passing by.

"Can you feel the earth turning?"

And I did. At terrifying speed, we were rotating and roaring through space. I felt a strong and familiar desire to make passionate love, but the desire was transformed into an entangling hug that felt more powerful than sexual passion. I don't think I had ever entered that zone before; where passion went from a physical pleasure into a spiritual place. Here we were barely sheltered in sand dunes littered with flotsam and jetsam, with the sound of the ocean like heartbeat of the planet, immense, and as compared to us strong, while we were fragile, and yet we were safe and would be forever.

San Juan Islands

I took every significant woman in my life to the San Juan Islands, in particular, Orcas Island, where my family went on vacations. But there were many obstacles to pulling off a trip with Jennifer: Rose, my mom, a failing car, money. Jennifer loved challenges. "No problem," she told me. Rose would stay with Helen; we would rent a car, and "don't worry about money.... ever, OK?" And my mother? I asked my older sister which wasn't easy because anytime I asked a favor from her the price was that I allow her to denigrate myself; clarification of her superior wisdom; and establish the pecking order of who my parents loved the most, with me on the bottom.

But then the day before we left, my mother had what her doctor called a "panic attack." My sister didn't deal well with crisis, and she drove my mother somewhat crazy, which would probably instigate more panic attacks. My sister read tabloids, so her nervous chatter was about strange murders in South Dakota or Elvis Presley sightings. We would have to postpone the trip. To Jennifer it was just another challenge. She paid for a nurse to stay with my mother. She called it magic or manifestation; I thought trust fund, but I knew I wasn't supposed to broach the subject.

My favorite place on Orcas Island, Beach Haven, was booked for 2 years, but Jennifer got us a cabin. It involved switching out two families, helping move the owner's mother-in-law across the island. Oh right, and a stage pass to a Grateful Dead Concert in Seattle, and $300 on top of the normal rental. We also had the same log cabin my family rented with the round pebble beach and quiet lapping ocean surf that was memorizing.

When we got to Beach Haven, I called my mother to tell her where we were. I held the phone out so she could hear the lapping sound of waves hitting the pebble beach. While I prepared lunch, Jennifer built a fort in the driftwood. One of the quickest born traditions in relationship history. This one had a mattress, a table made from a root wad, and in a small antechamber a shire, photos of Rose, Kathleen, my father, my mother, Bob Benson and my uncle. The photos formed a triangle. At the peak of the triangle there was a photo of Rose in one of her fairy outfits. "It makes it clear why we have to die, doesn't it?" It made me think of how many people had or were walking off the big cliff in the sky.

We were told the best place to eat was the East Sound Inn. A "cult" ran the Inn, as our proprietor referred to it, under the guidance of Guru Phil, who seemed to have the same status as Chief Sitting Duck. We were relieved, or at least I was, when it turned out to be a cozy restaurant and the only clue there was a "cult" was a pile of books. As we walked in and past Phil, he said, "wherever you go there you are." That doesn't make much sense I said to Jennifer. The server who overheard me, said with a smile that was just a little shy of cult dimension, "Exactly!"

As the server led to our table, we both realized a young couple who looked like natives, not tourist, glaring at us. As we sat down I said, "What's that about?"

But I didn't have to wait long to get an answer. The young man strode over to our table. He looked very serious, even angry. He got right to the point.

"That shirt you're wearing, he said, "that's mine. It was stolen from our car along with a cassette player and my backpack." He paused to let it sink in. I half expected the plain clothes detective woman who had caught me shop-lifting to show up.

Jennifer nudged a chair, "have a seat and tell us more."

Belligerently he refused, and continued, "I know it's mine because it is a Pendleton woolen pattern that my grandmother picked out and she was told it was the last of that pattern. She made it into a shirt with exactly that design, right down to the buttons." He pointed with his angular finger close enough that I pulled back.

"What do you want us to do about it?" Jennifer asked politely, and with a slight laugh, "take the shirt off his back?"

He said, louder, drawing the attention of wait staff and customers, "I want my shirt back and the other stuff you stole."

I turned away from him toward Jennifer, "Well this is a real mood killer isn't it?" He seemed like he might take Jennifer's suggestion literally. I imagined a tassel on the floor with turned over tables. I tried to remain calm. "First off, I don't think we're the same size."

"Bullshit!" he said.

I continued, "secondly I grew up within walking distance of a Pendleton outlet, which is where my first wife Kathleen, who has since died, purchased the material and made me this shirt."

"Double bullshit!"

That's when Guru Phil showed up. He was a gigantic man, somewhere between Buddha and Elvis in his later Los Vegas stage, dressed in bright purple. He glided over to the empty table near us and just sat there.

"Let's see what other details can I give you," I continued, "The Bishop family runs that store. It is along Johnson Creek. I planted alder trees in the parking lot." "Ah, let me show you this," I said, standing up, "this tear I got from Morgan our dog who has also since died...wow I guess I don't have many eye witnesses. You could call my mother, but she's almost 90. Her memory is unpredictable. She forgets my name but she can tell you her goldfishes' name from grade school." Phil smiled.

"We're going to go back to our dinner now," Jennifer said calmly. This is a special time for us, you know. We don't know how much we will have together. We came here to wait while specialists at the University of Washington are assessing options for me. And it doesn't look all that good."

Phil stood up and, with the pretense of moving a napkin holder on our table, came between us and the accuser. Without laying a hand on him, he guided the guy back to his table and then disappeared into the kitchen. It was an impressive move. The guy sat at his table, still glaring, but it was like there was a force field between us. Our server came by with two spectacular salads and informed us that dinner was on the house, and motioned to the couple, *The same for you.*

The accuser and his partner left. They glared as they passed our table but said nothing. We want back to our meal and tried to recreate our bubble. I had noticed Jennifer could make more abrupt mood shifts than me. I re-ran tapes about what I should have or could have said or done.

Jennifer distracted me by talking about Rose. "I think she is almost too good for this world. I'm afraid someone or something will crush her innocence. How do you suppose your mother did it? Imagine she went through 2 wars, the Great depression, Viet Nam, and you." She smiled, "I mean it. Not that you were bad. But can you imagine what it must have been like for her to imagine you in prison? She probably blamed herself for turning you into a peacenik."

Jennifer's Last Days in Hawaii

The last thing Jennifer ever said to me was, "Everything is perfect between us. You should go rest." She smiled and slightly turned away. I hugged her as best I could, avoiding life support tubes. She turned toward me. I stood at the doorway and looked back, but she was turned away from me.

I've reviewed this moment countless times. Did she turn away or toward me? How much? Was it significant? Was she saying goodbye? Why did she want to die alone? Or did she? Should I have insisted I stay? The nurses had moved a giant cozy recliner into the room. My hotel was within walking distance, so I never seemed far away. Was it like animals who instinctually wonder off to die alone? Would I have learned something else if I had stayed? But as she said, everything was perfect.

I was awoken at 6am by a phone call. A nurse told me I should come to the hospital. I knew Jennifer was gone, and I knew she knew, and she knew I knew.

I went to the hospital and sat on the edge of her bed. She looked finally peaceful. It wasn't quite a smile, but almost. The wrinkles of pain on her face were gone, as though she had plastic surgery.

I called the family. Before I could say anything, Jennifer's mom said, "I know. We'll be there soon. Rose has to take a shower."

Her mom seemed in control, as usual. But when she arrived, I could tell she was lost and not in control. When they got off the elevator Rose ran to me, and although she almost dangled to the floor, I picked her up and held her tightly. I realized, even though I was the newest "member" of the family, I was in charge. I carried Rose in my arms to a sitting area and told her, "Rose, this is very important." She nodded complacently. "I want to give you the choice. You can go into your mother's room to see her one more time." I placed my arms on her shoulder, and pushed hair off her forehead, "but you don't have to. Nobody is going to tell you that you have to." Then I wasn't sure what to say: it may be scary? She won't look like your mother anymore? She isn't really there anymore?

"What do you think I should do?" she asked. She wanted me to decide for her.

"No, Rose, it has to be your choice." I figured the best thing to do was to hug her tightly. I tried to imagine myself being her mother so I could give her Jennifer's hug, not mine. I added, "Your mother asked me if I would take care of you after she was gone. I told her you will be a part of my life forever."

With that, Rose abruptly stood up. "I want to go say goodbye by myself." She walked down the hall, past her grandmother, past her grandfather and brother, and with authority told a nurse, standing in front of her mother's room, "Excuse me, but I have to say goodbye to my mother." I heard her say, "Goodbye, Mom. Don't worry about me." Then she burst back out of the room, immediately to the elevator. She looked back at us impatiently. "There's nothing here for us anymore."

Later that day, Jennifer's brother David, and her dear friend Kay, and I went for a walk on the beach. I was not in my body. It was a typical Kona day, sun over the ocean and a thick layer of clouds just past the main highway all the way to the top of the island where it rained 350 inches a year. I did not exist. There was a droid operating in my place. I could move from place to place without hurting myself or others. I was crying off and on, but I wasn't grief stricken. When I cried it was like someone else was crying and I was watching them. We walked across the long beach toward the ocean. I started rubbing my hands obsessively, like I had a compulsive cleanliness disorder. I realized Jennifer had not died. She was inside me. There was no separation between us. If she had died so had I. Or if I were alive, so was she. It was like the way a character in a novel exists. There must have been a sizable landscape of synopsis dedicated only to her; they continued to fire off, not knowing she had left the planet. Actually she was waiting in Daffy's funeral service home waiting for our approval for cremation.

I walked blindly ahead toward the ocean while David and Sheila sat on a large blonde piece of driftwood. If I walked into the ocean nothing would happen. I sang Jennifer's meditation song out loud.

"I'm wearing my long-winged feathers as I fly
I circle around. I circle around.
The boundaries of the earth.
The boundless universe."

I walked to the edge of the sea. The waves came up and gently surrounded me with white and brown foam. I thought irrational things like wondering how many sand fleas there might be in each wave which led me to thinking about Crazy Michael and his sand flea theory of the universe which led me to a futile search for the name of girl I had a fling with in high school on the Oregon coast which led me back to reality as I thought why the hell would you call your mortuary, Daffy's. I was still rubbing my hands. But they didn't feel like my hands. It was like Jennifer was rubbing my hands, trying to warm them. I remembered she had done that the night at Twin Rocks on the Oregon coast. Oregon was out there, just a few thousand miles away.

Inside my physical envelope there was a person. Me. I was alive, and she was not. But that seemed no more real than that she was dead. The pull of Jennifer's soul inside me was strong. Stronger than me. It was the first time, among many that followed, when communicating with Jennifer or still being with her, seemed dangerous.

The ocean swept around my body, and I lost my balance. I was suddenly under water. I tried to breathe and salt water flowed down my throat. I remember a burning sensation, but no sense of fear. Then a hand reached out and pulled me to my feet.

"Hey," David said, "One death is enough for the day, OK?"

I hugged him and it felt like I was hugging Jennifer. I said, "She told me we couldn't hear the moon."

If I was fully attentive, then why did I leave that night. If I had stayed, I would have been there as she took her last breath. I was racked with guilt and uncertainty. Instead of me, there was a nurse who only knew her for a few days. Why did she turn me away? But she had also turned her family away. That was because she didn't have the energy to create her role as mother, brother, or daughter. I remembered how my mother felt heartbroken when her husband of over 50 years yelled at her during his last months, often. I reminded her that he did it to me as well. She broke down crying the day her son-in-law came to visit and father acted so cordial, even though just minutes before he had yelled at her, "Why is it that after 50 years I still have to explain things to you!" I told her that he was so close to us that it was like shouting at himself.

Jennifer clearly made a choice. I think. She had traveled to Hawaii to die. She wanted to die with just a few selected people, not her menagerie. But I knew I was also guessing. She had never said, "I will die soon and I want to be far away when it happens." Instead she said things like, "The sun will feel good. It will help heal me." If she had died in Portland, it would have been a chaotic. Her love would have been dispersed among many, like sharing a piece of bread with a village.

I wrote to the nurse who had been on duty that night asking her to tell me what happened after I left that night. She described how Jennifer was very restless. It felt like her entire body was vibrating. She refused pain medicine or sedation. And then she described a dream Jennifer told her about. In the dream she was all alone on the ocean in all directions. She's on a surfboard. She falls off it and tries to swim toward it but every time she almost reaches it; it is just out of reach. She feels desperate. But then she turns into a dolphin and jumps in the air and play. She is free.

Then she was in a box and we left Hawaii to go home. I had two carry-on items: my backpack and Jennifer in a box. We all slept off and on. I caught Jennifer's mother staring at me several times. She smiled bravely when I caught her. I wondered what she was thinking. Maybe she was thinking about how I—the newest kid on the block— was in charge of the ashes.

It seemed like every time I came back from crossing the Pacific. I wasn't sure where I lived. I always returned to the Shire, but the nature of home was always different. As a teenager returning from Japan, I was no longer who I was when I left; returning after touring with Metamorphosis in Japan, my father was dying. Now the love of my life was in a box and one home, Jennifer's apartment, was a still life, at the other my mother awaited me.

Jennifer had left a ten-page document about what to do with some of her stuff. When I moved the last box into my house, I entered our fort. I could smell Jennifer. Almost immediately I fell asleep. I had only catnapped since I got back from Hawaii. Most often when I closed my eyes I would face the image of Jennifer who looked naked and shrinking. The image of a struggling tiny featherless sparrow in a nest kept coming to mind. At first I had deep sorrowful crying that took my breath away. I would have to grasp for air. It felt like living was a willful act. When I look back on that time it seems odd how little I thought about Jennifer. She was all-encompassing, but I didn't have many recollections. It took all my strength just to stay alive. I felt like a weakened animal in the primeval forest; reduced to survival instincts, emptied of my higher level of reasoning and being. I also felt paranoid, as though there were a predator or demon was stalking me. If I remained still the demon would not find me. While I didn't feel suicidal, there was a fate just shy of that. I could not take care of myself. I ate, barely; I breathed, but no longer consciously. I took care of my mother, but only through a robot self. I tried to listen to her, and others too, but I couldn't seem to hear them as though my ears were plugged.

I alternated between liking and not liking music. I almost had to have it on or the silence seem to drive me right back to the wall of desperation., but I didn't like it because if the record changed then there would be a wall of silence. The sound of the needle moving back and forth over the shiny dead black space on the record stabbed at my heart. And when I knew I could not play it 24 hours; it would have to go off at some point then that was more terrifying than not having it. This one day I remember thinking I wanted to hear Bob Dylan's Sad eye lady of the lowlands. But I also didn't want to. It was perverse. I might as well have put on Pachelbel's Canon to drive myself to the precipice. The song would make me cry and wail; I knew, but I couldn't stop myself. I placed the needle carefully on the record. I put it down and took it off twice. I remember hearing kids riding by the house on bicycles. Then it seemed there was a glaring light. I wanted to close my eyes. I was upstairs, standing in front of the bathroom mirror, holding a rusty razor-blade in my hand. It was positioned to slice my left wrist. I only stopped because of a stupid insight or divine intervention, that I shouldn't do it with a rusty razor-blade.

It's Mabular

I went to the warehouse and collected the mail that had accumulated, mostly for Jack or his personas. But there was also a package from Jack. By the Crying of Lot 49 postmark, he must have sent it to me about a month before he passed. But it must have first gone to my house, then Jennifer's apartment, and finally back to the warehouse.

There were two reprints in the package. One summarized the differences between our short and long selves. In summary, the short self is one's biography, while the long self is the soul or what reached out before birth and after death. It fit my grandmother's death to a tee. Her small self was the one who thought black people were coons, the long self was the one who told me from her hospital bed, I was beautiful, eliciting from me, an "I love you," the only time I really meant it. The other reprint was from Laura Huxley's *This Timeless Moment,* an account of her communication with Aldus after he died.

Jack explained that Uncle Gus had offered his services in the persona of Unruffled Duck to guide me through a communication with Jennifer.

The Duck came dressed in his finest. A long-feathered head piece. Jennifer's song came to mind, "I'm wearing my long wind feathers as I fly..." If the head bonnet was any longer, he would have needed a tiny bridesmaid to carry the feathers like a veil. It was authentic except for the Nike running shoes with bright pink shoe laces. Part of me wanted to cancel. Was this a joke to him or one of Jack's multi-leveled, endlessly ironic and ambiguous performance pieces? I was having a hard-enough time taking it seriously.

We were making it up as we went along. The secular modernist paradigm had stripped us of meaningful ritual. Unruffled Duck explained his role. "I am a witness. That's all. I have no wisdom or guidance to offer. I did this for Jack when our mother died. I will be your anchor and reality check and I will take notes."

I had prepared as best as I could. We were going to do it inside the fort. Jennifer's smell aura was still strong. I had a box of Jennifer stuff. Photos, notes, watercolor journals, gifts, letters, clothing items. I knew nothing would hold a torch to smells and music. Inside the fort,

I could still smell Jennifer. Once when I came back from her apartment, in a mood of acceptance that she was going to die, I had sealed off the fort with duct tape. I knew each time I went in the fort some of her smell and her essence would escape. I added to the smells by laying out the peasant blouse she was wearing the day we met. I tried to add more of her clothes, but at some point it was like Easter egg dye. Mixing all the colors, it turned to an ugly brown.

The Unruffled Duck also brought a gift from Jack. It was a small ornate tin box, with a note, "To make up for the one you lost as a child." Inside were some old baseball cards. Not all the Brooklyn Dodgers, but at least my favorites: Duke Snider, Jackie Robinson, and Pee Wee Reese. I had recorded several songs on a cassette, some that were just evocative and some Jennifer-specific evocative. One in particular, Pachelbel's Canon, which was in effect our song. We used Ouspensky's guidelines in *The New Model of the Universe;* the chapter on Experimental Mysticism.

I told the Unruffled Duck I had two big fears. One was that nothing would happen and I would feel even more alone and the second was that I would be swallowed by grief and be frozen in time, unable to move on.

I told the Unruffled Duck how I thought questions were important. I told him about a dream I had that led me to this conclusion. In the dream I was in the lobby of a gigantic mountain lodge like Timberline Lodge on Mt. Hood. I was standing there with Jennifer's parents, Rose, and several of Jennifer's friends. A bellman who looked a like Crying of Lot 49 Currier, handed me a telephone on a gold platter. He told me to wait while he plugged it in. He disappeared under a giant table, making me feel like Alice after she had taken a bite from the make-large-side of the mushroom. Then inexplicitly she was there. Somewhere.

I was astounded, of course, and desperate to come up with a question. What do you ask a dead lover? If you only have one question, what would it be? The best I could come up with was, "Where are you?" Other things like, *do you love me?* Or *are you OK?* could wait.

She answered me by saying, "There are the most beautiful flowers. Odd though some of them are green. Are there green flowers? There's a snow field. And I can see some kind of tiny lodge. If I stay still, I may touch a frog in front of me. Orange."

Frustrated, I asked again, "But where are you? How do I get there?"

She continued describing details. I couldn't hear her well and shouted, "Everyone shut up. It's Jennifer and she is trying to tell me where she is." Everyone in the lobby stopped like they were playing Statue of Liberty, but then simultaneously started up again. I ran out of the lodge carrying the phone. I ran across a Heidi-like meadow, climbed over a rock face which was made of Styrofoam, encountered a cold blinding white glacier and glided up and across it effortlessly.

I was still running up a glacier toward a light when I woke up. "See," I said to Unruffled Duck, "asking the right question is important."

"Well, either that," he said, "or understanding the answer."

I went on, "Ask the right question and you establish the theory of relativity or solve a murder mystery. Ask a question too narrow and you might not see the trees in the forest or the other way around."

Sometimes I asked questions I don't think I meant to. It got asked for me. It asked her how it felt like to communicate with me. She showed me a tiny dried leaf on a branch in a vase falling. That was it. That's all. Get it?

The Unruffled Duck turned out to be a most excellent guide. Most of the time he just listened. It was like being given permission to talk out loud. After a while I forgot he was there. I began by describing the hospital scene in Hawaii in painstaking detail. I intuited that I needed to go completely to the dark side. I could have brought the full force of Jennifer's beauty and our love into the space, but that didn't seem like it would get me close to her. I told Unruffled Duck, " the only way to get past my ego is to go through the pain." When I thought about my ego, it made my neck and shoulders sore. My ego was a pain in the neck. I had to go directly and completely into the pain I felt through my loss and grief. I didn't know what the end looked like. How would I know if I had hollowed out my ego through pain? I remembered Ueda-san's metaphor of filling a bucket with water a drop at a time. When was it full? Or in this case, when would I be empty?

The pain I felt would have to be life threatening. An image came to mind of holding a knife to my arm and pushing the skin right to the brink; any further and the skin would pop and blood would pour out. I would need to reach a point where I was alone. Not the alone of a Friday night with no friends and nothing but popcorn and TV reruns, but the alone it feels like when you come close to losing your mind, or swallowed by the ocean as Jennifer felt in those last days. And when I would sink into the oceanic abyss, I had to have faith that I could hold my breath long enough to surface and gasp for breath, or that there would be a hand holding me as I held Jennifer's.

At one point I told Unruffled Duck that it felt like I had to breathe consciously. It was no longer an involuntary act. I had to think about breathing like I thought about moving my arm to pick up a cantaloupe at the supermarket. "Strange analogy," is all Unruffled Duck said. Then it felt like I was gagging. My tears turned into wailing. It hurt. My wailing felt like heart burn or I was having a stroke. "You will tell me if I am really dying, right?" I asked Unruffled Duck.

Time passed in incongruous leaps between less time than experienced and infinitely more time than experienced. I asked Unruffled Duck several times how long it had been.

"What?" he replied at one point. "You mean since we started? The last thing you said? Since you or the earth was born and when Jennifer died?"

Then I hit bottom. I could go no further. The grief was complete. There was no beauty in the world. The universe was nothing but pain.

And then there was no pain at all. I could go back and forth between all pain and no pain, voluntarily. I also wasn't sure if Jennifer was with me all the time or not. Did she go away and come back?

At one point I tried to get out of the fort to fetch water and tripped on the Unruffled Duck's feathers and fell against a chair. Blood streamed down my forehead, and I laughed. "Great, is this how I reach Jennifer; I kill myself tripping on a hippie Indian's feathers." It struck me as funny. I couldn't stop laughing. I wanted to tell Jennifer this story, but then the laughter ended as abruptly as it had started and grief swallowed me. But I also realized that someday I would laugh again. I would not just laugh at someone's joke or witticism, but I would see that laughter was at the core of the universe or an answer to the universal plight of dying. It was close by. There wasn't an obtuse wall separating sorrow from laughter, but a thin veneer that could move by the slightest breeze.

My expectations about communication with the dead were limited: moving chairs and tables, candles blowing out with no wind, channeling through a Madame Blavatsky behind her crystal ball. I was thinking about how Jennifer would wake me when she had bouts of excoriating pain in her stomach. It would usually happen several hours after she ate. I would sit by her and hold her tight, sometimes just her hand, and it felt like I was an electric conduit for her pain. I took the pain inside. I realized that was dangerous. I could feel it run up my hand and arm and into my body. And then I started rubbing my hands obsessively. I told the Unruffled Duck it felt like if I turned in one direction it was me and in another it was Jennifer. I told the Unruffled Duck that I was being re-programmed. It was as though my DNA was being replaced by Jennifer's. I told him it was very painful.

"Do you suppose," I said, "that is what Huxley meant by his book title, *Heaven and Hell*?"

I tried to explain how I asked questions. The image that came to mind was me standing in a meadow looking at the Milky way. And it wasn't just any meadow but Elk Meadow on Mt. Hood. Jennifer and I were lying on our sleeping bags. I asked Jennifer how I, the living, were supposed to ask questions of the departed. She showed me an image of constellations in the galaxy. There weren't questions but constellations of thoughts.

Then I realized Jennifer and I had never been to Elk Meadow. I was communicating with Kathleen. It was the last time we were alone; about a year before she died. It was a challenging hike for her. She'd had to rest every few hundred feet. But it felt like I was there with Jennifer, or Jennifer was Kathleen, or Kathleen was Jennifer. Right, it didn't matter, not at this constellation level.

When there is no longer a self than answers don't come in the form of words but a gestalt. There were other points when deep laughter returned. I asked Jennifer what this experience was, this DNA reconstruction thing. She showed me a small boy lost in the forest and a sign that just read "Signpost ahead." So wonderfully obtuse.

Again, I laughed until I cried. I think Unruffled Duck did the same. Then I added, "she told me the DNA reconstruction thing is called Mobular reconstruction. But I think it was her idea of a joke. Maybe I'm reading between the lines too much, but it felt like she was saying I take life too seriously. It should be fun looking for answers like hide and seek. It is more like a game than it is a battle."

"What?" I asked her, "you mean more like scrabble than the game of life? But that makes it trivial and puts wordsmiths and punsters at the top of the heap and anxiety driven existentialists at the bottom."

I was angry at her because she seemed to be indifferent to my pain and suffering. I asked her if she was bored. She didn't answer me directly, but told me she missed her body. She now knew with certainty what she was and was not responsible for, but she missed the ambiguity and uncertainty. She also told me it was difficult to be attentive to just me or any of us. There was no center anymore, no self, just countless connections and relationships. So, she had a new assignment, I asked?

No, she said, just a fuller understanding of her enduring assignment.

When I asked her why she died, she took me to a beehive. We stood there and watched the bees coming and going. Thousands of them. Then one bee fell off the hive to the ground. It landed on its back with legs kicking. I could feel the scorching sun on its stomach then its legs stopped kicking and almost immediately an ant crawled on top of it and we stood there and watched while dozens of others appeared and then carried it away.

I said out loud to Unruffled Duck, "So what we think is a big event, Jennifer's death, is just a minor event in her life, barely noticeable."

Gus replied, "someone else I am sure said the goal of living is leaning how to die."

I thought about that tiny out-of-body experience I had when staring in my junk drawer the day I met Jack. That was just a minute or less. This connection with Jennifer, when I felt out of my body, had been at least 2 hours. It was painful to leave her body and re-enter mine. I didn't have to go through the hell of the pain of her disease and dying, but it was physically exhausting as though I had been holding a contortioned yoga position. But I also didn't feel sad. I thought I might. Here I had been with Jennifer, really closer to her, after all inside her. We were closer than when she was alive, and now she was leaving.

But I wanted to get back to myself. I was reminded of St. Exupery's reflection on the ordinary. I needed ordinary life. Gus, no longer Unruffled Duck, and I watched a movie and ate popcorn, which seemed sacrilegious but necessary. Gus asked me what I came away with from the experience.

"That I don't have to believe anymore. I don't think when you die everything is suddenly resolved. From here it looks like you step off a cliff, from the other side it's just a baby step. Also, it may look like the body's struggle with pain is the worse part, but the most painful experience is letting go of yourself, and you can do that at any time, of your choosing."

We Talked While She Burned up her Life

The last time I visited Kathleen, it was late spring. It was the most difficult time to get into their compound. The road, not much more than an antelope trail, was impassable without 4-wheel drive. In the late spring there were patches of ice, snow, and troughs of mud hidden under ice. There were also booby traps to keep out anyone that might find the road— holes covered by branches; trees across the road that were on hinges. Roger also left strategic ambiguous messes, scattered animal bones, road signs and other targets blasted out by high-powered rifles (he had at least 5); piles of rusted cans, busted appliances, upside down cars. They didn't like to distribute such man-made ugly, but it was important to have a haven. Just beyond the reach of the road their part of the wilderness was well organized, even tidy which was likely more Kathleen than Roger. And just in case you missed the other clues just before their compound, a 4 foot by 6 foot sign, *Keep the fuck out. Turn Around Now before it's too late.*

The road started at a rest stop, which is where they instructed me to leave my car. When I arrived, there was a Californian in an RV. He had a Good Samaritan bumper sticker. The man wore a white panama hat, Hawaiian shirt, and brand-new hiking boots. He came over to me carrying maps.

"Can I help you?" he said cheerily.

Can you do radiation therapy? Got morphine or know why the fuck God is taking away a beautiful and bright 30-year-old woman? When I pointed in the direction I was headed he followed my gesture and then back to me with wonder and fear. There was nothing in the direction I pointed. Then suddenly Roger came barreling into the parking lot, the Jeep splattered with mud. He looking crazed. If I didn't know him, I would have been backing slowly into my car and hightailing it. His hair and beard were longer.

The Good Samaritan backed away. This wasn't covered in the Good Samaritan handbook.

Roger talked as we drove. I couldn't hear him. I was focused on this being my last minutes on earth as the Jeep flew this way and that. My head hit the top of the Jeep roof several times. Then he abruptly stopped. He stared out through the windshield, with no eye contact, and said, "No tears. You understand? We are trying to get past the illusion of this world to what really is. You understand? Kathleen won't tell you this, so I have to. You understand? It just is." Before I could answer his rhetorical question (is that what they were?) he started the car and continued on, but slower. In fact, very slow. I thought at first it was part of the road traction strategy. Then he looked over at me, making eye contact.

"I like you, Reed, you know that, right?"

Another "Keep the Fuck out!" sign on top of an upside car. It took me a minute to realize it was our old, trustworthy Volvo. Then another car skeleton. What looked like a wheat harvester. A tractor. A pile of junk, and a pile of dozens of car radiators. Then we went around a small knoll, and the chaos turned into a pleasant encampment. There were many improvements since my last visit. Two teepees, 3 sheds, and a vegetable and flower garden, no small feat since the homestead was on top of 4 feet of compressed volcanic debris from thousands of years ago.

"I'll leave you alone with Kathleen. Well, you and the raven," Roger said, pointing to a raven sitting on top a piece of obscure logging equipment, "if you know what I mean."

The compound was shaded, although, at least this time of the day, Kathleen's teepee site had direct sunlight.

She was sitting in front of her teepee with a small fire burning. She didn't move or look up when I got close.

"Roger told you the rules, right?" She still didn't look up.

"Of course," I said. Feeling a little awkward, I reached in my backpack for gifts from Michael and Mary's kids, origami animals and birds. Then I hesitated. Would this be construed as revealing sadness? Shit, maybe I didn't know the rules. Talk about having tea with an elephant in the room.

But Kathleen got up with some difficulty. She had gotten smaller and weaker since I had last seen her. But still radiant. If the end was near how could she still be so beautiful? If there was a war going inside her body, why was there so little sign on the outside? Other than her arm, which hung from her side, useless. But it was a good hug. OK, difficult. The hug brought up tears and a gagging feeling like I was going to vomit. As she sat back down I had to turn away to wipe the tears. Damn blue eyes.

While I felt sadness, I was struck by how we had done the right thing. There was an analogy to the road we had just driven to get here. With the booby-trap and "Fuck you" signs and piles of junk, one would never imagine this. A neat encampment, a beautiful woman with long blonde hair, a Native American teepee resplendent with feathers at the top blowing in the wind, a small fire inside a ring of carefully chosen rocks. And then to cap it off, music. It took me a minute to recognize it. Moody Blues. "Nights in White Satin." I remembered a description Kathleen had sent me about Roger setting up his stereo in his teepee with a 12-volt battery. The whole thing was strange to me, but what had struck Kathleen at the time was that the stereo and 12-volt battery with wires going this way and that was the only thing in the teepee. She wondered what Rolling thunder or Don Juan would have made of this.

She offered me tea and a joint and explained that she was burning all her diaries and official records of her existence. There were two boxes and stuff on the ground, including her passport, and a high school yearbook. I knew she couldn't erase all signs of her time on the planet. She had written for the environmental journal for several years. I also felt guilty. I had some of her diaries and several thick folders of letters, even papers she had written in college. It felt dishonest, but I rationalized it. Surely she knew I had some stuff. We had lived together for 10 years. She threw her passport into the fire and an eerie orange green flame shot up.

"Wonder what that was," she said, and laughed. "Maybe they have been watching me all these years."

We passed the joint back and forth and she continued to throw things in the fire. I knew Kathleen well and knew that she would appreciate being able to spend time with me in silence. A friend from college had visited a while back and had driven both of them nuts because she insisted on talking. All the time. Hyperactive. Myself, I thought sometimes Roger talked too much. But, I also knew he had been the magic custodian who had given her this time in the desert and a way to find peace.

Before coming I had been rereading diaries, some mine, some hers. One of the entries was about the first night we slept together.

Back at the shire, in Walden hut. Cheap wine, good cheese and sourdough bread. We had slept together but not made love because her diaphragm had sprung a leak, but it didn't matter. Even today I can remember the softness and warmth of her belly. It was sad that I knew I could not share this with her. The other entry I remembered was more disturbing. I had gone on an all-night drinking binge with friends and a professor-poet who could drink all night and remain coherent. In those days, to Kathleen, losing me was dreadful and inconceivable. Her entry read, "I went from picking at loose ends to pulling my hair out by the root. I had to put my head in a brown paper sack to keep from hyper-ventilating." I also thought about telling her about my crazy roommate who also wanted to erase all evidence he had been on the planet, but it seemed so cheap and crazy by comparison.

If you don't talk about death what is there to talk about? We talked about everyday life. She showed me archeological findings from nearby Ft. Rock, and about a road trip they had taken back to Malheur National Wildlife Refuge, where she and Roger had met. And how someone had blown up and sunk their barge home on Summer lake.

"Nothing lasts forever," she said. "I realized that you could say most anything and there was a double entendre. The last of this or that. No going backward...you just never know. Look how beautiful that is. Ever thought about?"

She sipped tea made from juniper berries and morphine. She worried that Roger might be addicted to the morphine tea. "But I can't worry about that now, can I?" she said. She looked at the raven who had moved closer to us. "We should always talk about dying, I think," she said with a light laugh and a smile I knew so well. "Not really. You know what I mean, though? One of my practices—and it's easy for me now, but it was before I really knew I was dying—that is, even if just for a second, about my death before everything I say. Try it and see how different it is."

We had a pleasant dinner in the main tent. Roger was the food preparer. Kathleen could do some cooking but her strength was unpredictable so in the middle of frying up a steak she might have to go to her teepee and then not rise until the following morning.

There were long periods of silence, at first that made me feel uncomfortable. I imagined the countless hours they must spend in silence. There was a raven, or maybe many, who flew about the compound. It seemed like it was always there. It became a game for me. Was it there? Where? Sure enough, anytime I thought to look it would be there, sometimes close.

I stayed two days. Toward sundown on the second day, after I came back from a short walk, Roger unceremoniously said, "You need to leave tomorrow morning. I hope you understand."

Understand what? I felt defensive. Why didn't Kathleen tell me? Didn't I have more rights than Roger? Had I done something wrong? Show me the handbook. I knew I couldn't make a big deal of it. When Kathleen wanted to be alone, she put an eagle feather fashioned to a large bone in front of her teepee. It was there the rest of the time. It was freezing cold that night and I spent it in my own small tent, wrapped up in every piece of clothing I had brought, sleeping bag, and blankets, even a ratty aluminum space blanket.

In the morning, just as the sun reached the compound, Kathleen woke me.

"Roger fixed you breakfast." It was a full western style breakfast: scrambled eggs, bacon, hash browns. Even the place setting was rather elegant. Considering where we were. Was this an inexplicable apology like my father used to give me by giving me the larger piece of meat at dinner after he had yelled at me?

They told me about their visit to Rolling Thunder in Northern California.

"He didn't really tell us anything we didn't know," Roger said.

Kathleen added, "Not true. He said the desert was the right place for me."

The longest conversation was about whether they should get some stuff, including a World War II Jeep, from Roger's ex-wife's new boyfriend's ranch. How odd. Kathleen had traded one kind of normalcy for another. But it was the ordinary that held us together, the gravity of an otherwise ethereal life. Living was just practice for what it was going to be like to find ourselves without a body.

I imagined that a lot of their time was just like this. Staring at the embers in a fire, talking about the mundane tasks of life, watching the raven move from branch to branch, preparing meals, washing dishes. To the naked eye there was little difference between life here and at Michael and Linda's. I almost laughed out loud. How could I say that? This was anything but normal. My junk drawer metaphor came to mind. Imagine the intertwining of string it would take to explain this journey. A straight-A student from Palo Alto, classmate of Joan Baez, ending up with a Harley Riding follower of Don Juan and a Raven. A random image came to mind. Kathleen had refused to obey an air-raid drill in the 1950s, probably about the same time I refused to pledge allegiance to the flag in third grade.

My wife (we were still married) was dying and living in a strange alternative world, and yet what I cried the most about was saying goodbye to Morgan. At first he had pretended indifference to me. Kind of flip attitude. Oh, you're back from the store. But then he just followed me everywhere. If I tried to make direct eye contact, he would look away. He allowed me to rub his belly and behind his ears, but it was as much tolerance as pleasure. But then, hours before I left, he stayed close to me and made a very soft wine. It sometimes sounded like a bird call in an isolated ponderosa pine. And he made eye contact. Then when I drove away he followed the car, but not frantically, as though he knew he couldn't catch it or stop it but just to show me how he felt. I didn't know that would be the last time I saw him.

Kathleen's Final Resting Place

If you think you're confused about who was dying, then imagine how I felt. So, let me recount it for you in boring factual detail.

My father passed, but not really. I woke up day after day thinking he was still alive. Every day it was a new nightmare. Sometimes dreams, but mostly I woke up fearful that I had just imagined his death. I would walk down the trail and encounter him. He would tell me how I hadn't cleaned up something right, or left a tool in the wrong place. It was always something I hadn't done right.

Linda and I had planned to make another visit to Kathleen. We had to postpone the visit because the girls had the flu. If we had gone when we had scheduled it we would have seen her alive.

Instead, I got a phone call from Roger. Without saying hello he said rather matter-of-factly, "I was washing the dishes and she was lying in the hospital bed. You know soon after your last visit she had to move out of her teepee. I had just noticed a crack in one of the plates. I dropped a fork, which made a loud noise." He giggled. "Well, everything is loud here. I went to pick it up and I knew she was gone. It was like a moth had fallen from getting too close to a light bulb. That's all. Not a lightning bolt or parting of clouds or shooting star." He paused. I sat down feeling light headed. "Just Like her, don't you think? You know what I thought of? There's a moment, at least out here, when the wind from one direction stops, it is replaced by the wind from another direction. I don't always catch it but sometimes when I am whittling I feel it. That's what her passing felt like."

He then told me the plan. I knew he was in charge, but I felt engulfed by confusing irretrievable sadness. Should I have been in charge now? I mean, wasn't I the closest person to her? It felt like I had been left out of my parent's will. But I was also grateful. I thought about how she had seemed peaceful when I was last there, and about all the ways she might have died. Also, she had been given a six-month prognosis. And it was 5 years. She had beat it. He told me that she was in Bend at a funeral home. Her parents were paying all those costs. They said they were just too old to make the journey, but I think they didn't want to see the reality of where their daughter ended up. Mary and I had to make it there in the next 36 hours or they would cremate her body.

We arrived in time to see Kathleen. She looked like Kathleen, but for one of the few times in her life she was wearing make-up. We looked at her, speechless for what seemed like a long time. Neither of us cried. I think from the day the doctors had told us she had cancer we knew she was going to die, no matter what cures she attempted.

Linda summed it up, "She's not here."

It made me wonder where she would hover if hovering was part of the transitional state.

We drove in a caravan out to the compound. There was Roger, his ex-wife, and two of his Harley friends. The Harleys had strings of wildflowers and juniper sprays on the handlebars. We drove through the rest stop parking lot past a family eating their lunch. They looked at us with exaggerated astonishment. It reminded me of Bob Benson's report on the memorial parade for King George of the Gypsies in Portland.

The Harley gang, who I suspect had already been drinking, passed around quarts of beer, shots of tequila, tokes of hashish and offered Linda and I magic mushrooms and peyote buttons. The tequila shots seemed just right. Warming in the cold air. The other intoxicants seemed utterly unnecessary. We were already in an altered state. We sat in front of Kathleen's teepee with Kathleen in the middle next to the fire ring, in a plain wooden box. Roger explained what was going to happen. It seemed relatively simple. They were going to dig a hole under the large rocks in front of the teepee where Kathleen would be put to rest. He had found a perfect round rock we would place over the box. It had taken him a week to find just the right one. And it was a long hike because the ceremonial rock was not in the neighborhood. It took us three hours to get there, another hour to find it.

As we hiked we told stories. It felt good. Even though the stories at times felt like it was about different people. They told stories about riding free over the desserts of Eastern Oregon and skirmishes with the law, and the best highs on mushrooms or mescaline. Linda and I recalled stories about Kathleen from Portland. The only common stories seemed to be those regarding Kathleen's abilities as a crafts person. She had made smoking pipes out of deer antlers and ashtrays from agates, quilts from garage sale rejects. The stories went on for several hours and then Roger stood up abruptly and calmy announced, "Time to start the service." I went off to pee, as did a couple of Roger's buddies.

That's when I realized there was a strange undercurrent to the memorial. At least I think there was. I recalled the Australian outback where sounds disappeared into the vastness. Although we were only standing 20 feet apart I couldn't quite make out what they were saying. Did he just say Linda has big boobs and he'd like to do her? Boobs or booty? Or something about wanting to get blotted? One of them turned to me. Are you guys together, you know? I said, "Linda's married." So? Or was it "that so?" Kathleen was sure a good looker, one said. And I'm pretty sure that is what he said. Roger yelled out, get your asses in gear. They responded like it was a military order. "Well, time to jump her," one of them said, or was that "jump to it?"

It was dark by the time we started back. Linda whispered to me, "if they try to rape me, don't stop them. I think Roger will stop them. And I would rather surrender than have you killed." That was so like Linda, choosing between 2 impossible choices and matter-of-factly selecting one.

I then wished I was on peyote or something. It was like we were in the movie *The Rose*[1] but there was a Billy Idol sound track. I realized the undertone I felt coming from the boys created a memorable ambiance. At a more normal memorial service back in Portland there would have been Pachelbel, flowers, crying, tastefully presented food, some of her photographs. I would have been crying, probably almost wailing. Instead, I was on high alert as though I were listening for Viet Cong or walking a dark street in the south side of Chicago or part of the movie *Deliverance*. It was more like a service when humans were low on the food chain. Even in grief, you couldn't let your guard down. I watched the hombre's every move and tried to listen to everything they said.

By time we got back to the compound everyone was exhausted and injured. One of my fingers was numb from when the rock rolled over it. Roger had a gash on his forehead. In the firelight I could see one guy had a black eye. Roger read several passages from Don Juan and Rolling thunder.

Before we separated to our sleeping areas, Roger took me aside and whispered, "The brothers are crushed. They really loved Kathleen, and it's just their way of expressing things."

Linda was right. He had come to her rescue. This was his kingdom, and he had carried out rules of the domain regarding princesses from a faraway land called Palo Alto, who had died of wounds from a triumphal battle with invisible enemies.

In a Tiny Blue boat on the Sea of Eternity

My mother did most of the heavy lifting of her own dying. I had to make sure her mind and body were dying at the same pace. No small feat, but mostly it was working. I reminded myself that the old die to make room for the young. My mother was in her 90th year. It was time she died, like giving up her seat on a streetcar. I was confident that when she died, I would not have nightmares about her, maybe dreams, good memories, but no unsettled psychic business.

My mother's world kept shrinking. She was small and getting smaller (4' 11", 95 pounds). She drove until six months before she died. But her range changed from anywhere except freeways, down to the local grocery store and hair salon. In the last months she inhabited a small part of her house—a well-worn path with a walker between her bedroom, bathroom, kitchen, and couch in the living room. Routines were critical.

One day I overslept. I scurried up the hillside and fell; no injury but a torn shirt and muddy pants. My mother was leaning on the kitchen drainboard; lost in thought, she didn't see me until I was standing next to her. She looked up; her face stricken with horror.

"Oh, dear," she said, with blue and red eyes barely visible through her deep wrinkles, "I'm losing my mind."

She had said this before, but usually in a kidding way. This was different. She was terrified. I put my hand on her shoulder, thinking either to hug her or guide her to the couch.

"Why do you think that?" I asked. I could feel her tiny self that was shrinking by the day under her baggy blue sweater.

She shook her head repeatedly, "I was going to get something and I don't know what it was." Then, she pulled away and stared at me, "Why is this happening to me?"

I guided her to the couch, and as we took shuffling baby steps, I said with a light laugh, "But we all do that. Just this morning I couldn't remember why I went into my kitchen." I sensed what she meant, the difference between her lapse and mine. This simple act of forgetting was not like mine. When she forgot what she was doing her familiar self, of almost 90 years, had disappeared and she had fallen into the abyss. When I forgot something, I didn't leave myself but looked at myself with laughter or critical disdain. She hadn't. For a moment there had been nothing. No self. No memories. No personality. No place. Just darkness forever.

That day I didn't know what to do about her encounter with nothingness. I felt it deep inside my genetic connection to her, but all I could do was treat it with the simplest of remedies. I heated soup. We watched a movie together. I made up a list of household maintenance chores so I could be around all day. I figured the noises might be comforting. The sounds of the ordinary. Most of the time she was napping. She was also reading her favorite book, *My Antonia* by Willa Cather. She had read it many times. More disconcerting: she was reading the same page over and over. When I thought it might be time for dinner, I came into the living room, but she was gone. Already in bed, even though it was still light out.

I sat on the edge of her bed, trying to think of the right thing to say or do. My mother was like a sand castle in the incoming tide; she was slowly being erased. There was nothing I could do but be her guardian angel and play minor god by balancing the dying of her mind and body. In her look of horror, I knew her mind had taken a leap forward, and I needed to find something to bring it back into balance with her body.

That night I couldn't fall asleep. When I closed my eyes, I saw her haunted small blue eyes looking to me for help. She wanted something from me. But what could I give her? Then it came to me in a shiver that went up my spine.

Before telling you the story, I told her I have to confess and explain something. My mother loved Kathleen, at least as much as I did. When I would tell her about the latest events, such as bouts of chemotherapy, the wrinkles on her face would deepen and turn black, her eyes would close involuntarily. When Kathleen moved to the desert, I decided I had to make up a story. Everything about her life with a motorcycle gang, living in a teepee in the desert, following Native American religious ways, would not make sense to her. She would probably have told herself I was talking about a friend. So, I "made up" a story about how she died in Hawaii.

After our encounter with nothingness, I woke up early and sat on my deck watching a blue heron stalk fish on the pond, the pond that figured in the story I was going to tell my mother. I held my mother in my thoughts and waited for the hour when I knew she would be awake. She was lying on her couch, reading *My Antonia*. When I greeted her, she struggled to sit up.

"Good morning," she said, the first words she had spoken.

"I want to tell you a story," I said, sitting in the stuffed chair my father always sat in when he was reading. She smiled. "Oh, goody." There was no horror, just the calm acceptance she usually had about all things to do with her life, but I knew it was still there, like a phantasmagoria in the ancient forest.

"When Kathleen was dying in Hawaii," I said, "she would go away and come back. I don't know from where, but it wasn't the same as when she woke up in the morning or came back from a nap in the afternoon. She went away. Far away."

I had to say this carefully because my mother prided herself on being an agnostic. It was important that people understood she wasn't an atheist. She believed in something greater than herself but not a god in white robes or the man called Jesus. To tell her that Kathleen went away and came back was like telling her there was a miracle, like Lassie finding her way home from a thousand-mile journey. You couldn't explain, but it made you feel good.

"Well sometimes," I continued, "when she would come back from somewhere she would look scared."

It was more than scared. It was a horror. But I couldn't say that to my mother. And I couldn't describe how Kathleen looked then. Nearly starved to death by the cancer, she looked like a struggling sparrow in a nest, yearning for food and nothing else. Terrified like my mother had been the day before.

I continued, "Kathleen looked at me and in a weak voice, said, "I'm scared. When I close my eyes, I am alone on an ocean that goes on forever and then I start to sink. It feels good at first. I can see light and the ocean is blue and warm, then it turns dark and the further I sink the more I disappear. I can't stop it from happening. If I close my eyes, I fall forever and disappear."

"So, here's what I did," I continued with my mother, now more alert. It was as though I had said to a child, *it was a cold and dark night in the forest...* So, I told her, "Remember how in summer we floated around in the tiny blue plastic boat on the pond? So instead of the ocean, imagine you are on the pond and we are in the boat together. And imagine that I am holding your hand I grasped hers and that I will forever."

She smiled. In a short while her eyes closed. I held her hand tightly. I felt her hand tighten and let go several times. Then she slowly opened her eyes; looked at me and said, "It worked." I could tell she was alert and not afraid. "What a delightful story," she said.

That's all. We shuffled around; ate lunch together, talked about everyday things. It all seemed very normal.

The next day I came up to the house to fix her breakfast. From the couch as soon as I walked in the door, she said, "Dear, can you tell me that story again?"

My mom died soon after the tiny blue boat story. It seemed from then on her mind and body were moving at the same pace. She had no panic attacks. One day she got up from her couch in mid-afternoon, said she felt like going back to bed. She never got out of bed again. I slept on the floor in the living room for several days as she drifted in and out of consciousness. When she was in this coma-like state, I would come into her room and say, "Mom, it's your son, do you recognize me."

At first she was indignant. "Of course, I recognize you."

I said, "humor me. It just helps me know how awake you are." She knew I meant "alive" not awake. But that was an OK secret. As she slipped into a coma it became more and more difficult to get an answer. Just hours before she died I came into her room and said, "it's your son do you recognize me?" She didn't open her eyes, but, with difficulty, shook her head. I said, "No? Are you kidding me?" With a thin but definite smile on her face, she nodded. That was the last thing she said to me.

So now I hope when I die I can be in a state of mind to tell a joke. I suppose if that fails I will go for something enigmatic like Thoreau's last words, "Moose. Indian."

Thanks to Tinkerbell and Supreme Court Judge, the Missing Box is found

I gave Uncle Gus the task of distributing the last of Jack's stuff to the receivers so I could focus on finding the missing box. Also, ironically, I wanted no more random encounters. But Gus led me to the box. He had visited one of Jack's friends, Waskow, who had gone from being a feral hippie, getting his salads from parking lots to life in the suburbs. The ranch-style house in the suburbs would have been one of the last places I looked. While I spent days at the warehouse rationally trying to figure out where the box was, Gus had discovered it by chance when Waskow showed him his 1948 Indian motorcycle in his garage. The box was under a pile of plastic destined to be recycled. If he had come just 2 days later, chances are the box would be gone forever, or maybe in the hands of an unscrupulous dumpster diver, wanting fame and fortune. Waskow did not understand how it got there. He was having a Halloween party, although it was almost Christmas, and he would be there to hand over the box as long as I could remember how his prototype of a perpetual motion machine was powered. His way of making sure I had a right to the box.

"Jack came up with the idea," Waskow told me. "the Answer is

Twinkies." It was right there on the outside of a file folder about Waskow.

I was ready for this quest to be over, so I immediately drove to the suburbs. Stranger in a Strangerland. I got lost; couldn't find my way out of a parking lot; ran over a skateboard; couldn't understand house addressing schemes. It was an amazing landscape. As far as the eye could see in every direction, the same houses with green yards. How could this only be a few miles from my comfortable inner-city grid of disorganized houses and roads? It was like stumbling into another country. If I asked directions I was sure they would speak in a foreign language; incarcerated for not having a passport, one of those inner-city grid people. I would come back with a tiny scar on the back of my neck where aliens sucked blood and implanted a microchip.

Dusk was settling in and lights were turning on, which is when I remembered it was Christmas season. I knew it was since Waskow was having a costume-oriented Christmas party. But, as I came to the top of a long hill and looked down the long slope ahead, there were lights everywhere. It was magical. Like Aldous Huxley once remarked, that if a resident of the middle ages was transported into a modern city, with all its movement and light, he would have thought he had died and gone to heaven or Shangri la. There were the evenly distributed street lights and glowing houses, and the amber lights ahead on the very straight road resembled an airport runway.

It was breathtaking enough that I had to pull over. I think years before I had been on this road, but then it was farmland. I felt old. It reminded me of the time I took my mother downtown and showed her the building she used to work in. She hadn't been there in 10 years. I could tell she had no recognition of the building or surroundings. To me, the area had slowly changed. For her, it was instant and complete.

I checked the address. Correct one. And more telling the old-fashioned St. Nicholas statue in the front yard. Other yard decorations in the neighborhood looked like they came from Wal-Mart; this St. Nicholas looked like it might have come around the horn of South

American in the 19th century. There was loud music and people in the yard. As I got out of the car, I could hear someone barfing their guts out as someone else sang to them, "Deck the halls with bowls of pasta..."

The front door was wide open, and I spotted Daffy Duck, Mickey Mouse, a mobster, Rudolf (or some creature with a bulbous red nose), and sitting on a large platter with four legs, a turkey with dressing falling out of its fake mouth. I felt dazed for a minute.

The entire hallway was lined with ornately framed documents, sketches, lithographs and small paintings. Several of them looked familiar. Who was that artist? Paris. Moulin Rouge. I was trying to remember the artist's name when I spotted a bedroom with coats piled on a bed.

There was a topless young blonde woman sitting in a yoga position on the bed. Then Mickey Mouse entered.

"Shit", he or she said, "Last time I'm bringing my mom along to a party."

"Do you know where Bill Waskow is?" I asked.

Mickey looked at me suspiciously, then led me out into the living room and pointed me to Groucho Marx, whose nose and mustache had slipped down to his chin so he looked more like Rumpelstiltskin, Marilyn Monroe was sitting on his lap engrossed in a conversation with Clark Gable and a young woman without a costume — either that or she was dressed up as a typical college student of the 1970s. I asked Marilyn if she was sitting on Bill, who owned the house. She looked down at Groucho, surprised, as though she hadn't realized she was sitting on someone.

"No, that's another Bill. He's a retired supreme court judge."

Someone else shouted, "Bill's in the kitchen with Tinker Bell." In the kitchen, Tinker Bell was shouting about her love for David Bowie. She was tall and gorgeous and totally ruined my image of Tinker Bell for life. I asked her if she knew where Bill was.

She looked at me as though I had asked about the Flying saucer in the kitchen. "And who are you?" she said swooping close to me. "Now where the hell did I put my wine?," she said as she tossed her glass of red wine over the top of her head, brought the glass back and examined it, "Shit, I guess I need a refill."

A short man who might have been Harpo Marx came up to me, "You must be The One. I'm Bill."

He took me on a tour of his house. Down a hallway, a document signed by John Adams freeing slaves on Bill's—a great or great-great-grandfather's—estate in North Carolina. Renaissance music instruments. A Stradivarius violin. "Lots of old furniture," Bill said, distractedly. He led me out to the garage.

There was the box.

I expected it to glow or be shrouded in an invisible force field; but it was disappointing. The sumo wrestling wrapping paper was almost all gone or soiled by car oil. I wanted Bill to know how important the box was. Like my friend who unknowingly carried the Pentagon papers[2] to the *New York Times*, playing a critical role in history, Bill had had the secrets to the known universe buried in his garage for 20 years. I opened the box.

Remarkably, the contents seemed dry and intact. We stared at them for a few minutes. "so, this is what the fuss is about huh," Bill said. "So, look, let's get together. I have some Jack stories I'd love to tell someone. Loud sound of breaking glass. "But hosting duties you know."

When I tried to find Bill about a month after that, he had disappeared. Well, more to the point, the house was gone. Just bare ground. There was a pair of water-logged Mickey Mouse ears. OK, so it was real, I guess.

---

1. Movie, The Rose. 1979. The tragic life of a self-destructive female rock star.
2. Conveyor Howard Rheingold, author of *Smart Mobs*. Narrator and Howard sat on a US Congressional committee at the time mapping out the coming information age.

THE HOLY GRAIL: IS IT JUST A CRACKER JACK PRIZE?

S o here we go. The box. First off, there were baseball cards, the same ones I had in the collection I lost as a child. A bag of marbles, labeled, "we finally found his lost marbles." There was a copy of Dr John's Random knowledge manuscript, 25 photos of Dr. John with famous people, including Einstein, Abraham Lincoln, Sniffy Doolittle, Betsy Burkham (I don't know the last two but Gus told me they were going to be famous someday).

Summary of the Mad Lib Adventures

I think the Badger Manual is the heart and soul of Dr John's philosophy. He had some other techniques for understanding the world from a random point of view, but there is something lacking. Most of the papers were worksheets, that seemed like surrealistic mad libs. I don't know if he knew about Mad libs. They have been around since 1953, so he might have. The basic premise is simple. With a list of words or concepts, the user searches the vast store of human knowledge to find pointers—what for some inexplicable reason Ainsworth called "whispers"—that would not be accessible through rational means.

To carry out the instructions today, with Google, takes minutes or hours at the most. It would have taken Dr. Ainsworth days, weeks, or even months. He predicted the Internet, what he called the Mosaic, but it was not available to him. The equivalent was the public library, a place where Ainsworth lived for weeks at a time. There were a handful of online databases available before he died, such as ERIC. And, according to Jack, he had occasional access to ERIC at a university library. Ainsworth used a battery of common reference works for his own random searches. He did not leave behind a guide about how to use the reference books. Randomly? In the order, he listed the reference book?

He had over 100 of them. He called this one the "Clapp drop."

You should conduct a Clapp Drop by yourself and when you are clear about what you are looking for. Remember, a Clapp Drop will not help you find what you think you are looking for. But you will hear a whisper about what you didn't know you were looking for that will lead you to what you are looking for.

Clapp Drop Reference Materials

City phone directories
Who is who
Book of quotations
Books in Print
Encyclopedia Britannica, 1911 edition
Local Newspaper clippings files
Collections of graphics
Book review Digest
Index to Poetry
New York Times Index
Oxford English Dictionary

Almanac—last year in print

Atlas—the most reputable one possible

Concordance to your favorite writer

Random Knowledge Worksheet #1

_____ (your name) has published a novel _____. It takes place in_____. It is a story about _____. The main character is _____, whose job is _____. He/she has one child _____. His/her life changes when_____ moves in next door. He/She is a _____. They become involved again because of their common interest in _____. The story has a _____ ending. It is well worth reading because it is _____.

Instructions:

Your name: Use only your first name

The novel: Use the most important word. You may also use up to two words if it is a concept

Takes place in: Name of place you lived when you were 18

It is a story about: The first word that comes to mind

The main character: Your Father's first name

Whose job is: What you would like to be but have not become (or may never)

He/she has one child whose name is: Your middle name.

His/her life changes when: Name of your first girl/boy friend

Two of them have an affair/common interest: Your favorite hobby or activity

Story ending: Is it sad? Happy?

The Badger Manual

The Badger Manual, Dr. John's edition, is a splendid work of art, kind of like the naïve works of a 10-year-old autistic artistic genius. Childish water colors, decent replicas of great works of art like Mona Lisa. Pages and pages of 2 point calligraphed descriptions—one has to assume—of all the knowledge of the world. A lavish use of pop up collages inside one another like Babushka (stacking) dolls.. There is a collage for each country in the world, containing smells, sights, sounds, and tastes (not perishable like honey, according to the labels) in tiny boxes. I haven't had the heart to open any of them. On the outside of the box it states, "There is more stuff in here then can fit. You may ask, how did he do that?" All the boxes were attached to one another with multi-colored twine. Some boxes have only one or two connections while others were attached to multiple pieces, as many as fifty. The boxes and string reminded me of my cat's cradle arrangements so many years ago. The more important boxes (by twine count) were labeled "secrets of the universe." Inside the boxes were smaller boxes labeled "random stuff. Do not open death or enlightenment may engulf the opener." I opened those. Inside the tiny boxes was junk. Meaningless junk as far as I could tell, either that or the beginning of another novel or universe.

Inside box #1, the only one with a number, was a brief note, "This manual was first put together by Diana Rosa, sister of Don Rosa, ten years before he published the manual appearing in *The Secret of Atlantis.*[1] Dr. John found it in a shipping crate of women's shoes in garbage at the Amex Shipping Company in Ashland, Oregon."

While rummaging through the box and thumbing through the manual, it reminded me of what Jack told me, when we talked on the phone and met for the first time. How, in "A New Model of the Universe," describes his stages of enlightenment, from a multitude of voices, to a single voice (God, Mohammad) and then to—what he considers the highest level of consciousness. Where awareness and communication are mathematical. He observes that infinity is not continuation in one direction but infinite variation at one point. He stares at an ashtray for a long time. He realizes it is connected to everything in the universe. He finds a note to himself the following day, "a man can go mad from one ashtray."

Comic book scholars will know—heck many others as well—that the Badger Manual is a lot like the Disney cartoon's Woodchuck Manual. The badger manual does not have information that would be appear in an encyclopedia or Spangler's History of the West. But, the Manual can answer questions ranging from what is at the edge of the universe and why on January 20th, 1880, Frederick left his tuna sandwich half eaten in a cafe shaped like Elvis's pink Cadillac in Havana, Cuba.

The manual is 880 pages. There is also a hint that this is only 1 out of 24 volumes. The most interesting take away, so far, is the Time Scrambler. Keep in mind that in Dr John's historic period, as with his proposed "mad libs," you would have to this manually; making what today might take seconds or minutes, at the most hours, into a multi-month and several data slaves. But he predicted there would be the Mosaic, the Internet and other online tools.

There are 12 universes. In a manuscript, like this novel, one can tap the parallel universes by replacing conjunctions. (1) Replace all "and" with "or" (2) Replace all "for" with "and yet, and (3) Replace all "but" with "so." This is the conjunctive universe. There is also the quantum universe in which meaning spreads out horizontally, not vertically. Imagine Ouspensky's ashtray. In this case, you have to imagine everything in the book happening at one time in one place. The reader then must disentangle the quantum moment, finding the beginning and end of events, and creating an event over time which is vertical from a horizontal one. There are others.

---

1. *The Secret of Atlantis* is a 32-page Disney comics story written and drawn by Carl Barks, and lettered by his wife, Garé Barks. The story was first published in *Uncle Scrooge* #5 (March–May 1954)

JACK'S MEMORIAL SERVICE

J ack wrote up instructions for his memorial service, 30 years before it was needed. He also got his obituary published in over 200 small newspapers with his name as byline. Keep in mind, he also wrote up obituaries for the people he had created. Gus and I are still tracking those down.

Uncle Gus and I discussed many closing ceremonies, ranging from Native American to Zoroastrian and Emily Post, but I made it up at the last minute, and without Uncle Gus. Things like: "Setting: trees older than me; grasses more numerous than my offspring. Music track—Pachelbel canon, played until everyone is laughing."

But how I found out he had died was anticlimactic. A homeless woman handed me the Oregonian, folded back to the obituary page.

"Jack Ainsworth, of Portland, Oregon, 78 kicked the bucket (Gus insisted they use this term) Wednesday, June 15, 1990, at Providence Hospital. He is survived by his wife. He was born in Salem Oregon; the son of Dr. John and Sarah Ainsworth. He graduated from Linfield College. He was a lifelong Mason. He was a carpenter and artist. A memorial service will be held at the Unitarian Church on July 4, 1990." Almost every word was a new fact about Jack. I calculated he was 65, not 78. He was a Mason, huh? Linfield College?

I had gone to the warehouse two weeks earlier intending to visit Jack, but when I parked I was overwhelmed with a feeling of chaos. I didn't want to visit. My life was full. The days of screaming fits of creativity and strangeness of the salons seemed like a long time ago. I was about to drive away when I noticed something weird in Jack's RV. Curiosity got the best of me. I ran across the street. There was a moss garden in the RV bumper with lively mushrooms and one very green fir tree several inches high. I climbed on the bumper, carefully avoiding the mushrooms and tree, to look inside. The dashboard had been converted into a Japanese garden. A coincidence? Was this a message to me? But I lately had been thinking the whole world was created just for me. Messages and messengers everywhere. It wasn't just the Japanese garden; the bumper was like the one I created on Fred Jett's surfer wagon bumper. Did I tell Jack about that one?

A black sedan pulled up. It looked a lot like Mrs. Oglie's Cadillac. Just another coincidence? A short, swarthy guy in a suit got out, jumped up on to the loading dock, and helped the Caddy back into a position against the loading dock. Another short guy in a suit got out, who looked vaguely familiar. They unloaded boxes. I thought Jack was trying to distribute, not receive? I ducked down in the front seat. Feeling stupid like I was a private detective waiting to observe a secret rendezvous. They filled the freight elevator and disappeared.

I realized it was Uncle Gus, and his friend, the reformed Nazi sympathizer.

I thought about how we were connected. At one time jack, in his private investigator persona, provided me his own report. Apparently, the first time Jack and I almost met was when Jack hung out at the Folksinger Cafe in the Sellwood neighborhood a mile from the Shire. I would have been an early teen. I was hanging out with a gang of geezers led by Zippo, a transplant from New Orleans who popularized sequined shirts and white buck shoes at my school. Jack knew about the night that Zippo started a riot at the Sellwood movie theater a few blocks from the Folksinger by strewing a garbage can over the people in the first rows of the theater and then diving through the screen showing a John Wayne movie. He knew about it because that same night Zippo had beat the shit out of one of his "Reedie" friends because he was a commie.

I ended up traveling to the ends of the earth through Jack's networking skills. Through the Gertrude Stein Fellowship Salons, I met many of the most colorful characters in my life. But how did it work? That we almost met in Sellwood when I was thirteen was a coincidence, right? If we had, would it have made any difference in my life? The reason we did finally meet had something to do with me delineating and announcing my mission in life; and it didn't matter if that declaration really made any sense. When Kathleen and I moved back to Portland with our fantasy of a technological laboratorium, it was stupid and naive, but I had created a mission or quest that was my own. Jack couldn't help you if you just wanted to find other dentists, but if you were a dentist that wanted to sculpt utopian villages out of dentures, then Jack was your man.

It's probably just as well Jack passed on when he did. The glory days of networking were fading. The Crying of Lot 49 postal service, and underground organizations like the Entropy Evasion League, were anachronistic. Rather sad that the very thing that Jack envisioned, and I, a worldwide global social network (Myspace) and online storehouse of knowledge eliminated the need for people like Jack. Scarcity of information and difficulty of finding like-minded people has been displaced by the Internet. I Instead of seeking scarce information like a needle in a haystack, now we spent our time trying to filter out all the unnecessary or obtuse information or people. The world was filled with too much granfalloon, making finding one's karass, in some ways easy, in other ways more confusing and less interesting.

I was to work with Uncle Gus on The Last Roundup to return whatever Jack had taken from people over the years. Also, I was to organize the boxes and a shitload of other stuff—some valuable, some not. Whatever people had given Jack instead of money, like a roasted chicken. And I was to continue to search for Dr. John's missing box.

About the memorial service announcement, "Just a sham," Gus

said. "You know Jack had some groupies and people that might be expecting some of his fortune."

"Fortune?" I said.

He explained that Jack had a number of patents, including ones he shared with Gus for carnival rides, and maybe $1 million in other assets, including paintings, and sculpture, rare stamps.

The memorial service was going to be at the Funny Farm in two days.

While Jack was an invisible person, there still might be hundreds of people that would attend his memorial. I also felt the need to do something more private. I remembered how when I gave up shoplifting in high school I had gathered everything I had stolen and put it in a box and floated it down the creek in the Shire. It was wild and natural in those days. I could imagine the shoplifting box disappearing into a wilderness. If I floated a box, now someone would find it in days or even hours. But maybe that was the point. I wanted to create a floating junk drawer that would contain icons of my relation with Jack. I hoped the box would be found and contents might change someone's life, giving them mysterious marching orders from a crazy God.

I had no idea what to expect when I arrived at the Funny Farm: images of something between a Grateful Dead concert or tribute to a union organizer came to mind. There was little fanfare at the gate. A red balloon which looked like it might have been left over from a previous event and a hastily written sign, "This way" with an arrow; which seemed useless since the road was surrounded by thick Oregon jungle. There was only one way to go. But no cars, no bikes. No people. No noise. But then as I approached the sweeping lawn of the estate manor, row after row of seats. And full. 300 people or more. Uncle Gus was on stage with some men doing what looked a sound check.

There was something odd about the gathering. Other than Gus and his colleagues, it was silent. Then I realized the "people" were mannequins. As I walked past the last row I realized each "person" had a name tag.

Gus saw me, waved, "Great, isn't it? Just the way Jack wanted it, I think."

Gus and I had cataloged at least 125 rumors that Jack hadn't Jack passed along but just disappeared. We figured at least 100 of these were likely created by Jack or one of his minions.

It was closed casket but Charles, the crematorium director, swore it was really him. There were also two other memorial services, one in Gresham, a town about 20 miles from here and another in Tokyo, a place called Moon Island. Gus and I thought we saw him digging through the dumpster at Quality Pie. Fitting. Afterall a dumpster is what happens when a junk drawer has lost to entropy, enters limbo until reincarnated into other stuff to become a part of another story.

POSTSCRIPT

So, there was the matter of what to do with the archives, now reduced and organized. Maybe there would be a Ph.D. student who wanted to create a concordance to the most under-appreciated author of the least century or someone who wanted to create an alternative history to Portland, Oregon, or the universe. So, I offered the proprietor of The Spork storage facility a deal. I offered to pay 25 year's rent in advance if he would give me a 10% discount. Without hesitation, he got out a form. I signed in 30 places and gave him a check. He ended the transaction with a handshake, and "You know with climate change this might be all under water." And then added with a wry laugh, "but don't worry, we make the sheds to float." Comforting. I could imagine someone in Hong Kong finding the archives and publishing the manuscript in Chinese. Or if it stayed here and someone bought it at an auction, they might at least wonder how the hell a papal decree end up in a storage shed near where Arlo Guthrie wrote "Roll on, Columbia"?

I put the last box down. The shed was full; just enough room in the middle to sit at a kid's school desk that belonged to Kathleen, along with the clock that used to hang in the San Francisco Chronicle office (just to throw off archeologists again). Most people should die when they do. Eventually, I think Jack would have saved the planet and scored the meaning of life.

The thing is, with Jack, you could see him in a coffin with every unique birthmark, or even could have been there when an arrow went clean through him and killed a chipmunk climbing a tree which felled a green apple that hit your mother who also died, and you could dig up his grave and yelp, "Sure enough!" there was his diminishing body with the same birth marks and his well-known black thumb nail, and even then you might figure he was still alive concocting plots, meeting new people, hidden away in Superman's ice fortress.

Almost 20 years passed between when I finished this manuscript and figured out what to do with it. Most of the time it just sat in a box. Also, I spent a lot of time using the Badger Manual to change my life. It was like having Aladdin's lamp, but not knowing all you had to do was rub it.